Jodie Mae

ROBERT G. ROGERS

STRATTON
—PRESS—
Publishing Life

JODIE MAE
Copyright © 2019 **Robert G. Rogers**

All rights reserved. No part of this book may be used or reproduced by any means, graphic, electronic, or mechanical, including photocopying, recording, taping or by information storage and retrieval system without the written permission of the author except in the case of brief quotations embodied in critical articles and reviews.

Stratton Press Publishing,
831 N Tatnall Street Suite M #188,
Wilmington, DE 19801
www.stratton-press.com
1-888-323-7009

Because of the dynamic nature of the Internet, any web addresses or links contained in this book may have changed since publication and may no longer be valid. The views expressed in the work are solely those of the author and do not necessarily reflect the views of the publisher, and the publisher hereby disclaims any responsibility for them.

ISBN (Paperback): 978-1-64345-424-5
ISBN (Ebook): 978-1-64345-667-6

Printed in the United States of America

Also by Robert G. Rogers:

Bishop Bone Murder Mysteries
Tale of Two Sisters
Murder in the Pine Belt
Killing in Oil
Jennifer's Dream
The Pinebelt Chicken War
The La Jolla Shores Murders
Murder at the La Jolla Apogee
No Morning Dew
Brother James and the Second Coming

Murder Mysteries
The Christian Detective
That La Jolla Lawyer

Suspense Thrillers
Runt Wade
The End Is Near

Contemporary Drama
French Quarter Affair
Life and Times of Nobody Worth a Damn

Juvenile Adventures
Lost Indian Gold
Taylor's Wish
Swamp Ghost Mystery
Armageddon Ritual

Children's Picture Book
Fancy Fairy

I thank all those women who have had to struggle to find their place in a society, which has placed unnecessary obstacles in their path. Those women were an inspiration for this story. Perhaps it will encourage them to break free of whatever stigma was imposed on them at birth.

I also want to thank my sisters, Phyllis and Brenda, and my brother, Curtis, for their inputs and suggestions.

And I'd like to thank all those who read the story and encouraged me to get it published including Eva, Bill, Galina, Yarka, and Nadine.

CHAPTER I

The old truck lurched to a halt, half a steering wheel's turn off a muddy, gravel road. It idled rough and waited as if a human thing pondering what to do about the rusted barbed wire gap blocking its way.

Overhead, jagged yellow streaks, chased by tumultuous thunderclaps, tore through swirling black clouds. Gusts of wind laden with icy pellets buffeted the truck and raked puddled potholes in the ruts of the dirt lane beyond. By then, the day was little more than the tarnished silver twilight that comes with a day's end.

Lizzy Phelps, thirty something, swung out of the cab onto the running board. "I'll git the gap," she said of the barbed wire strands and leaped onto the gravel with a loud crunch. She was thin with blond hair that came from a bottle. Her only protection from the cold rain was a skimpy brown jacket and floral print dress. She yanked to free the gap's sapling pole from its wire loops, but with the wire strands tightened by the cold, it seemed frozen in place.

Lizzy's four children shivered under a patchwork quilt in the truck's bed with their furniture and furnishings. They threw back the quilt to steal a quick look over the truck's cab.

Jodie, the oldest at sixteen, swept the stringy, light brown hair from her eyes and pointed. "Look yonder!" she said.

Directly ahead, in the pale shadows of the coming night, sat a bare wood shack. Wooden shutters covered the front window openings. Scrubby blackjack oaks grew here and there around the shack and into the pasture in front of it.

Jodie's pretty face showed pink from the chilling wind and a glistening sheen from sprays of rain. The faded blue, print dress she wore under a red sweater, a hand-me-down from one of her mother's friends, was two sizes too large; obviously so over her tall, willowy frame.

"J-j-just another shack," Taylor, beside her, said with a stutter he'd had since birth. He was a year younger than Jodie with brown eyes and thick dark hair that drooped over his ears. "Favors his pa," most said. His height, a few inches over five feet, brought mocks of "runt" from other boys, and some girls, though usually only once from the boys. The pair of worn overalls and a frayed cloth jacket he wore over a khaki shirt offered little resistance to the freezing cold. His teeth chattered, and he couldn't remember the last time he felt his toes.

The smaller children, Emma, eight, and Ted, six, jumped up and down with the excitement of a new home, their cold temporarily forgotten. Lizzy had eyed the shack as vacant a few days before, a habit she'd acquired since her divorce, when the little money she had never seemed enough to cover their needs.

The shack was one of many and was left over from the days when men lived in the woods while they logged old grove pines in south Mississippi. The elongated shacks were fitted with wheels and moved on railroad spurs from location to location. When all the timber was cut, the wheels were removed and the shacks left in place, held off the ground by tree rounds or bricks. Landowners used them for storage or itinerant farm workers.

Log rounds laid on end provided steps into the front room at the middle of the shack and out the rear door of the kitchen. The third room, at the opposite end, was used for sleeping. The shack didn't come with an outhouse, but the cluster of dense bushes within hurrying distance of the back door served the purpose.

It was December 1941, less than a month after the Japanese had bombed Pearl Harbor.

"Son of uh bitch is tight!" Lizzy hollered.

Stubbs, the driver, a fat balding man in coveralls and leather jacket, turned on the truck lights as if that might help. The white light infused an eerie glow to the blue-gray fumes that poured from rusted holes in the exhaust pipes and wrapped the truck in an eerie cocoon.

Lizzy slammed her shoulder hard against the pole. It moved just enough to free it from the wire loop holding it in place at the top of the fence post. That done, she dragged the wire strands to one side and jumped onto the running board and hollered for Stubbs to "Git goin'."

The truck shuddered violently as it took the lane's deep, twisting ruts. Each bump threatened to fling the Phelps's belongings over the truck bed's bulging, wooden extenders.

Stubbs braked to a halt in front of the shack, his lights on the door.

Lizzy smashed the door open with her shoulder and disappeared inside. When she reappeared, the truck's headlights framed her in the doorway. She was not wearing a slip and in the light looked ghostly naked. Her hair lay flat against her head and shadowy slices from the truck's lights grew about her protruding ears like tankard handles.

The children leaped off the truck's bed and raced for the shack. It had to be warmer than the outside.

"Git a lamp lit, Jodie Mae!" Lizzy shouted. "Taylor, git a fire started! They's a heater in the front room. I seen some lightered knots 'round here t'other day." Lightered knots, twisted pieces of resin-filled wood from decayed pine trees, ignited quickly and were used as kindling wood by country folks everywhere.

Jodie lit a kerosene lamp to fill the middle room with golden light. Gusts of wind pushed the flame to and fro and sent shadows creeping along the walls and floor. Ted and Emma stood behind the heater bundled in a quilt to wait for the heat. Frigid air through cracks in the pine floor curled around their legs and sent shivers over their bodies. Flurries of rain whistled through cracks in the wall to decorate the floor with wet streaks. The roof's rusty tin sheets flapped up and down like the wings of a huge bird struggling to take flight.

Stubbs, fearful of not being able to restart his engine as cold as it was, left it running and the lights on to help with the move in. He unhitched the tailgate and gave Lizzy a hand unloading. The sooner the stuff was inside the shack, the sooner he could hit the road home.

"Thump!" Taylor dropped a load of wood on the floor by the round tin heater and lifted its lid. He shoved as much as would fit into the heater on top of the newspaper Jodie stuffed in. With a match struck against his thumbnail, he lit the sheets. The wet wood hissed, popped, then burst into flames.

"I'm cole, Mamma," Emma told her passing mother. Stubbs was a step behind with a box of belongings, which he dropped against the wall and hurried out for more.

"And hongry," Emma added. They hadn't eaten since morning.

Lizzy, wrestling a chest of drawers, said, "Goddamn it to hell, the Lord's a'punishing me. Taylor, git some more lightered knots and make a fire in the kitchen stove."

Taylor frowned, but disappeared out the front door to do as she'd ordered.

With the truck finally unloaded, Stubbs placed the extender panels flat in the truck bed and rehitched the tailgate. Lizzy watched from the log steps, a quilt wrapped around her shoulders. He checked the straps holding the mirrored wardrobe, his payment for the move, to the cab then climbed out. Each move the Phelps made meant the surrender of another piece of furniture. What money they had went for food.

Stubbs made a head gesture toward the mirrored piece of furniture as he faced Lizzy. "My ole lady's gonna be happy to git this." He smiled with a half-wave, then reached for the truck's door handle to get in. His smile faded though when he saw Lizzy shiver in the cold. He cast his eyes down as if to search from something on the wet ground. "Uh, shore sorry to have to take it though, 'n everything. Must be hard on a woman raisin' younguns by herself. You reckon you 'n Chet'll ever git back together?"

"Ain't no hope of that, Stubbs. Going on three years now. Once them younguns started comin', he took to drinkin' 'n laying out, stickin' his thang where he shuddn't. He ain't likely changed."

"I reckon not," Stubbs said. He managed a darting look at her now and then, between sentences. "I reckon not."

"Payday 'ud come 'n I wudden't see 'im for two days," she said and pulled the quilt tight. "Them no good friends of his from the plant 'ud leave him in the driveway, passed out cold, wudden't have a nickel to his name. If I said anything, he'd—"

Tears came into her voice, and she turned her face for a second. "Hell, I stayed black 'n blue half the time after Jodie Mae came. I had two black eyes when we went for the chile support hearin'. You know whut that sorry bench-legged son of a bitch tole the judge?" Chet had short, stubby legs, bench-like.

Stubbs shook his head.

"He—" She wiped her eyes and nose with the back of her hand. "He said them younguns wudden't his. 'Ain't none of 'em mine' wus what he tole the judge. Ain't none of mine,' I'd shore like to know whose they wus!"

Stubbs shook his head again. "Ain't it so. Un huh." He glanced up. The cloudy sky had calmed some, but the clouds' underbellies were no less black and threatening. "Reckon I better git on home, Lizzy." He yanked at the door handle and pulled himself onto the running board.

"Might better wait and git a cup of cawfee 'fore you do," Lizzy said.

"Can't. Ain't got no taillights on this thang! Don't wanna be on the road longer 'n I have to." He crawled inside and slammed the door. "Ain't a bad-lookin' woman," he mumbled under his breath and began a careful turn toward the road. "Got a good build."

In truth, at first glance, Lizzy was not "a bad-lookin' woman," particularly with her hair done and fluffed out to cover her ears. But up close, her eyes were red and swollen and her cheeks puffy from working long hours in smoke-filled honky-tonks and going nights without sleep.

The truck lumbered out the way it had come, lurching over the ruts like a boat in a hurricane and trailing gas fumes. Stubbs stopped long enough to rehitch the gap.

The fire crackled in the kitchen stove and sent waves of warmth into the room. Outside, the wind howled and drove sprays of rain and sleet against the tin roof and walls of the shack. Taylor found a hammer and attached the front door latch knocked off by Lizzy.

"Jodie Mae, dig that skillet out and fix some hoecakes and brown gravy," Lizzy said as she picked up a one-gallon syrup can and filled it with water from the rain barrel by the back door. It was fried bread, but they called them "hoecakes" or "flapjacks" depending on, well, just depending on which name they used that day.

There was a hand pump in the yard, but it had to be primed, so dipping water from the rain barrel was quicker. Taylor would get the pump working after they settled in.

She set the can of water on the stove next to Jodie's skillet. "Tho' a handful of cawfee in 'nare when it gits hot," she said and hurried to make the beds in the back room.

Jodie shook her head and mixed the flour batter for their hoecakes. Emma and Ted gathered around to watch. She spooned lard into the cast-iron frying pan, and when it had melted to a clear layer of oil, she poured in white batter to cover the bottom. It brought a sizzle from the pan. After bubbles began to pop through the batter, she flipped it over.

"Hurry, Jodie," Ted said.

"I'm hongry," Emma said.

"Git some plates," Jodie told Emma when the hoecake was fried brown. She tore it into two pieces and gave each half.

"Wait for the gravy," she said. They didn't.

She dropped a handful of dry flour and a little water into the greasy skillet and stirred till it turned brown and creamy. Hoecakes and brown gravy were a staple item in their diets. She poured a puddle on their plates and poured more batter into the pan.

Ted and Emma sopped the gravy with torn pieces of fried bread. At first, Taylor sulked to one side, not willing to admit his hunger, but eventually the smell of hot food got to him, and he picked up a plate to wait for the next offering.

On her return, Lizzy grabbed a bite of hoecake and swiped it through the gravy in the pan. Then, she went to the front room to comb her hair. A piece of broken mirror propped on a two-by-four bracing beside the heater thus became their dressing table. It held a comb, box of face powder, and lipstick. Satisfied with her hair, she pulled on a dry dress, pink with red flowers, and dabbed a fresh layer of red lipstick on her lips.

"Git me that red tablecloth," she told Jodie. "I'm gonna hitch a ride to the County Line Inn."

Jodie heard the tired, hoarseness in her voice and wanted to choke up, but left to get the tablecloth; Lizzy's protection from rain.

The honky-tonk, just up the highway, straddled the county line. When there was a raid, the whiskey, which was illegal in the state, was moved from one end of the bar to the other, from one county into the other. Since the tonk was always called before a raid, there was plenty of time. About a quarter was added to the price of a bottle for each sheriff's retirement fund. Since both intended to retire well, they never raided at the same time.

Emma and Ted grabbed her legs and said, "Don't go, Mama! Don't go! We scared."

She patted their heads and switched her eyes to Jodie and Taylor. Both stared at Taylor accusingly.

"You know as well as me twelve dollars a week chile support ain't gonna feed us." She turned to rearrange the padding in her brassiere to push her breasts suggestively outward.

"Y-y-you gonna b-b-brang men to the house?" Taylor asked.

Her face flashed with anger. Another time she might have grabbed him by the hair of his head and whipped his behind till she was tired, but it was late, they were out of money, and it was nearing Christmas. She whirled the red oilcloth over her head and stepped into the inky, storm-filled darkness and disappeared.

CHAPTER 2

Trailing black smoke from a lamp, Jodie led them to their mattresses on the floor in the far room. Lizzy's was in the front room with a couple of cane-bottomed, straight-backed chairs, a tattered sofa and two small tables.

With Taylor's help, Jodie strung a quilt from a rafter at one end of the room to give the girls privacy. Mostly only Jodie and Emma used it. Ted and Taylor changed wherever it was convenient. Often they didn't bother to dress for bed, as was the case that night.

For a while, they listened to the Grand Ole Opry on Taylor's battery radio. Little Jimmy Dickens wailed on about having to take an "ole cole tater" and wait for a turn at the table. Ted and Emma laughed at his plight, but Jodie and Taylor heard it as a depressing reminder of their own.

They turned the radio off and pulled the covers over their heads to shut out the fear that their mother might not return and they would be left alone, not knowing where they were. Jodie prayed for her mother's return and that they would be safe. Taylor, on the other hand, cursed every "son of a bitch" he could remember.

Sometime after midnight, Jodie and Taylor woke to a woman's raucous shout. "Whoopee!" Relief came when they heard Lizzy laugh, but that was crushed by cursing exchanges between two, obviously drunk, men.

Emma awoke and asked, "Is Mama home?" Ted didn't stir.

"She's h-home," Taylor said.

"Why don't Taylor call her mama?" Emma asked Jodie. "He ain't never called her mama."

Jodie had asked Taylor the same thing months before.

"She ain't n-n-no mama uh mine, jes uh alley cat," he had said. "I ain't got no m-m-mama, no pa either, hear him tell it. You a-a-all I got, Jodie Mae...'n the younguns."

Emma fell asleep without hearing an answer.

Jodie and Taylor usually found crumpled dollar bills on the kitchen table in the mornings. With that, plus money Lizzy got from waiting tables and the few dollars of child support, and the little the children made from fieldwork, they bought food and a few clothes. When things got really bad, Lizzy begged for food allowances from the Welfare Department, a last resort, because before food coupons were handed out, she had to explain what she did for a living. She feared that sooner or later, they'd find out the truth and take away her children. There was never enough for rent, so Lizzy moved them from one vacant shack to another, always just ahead of the law or an angry owner.

Taylor lay awake for a while and imagined bashing in the heads of the men and dragging their bodies into the woods to rot.

In the morning, Taylor and Jodie tiptoed past four people covered by blankets on the front room mattress and a pallet made of quilts. On the floor beside the heater were two empty sardine cans, a half-eaten box of crackers, a piece of cheese on wax paper, and two pint-sized whiskey bottles, both empty.

Taylor paused long enough to search the pockets of the men's pants strewn over the chairs. He did it more for revenge than the scant bits of money they yielded. He found a red handled switchblade knife, a nickel, and several pennies. A grunt from one of the men froze him. The man did not awake however, and Taylor crept into the kitchen to help Jodie get a fire going in the stove.

"L-look." Taylor held up the red knife.

"It ain't yours, Taylor. They gonna be mad."

"It's m-mine now," he said. He pressed the button that kept the blade inside the red knife's cover. The long steel blade snapped into place with a click, ready for action.

"I-I'm calling it Devil." Taylor's face twisted to an angry rage as he thrust the sharp blade into an imaginary enemy.

Jodie frowned but continued to break limbs they'd gathered the night before into small pieces for the stove.

After the fire began to crackle, Taylor picked up the large can he'd hidden behind the wood box and waved it at Jodie. It was his "New Orleans' can," one he'd found on the highway two summers before.

"W-w-when it's full," he had told Jodie, "I-I-I'm going to New Orleans and git a job."

While Lizzy got what he made doing fieldwork, the can got what he made on the side for after-hours work and the occasional extra dollar or two a farmer threw in "for a good job." Nobody ever complained about Taylor's work. He dropped the coins from the morning's search into the can and, after a glance to see that nobody was up, took it outside to hide. He always let Jodie know where it was in case anything happened to him.

"Y-you coming with me," he said when he returned.

"You ain't never gonna save enough for both of us, Taylor," she said with tears in her voice. "Besides, Mama needs me to take care of Emma and Ted…till they git…get older."

"With u-u-us gone, she can make enough from a regular job to take c-c-care of 'em. Sides, all she does is holler and whip us ever time we look cross-eyed."

"She works night and day, Taylor. Stays wore out."

He saw the tears in her eyes and said, "I'll c-c-come back and git y'all, after I find work. You…ain't gonna have to p-p-put up with whut Lizzy's doing!"

"It's the only way she can get enough money to feed us. When I learn how to talk good, I'll get a job in town and help out. I ain't, I mean, I'm not going to end up like her!"

The year before, Jodie had noticed how radio announcers completed each word perfectly and never used country slang or bad grammar, except on the Grand Ole Opry where sounding "countrified" was expected. She copied a newscaster whose delivery was in the main, smooth and polished, but when it suited his purpose he could cut a syllable or sprinkle in a little slang. It made him sound real, not prissy like some of them. Taylor scoffed at her efforts, but admired her more than he would say.

Since then, she practiced when she was alone and found that she could sound something like the newscaster. Even so, when she wasn't careful, she lapsed into her old habits.

"A-ain't gonna do you no good. You gonna be white trash no matter how prissy you talk. Ain't n-n-nobody gonna forget you one of them trashy Phelps."

"I got to…have to try, Taylor."

"Well…go on t-t-then. Might hep git you a job in New Orleans when I come back for you." He paused. "Y-you sound real good though."

She hugged him and smiled.

He put more wood into the stove and deliberately replaced the stove lid with a loud clang. Movement and curses from the next room brought a grin to his face. Seconds later, Ted and Emma burst into the kitchen, and Jodie began breakfast, hoecakes and syrup.

It was more exciting than usual because the syrup can was almost empty, a condition much anticipated by the Phelps children. At the bottom of the galvanized can were small, crystal clear cubes of sugar, which the children loved to chip out and eat like candy when the syrup was all gone.

Jodie made a pot of coffee for her mother and the others in the front room. She was relieved when the other woman took it in there to drink. Bess, she said her name was. She laughed as she took it away. It seemed to the children that she laughed at everything. In fact, for the whole time they would know her, she never seemed sad. She looked to be Lizzy's age, maybe a year or so younger.

Tall and coarse-looking, Bess had big hips and shoulders. And as if her shoulders were not prominent enough already, she always wore dresses of one loud print or another, all with puffy, padded shoulders. Her dark hair hung straight down, usually with a curl or at least a curve, sometime in a bun, depending on how much time she spent on it.

The two men, Slim and Smiley, Bess had called them, talked about leaving. Both were married but were going directly to work. They didn't want to face their "ole ladies" after "layin' out all night."

"Goddamn it!" they heard Slim shout. "Somebody stole my goddamned knife! Lizzy, one of yore little farts took my switchblade."

Bess laughed and said, "Ain't nobody took your knife, Slim. You just lost it."

Lizzy opened the kitchen door and said. "You younguns git on in here!"

They did and stood in a line along the wall in front of the kitchen door.

"Any uh y'all take Slim's knife?" Lizzy asked with a wag of her hand at the shorter and more compact of the two men. Both were in their forties, too old for the draft.

Slim had the narrow face of a weasel and stood with his hands on his hips. He stared at the children. Smiley was heavyset and had a broad face etched with deep smile lines. Both wore grease-stained khakis. Both had oily hair, dark and uncombed; both red-eyed and smelled of something dead from working in stockyard mud all day. Their faces, covered by thick black stubble, looked permanently dirty.

Ted and Emma said, "No!"

Jodie mumbled something, and Taylor yelled, "W-w-we ain't g-g-got no damn knife."

"I had it last night eatin' sardines, and I ain't got it now," Slim said. He shook the blankets and lifted the mattress. He dropped it with a thud. "Son of a bitch!"

"Ain't no damn knife," Smiley said. "Let's get on, Slim." He reached for the door latch.

Slim dropped to his knees and swept his hand around under the sofa. A splinter ended that. "Shit!"

"M-must uv fell through a c-crack," Taylor said. "W-why don't you crawl under the house and look?" He grinned.

Slim took a step toward Taylor, eyed him hard, and said, "You shit ass. You took it, didn't you?"

Lizzy got between them and said, "If they took anythang, I'll skin the hide right off their butts. If any of y'all did it, you'd best own up to it, 'cause if I ever find out, I'll beat you till yore blue."

"We ain't took it, Mama," Jodie said.

Emma grabbed her mother's legs and cried. "Please, Mama. We ain't done nothing."

Ted tried to do the same, but Taylor held his arm. "W-w-we don't beg," he said.

Slim leaned over so that his face was inches from Taylor's. "You little runt!"

Taylor's face flushed red. He pushed at the man and drew back with his fists, but Jodie put her arms around his shoulders and pulled him into the kitchen.

"I'm going to work, Slim," Smiley said and left through the door. Slim cursed and followed him out.

Bess stayed behind.

For Christmas, Ted got a cap pistol and roll of caps that he fired in everyone's ears. Emma got a rubber doll baby and crib. With a cry in her voice, Lizzy hugged Jodie and Taylor and said, "I ain't got no Christmas for you."

Neither minded. They'd overheard Bess brag how she'd distracted a clerk long enough for Lizzy to get the "presents" out of the store. It scared them to think she might get arrested for their presents.

CHAPTER 3

The Christmas recess ended, and the Phelps children faced a new school, something they all dreaded. They'd gathered in the kitchen for breakfast. Lizzy slept in the next room.

"I a-a-ain't goin'," Taylor vowed. He always threatened to run away or quit each time they had to go to a new school.

"I h-h-hate it! Always callin' us white trash! B-b-bastards!"

Jodie wanted to say no, but she knew he was right. She hated it too.

He mumbled a curse under his breath.

Jodie sprinkled sugar over the brown flakes she'd poured in their bowls and poked holes in a can of condensed milk with their ice pick. She poured the chalky-tasting liquid over the cereal and added water.

"Ain't never got no sweet milk," Ted said with his first bite.

Store-bought milk was too expensive, and besides, the icebox went with the first move.

After breakfast, Jodie used a fork to comb her hair. The real comb was in Lizzy's purse, and no one dared wake her up. Taylor didn't bother with the fork, just pushed what he could to one side.

"I-it ain't my hair they'll be talkin' 'bout," Taylor said. He led the way out the front door. The sun was out, but it was still winter and cold.

The school—a small, white-framed building on a flat, barren rise—was half a mile away on the muddy, gravel road that ran in front of the shack. Cold water from the road seeped through the newspaper in Jodie's shoes right away and brought giggles and stares as she squished to her seat after the morning bell. A month would pass before Lizzy "earned" enough to buy her a new pair. Jodie doubted she'd bought them, didn't dare ask questions.

During the first recess, the biggest and oldest of the four Cochran brothers shouted at Taylor. "Hey! Phelps' runt! Come over here and t-t-talk f-f-funny!" In class, he had snickered, along with others, every time Taylor was called on to recite.

The brothers bumped shoulders and doubled over laughing. Taylor flew into them. He knocked the first boy flat on his back and bloodied the nose of another as he turned. A third boy took a fist in the mouth before they regrouped and circled him.

"We gonna whup you good now!" the big Cochran boy said.

Taylor motioned them on. He took a lick in the face and another in the back, got knocked down, but got up and traded licks, his harder. Soon, the younger Cochran backed off holding his bloodied mouth with both hands. Another retreated after Taylor elbowed him in the stomach. Taylor's knee to the oldest boy's groin doubled him over and made him stumble away. The remaining Cochran just faded into the crowd. The fight was over.

"Don't reckon he's a sissy," Leroy, the second oldest Cochran said, with a glance back.

"We whupped him real good, didn't we, Elmer?" the youngest boy asked his older brother.

The tall, stooped shouldered boy who'd first shouted at Taylor stared at his brother for a second, rubbed the knots and bruises on his head, and said in a hoarse whisper with a nervous glance at Taylor, "I reckon we did."

Boys gathered around Taylor to laugh and slap his back and punch his shoulders and to tell him how glad they were he was there. His right eye was black and swollen shut, but no one at that school dared call him a "runt" or "tongue-tied" ever again.

Jodie wished she could trade a black eye for a friend. *That'd be easy*, she thought. Instead, she traded with compliments.

"That's a real nice dress you wearing." Jodie would say even if it were one cut from a colored feed sack with an irregular hem. After a few of those, the girls were glad to see her. "What nice things you gonna say about me today?" their faces said. Good things to say about anybody were hard to come by in the country schools but always welcomed.

It got her by.

Bess moved in to stay. Taylor didn't like it. Neither did the others, mainly because she insisted on helping out in the kitchen.

"Makes me feel real good cooking for y'all," she said.

"She's m-m-mixing biscuits with her dirty hands," Taylor told Jodie. "Gets out of bed with Slim and sticks her hands in the dough." Bess tried to brush back loose strands of her thick black hair, but with sticky, dough-covered hands at least one or two strands ended up in each pan of biscuits.

Taylor dismantled each biscuit before he'd take a bite. If he discovered a hair, he dangled it between his fingers, walked to the back door, and let it float to the ground. If Jodie found one, she'd flip it onto the hot stove where it crackled and singed. Bess never let on that she knew what was going on, if she even knew. Just hollered, "Whoopee!" when she smelled one singe on the stove.

Lizzy and Bess "hired out" to Ma Bradley, the owner of a seedy Jordan café across the tracks. At Ma's, a few dollars bought a man a beer or a pint of bootleg whiskey and a sandwich and a trip upstairs "for a good time," usually fifteen minutes or less. Ma got a cut that she divided with the police chief and the county sheriff. Ma's was never raided, and her girls had steady work. They made more when they freelanced, but Ma's was a lot less dangerous.

Nellie, a tough, bald old woman with one eye, controlled the juke joints in the county. If a girl didn't work for Ma or Nellie, they were independents and fair game for razor blade slashes and broken beer bottles in dark hallways and bathrooms.

Until the spring vegetables "came in," lunch at the school was a plug of corn bread, syrup, and sweet milk donated by the local farmers. The corn bread crumbled during the "soppin'" and made a sweet, crumb-filled paste, which the children scooped up with spoons, if available; otherwise, with their fingers.

Jodie, Ted, and Emma rarely missed school, but Taylor played hooky anytime he found work and his New Orleans can got every cent he earned since Lizzy didn't know anything about it.

One afternoon, the school principal came by the shack and talked to Lizzy at the front door. Anybody who passed on the road would see that he had not gone inside. Otherwise, he might just as well have packed up that night and left the county. The women would see to it that their men folks watched his backside cross the county line.

When Taylor came home that afternoon, Lizzy grabbed him by the arm and asked, "Whur you been?"

"S-s-school!"

"No you ain't! You been layin' out. The principal told me!"

He pulled away, but she jerked him back. As she did, the plug of chewing tobacco he'd taken from the pants of one of Lizzy's overnight visitors fell out. He didn't chew but liked to show the plug at school.

Lizzy saw the black plug. "You ain't goin' to school and you been chewin'!"

Taylor picked up the plug and shoved it into his pocket. He began to walk away, but she grabbed him.

"I ain't havin' you end up like that bench-legged, son of a bitching, good for nothing, low down, lazy bastard you call yore pa!" Chet chewed, even more proof that he "wasn't worth spit."

Taylor opened his mouth to say he didn't have a "pa" but never made it.

She slapped him on the head and shoulders. And when he covered his head with his arms, she grabbed a leather belt off a nail in the wall and blistered his back and behind with it. Ted and Emma watched with their hands over their mouths. They had been where Taylor was and didn't want to be there again. Jodie opened her mouth to complain, but Taylor silenced her with a look. One word and she'd be next.

He made no sound, not a cry or protest while she swung the belt against his behind. His silence sent Lizzy into a fury, but she couldn't swing the belt any harder than she already was. Finally, exhausted, she dropped the belt to the floor and collapsed onto the sofa.

"Ain't gonna have no youngun of mine takin' up bad ways… have to git uh education. Have to," she said. "Ain't nobody can take that away." Then, she began to cry and continued until she fell asleep. She usually did that after beating one of them. Taylor could never understand it.

Jodie followed Taylor outside. "She didn't go…mean it, Taylor. She just wants you to get an education."

"Don't matter none to me. R-r-reckon I'll trade a beating for money, if I have to," he said. "Especially if it g-gits my can filled."

After that, Taylor got his teachers' permission before he left school. He told them he had work at home that needed "tendin' to." None argued. Most were glad to see his behind out the door anyway. Jodie did his homework to keep Lizzy from finding out. His New Orleans can was the better for it.

Taylor got the pump in the backyard to work, but the water was rust-colored and bitter so they used water from the rain barrel till it got stale and full of dead bugs. He and Jodie searched for the spring they knew was in the woods someplace. Every shack they've lived in so far had one. They found it in a small ravine at the base of a tree-shrouded hill covered in pine straw. Taylor scooped out the silt left by the winter rains and crystal clear, cold water bubbled into the spring's sandy-covered basin.

It would keep their milk, butter, and vegetables fresh, not to mention the watermelons Taylor "found" when nobody was watching. The rain barrel behind the shack was emptied and cleaned and made ready for the fall rains.

Shortly after the last day of school, a brown pickup truck drove up the dirt lane and stopped near the front of the shack. Jodie and Emma were shelling peas in the front yard. They knew the truck meant trouble. Anyone not holding a bottle or staggering or cursing was suspected by the children as being up to no good because "They might be the law."

Emma ran inside. "Mama! Mama!"

Jodie watched a stout, red-faced, middle-aged man get out of the truck. On his head was a broad-brimmed straw hat that left a streak of shade across a face twisted into an angry frown. He had a stomach that strained the wide leather belt around his girth.

Lizzy rubbed the flour from her hands and hurried outside. She had been flouring the half a dozen or so perch Taylor had caught at the creek after "middle bustin' some new ground." Bess was in town "working," she had told them. They all knew what that meant.

"Yes, sir?" she said as she met the man halfway. Her blond hair was frazzled in spite of a hasty effort to restore it as she passed the mirror.

Taylor came from the back to stand with Jodie. Emma and Ted sat in the front door to watch. All were barefooted and all wore as few clothes as possible, ragged overalls and oversized print dresses.

"Whut kin I do for you?" she asked.

"Name's Caleb Anderson. This is my land." He gestured with his arm.

Taylor kicked at the earth, and Jodie's face dropped. It meant another move, another school, more jeers.

"We been takin' real good care of it," Lizzy said. "Ain't hurt it none."

Without looking at her directly, he said, "I'm gonna need this shack for my field hands. Y'all just gonna have to find some other place."

"We ain't got no other place, Mister." Lizzy glanced back to see if "her younguns" had heard.

"Can't be helped. I sleep fifteen field hands in there come summer." The man adjusted his straw hat. A sudden breeze rattled through the leafy trees around them.

"Mister," she said, choking up as she did. "I got me four younguns. We shore need a place to stay…bad. That ole shack is the only roof we got over our heads. Could you see yore way clear to—"

The man interrupted. "I'm gonna move them field hands in here in three weeks. Y'all be out by then or you can sleep with 'em!" He got back into his truck and left.

Lizzy turned to the children and said, "Don't y'all worry none. Ain't no potbellied varmint running us off."

That satisfied Ted and Emma. Jodie and Taylor knew better.

The birds, which had retreated during the confrontation, resumed singing and fluttering between trees and bushes in search of something to peck. A favorite place for birds and children alike was a huge blackberry patch off the dirt lane, always heavy with plump berries. Though the children got most as they ripened, the birds didn't mind taking the leavings.

After supper, Taylor and Jodie went outside to stare into the star-filled night sky.

Jodie asked, "You reckon the law'll come?"

"Always do, d-d-don't it?" He threw his knife into a block of wood on the ground. The blade sank in half an inch and quivered. "This time, I mean to get me one. B-b-bastards always laughing at us." He pulled the knife from the block of wood and thrust it upward.

"You ain't gonna! 'Sides, you don't know how."

"I reckon I do. You stick the knife right there and shove it up." He pointed to a spot on the left side of her chest just below the ribs. "Saw it in a picture show."

"Please don't kill nobody, Taylor! Soon's I can, I'll get a job. Get us a real house."

He put his hands on her shoulders and said, "We ain't never gonna have nothing, Jodie Mae. 'Cept what we take. Why you think they call us white trash? We're like them w-wild animals out yonder." He waved at the woods behind the shack. "When we git hungry, we find us something to eat. Don't matter whose grub it is. We get sleepy, we take the first place we can find. It ain't never ours."

"We gonna have something someday! I know we are! We just… have to keep trying."

Taylor didn't answer.

"You don't hardly stutter so much no more, Taylor," Jodie said.

He looked at her. "When I get mad, for sure I don't."

No field hands showed up in three weeks. Likewise, Lizzy ignored the warning to move. She usually ignored the first anyway and sometimes the second.

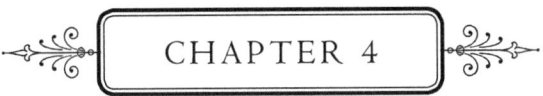

CHAPTER 4

The Phelps' children hired out to farmers who always needed extra hands since the war had taken so many in the draft. For a day's work, Jodie and the younger children brought home fresh vegetables, sweet milk, eggs, and sometimes a piece of stew meat or slab of bacon. Taylor was usually paid in money. He put most on the old wooden table in the kitchen for Lizzy to pick up. The rest he put in his New Orleans can. Each time he shoved money in, he bounced the can up and down as if measuring how much was in it. Jodie feared the time would come when the can would be silent, and Taylor would have enough to leave. She wanted him to go but hated it all the same.

One day the brown pickup truck stopped on the gravel road in front of the shack. The man rolled down his window and stared at the shack. The afternoon heat waves from the road made the truck look like it was wiggling back and forth. Lizzy stormed out front and stared at the man with her hands on her hips. He tore away, spraying gravel as he did.

After supper, Taylor drifted outside to check his can. The air was still like it got in summer and so hot that even the slightest breeze brought a prayer from any it caressed. A "slap," another dead mosquito, reminded him that Jodie was in the back door "standing guard" while he checked his can.

He walked back. "Still ain't enough," he told her, even though he knew there was.

She shook her head, but she also knew.

Twice the children saw the brown pickup truck drive by slowly. They also saw other pickup trucks do the same and told Lizzy.

She cursed and said, "Don't matter how many times they drive by, we ain't moving."

Bess and Lizzy decided to have "parties" at the shack Friday and Saturday nights, sometimes Sundays if anybody showed up. Some of the men from the juke joints they'd worked came by for a beer and a greasy hamburger, and a few minutes of jukin' to the radio in the bedroom. The children stayed in the kitchen till the parties ended. Bess "found" an extra radio for them. She bought bootleg beer and bottles of "pop skull" whiskey from a sheriff's deputy and a case of blackberry wine that nobody wanted. Some old man she knew gave her a "rattle trap" of a car so she and Lizzy didn't have to hitchhike to get back and forth.

Jodie and Emma managed the cooking for the parties and mostly stayed out of the way. Taylor did the same but cursed anybody who dared stick their heads through the kitchen door to ask for anything.

Late one night, as Taylor and Jodie cleaned up, they heard Lizzy ask Bess, "You ever wonder why they pay us two dollars when they could get all they want at home for nothing? I betcha their ole ladies'd like to feel some hard peter once in a while."

"It ain't like ours is fresh!" Bess laughed. "Ain't none of 'em studs, I reckon. Can't recall the last time one grunted more'n five minutes before he rolled over."

"That don't stop them from bragging about how we done hollered and screamed a 'whole hour.'" Lizzy laughed. "Reckon none of 'em can tell time!"

Bess laughed. "Ain't that the truth, Lizzy!"

"At least we git two dollars for our trouble. I reckon their wives got a right to expect a little more for their five minutes."

Bess slapped her hands together. "Mos' likely they want some loooove talk, maybe feel gooood now and then. Whoopee!" She tilts her head and said, "Hand me that bottle over yonder, Lizzy. It looks like it's got a swaller or two left in it."

Lizzy made a noise as she raked the bottle off the floor. "Get right down to it, I don't know why anybody goes to a honky-tonk. Stinking smoke and stinking men slobbering 'how much' in your ear. The whole thing's a barrel of shit."

"Ain't that right!" Bess said. "And you can't tell one dipper full from another."

"Hell, Bess, ever man in 'nare is just one big peter looking for a place to put it. I reckon they like a tonk 'cause there ain't no younguns standing around to remind them they should be home."

Bess agreed but knew there was more to it than that. A man wanted to climb into bed with a "young thing" to prove he could still cut the mustard, not so with the old "thing" he had at home. And she thought, *Me and Lizzy are getting close to being old things*.

Lizzy said, "I got to get me some other way to make a living, Bess. Emma's already wanting to go jukin' with us. Thinks it's fun. I got all choked up."

"That's pitiful, Lizzy. Downright pitiful."

Lizzy bobbed her head. "This ain't no kind of life for my younguns, Bess. Ever time I go to the welfare, they hem and haw 'bout taking 'em away from me. I shore ain't wanting to end up in the pore house." Jodie had heard Lizzy talk about the "poor house" more than once, but never learned what it was or even if it was. Just figured it was something Lizzy had heard from her family long before.

"Whut else can you do? Garment factory ain't regular. Work you to death one week and starve you the next. All marryin' got you was a house full of younguns and a strang of black eyes." She laughed, though not nearly as loud as she usually did.

"Ain't nobody ever asked me to marry," she said in a low voice. "Don't reckon they will now. Anyhow, we ain't got no education, Lizzy, and ain't got no skills." She slapped her hands together and laughed loudly. "Except one. We can wait tables and wiggle our behinds."

Bess went to town to meet somebody coming off the night shift at the plant. Lizzy put Ted and Emma to bed and cleaned up the front room.

Jodie and Taylor went outside and sat on a log in the yard to talk. The night air was cool, a refreshing change from the smoke and liquor smells of the shack. Crickets and creatures sang from the woods. The stars were out with a full moon.

Both were exhausted from working over the hot stove since early afternoon. Jodie's hair was stringy and coated with grease from the frying pan. Taylor reassured her with a pat on the back.

"I reckon you was right, Taylor," Jodie said. Her head bent low to stare at her feet. "We always gonna be white trash. Ain't no way to get away from it. Mama lets Ted bring in beer, and Emma can't wait to be like her. Mama…" Tears in her throat stopped her from saying more.

Taylor finished for her. "Might as well come right out and say it, she's a goddamned whore, and if you don't get outta here, you and Emma'll end u-u-up just like her."

A rustle got their attention. They turned to see Lizzy in the back door with a cigarette. She threw it down and went back into the shack. Her sobs kept Jodie and Taylor awake until the early hours of the morning.

One Saturday, when Taylor worked late and Bess was busy in town, Lizzy had to do the "party" by herself with help from Jodie. Only Slim and Smiley showed up. Slim was already half drunk and smelled of stale sweat. His khaki shirt was permanently stained with sweat rings under each arm. The dirty pair of pants he wore were more the color of black stockyard mud than the blue they had been on Monday.

About seven, Jodie brought in a skillet of fried eggplant for them. Slim swiped at her bottom. "Look at the wiggle on Jodie Mae's ass, Smiley!"

Jodie gave him a dirty look. Her cotton dress was so thin it was practically invisible. Her buttocks were nicely round and her breasts showed even in Lizzy's old, oversized dresses. Hidden behind a mat of uncombed hair was a face with finely formed features and emerald green eyes, not that anybody cared. Visitors in that house weren't interested in her face.

"Just a girl, Slim," Smiley said, but he said it with a smile and took a look.

"Shit! If she's big enough, she's old enough. And she looks plenty big to me. Hey!" He clapped his hands together and hollered, "Jodie Mae! Let me fix you a boilermaker. Make you feel real good." He picked up his glass of beer and pop skull and waved it about. Some spilled onto the floor and sent the raw smell of corn whiskey and beer about the room.

"Look at them titties jiggle, Smiley?" he said. Jodie didn't have a bra. "I'm gonna get me some of that!" He pushed up out of the chair. Jodie dropped the hot frying pan onto the table and dodged into a corner. White smoke, from burning wood, curled around the pan. Smiley got up to help. Her eyes searched the room for the hickory club Taylor had fashioned as a snake stick, but it was behind the door, out of reach.

Lizzy heard the commotion and stomped in from the kitchen. She pushed between Jodie and the two men and shook her fist in his face. "That goddamned pop skull gone to yore head? That's my youngun there!" Her hand made a gesture toward Jodie.

Slim pushed her back with the heel of his hand and said, "Me 'n Smiley 're looking to get us some of that." He bobbed his head toward Jodie. "You'd best get the hell out of the way."

She hit him up in the face with her fist. He barely moved, just grabbed her shoulders and shoved her hard against the wall. Her head bounced off the wall, and she fell to the floor, glassy-eyed.

About that time, Taylor came in to see Jodie backed into the corner. Slim and Smiley, with shit-eating grins on their faces, blocked her way. Lizzy, on the floor, struggled to get to her feet.

"You okay?" Taylor asked Jodie who nodded yes. Slim and Smiley turned to face him.

"Assholes!" Taylor said.

Slim shoved his fists out. "You tongue-tied little bastard! Come on. I'm gonna whip yore ass!"

Taylor pulled the red knife from his pocket and snapped the blade into place.

Slim's jaw fell open.

"Yeah! I took it you yeller-bellied, pile of worthless dog shit! You son of a bitch! You want it back? Here it is!" He jabbed it at them.

Smiley bolted toward the front door but, in his haste, stumbled over the sofa and landed on his knees. Without breaking stride and without looking back, he half knee-walked the rest of the way out the front door.

Taylor turned to watch, and as he did, Slim charged past and didn't stop until he was in Smiley's car.

Taylor cursed them from the front door. "Yeller-bellied bastards!"

"Could have whipped his ass," Slim said as he locked the car door. "Should've."

"Yeah. We could have." Smiley pressed hard on the accelerator, spraying gravel.

"Sooner fight a mad dog," Slim said.

"Be 'bout the same I figure," Smiley said. "Little shit's got your knife."

Slim glanced over his shoulder. "Hav'ta get another one."

They didn't stop to close the gap, and they never came back.

Lizzy and Bess quit the parties and went back to working the honky-tonks.

CHAPTER 5

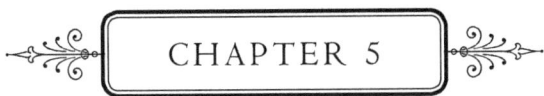

One afternoon, when the Phelps were halfway through an early supper of turnip greens and corn bread, the brown pickup truck pulled up in the front yard. The red-faced owner, absent his straw hat, rolled out of the brown truck holding a German Shepherd on a leash. His face was like stone, his eyes hidden behind dark sunglasses.

Nursing a hangover, Lizzy stormed outside. Bess was on the coast with the old man who'd given her the car. She'd hinted that he might want to "hitch up," but it never happened.

Like two gladiators, the man and Lizzy met halfway between the shack and the truck. The children crowded into a window to watch.

"Now I done told you to get!" the man said.

"Well, I ain't gettin'!"

The dog strained at the leash and bared his fangs.

"I ain't havin' no whores live on my property!"

Lizzy hit the man in the face and knocked his glasses to the ground. He staggered sideways and cracked one lens under his shoe. The dog lunged forward, almost breaking free from the man's grip. With that, Taylor ran for the front door. His hand searched his pocket for the knife and handed it to Jodie.

"Stay!" the man ordered the dog and lashed out with his free hand to knock Lizzy to the ground. She bounced up screaming and cursing.

"You motherfucker!" she hollered and began to cry like a hurt child. Tears streamed down her face. Her right arm, the one he had hit, hung limply by her side. She bent over to claw at a brick in the ground with her left hand.

The dog growled and whined to be turned loose, but the man yanked back on the leash. "Shut up, Max!" He looked at Lizzy and said, "Didn't go to hit you, ma'am."

Taylor grabbed a hickory club he kept behind the front door and leaped into the yard. "Let's get 'im!" he said.

Ted and Emma flew through the door behind Taylor and Jodie. Ted waved the stove poker, and Emma held a big cooking fork in her hand.

"I don't want no fight with children!" The man retreated to the truck where he jerked the snarling dog into the cab and started the engine. He threw it into reverse and drove backward toward the gap. The dog stuck his head out the window and snarled.

"Cocksucker!" Lizzy threw the broken brick, but with her left hand, it lacked force and bounced off the truck fender to leave little more than a red scrape mark.

Taylor got close enough to take a swing with his club but tripped on a root and sprawled flat on his face. Ted and Emma fell on top of him.

The truck crushed a rear fender against one of the fence posts as it slid onto the gravel road. The dog barked at the post and strained to climb out the window. The man whipped the truck around and streaked away. The dog barked until they were out of sight.

In spite of it all, Jodie laughed at the sight of it.

Lizzy, cursing and crying, gripped her aching right arm and staggered toward the shack. Jodie helped her to bed and gave her a headache powder.

Taylor retrieved the broken sunglasses and put them on, not bothered about the cracked lens.

The next day, Bess came back.

That night, Bess and Lizzy sat barefooted in the front door, each with a beer, and watched the cars and truck on the road. None slowed down or stopped.

Lizzy said, "I get tired uv being one step ahead of the law. Ain't never got enough grub. Can't remember when I bought my younguns anything new to wear. The ole biddy at the Welfare said she was gonna put 'em in a fit home unless I got a regular job. God help me! I wish I could find me a regular job!"

"Ain't it so, Lizzy!"

"It's a goddamned shame, Bess. A man can stick his goddamned tally wacker in a woman's crack for five minutes and get up and leave. A womern has to spend the rest of her life payin' for it. I'm tellin' you, a womern has a lot put on her."

"Whoopee, Lizzy! We shuda been born with tally wackers!"

Not long after the fight, almost midnight, the random slam of car doors woke them. They hurried to the windows to look out. Bess was on the Coast, working. Cars and trucks lined up along the road with their headlights on high beam, pointed toward the shack.

The children watched with their mouths open, too scared to say anything.

"My god!" Lizzy said.

Hooded men in robes walked down the lane. Their work shoes kicked at the long white robes around their legs and stirred dust. Some carried rifles, others shotguns. Two men dragged a large cross, wrapped in white cloth.

"Do they mean to kill us, Mama?" Ted asked. Emma sobbed.

"I don't know," Lizzy said and hugged them. "Please, Lord God, you can take me, but spare my younguns."

"It's the…Ku Klux Klan!" Taylor said. The blade on his knife clicked open. "Let 'em try."

They didn't. Instead, the hooded men formed a line in front of the shack, their outlines silhouetted in the headlights. They dug a hole and planted the cross in it. One, with a red patch on his hood, strode forward and touched a match to the cross's padding. It burst into flames. Heat and fumes wafted into the shack.

"When this cross stops burning, y'all have till sundown next to clear out! This is your last warning!" the one with the red patch shouted over the crackling flames. He pointed at the house and raised the shotgun in his hand. The others did the same. Metallic clicks rippled down the line as they cocked their weapons.

"Get down, younguns!" Lizzy pulled them to the floor as a hail of bullets cut holes in the tin roof. Then, doors slammed and the cars drove away.

Lizzy collapsed on her bed. Jodie brought a headache powder and dipper of water. Like little chicks with a mother hen, the younger children huddled around their mother on the bed. Taylor stood guard in the kitchen the rest of the night. Jodie dozed in a chair. He stared out at the burning cross. The flicker of red flames and the smell of coal oil and burnt wood filled the shack.

"B-bastards," he said. "Low-down bastards."

The cross was charred rubble with smoky embers when Stubbs moved them out the next day, long before the "sundown" deadline. The old shack mysteriously burned to the ground weeks later.

Four shacks later, they moved into little more than another shack a couple of miles outside of Whitfield, a little town south of Jordan, the county seat where Jodie went each week to pick up their support check from the courthouse. She caught the Jordan bus in Whitfield when they had the money. Otherwise, she hitchhiked.

To get to town from the shack, she had to cross a narrow bridge of loose, warped planks laid end to end and held high over Whitfield creek by a canopy of rusty iron girders. And before that, she had to walk a gravel road built up some ten feet above the creek's high watermark. She exchanged "hellos" with the two black families, the Browns and the Hansens, who lived on the other side of the creek.

Jodie chopped cotton that morning. In the afternoon, like she did sometimes, she picked up her fishing pole and headed to a good-sized branch that fed into Whitfield creek, not far from the back of their shack. A few minutes after she'd baited up, she heard a strange sound from around the creek bend. She drove the end of her pole into the soft mud of the bank and eased through the brush to see what it was. A full-faced young man in short khaki pants and shirt stood on the opposite side the creek casting with a fly rod. He was lean, on the tall side, and tan. His dark brown hair was cut flat on top as was the fashion then.

Gosh, she thought, *he's pretty.*

Her stomach fluttered. She watched him cast, again and again, without success. The muscles in his arms flexed with each cast.

Can't get no fish along there, for sure, she thought. She'd already tried herself.

"Slap!" Her pole hit the water behind her. It scared her so she almost fell into the creek.

When she looked up, the young man smiled across the creek at her. He waved. Flustered, she didn't think to wave back, just ran back to her pole. She picked it up to pull in what she'd hooked. Whatever it was, it was big. The end of her pole twisted left and right as the line cut through the creek and made a sound. Finally, the fish tired and Jodie hauled in a large trout.

"Must weigh four pounds." The voice came from across the creek. The young man she'd seen had come up the creek to watch.

"Huh?" Jodie looked up and blushed.

He said, "I was beginning to think there were no fish in this creek. By the way, my name is Steven Jefferson. What's yours?"

"Uh, Jodie Mae." She hesitated then added, "Phelps."

He didn't frown. Maybe he ain't heard of us, she thought and immediately scolded herself for the lapse. *I mean "hasn't heard of us."*

"Beautiful spot. First time I've seen it," he said with a nod at the sandy-bottomed pool in the elbow of the small creek. Trees grew to the edge and dipped their branches into the steam. Shadowy outlines of fish streaked about in the clear water.

Jodie felt tongue-tied. The way he smiled when he talked made her feel funny. And his dark brown eyes seemed to reach out and touch her face. "Steven," she repeated to herself.

"Fish, uh, come up here from Whitfield Creek to catch the bugs and things that fall out of the trees," she said.

As she spoke, a large trout struck at a bug that fell from the willow tree. Right away, Steven flipped the fly at the end of his rod in that direction. It landed on the water with a soft "plop."

"You don't mind, do you?" He pulled at the rod to make the fly dance on the water like a bug swimming for safety.

"Naw. I gotta get anyhow." *I'm never going to get it right*, she thought.

He took the time to tell her what he was doing and talked until she told him it was time for her to go.

"I hope to see you again," he whispered, so as not to scare the fish.

Jodie's smile almost exploded off her face. *He wants to see me again*, she thought. She sang as she skipped along the trail home. "I won't sleep a wink. I'll be walking the floor thinking about you."

Everyone thought the fish was the reason she was so happy. She didn't tell anybody, except Taylor later when they were alone.

"He's a college boy, Taylor, from Jordan. He's spendin' the summer with his grandma." She repeated what Steven had told her.

"Damn city boys ain't worth shit!" Taylor said.

Jodie didn't agree.

She couldn't wait to get to the creek each day. Sometimes Steven was there. Sometimes he came later and sometimes not at all. On those days, she looked for him more than she fished. She showed him a way to get across the creek.

Gosh, I love to hear him talk, she thought. And he was the first boy ever to say more than three words to her, let alone stand right beside her when he did.

CHAPTER 6

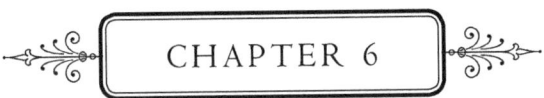

It was the time in the summer when farmers "laid-by" their crops. That's when they dropped a scant handful of sodium nitrate, "soda," alongside their row crops and prayed for rain. Afterwards, they hired out for day work at temporary sawmills around the area and waited for the harvest. And, they caught up on their fishing and hunting and repairs they'd been putting off.

"Hoa up!" Big Myrick, a leather-tough old farmer without an ounce of fat on his body, called to the mule hitched to the ground sled. Taylor, shirtless and tan from the summer exposure, walked along side. He'd worked for Myrick since they'd moved there. The mule, black with sweat and showing white salt rings on his flanks, willingly obliged and seized the opportunity to relieve himself, loudly.

"I'll git the soda," Taylor said. He pulled a leftover bag from the sled, threw it over his shoulder, and lugged it to a storage shed a few steps away. His lean, muscular torso, as hard and tough as a hickory pole, gleamed through a layer of sweat. He had grown to five feet, seven inches, as tall as he would ever get. Chet was no taller.

The mule's long ears turned backward to listen. He swished his coarse black tail to momentarily dislodge biting flies from his back. The flies stirred briefly in the lazy, hot afternoon air then resumed their places.

The old mule turned his wall-eyed face and hairless dull gray nose and mouth toward the farmer at the rear. His soulful mouth watered for a bite of the fresh green stalks of corn rustling in the breeze well within reach of his long neck. All day long, hundreds of the green, tasseling stalks had tantalized him and all day he had waited for his chance.

The old farmer removed his straw hat and shaded his eyes from the sun to search the sky for rain clouds.

Without hesitation, the mule swung his head over the row of corn and "chomped" the top out of a stalk. He got a swift, stinging slap of the reins across his backside, a reminder not to do it again. But the mule's memory was poor. Yesterday, he had done the same thing.

When Taylor returned, the old farmer handed Taylor some bills, his pay for the week's work. "I put a little extra in." He usually did. "You done some hard work for me."

"Thank you." Taylor slid the bills into his pocket.

The old man stared at the ground and talked about the rain, without noticing or caring that the mule helped himself to another corn stalk.

"I know you been talking 'bout going to New Orleans 'n all before the war ends. I heard it has a ways to go yet. If you was needed at home, uh, didn't want to leave, the plant needs men. Been hiring women. Ain't nobody gonna look at your birth certificate. 'Sides, you as much a man as anybody, more 'n most."

"Yes, sir. I appreciate it, what you're saying 'n all, but I don't reckon I can work at the plant," Taylor said. He spit on the ground. "Chet works there. He's my pa, even if he runs 'round tellin' that I ain't. Don't know if I could work in the same building with him."

"A shame," Big Myrick said. "My boys are growed up and gone. Lost one…in the war. I'd be proud to have you as my son."

For an instant, Taylor choked up. "Thank you," he said. "I'm much obliged."

When Taylor turned to leave, the old farmer said, "Good luck to you. In New Orleans, 'n all. Can't say I ain't wished I'd 'a gone off when I was your age. Been working the ground all these years…no better off than my pa." He stared out over his cornfield and sighed. "You gonna do good, Taylor. I know you are."

Taylor thanked him.

JODIE MAE

Jodie had boiled clothes in their washpot that morning. Afterwards, she cooked dinner, hung the clothes out to dry, and then dug worms for fish bait. She had promised to show Steven a cave not far from the creek.

Lizzy sat down to sew a dress for Emma when she heard Jodie holler that she was going. Taylor walked up as she skipped toward the trail. "Where you headed?" he called.

She stopped and motioned with her head toward the creek, unable to suppress a smile.

"Your boyfriend from the city!"

Jodie blushed and looked at the ground. Emma, in the kitchen, saw the look on Jodie's face when she answered, "Maybe."

Jodie wanted to think that, but so far all they had talked about was baseball, fishing, and his plans to go to law school in the fall.

Emma yelled at the top of her voice, "Mama, Mama, Jodie Mae's got a feller!"

When the words reached Lizzy's ears, she threw the half-completed dress on the floor and stormed outside. She jerked Jodie's arm and pulled her roughly into the house.

"Ain't I told you about boys? Ain't I?"

"I ain't been doing nothing bad, Mama. Really, I ain't."

Taylor growled at Emma, "Next time keep your mouth shut!"

Emma stuck her thumb in her mouth, burst into tears, and crawled under the porch to hide. Ted followed. They knew a major whipping was about to begin and none wanted to be close. When riled up, Lizzy sometimes forgot herself and whipped all within grabbing distance.

"Raise up yore dress and bend over!" Lizzy hollered.

A loud scream followed. "My god! You ain't got no step-ins on. You was sneaking into the woods without step-ins to see a boy! You done let a boy touch you!"

She yanked a wide leather belt from a nail in the room and cracked it against Jodie's bare behind. Jodie cried out as the belt cut into her flesh. An enraged Lizzy swung the belt even harder. "You ain't been hearing nothing I been saying. You ain't learned nothing."

With each loud pop, Taylor felt worse and worse.

Unable to stand it any longer, he stormed inside and grabbed Lizzy's raised arm. When he saw the crimson sight of Jodie's back and behind, he pushed Lizzy onto the bed. "Goddamn it!" he shouted. "Stop it!"

"She ain't got no step-ins on!" Lizzy screamed with tears in her voice. "Done let a boy—"

Jodie pulled her dress down. The cloth on her wounded flesh brought fresh tears to her eyes.

"She ain't had no goddamned step-ins since last year! She didn't want to tell you 'cause we ain't got no goddamned money to buy any! 'N we didn't want you and Bess out stealing 'em."

Jodie pulled at Taylor's arm. "It's alright Taylor. It didn't hurt me none." She had never seen him that angry.

He followed her outside. Inside, Lizzy screamed and beat at the wall with her fists.

"My own flesh and blood hitting me! God, strike me dead if I ever done anything to deserve it! Strike me dead!" she cried over and over. Finally, she opened a bottle of blackberry wine and drank and cried till she fell asleep.

Taylor sat down with Jodie on a log at the edge of the backyard to wait it out. He would apologize later or she'd cry for a week.

He saw Jodie stare at the trail. He said, "Go on. I reckon he's waiting." He waved in the direction of the creek. She hesitated. "Go on. Ain't nothing gonna happen here." He picked up her fishing pole and handed it to her.

She dabbed the tears from her eyes with the hem of her dress, forced a smile, and hurried away.

Steven had caught two perches by the time she arrived. He propped his fly rod against a small pine and offered her a hand down the slope. The pine straw made it slippery.

"You've been crying," he said.

"It ain't nothing."

He touched her tearstained cheeks gently with his handkerchief. Since the first time they'd met, he had become accustomed to her country twang and her stringy hair. She had been a welcome diversion from the chores he did around his grandmother's house. *How funny*, he thought. *Till now, I never thought of her as a girl. Must be the tears.*

His touch, as casual as it was, passed over Jodie like a warm blanket. No boy had ever shown her affection before. She loved the feel of his hands against her face.

"There," he said. "Is that better?"

She nodded and looked into his eyes.

The air grew cool. Thunder and lightning filled the dark sky. Then, rain poured down. They took cover under the broad branches of a large pine but were drenched. When she trembled, Steven put his arms around her. The rain all but made her dress transparent. The dark tips of her firm breasts protruded visibly.

He leaned over and kissed her cheek. She sensed a change in him. His touch was different, more demanding. She felt strange too. She enjoyed his soft caresses as she had never enjoyed anything before.

He pulled her close and kissed her full on the lips, at first with a tenderness that melted her resistance, then with his strong arms locked around her, he kissed her harder. Her breath came in pants though she tried to control it. His hands slipped first one, then the other strap of her dress off her shoulders. It fell to the pine carpeted ground under their feet, leaving her slender body completely naked. He kissed her neck, her lips, then her shoulders, while his hands moved over her arms and waist. A strange glow built within Jodie as she responded to his kisses and touch.

She recalled what her mama told her about boys, but it was lost, as was her resistance. She kissed him back with passion. She answered his demands with her own. He eased her to the soft carpet of pine needles where they consummated what nature had set in motion.

The rain ended before they knew it. She forgot about the cave and even went home without her fishing pole. It was Steven's last day, but she barely heard when he told her.

Jodie didn't eat that night. Lizzy figured she was still upset over the whipping. Jodie stared at the ceiling half the night. Pleasant memories mingled with feelings of guilt. Steven had made her newly aware of the difference between talking "countrified" and talking "citified." She vowed to talk good, like him, and prayed she'd see him again but held little hope that she would.

That night, Taylor counted the money from his New Orleans can on the kitchen table. It came to a little over four hundred dollars, plenty enough for room and board, he figured, until he could get a payday. Jodie watched.

"Leaving half for y'all," he said with a jerk of his head toward the front room. "Anything happens y'all catch the bus and come to New Orleans."

"No, Taylor, you need—"

"It's been said, ain't it! White trash makes do!"

She didn't like what he'd said but couldn't find the words to dispute it.

After supper that night, Taylor and Jodie stared into the sky on the outside steps and listened to the night. Fireflies filled the dark around them with bursts of yellow light and wild creatures screamed in the woods from high crescendos to low ebbs, over and over.

He left before daybreak the next morning. Jodie cried as she watched him head out; a sack of his belongs dangled by his side. He cried too, but not until he was well down the road.

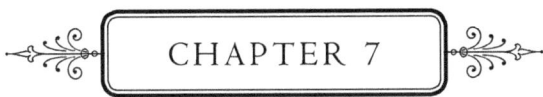

CHAPTER 7

Jodie went back to finish her senior year of school. She felt confident enough to write letters to Steven. She pledged her love, but he never answered and some were returned unopened. She even walked to the Jefferson's home to see him when she went to town for the support check, but Steven was "not here just now." After a while, she quit writing, quit going by his house, but she never forgot.

Cold, wet weather came early in November that year and stayed. Frost killed the grass and the freeze that came later stripped leaves from the trees. Taylor did not write. No one expected him to. Late one night, Jodie heard the lid of the tin heater clang shut and Lizzy's fretful voice. "I got it alright, the goddamned clap. Burns when I pee."

"Whoopee," Bess said.

"They say if it ain't cured, it'll eat yore brain," Lizzy said.

"You been taking that brown medicine?"

"It ain't worth pee doodily." A warm fire popped and sizzled in the heater. No one spoke for a while.

"Don't reckon I got a choice. I got to go to that colored doctor in Alabama."

"You could go to the health department."

Lizzy scoffed. "They'd call the welfare and they'd say I was unfit. You know that." The Alabama doctor didn't report things to the authorities.

The next morning, she announced to the children that she had to go to the hospital. She didn't say why. With tears running down her cheeks, she promised to be back in a week. She wore her favorite outfit, a dark brown wool skirt and tan blouse with long sleeves that she had sewn herself.

Bess stuck her head out the car window as they drove away and said, "I'll come back and stay with you." Her heavy tangle of dark hair barely moved.

She didn't come back. Her car broke down in Meridian. That was Monday. On Friday, Jodie went to Jordan for their support check. They were out of food.

It had drizzled cold rain off and on since daybreak. The sky stayed dark and threatened to storm. Clouds churned and swooped so low, they brushed against the barren treetops. To keep out the cold, she pulled a red sweater over her long-sleeved cotton dress and put one of Taylor's jackets over that.

She picked her way along the heavily rutted gravel road toward town. She hadn't heard a car or truck since early morning. Thankfully, the rain stopped.

She squished along and tried to avoid mud holes to keep her feet dry. As the bridge came into view, she saw a big, shiny black car parked where the raised roadbed broadened. Its doors open, its lights on.

In the summer, men often parked their cars or pickups there, or on the ledge below the roadbed, to hunt squirrels or to fish, but no one ever parked there in winter and especially in a car like that. The roar of raging creek waters reached her ears and sent a shiver over her body. Her pace quickened.

"Agh!" she said. In her haste, she almost stepped in a pool of bright red blood in the mud in front of the car's headlights. A red trail led from the pool down the incline to the ledge below. She heard a thump and a pitiful cry. She inched to the edge and peeked over.

Three men in khakis, each with bloodstained knives, circled a huge, heavyset man with a baseball bat. Blood streamed down his arms and back and his white shirt was crimson red. The man's back was to the road, as was that of the tall man who lunged at him with a knife. The big man turned and swung the bat to drive him back. The faces of the other two were smeared with yellow road mud and blood oozed from cuts on their heads.

Like wolves, they inched in. One by one, they jumped forward to stab at the dark-haired giant with their knives, only to be driven back by his bat. The man gasped for breath and staggered with each swing. The arm of one of his attackers hung limply by his side. Another, whose bloodied face was twisted in pain, dragged one leg. He cried out with each thrust of his knife. A leather bag lay on the ground a few feet from the melee.

The man with the limp arm looked up and saw Jodie. "A girl!" he said. As he did, he took his eyes off the man with the bat.

The big man swung his bat against the man's head. *Pop!* The sound almost made Jodie throw up. The knife fell from the man's lifeless hand as he dropped to the ground.

The tall man began to turn but stopped short when he saw the big man look down at the man he'd just hit. Taking the opening, he plunged his knife into the big man's back. The big man spun around with his bat and caused the tall man to stumble back and fall. As he did, Jodie glimpsed the side of the tall man's face, saw his crew cut.

The other attacker jumped forward on his good leg to finish the giant off, but he wasn't nearly fast enough. The shuffle brought the big man around, the knife still buried to the hilt in his back. He twirled around, his bat was already slicing through the air to smash his attacker squarely in the face with a loud *plomp*. The man unconsciously reached for his crushed nose, but life left his body before his hand reached it.

The big man's face suddenly stilled. He took half a step forward, more a stumble, and crumbled to the ground, jerked a few times, and then lay quiet. The bat rolled from his hand.

The tall man looked up, but Jodie was gone. After the man stuck his knife into the big man's back, she began to run and didn't stop until she was at the state highway. There, she hitched a ride with a logger and his wife to Jordan. No one followed.

At the creek, the survivor, the tall man with the crew cut, pulled his knife from the dead man's back and wiped it on the last patch of white on the man's shirt. No cars had passed. He breathed a sigh of relief.

"You thieving son of a bitch! Why didn't you just hand it over?" He kicked at the leather bag filled with money for a bootlegger pay-off the huge man tried to keep for himself. He checked the dead men's pockets then rolled their bodies into the creek and watched as the mud-yellow water swept them away. When the last body was gone, he turned back to the road.

Who was that girl? Did she see me?

Jodie hurried into the Chancery Clerk's office and told the elderly lady behind the counter. "Lizzy Phelps' check, please." She said it faster than usual because she wanted to get back to Ted and Emma as soon as possible.

The clerk went to a desk in back where she spoke to a man in a dark suit. He shook his head and gave her a note from his desk. The woman handed it to Jodie. "Plant's on strike. No money. Chet," the note read.

God! Jodie reeled back. *No money!* What would she do? There was no food in the house. Bess hadn't come back, and she was still scared from the fight.

"Did he see me?" she asked herself. "What if he comes for me and finds Ted and Emma?"

It was pitch dark by the time she hitched a ride back to Whitfield. The only sign of life in the little town was the lone light on the main street. She wished for a ride to take her home but no cars were in sight. Her teeth chattered with fear. Her face and hands were numbed by cold. She eased into the pitch-black night at the edge of town and headed home. Unable to see more than a foot ahead, she went by the crunch of gravel to stay on the road.

She came to the creek. The Brown's and Hansen's houses were dark. Bad weather had sent them to bed early. The roar of the creek hit her. Was the man with the crew cut on the other side? Every step she took on the bridge was a nightmare. The planks of the creek bridge rattled and squeaked.

Her toe stubbed the end of a warped plank. She fell to her knees. Terrified that she had been struck, she waited for the next blow, but none came. She got to her feet and hurried across. The roar of the creek was behind her. Gravel from the road crunched again under her shoes. Her knees quivered. She wanted to cry but knew it would do no good. Was the car still there? She strained her eyes but could not see.

She wanted to stop, wanted to turn around, but knew Ted and Emma were alone. Instead, she ran. Cold air hit her face and legs and the bottoms her shoes slapped on the gravel as she flew past the spot. The car was gone, but she didn't slow down until she was inside their shack.

Ted hugged her legs. Emma sniffed behind him. "They was a man here," she said.

Jodie closed the door. "What'd he want?"

"Wanted to know who lived here," Emma replied.

"And if our mama was home," Ted added.

"We told him mama was gone, but our sister'd be back in a while."

"Did he have a flat top?" Jodie asked.

Ted shook his head yes. Jodie trembled and blew out the lamp.

"We didn't know what to do," Ted said. His voice quivered. "Did we do wrong?"

"No," she said. "It's okay."

She put them to bed and stayed by the front window till after midnight. No one came. Maybe it would be okay. "Please Lord, help us," she prayed, exhausted, in a chair by the door.

Much later, a car door clicked shut on the road. *Mama...Bess?* She hoped. Another, heavier, door shut. A truck. She looked out the front window. Shadowy figures slashed the night with flashlights. The shadows drew closer. Hushed voices came with them.

Jodie shook Ted and Emma. "Shhh!" she whispered. "Somebody's outside."

"Is…is it Mama?" Ted asked.

"No."

Footsteps moved around outside the house. Metal bumped against the wood siding. With each bump came a splash. The smell of coal oil filled the inside of the house.

"It's coal oil," Ted whispered. "They mean to burn us out. I w-wish Taylor was here."

Jodie clamped her hand over his mouth.

"I'm scared," Emma said. Jodie shushed her. She asked, "Can we go outside?"

Jodie heard the familiar metallic click of a weapon being cocked and gasped.

A voice asked, "What you doing that for?"

"In case a varmint comes out," a man with the fuzzy voice said. The other man laughed.

Was it the man from the creek? Jodie's knees threatened to buckle. They could not go outside. She herded Ted and Emma into the kitchen as the sound of flames reached their ears. Dense, black smoke poured inside. Orange-red flames knifed through cracks in the walls and cast a smoky glow about Jodie and the children.

"Get down," she told them. Heat from the fire brought sweat to her face.

Jodie pushed the kitchen table aside. They'd set it over a rotted-out place in the planked floor. She ripped out one board, then another to widen the hole. The walls of the old house were engulfed in flames. Smoke, filled with pine tar fumes, pushed into every room.

"I'm burning up! I want Mama," Emma said.

"It's okay." Jodie urged them into the hole onto the musty earth under the house. The house was on blocks, two feet off the ground. She eased in after them and crawled to the nearest edge. The air was breathable under the house and cool.

The house groaned and creaked like it might collapse any minute. Flaming globs fell like fiery raindrops from the sides of the house to the ground. Jodie peered through the smoke and balls of flame that fell from the sides of the house. She saw no pants' legs! Timing the flame balls, she rolled out, then reached back for Ted and Emma out as the house exploded behind them. They sprinted through a cloud of smoke and ashes into the woods. Seconds later, the tin roof of the house collapsed into the flames and sent a wave of smoke outward.

"Better get on back, case we have a fire to investigate," the fuzzy voiced man said. The men walked back to road and drove away.

Jodie, fearful that they would return, hurried the children down the muddy road to the Browns. Holding back her tears, Jodie told Mr. Brown the story. They stood on the front porch. Mrs. Brown listened from inside the house, her face visible in the lamp light.

"Warn't wearing no sheets, you say?" He rubbed a hand over his balding head. He knew what Lizzy did for a living, so the burning did not surprise him. Usually it was the KKK, but if they didn't do it, it was most likely "the law."

Jodie nodded.

"Come on in," he said. His eyes looked up and down the road. "Ain't wanting no trouble with the law."

Jodie kept quiet about the killing she saw though she suspected it had more to do with the burning than "the law."

"Lillian, you gives these white children your bed," Mrs. Brown told her daughter. Without argument, Lillian crawled onto a small army surplus cot with her brother, Thomas. Jodie, Ted, and Emma piled onto Lillian's small bed placed against a wall. Jodie slept rolled up against the bare stud wall to give Ted and Emma, who slept foot to face, more room. Mr. and Mrs. Brown went back to bed. Neither wanted a light on if a car passed.

Early the next morning, Mrs. Brown called them to a hot breakfast. Except for the bedrooms, everything else was in one big room, the kitchen with its wood burning stove, the eating table, a few easy chairs, and sofa. A fire burned in the mud-straw fireplace along the back wall and gave off a smell. Ted fought for Mrs. Brown's large biscuits with Johnny, George, and Thomas, the Brown's sons.

Though Ted and Emma barely knew the Browns, Jodie and Taylor had picked cotton for them last year. Also, Jodie sometimes stopped for a dipper of cold water on her way to and from Whitfield. Thomas was about Jodie's age, Lillian Emma's. The other boys were older.

"Yo mama working?" Thomas asked.

"She's been sick. Had to go to the hospital," Jodie said. "Taylor went to New Orleans." She could see by the expressions on the older boys' faces that they were envious. They had talked to Taylor about it, but couldn't go anywhere. They were needed on their forty-acre farm.

"You children is mighty lucky to get out alive," Mrs. Brown said. Unlike her lanky, leathery husband, she was short and rounded.

"Thank you for letting us stay with you," Jodie replied.

"You can stay as long as you needs to," Mr. Brown said. He pushed away from the table and snatched his old felt hat from its nail perch on the wall. He had to walk to the small lumberyard where he was doing "public work" in Whitfield.

"We don't want no charity," Jodie said, remembering too late to say "any charity."

"Reckon I got enough work to keep y'all busy." Mrs. Brown smiled. In a big family, there was "a Lord's plenty" of clothes to be boiled and scrubbed.

That evening they played a version of Red Rover. "Red Rover, Red Rover, come on over!" One or the other of them yelled and threw a small ball over the house. Whoever caught it tried to run it to the other side without being touched.

Willie Bea Hansen, an only child from across the road, joined in. She was a year younger than Jodie and a few inches shorter. Her father, a railroad brakeman, had been killed several years before.

As she dodged past Jodie's outstretched arms, Willie Bea slid and fell in the mud and messed up her freshly starched dress. She rarely wore anything else, thanks to her mother Beatrice, who swore to give her child a "Christian raising" after her husband died. Beatrice worked as a nurse's aide at Whitfield Hospital. Willie Bea, who rarely lacked for anything, was the envy of all the children.

"I'm sorry, Willie Bea," Jodie said and tried to brush the mud off the dress. It didn't help.

"No, you're not. You did it on a purpose. 'Cause you're jealous," the black girl said. The children formed a circle around them.

"I did not! And I'm not jealous!" Jodie said.

"You're just a white cracker," Willie Bea said. "Mama says."

"Well, you're a black cracker," Jodie said, the only thing that came into her mind.

"No such thing," the black girl said and shoved Jodie.

The Brown children egged them on. A fight was always good. And Willie Bea did put on airs, even bragged about going to college after she finished high school. And "she never did no fieldwork," they told Jodie.

"Hit her back Jodie Mae." Lillian jumped up and down to see over the heads of her taller brothers.

Jodie pushed Willie Bea, and they pulled each other's hair and rolled around on the ground until Beatrice Hansen broke it up.

"Come on, child," the slight black woman told her daughter. "You don't fight with the likes of these." She pointed a finger at Jodie.

Jodie watched her stalk away. Her feelings were hurt. *Will we always be white trash?* Taylor said they would.

Chicken and dumplings simmered on the Brown's stove, beside a pot of field peas and a pan of corn bread two afternoons later when a car sloshed past on the still wet, gravel road. Ted rushed in and hollered. "It's Mama!" He turned and ran down the road, Emma a step behind.

Mrs. Brown told Jodie, who scrubbed at a dirty pan. "Go on, child. You don't need to finish. Go see yo mama."

Jodie lit out after them.

CHAPTER 8

Jodie and the younger children came off the road to see Lizzy on her knees in the charred remains of the shack. Black ash covered her arms and clothes. Her mouth moved, but the only sound came from the dull thump of her tears that fell into the ashes. Bess, also covered in ash, stood and shook her head. She rubbed at her eyes with the backs of her hands.

"Mama, Mama," Emma and Ted shouted. Jodie was a step back.

"Oh my god!" Lizzy ran to meet them. "Oh my god! You're alive!" She did not bother to wipe her ash-darkened hands, just hugged them hard.

"We thought y'all was dead," she said between sobs.

Bess also cried, the first and only time Jodie ever saw that.

"Praise the Lord! My younguns weren't took!" Lizzy said. She looked up and said, "I swear I'm gonna do better. So help me God."

They piled into Bess's car to see Ma Bradley but stopped first to thank the Browns.

Ma gave her the key to a house she owned in a rundown part of the town.

"Ain't got no work for you," the tough old woman told her. Her face was deeply lined and wrinkled. She had lost a lot of her hair and covered her head with a white scarf. "Since the plant's been on strike, ain't had no customers." The "plant" was Jordan Hardboard.

With no food or money, Lizzy begged the Salvation Army for whatever she could get. They gave her a few clothes and food enough for a couple of days. Most of the clothes were better than what they lost in the fire.

When the food was gone, Jodie went with Lizzy to the welfare office where they met a stout lady with white hair. For some strange reason, she wore a tiny, cloth hat with a pink ribbon on one side. She stared at them over her wire-rimmed glasses. Lizzy had fixed her hair, even put on makeup and a starched, ironed dress. Jodie had done the same.

"You say Taylor isn't living with you?" She read from the information sheet Lizzy had filled out.

"He went to New Orleans."

"And you aren't working?"

"I been looking," Lizzy said. "But with the plant on strike, ain't nobody got any."

"I'm going to give you a slip for groceries." The woman handed her an authorization slip. "There's been talk about how you make your living."

"You just try raising four younguns on twelve dollars a week."

"Uh-huh." The lady said, "These children were seen living with a nigra family. We just can't have that!" She looked up sharply. "I'm going to start papers in the court to put these poor, mistreated youngsters into a proper home. I know a family here in town that can use this girl." She nodded at Jodie. "The others can live with their pa, if he'll take them."

"Ain't nobody taking my flesh and blood!" Lizzy shouted, "You goddamned lily-livered, low-down, yeller-bellied bitch. You'll have to kill me first!"

Lizzy grabbed Jodie by the arm and dragged her away. Lizzy bawled like a baby all the way home.

They didn't hear any more about it, but Lizzy expected somebody to show up any day and tell her to "hand 'em over." But nobody did and it was time for Christmas. She never had much for "her younguns," but the children didn't seem to care. They were happy to be out of school.

A few days before Christmas, Taylor strolled through the front door with a sack of groceries. He had picked up a leather jacket, pair of boots, and blue jeans since they last saw him. The burned out remains had sent him to the Browns who directed him to Ma Bradley. Ma told him where they were.

"Figured y'all could use this," he said. "Merry Christmas."

Jodie was overjoyed to see him. So were Ted and Emma, even Lizzy, who was so choked up, she could barely call his name.

"My barge's in dry dock with a bent propeller shaft. Got a few days off," he said. "Shore glad to be home to see y'all."

The next day, Taylor and Jodie sat on the front porch and talked. Lizzy and Bess took Ted and Emma into town with them.

"Lizzy says the welfare's gonna try to take y'all away."

"I think it's going to blow over. We ain't, uh, haven't heard anything about it since we went down there." She was afraid he might want to stay. With his temper, that would only mean trouble.

"I'm happy you found work, Taylor. Not much to do around here. The union voted to end the strike at the plant, but they won't go back to work till after Christmas. Don't want to pay them for the days off."

"Bastards!" Taylor cursed.

He looked at her and said, "I wish I could take y'all back with me."

Jodie leaned over and hugged him.

Two days later, Taylor slipped away before daylight. Jodie woke when he kissed her cheek goodbye, but he shushed her. The floor creaked under his departing steps. Tears filled her eyes and rolled onto the pillow when she heard the door close behind him.

Lizzy accepted his departure without comment.

A week later, Lizzy sat at the kitchen table in a housecoat. She rubbed her bloodshot eyes and stared at a crumpled sheet of paper. Her thin hair was twisted and matted and overdue for a shampoo and bleach. Jodie asked what it was.

"This here's a court order," Lizzy said on the verge of tears. "The law's taking y'all away from me. Ted and Emma's gonna live with that bench-legged son of a bitch, Chet. That way he won't have to pay no child support for them."

"What about me, Mama?"

"Oh Jodie Mae, I'm—" Lizzy reached out to hug her but was interrupted by a loud rap on the door.

"Lizzy Phelps," an authoritative voice yelled. "Deputy Sheriff!"

"My god," Lizzy said. "They've sent the law?" Her shoulders slumped forward. She tightened the cloth belt around her housecoat and headed to the porch.

Jodie frowned. The voice was familiar. With Ted and Emma close, she crept into the front room to listen. Ted and Emma chanced quick peeks around the corner of the door.

"This ole boy says Taylor took his car. He in there?" the man asked.

His voice had a fuzzy sound. His words came out round and indistinct. Jodie felt sure she had heard it before. Ted looked at Emma and whispered to Jodie, "He's the one who come by the house, before we was burned out."

"Are you sure?" Jodie asked.

He shook his head. "Ain't it, Emma?"

Emma nodded yes.

Then she remembered. It was the voice of the man waiting for "a varmint" the night of the fire. Was he also the one she saw at the creek? She pushed aside the curtain to see.

She saw a tall, young man in a county sheriff's uniform and badge, his head covered by a sheriff's cap. He stood with one foot on the doorstep. His hand rolled around on the butt of his holstered pistol. Behind him stood an old black man.

Jodie had an instant dislike of the man. Aside from the fact that he'd burned their house, he had a smirk on his face.

She searched his face for anything to identify him as one who stabbed the big man at the creek. That man had a crew cut but wasn't in a uniform and hadn't said anything. He was tall and young like the deputy though and favored him, she thought. She wished he would take off the cap.

Lizzy, relieved that he hadn't come about the "court order," said, "Taylor's been in Memphis for a month."

The man scoffed and said, "This ole boy says the one who took his car was a pint-sized runt with black hair down to his shoulders!

The only thug in this county who answers to that description is your little bastard."

The black man nodded.

"My boy ain't no thug!" Lizzy stamped her foot.

"And I suppose you ain't no goddamned whore?" He straightened and pointed a finger at her. "I'll drag your ass to the jailhouse right now if you threaten me, woman!"

Lizzy slapped both hands on her hips and snorted.

"Where's your little shit asses? I want to question them."

"None of your goddamned business."

"I have an arrest warrant for Taylor. You want me to bust up the house, and you too, serving it?"

Jodie urged Emma and Ted through the door. The deputy stared hard at all three.

"We don't know where Taylor is. It's like Mama says," Jodie told him. Ted and Emma, held on to Lizzy's legs and shook their heads.

"Shit," he jeered. "One of you would lie and the others would swear to it. But I ain't doubting that if he had been in there, he ain't now."

Without a smile, he stared at Jodie, his eyes narrowed.

He leaned forward as his hand slid down the holstered pistol. "I thought maybe we'd met, but I guess not. Have to throw you in jail if I catch you out whoring…like your ma."

Jodie grabbed her mother's arm to hold her back.

The deputy looked at her then told the black man, "Come on. We'll check out the tonks."

When they were out of sight, Jodie told her mama, "He's the one who burned us out for sure. I remember his voice. I think he killed that man at the creek too."

Lizzy's face snapped around. "Listen here, Jodie Mae, all you younguns!" she said. "It ain't right what he done, but he's the law! They say he's a real mean 'un. If he thought y'all knowed anything, Lord knows what might happen to you. Most likely end up in the crazy house, or in the swamps somewheres with a bullet in yore head. They's some things you just have to forget, no matter how bad! You hear me?"

"We will," they promised, but Jodie knew she would never forget.

Lizzy told Jodie, "Might as well throw another handful of coffee in the pot." Jodie followed her into to the kitchen.

"The welfare says you can live with Elmore Jackson and his sickly wife. She's messed up bad inside, maybe got a cancer. You'll have to take care of her, I guess, till you come of age." Lizzy told Jodie where she had to go.

"When, Mama?" Jodie asked.

Lizzy didn't answer right away. Tears dropped from her cheeks and fell on the hot stove and sizzled. "Today," she answered. "You gotta go today."

Close to tears herself, Jodie packed her belongings in a paper sack and sat on the front porch to wait. Ted and Emma sat with her, their bags of clothes by their sides. It was one of those days in December when the weather felt more like early fall than winter. Lizzy stayed at the kitchen table. No one said a word.

Chet came by with his new wife and picked up Emma and Ted. Both children walked backward to the car. Lizzy sobbed on the porch as the car rolled away. With slumped shoulders, and a tear-streaked face, she went inside and collapsed on her unmade bed and cried like a whipped child.

"I reckon I'll go now, Mama," Jodie told her in a whisper.

Lizzy struggled out of bed and hugged Jodie. "I'm sorry, Jodie Mae. As God is my witness, I'm sorry. He's a punishing me. I hope someday you'll understand. They's things you don't want to do, but sometimes you ain't got no choice." Later, she got drunk.

CHAPTER 9

Jodie trudged along Front Street with her paper sack of belongings. Christmas carols, mournful to her, came from the stores she passed. Each one seemed to hang on until the next had its turn. Then, she stood in front of the Jackson's store, where Lizzy told her to go. It occupied the lower floor of an old two-storied brick building and offered men's and women's clothing.

The bricks, once bright red, had faded to a dull pink and were streaked with black tar and orange rust from the roof and rain gutters. An overhang, secured to the front of the building by rusty steel cables, extended over the sidewalk. A plain wooden sign bearing the name "Elmore's Discount Clothes, Men's and Women's" in black and white letters, rested along the front edge of the overhang. To confirm years of neglect, white paint curls clung in patches to the sign. Most stores along Front Street were run-down. Their main customers were country people, plant workers, and blacks; people who wanted bargains, not fresh paint.

The store had three plate glass display windows and two glass doors, one for the men's department and one for the women's. Jodie sighed and went inside. Three centrally located columns supported the store's ceiling and divided the men's department from the women's. The cashier's stand, near the rear of the store, was a square enclosure with counters elevated two feet off the floor so the clerks who sat inside could watch customers in the store. The men's and women's shoe departments, separated by a hallway, were at the rear of the cashier's stand. Behind the men's shoe department was a storage room for extra inventory. There was a small office and bathroom behind women's shoes.

Jodie made her way to the clerk's stand where a stout woman in her fifties gossiped with a younger woman and man. Her hair, piled on top and frazzled, was completely white. Her eyes had followed Jodie from the moment she entered the store. She was on commission.

"Beg your pardon," Jodie said.

"Yes," the woman replied. She didn't smile as was her custom with a customer. The sack by Jodie's side told her Jodie was not a customer. Her name was Myrtle Ralston. She had been with the store since it opened.

"I'm looking for Mr. Elmore Jackson."

"He's not hiring. Business still down from the strike," Myrtle snapped.

"The welfare sent me."

"Oh, you must be the new nurse." Her tone softened. "You go right through there to the flight of stairs outside." She pointed to the narrow hallway at the rear of the store. "The apartment is upstairs."

The apartment had been storage space for the store but was never used for that purpose. It was renovated into a modest-sized living room, two bedrooms, and a bath. A kitchen and dining room overlooked the alley.

Jodie went up the steep stairway. It was exposed to the weather but had a covered landing at the top. She caught her breath and knocked.

Elmore Jackson, a hulk of a man with broad shoulders and square face, answered. He wore a white shirt and dark pants. "Yes?" He was hunched over as he opened the door, but straightened up when he saw Jodie. His face was lined with a sad, serious look, but his dark brown eyes were alert. He brushed his brown hair into place with his fingers. A scant amount of gray showed at the temples.

"I'm from the welfare," Jodie said. "Jodie Mae Phelps."

"Come in. Come in. Turning cold." He looked behind her. A gust of cold wind whipped up debris in the alley behind the store.

"I guess they told you what you'd do. My wife is in bed these days. She's weak," he said and gestured for her to follow.

He opened the door to her room. A thick curtain kept out most of the light and everything inside the room—the bed, chairs, tables, everything—was covered in pale shadows. The air was stale, but it was the smell of medicine and the stink of sickness that Jodie noticed.

Mrs. Jackson sat up when she saw Jodie. She was thin and delicate. Her hair was as white as her face was pale.

The sickness, Jodie thought.

The woman pulled the bed covers up and frowned slightly when Mr. Jackson introduced Jodie as "the new nurse."

"I'd like a word with Mr. Jackson," the frail woman said. She was younger than Elmore, but looked years older.

Jodie closed the door behind her and waited in the living room. A layer of dust covered everything she saw. Newspapers and magazines littered the chairs and tables. Dust curls lay everywhere. A couple of pictures hung lopsided on the walls. It looked as sad and neglected as the outside of the building.

Jodie overheard Mrs. Jackson complain. "I thought they were going to send a colored. I don't want a white girl to see me like this."

Mr. Jackson's gentle reply was muffled. "Now Ruthy...didn't have one. Phelps...country girl. If...work out, I'll get a colored."

When the bedroom door opened, Elmore motioned Jodie inside. He recited her duties—give medicine, help Mrs. Jackson to the bathroom, dress her in the mornings, wash clothes, and keep the apartment clean.

The Jacksons' children, Virginia and Marshall, came up from Mobile the day before Christmas. Marshall was thin and slight like his mother. He had a small face and sandy hair with curly ripples. He was no taller than Jodie, months past thirty, with a high-pitched, grating voice.

How can a rough man like Elmore have a sissy like Marshall? Jodie wondered.

Virginia, a few years younger than Marshall, was large and dumpy from top to bottom with frowzy light brown hair. It looked as if parts of her flesh tried to roll through folds in the extra large dress she wore. She had two children but, out of deference to her mother's condition, had left them with her husband. She was almost a head taller than Jodie.

Jodie stayed in the room with Mrs. Jackson while they visited with Mr. Jackson in the living room. Mrs. Jackson slept most of the time.

"Well, I agree with Mother!" She heard Marshall say. "It's not right to have her waited on by a white girl."

"It does seem bad to force Mother to accept someone she doesn't like," Virginia said with a tone of pained concern.

"I'm not going to send her back," Elmore said. "Can't. I gave my word."

Jodie walked to the window, parted the curtain, and stared out at the birds fluttering about in the cold outside. She preferred that cold to the kind she felt.

Virginia dismissed her for Christmas day. "We'll have our dinner as a family."

What a relief, Jodie thought as she walked home. Taylor was there!

"I'm so glad to see you!" Jodie said and hugged him. "You look so good!"

He flexed his muscles. "Hard work, Jodie Mae."

"I didn't expect to see you so soon. When'd you get in?"

He drove from New Orleans the night before.

"Had that...borrowed car," he said with a grin. "Figured I'd better bring it back. It being Christmas 'n all. 'Sides, the tag expired."

They laughed at that, and it felt good. It had been a long time since they had laughed together.

Thanks to Taylor, they had a ham for Christmas dinner. Chet brought Ted and Emma by while he visited his new wife's family. Bess ate with them. As far as Jodie knew, they were her only family. Taylor was up early the next morning, as was Jodie. They both had work to get to.

"Have to hitch back," he said.

Jodie held back tears as she hugged him goodbye.

"Don't know when I'll get back," he said then pressed his red switchblade into her hand. "Use it if you have to." He was gone.

Jodie overlooked Mrs. Jackson's resentment and saw to her every need. Then, there was a change. It happened when Jodie told the woman that she couldn't cook.

"Hoecakes and brown gravy are about all I know."

Mrs. Jackson smiled. "I'll show you! I love to, used to anyway, love to cook."

Mrs. Jackson sat in a soft chair Jodie brought into the kitchen and told her what to do. It was the first time she had been out of her room in months, and she seemed to come alive.

In the spring, she gained strength. With Jodie's help to get down the stairs, they went for walks in the park. Her color improved. The bedroom window curtain was opened. While it was only a remission, the doctor said, it was welcomed; and Elmore believed it was Jodie's doing.

Mrs. Jackson also took an interest in Jodie's appearance. She showed her hairstyles, helped her select and apply makeup, and even gave her a couple of dresses. Lipstick and rouge, the few times she used them before, was whatever Bess or Lizzy had left lying around, something dark red.

Jodie was paid fourteen dollars a week plus room and board, some of which she gave Lizzy to help out. She slept on a cot in Mrs. Jackson's room. Elmore slept in the extra bedroom. On Sundays, her day off, she visited Lizzy.

Men were not as interested in Lizzy as they once had been. So "to make a living," she turned the rented house into a beer parlor. The payoff to the police chief to sell beer was much less than for whiskey. A man called Tex, big and stooped-shouldered with whiskers that stayed black even after a close shave, gave her money for the payoff and stayed around afterward to help. Not married, they fought anyway.

The next Christmas, Ruth directed and Jodie cooked Christmas dinner for the Jacksons.

"We'll cook all their favorites!" Mrs. Jackson said. With decorations from boxes under her bed, she and Jodie decorated a five-foot pine tree. Placed just inside the living room, a fresh pine scent greeted all that entered. Jodie took care in draping red and white tinsel ropes over and around the boughs, and on spots pointed out by Mrs. Jackson, she hung treasured glass ornaments unwrapped from tissue paper by the frail woman. They added gossamer webs of angel's hair. Jodie placed a well-worn silver star on top.

Jodie stood back and admired the tree. "It's my first really," she said. Before the divorce, Chet might not show up for Christmas; and if he did, he was drunk and "they" fought. After the divorce, it seemed they were either moving, about to move, or had just moved. Christmas became just another day.

"It's beautiful," Mrs. Jackson said. "Last year Elmore did most of it. You should have seen that one." She laughed.

In the spring, Jodie turned twenty-one. She had been there for almost a year and a half. It was 1947.

One day, when she bent over to lift a box of dirty clothes, she turned to see Elmore staring at her. Then he walked away. He began to drink more after that.

In the summer, instead of a visit with Lizzy and Tex on Sundays to witness their drunken brawls, Jodie walked in the country. She wanted to buy a piece of land, something that would be hers alone, a place no one could run her "off from." On other days, she read the classics and Robert Browning's poetry to Mrs. Jackson in the park. She loved to read.

Steven's handsome face popped into her thoughts when she was alone. She'd remember the wonder of that summery afternoon, the rain, his embrace. Once while she and Mrs. Jackson were in the park, she thought she saw him. After a while, she didn't remember so much. It felt better not to. "I don't care," she told herself. "I don't care about anything."

Ruth's favorite was a stanza of a poem from a wife to her husband. She had taken a pencil and changed a few words. "Thy love shall hold me fast, until the last minute's sleep is past, and I awake saved and yet it will not be." Tears ran down the cheeks of the dying woman and Jodie's as well. Both wished that she would "awake saved," but knew that she would not. Remissions were always followed by periods of accelerated deterioration.

She died in October. Before she fell asleep for the last time, she put a gold locket into Jodie's hand. "It's yours," she whispered.

Ruth Jackson was dead. Elmore's sobs filled the apartment. The store closed for the funeral. Virginia and Marshall came to help with the arrangements. After the funeral, Elmore took a fifth of whiskey and went into her bedroom. When the bottle was empty, he passed out. Jodie, with Marshall and Virginia, kept the wake in the front room.

Seeing his mother's locket around Jodie's neck, Marshall pointed and said, "You took that from my mother!"

"I did not! She gave it to me." She clutched it to her chest.

"Ha," Virginia scoffed. "Stole it, I bet."

"We'll see about that!" Marshall pranced into the bedroom, but Elmore couldn't be roused.

"Well, I know Mother would never give you her locket!" he said when he returned. Virginia agreed with a sharp nod of her head.

Jodie decided not to argue. It didn't seem right. Ruth Jackson's last sleep had passed, and she had not awakened.

Before the rest of the Jacksons were awake the next morning, Jodie gathered her clothes and went home. Lizzy and Tex were still in bed. When Jodie announced at the bedroom door that she was back and why, Lizzy, her voice hoarse, told her, "Since you're here, fix the coffee."

"Shut the hell up! I'm trying to sleep." Tex groaned.

Lizzy got up when she smelled the coffee. "So the Jackson woman upped and died, did she?" Lizzy's bleached blond hair, matted in prongs by greasy fumes from last night's hamburgers, protruded from her head like barren tree branches.

"Didn't figure she'd last this long, no how. He pay you regular? Elmore?"

Jodie nodded.

"We behind in our rent. Could use some help."

Jodie winced. She had one hundred dollars, enough for one acre of land.

"You hear me, Jodie Mae? I said we need money. If you coming back here, you gotta help out. We don't make much, not after we pay everybody off. Low-bred bastards, living off my sweat. It ain't right!" She sat her coffee-stained mug hard on the table and stared at Jodie through bloodshot eyes.

"I only have twenty-five dollars left," Jodie lied.

"Ain't enough for what you put up with. I'm gonna go see that Elmore Jackson and get some more."

"Don't do that."

Lizzy took a mug of coffee to the bedroom for Tex. While she was gone, Jodie hid all but twenty-five dollars in her shoes. She had seen her mother go through pockets before, and she didn't trust Tex.

Elmore was up by then. He had a headache, but he also had a store to run.

Jodie had left a note. It read, "Dear Mr. Jackson, I just want you to know how much I enjoyed taking care of Mrs. Jackson. She was a nice lady and you are a nice man. I'm going home now. I only took my clothes and things. I'm leaving the locket Mrs. Jackson gave me. She must have already promised it to Marshall."

Elmore stumbled into the dining room where Marshall was sitting. "You tell Jodie Mae your mother gave you this locket?"

Marshall hated it when his father raised his voice. He squirmed in his chair and said, "Uh, well, we, I just thought it should stay with the family. That girl would...well, Father, really! Everybody knows the Phelps are trashy people. Her mother even—"

"Don't you ever say that again, boy! That girl worked hard for your mother and me. If she's trash, we all should be."

Marshall didn't argue and, of course, neither did Virginia. Besides, Jodie was gone, and they had the locket.

"I sure need somebody to help me in the store," Elmore told Marshall at breakfast. His anger had passed. He and Ruth had wanted Marshall to learn the business and take it over when they were gone, but Marshall always refused.

"For God's sake, just sell the damn thing and retire!" Marshall said.

"Then, what would I do? A man has to stay busy. Hell, I'm too young to retire! Barely fifty!" He straightened up.

More than "barely," Marshall thought but didn't take issue and the discussion tailed off. Marshall pocketed the locket before he and Virginia left that afternoon. Elmore packed his wife's things and folded the cot. Within a few days, the only traces of his wife were his memories and the photo he kept by his bed.

He went to the store and wandered around without speaking to anyone.

CHAPTER 10

In another part of town, where no one ever drove on Sundays to see how the well-to-do were doing, Lizzy poured herself a mug of coffee and sat down at the table with Jodie. There was a chill in the room, and it was like the dank air was sticky with smells—beer and cigarettes dominated by the greasy smell of fried hamburgers.

Jodie waited for her to say something. She didn't, just sighed and stared at the stained table.

Jodie asked, "You want me to go to the welfare?"

"No, I reckon not. I'll put up a cot for you in the kitchen. You can help out nights waiting tables," Lizzy told her.

"I don't want to," Jodie protested.

"I guess you think you too good for that! Well, let me tell you something. I wasn't too good to do lots worse than that when I was putting food on your table," she said. She did not try to disguise her bitterness. "Lots worse." Her voice trailed off. She stared into her mug.

Jodie waited tables that night.

"You can have old Lizzy, but I'd shore like me some of that Jodie Mae," a customer said and pinched her behind as she passed.

"Ouch!" When she gave him a dirty look, he laughed and slapped the table.

"Why do they do that? They know I don't like it," she complained to her mother. "If it's not that, they slap my behind or squeeze my leg or ask me to go to bed. One man even put a five-dollar bill on the table."

"They just want to get a rise out of you. My butt used to look like it'd been hit with buckshot."

Tex leered from his straight-backed chair but said nothing. As tough as he was, he was wary of Lizzy's temper.

One afternoon, Lizzy went out to buy hamburger buns while Jodie ironed bed sheets. Tex lay sprawled on Jodie's cot in a dirty undershirt and pants and sipped a beer. The loose-fitting blouse she wore gave him an occasional glimpse of pink flesh, enough for him to imagine the glimpse was meant for him. He stared for a few minutes, then got up and rubbed his crotch against her behind. She twisted around and shoved him away.

He grinned. "You ready for some of that? I bet you ain't never had any dick, have you? You probably just stick your finger in it, don't you?"

Jodie was horrified. She slapped at his face, but he caught her hand and pulled her toward him. His breath came in lustful pants. With her free hand, she pushed at his whiskered face.

"Leave me alone!" she shouted. Fear kept her from being nauseated by the foul smell of cigarette smoke and stale beer on his breath. "I'm going to tell—"

"Quit your damned wiggling!" He twisted her arm behind her back. She grimaced but did not cry out. Frustrated by her lack of cooperation, he ripped away the front of her blouse and slapped her hard across the face. Dazed, she staggered back a step. When he yanked her toward him, she hit him full on the jaw with a stinging pop. He blinked and threw her across the cot.

"Goddamn you!" He began to unbuckle his pants. "You gonna get what you need. We'll see how goddamned feisty you'll be then."

Fear filled her mind. Panic and helplessness. Tex stood between her and the door and anything she could use as a weapon. She wanted the flat iron, but it was out of reach on the ironing board.

He kicked off his pants and rubbed his jaw. "Now." He grinned and spread his arms wide to block her escape. He licked his lips in anticipation; the bulge in his shorts grew. Devil! She remembered and jerked it from under the pillow. She pressed the button to let the old blade swing into place, shiny and lethal. At the same time, she jumped up and pushed the blade toward his stomach. Her breasts fell loose from the ripped brassiere, but she was so angry she didn't even notice. Tex's lust was gone. The first click of the blade saw to that. He stepped back and held out his hands.

"Now goddamn it, Jodie Mae! I was just joking, really. I wasn't gonna do anything."

"You sure as hell aren't now, are you?" Jodie jabbed at his flabby stomach and sent him jumping backward.

"That thing's e'legal!"

She backed him across the room, past the ironing board. She picked up the iron, still hot, and swung it against the meaty part of his shoulder. It left a nice red tattoo. He ran cursing into the bedroom and slammed the door behind him. He shouted, "I'll get you for this, you prissy bitch. You'll be begging me for it 'fore I'm through."

"You worthless piece of dog shit!" she cried out, recalling something Taylor had called somebody years before. "Open the door and see who'll be doing the begging!" She screamed and slammed the iron against the door again and again. Her energy drained, she collapsed on the cot and sat mute till Lizzy returned.

Tex answered Jodie's accusations with some of his own. "She was coming on to me, Lizzy. I swear to God. Get me the Bible. I'll put my hand on it! I hope God'll strike me dead if I'm lying." By then he'd had several beers. The raw red mark on his shoulder had bubbled.

"Liar!" she shouted at him and pointed her finger in his face. She turned to her mother. "He's a liar! He's been staring at me since I came back. He's no better than a egg-sucking dog."

Lizzy eyed the man and nodded. "I can't have nothing." She began to cry. "God don't want me to have nothing! He's still a punishing me."

She took a beer from the refrigerator. Tex did the same.

Lizzy faced him and screamed at the top of her voice. "You a cock-sucking, low-down son of a bitch!"

"Don't curse at me, woman! Shut yore goddamned mouth or I'll shut it for you."

Jodie retreated to the dark front room and listened and waited for what she knew was coming. Tex and Lizzy matched each other beer for beer, obscenity for obscenity. They circled about the kitchen and eyed each other like two spitting alley cats ready to fly at each other. Nearing midnight, the cursing stopped. The room grew silent.

First the table was flattened and the legs used as clubs. Chairs were splintered and Jodie's cot wrecked beyond repair. Finally, when the clubs grew too heavy to swing, they slugged it out, toe to toe. Lizzy gave two or three licks to his one, but his were worse. He lost a tooth and blood poured from cuts on both lips. Her eyes were blackened and both eyebrows gashed.

The sirens sounded. Jodie hid in the closet. The police burst through the back door and carried them away. It took four officers to subdue Lizzy. The beer bar was closed that night.

Jodie walked to the jail after dark. Prisoners were in an upstairs cellblock that overlooked the street. Tex was passed out, but Lizzy, still drunk and raging mad, smashed out the windows of her cell with her fists. Lit by the streetlights, blood streaks glistened on the fallen glass. Not content, Lizzy ripped the bed from the wall and threw pieces of it and the bedclothes through the window. Next she threw out the prison smock and stood completely naked in the window.

"Goddamned cocksuckers!" she screamed at anybody walking by and then, for some unaccountable but merciful reason, passed out. Someone came to bandage her bleeding wrists. Jodie wanted to cry, but the episode left her without feelings.

The next day, Lizzy and Tex appeared before Judge Harvey, a small man with glasses and a crooked mustache. He spoke rapidly and in a deep voice.

"Mrs. Phelps, I'm going to let you and this man go. However, I want you to know I regard you as a bad influence in this city. If you ever appear in my court again, I'll levy a stiff fine and add jail time." He rapped his gravel and reached for the next file.

"You goddamned hypocrite," Lizzy screamed as the bailiffs dragged her away. "I've seen you come in the back door of Ma's many a times!"

Jodie, who sat at the back, cringed. The courtroom, filled with lawyers and clients, broke into laughter.

"Put that woman in jail till evening," the judge ordered.

Jodie waited by the front door of the jail until well after dark when she was let out. Lizzy staggered out. Tex had long since left town, never to return.

Lizzy reopened the beer bar.

"Ain't got no choice. We gotta eat," she told Jodie.

Bess dropped by to help when she could, still smiling as always. She'd taken a job as a maid in a boarding house. Like Lizzy, she had aged and not much in demand. Lizzy was her only friend as Bess was Lizzy's.

Jodie cooked when Bess worked the beer bar with Lizzy, which wasn't often. When Bess wasn't around, Jodie and Lizzy did it all. Jodie felt her mother blamed her for Tex's departure.

Mr. Jackson sent a card at Christmas. Two months had passed since the funeral. It seemed a year to Jodie. Each night that she wiped tables and fended off customers took a little more of her self-respect. When she had time, she read the classified ads. The only jobs she was qualified for were as bad as the one she had.

"You ain't taking care of your hair no more," Lizzy complained. "Can't catch no boyfriend looking like that. Customers don't like it either. You ain't bad looking. Beats me why you try to look so god-awful."

Jodie walked away. That night, after the café closed, she looked at herself in the bathroom mirror and cried. Her hair was stringy and greasy, uncombed in…she couldn't remember when. She felt as dirty as the tables that she cleaned of spilled beer and catsup, no better than the men whose tables she served, men with day-old beards and week-old body odors.

How long will it be before I get so sick and tired of this that I'll say yes when somebody asks me to go "juking" or maybe even "marry up with them"? she thought. Six kids, a potbelly to go with them, a mongrel dog or two, and a garden to tend while he's out drinking and pinching behinds.

"I wish I was dead," she said. But with no other choice, she kept on.

CHAPTER 11

By mid-March, the winds had died down and spring blooms opened. Birds sang in the sweet perfumed air outside while inside the foul-smelling beer bar, Jodie picked up the pieces of a broken beer bottle left over from a ruckus the night before. It was Sunday, a day of rest. Jodie used it to catch up, to get ready for Monday night. Mondays were slow. She liked Mondays.

The door opened behind her and let a shaft of bright sunlight inside the room.

"Jodie Mae?"

It was Elmore Jackson. He stood just inside the door and stared, as if not sure what to do next. His gray felt hat was clutched in his hand. Ashamed of the way she looked and felt, she blushed.

She stood and offered him a chair. "Can I get you a cup of coffee, Mr. Jackson?" There was no feeling in her voice.

He declined her offer and asked, "Uh, is your mother at home?"

Lizzy barged in from the kitchen. "Howdy. Sure sorry to hear about Mrs. Jackson. Get us some coffee, Jodie Mae. I got some things to say to Mr. Jackson."

Jodie frowned at her mother and shook her head.

Elmore's lips moved like he wanted to speak, but no words came. He looked about the place. Finally, he said, "I've been thinking. Since Ruthy passed on, I've, uh, been kind of lonely."

She scoffed. "Don't have time to get lonely around here."

Jodie returned and handed each a cup of hot coffee. Saucers weren't used in the beer bar, just an extra dish to wash and nobody minded. He wrapped his hands around the warm cup and sat down. Jodie retreated to the kitchen doorway.

He glanced about the shadow-filled room and said, "No, ma'am, I don't reckon you do. Uh, what I want to say…I've missed Jodie." He sighed, relieved to say what was on his mind.

"What? Huh! Is that why you…Well, you can just get notion that out of your head right now. You—"

He waved his big hands slowly across the table and interrupted. "It's not like that, Mrs. Phelps." It was one of the few times Jodie had ever heard her mother addressed as Mrs. anything. "Uh, uh, you see, I'd, uh, like to marry Jodie." He lowered his head and stared into his cup.

Lizzy looked at Jodie but said nothing, then back at Mr. Jackson. Jodie was too stunned to say anything.

He said, "Mother used to tell me Jodie wanted to go to college. I'd let her go to JC." JC was a two-year college near town. "And someday, maybe when I get ready to retire, I'd let her do a little in the store…when I get ready to retire. Not any time soon, of course. Wouldn't that be better than this for…Jodie?"

Lizzy lit a cigarette and stared at the wall. Jodie wanted to run through the front door and not stop.

"Ain't you forgetting your age? You gotta be—" She wasn't sure how old to say really. Looking at his lined face and the way he stood sometimes, hunched over from arthritis, it was hard to tell.

"Mrs. Phelps," he interrupted. "I'm as strong as I ever was. I work twelve hours a day just like I always have." He stood as if to demonstrate how robust he was. "A man is only old if he lets himself go."

Jodie frowned. He was old!

"I'm counting on Jodie Mae to help me out here," she said. "Got rheumatism in both hands, need help."

It had come on when she knocked out her jail cell windows with her fists, Jodie remembered.

"I reckon it'd cost me better than a couple of hundred dollars to get somebody trained as good as her."

"What!" Jodie said. It just came out. She backed into the kitchen, out of sight. Was her mother negotiating her away for two hundred dollars!

"I could loan you a few hundred, Mrs. Phelps," he replied.

"Don't know when I'd get around to paying you back."

Elmore acknowledged with a nod of his head. At first, he was ill at ease, but now that they were bargaining, he relaxed.

Lizzy turned and said, "Jodie Mae! Where are you?"

Jodie came to the kitchen door, but said nothing.

"What do you think? You can't expect to spend the rest of your life frying burgers and opening beer bottles. You're almost twenty-two."

Jodie's birthday was in April. She fought back the tears, slowly shook her head sideways, and then stared at the floor.

"Let us think on it, Mr. Jackson," Lizzy said.

Elmore waved goodbye to Jodie, but she never raised her head.

"What's wrong with you, child?" she asked Jodie when he was out of sight. "The man's offering you a roof over your head. Ain't seen nobody around here offer better. He ain't bad looking, all things considered. Can't be more than fifty, well, maybe a little more."

"I…" her voice choked. "I…you need me here. You said."

"Old Bess can help me. She's about had a belly full of that boarding house."

"Mr. Jackson's old. He's…I…" The thought of marriage sent a churning to her stomach.

"Shit, you worried about sleeping with him?"

Steven's face flashed through her thoughts.

"You get used to it. First couple of times it hurts some then it's okay. Just spread yore legs, the man does the rest. Now and again, you get a little fun out of it." She paused as though trying to remember. "Now and then."

Jodie stared at her. Although she had heard her say worse about sleeping with men, it had never been real until then.

"Don't last long, no way. If you get a mind to, moan and wiggle some, they get their gun faster that way. Have to get you a douche. Keep you from stinking. God, a womern has to put up with a lot of shit." She shook her head in disgust.

Unable to stand anymore of it, Jodie ran from the house and stayed away until after dark. Lizzy was asleep when she returned.

The next morning, Lizzy asked, "You made up your mind? It ain't the money, the two hundred. Just a way for me to get something out of it. I'm thinking of you, Jodie Mae."

"Me?"

"Well, you're always saying how you don't like working here. That old man's offering you a way out. Go to college. Make something of yourself."

Jodie shook her head, still unable to believe Elmore's proposal and her mother's response.

"I can't make you go, but if you stay here, you know what it's gonna be like. Sure don't want another thing like with Tex. I'm too old to be fighting a man off you."

"You weren't fighting him off me. You were fighting because you were mad at him."

"I ain't saying that ain't partly so, but next time I get a man, I want to keep him. Long as you around, they gonna look and think. Look and think and wonder. That's the way a man is. They can't help it. Get a couple of beers in their gut, they start seeing things they ain't seeing."

She patted the tabletop where she sat, stared off, and then said, "Tell you the truth, Jodie Mae, I'm getting tired of this way of life. I'm looking to get married myself…if I can find anybody who'd have me. There was a time…" She shook her head. "Not anymore. Plum wore out now, I reckon." She turned away to wipe a tear.

"Well, you marry him! I don't want to! He's not…"

Lizzy looked at her for a pause then said, "If you'er thinking about that Jefferson boy you…met when we lived in Whitfield, he's marrying that Jordan gal. Just read it in the paper." She pointed at the newspaper on the table.

Jodie grabbed the paper. The story was on the front page. "Steven Jefferson will wed Victoria Jordan after his graduation from law school in June." She slumped forward. She dreamed that he would remember and come for her. That dream died.

Lizzy, seeing the desperate look on Jodie's face, said, "Child, I'm sorry. I guess I knowed how you felt, writing them letters and all, but it wasn't never gonna be. Them kind of people marry their own kind. We ain't—"

"I know what we are," Jodie interrupted. "We're white trash. Enough people have told me."

"Well, you know a womern can't do much in this world, wait tables or clerk somewheres. I ain't wanting you to get mixed up with Ma and her kind."

"I'd rather be dead," Jodie said and wished she were. "I'll start the burgers for tonight."

"Think on it. Lots of old men marry younguns. Ain't nothing wrong with it. They die and you get their property. He does have that ole store."

"The bread's on top of the ice box." They mixed in stale bread to stretch the ground beef. Covered with catsup and onions, and washed down with beer, nobody ever complained about the taste.

Jodie lay in bed that night and stared at the ceiling. She was Jodie Mae Phelps, poor white trash, not somebody Steven would marry.

It's like Taylor said, she thought, *we're always gonna be white trash. Elmore's offer is the only escape I have. God!* She recalled something else Taylor had said: "The only thing we'll ever have is what we take."

Well, by God, she thought, *I'll take his damn store. At least I'll have something. I don't care anymore. God, I don't care. I just wish I could die.*

The next morning, she told her mother, "I'll do it."

She married Elmore in June 1948. Marshall and Virginia objected and refused to come to the wedding. Jodie didn't invite Lizzy and didn't know how to reach Taylor.

A year later, Jodie Mae Jackson worked to finish Christmas dinner before Marshall and Virginia showed up. Elmore expected it.

Drizzling winter rain covered the asphalt in front of the store in an ebony shine. Cars and pickup trucks bumped over the water-filled potholes that peppered the street with bone-jarring jolts and rhythmic regularity, but they barely slowed. There was no time. Christmas was only days away and gift lists had to be completed.

Jodie smiled as she peered at the apple cinnamon pie that was baked in the oven. She slid the bubbling pie out to sit on the range top to cool. Its aroma wafted into the apartment.

"Umm..." Jodie could not resist a taste of the fresh apple filling that oozed through narrow slits in the golden brown crust. She kissed the tiny patch of sweetness from her finger and wiped perspiration from her forehead with her apron tail.

The small kitchen, accessible through the dining room, stayed hot regardless of the season from heat given off by the gas range and the apartment water heater. Its single window remained propped open with a stick in summer and winter to emit as much heat as possible. Jodie suspected not much ever escaped. The orange and yellow kitchen floor linoleum was trail worn to its black asphalt base. Only the keen eye of one who washed dishes would know the sink once had a complete porcelain cover. The pale Formica countertop was chipped and unglued at the corners. The white refrigerator had a long history even before it was lugged up the stairs from the Jackson's first home.

But, Jodie had mopped the floor to a sheen and the lace curtains over the kitchen window were starched and ironed. Every curtain in the apartment hung with renewed crispness. In the dining room, on an oak sideboard, were yet another apple cinnamon pie and a plate heaped full of oatmeal cookies. A fresh ham and baked turkey would soon join them, along with all the salads and vegetables Jodie's kitchen could produce.

"Marshall and Virginia are driving up!" Elmore announced a few days earlier. They would arrive three days before Christmas to spend time with Elmore. That'd leave time for Virginia to get home for a Christmas celebration with her family. Marshall spent Christmas with Virginia's family.

It was the first visit for them since the wedding. In reprisal for Elmore's marriage to Jodie, they had shunned him last Christmas, and he wandered about the apartment in lonely gloom. So the day was a special one for him and a responsibility for Jodie that she viewed with anxiety and apprehension.

"Better fix everything Mrs. Jackson would have," Jodie thought out loud as she began her two-day toil. "A feast for the wayward children."

Jodie's work was interrupted by "Joy to the World" coming from the living room radio, a floor console. She strode into the room to switch it off.

She refluffed the cushions of Elmore's brown leather easy chair placed within arm's reach of the radio knobs. Then, she inspected the effect of the white lace doilies on the two red velvet chairs and matching sofa. Like the curtains, each had been washed, starched, and ironed. The mahogany accent table in the middle of the room was waxed and crowned by a vase of green and red carnations from the florist. A framed picture of Ruth Jackson sat on it. Jodie figured it was up to Elmore to put it away. Nothing would be changed from when their mother kept house. Even the white crinkled shades over the sofa lamps were wiped clean.

The wooden "what-not" stand in the corner was as Ruth had left it. Miniature crystal and porcelain figurines occupied their same positions. Only the dust had been removed. Jodie glanced up at the white ceiling light globe. It was clean, but the wallpaper sagged.

"Was it sagging that first day?" She tried to recall what it had looked like when she first arrived to care for Ruth. It did not matter really, as she could not repair it anyway, and Elmore did not seem to care. The wallpaper was a concession to Ruth. Plain white paint would have satisfied him.

Using Ruth's decorations, Jodie recreated the Christmas tree they had decorated together. "It looks the same," she said, pleased with her effort. The scent of pine drifted through the apartment. The slam of a car door jolted her back to the present. She rushed to the dining room window and looked out.

"They're here!" She sighed and tried to smile in spite of the feeling in her stomach.

Marshall twirled out of the car.

"He hasn't changed," Jodie said. He still carried the youthful build of a teenager with an unblemished, dainty face. The red tie he wore with a green plaid sports coat matched his curly sandy hair and his fiery temperament. Virginia drove her car. Marshall did not own one. Her brother's opposite, she slid out of the car slowly.

"She favors Elmore. Unfortunately."

The seams and folds of Virginia's black and white dress hung in bunches and gathers. Marshall paced and fidgeted as he waited for his sister to push her arms into a shapeless, black wool coat. They divided up brightly colored packages from the back seat.

As she peered out the window, Jodie's thoughts flashed back to a time shortly after her marriage to Elmore. The recollection sent a shiver over her body.

CHAPTER 12

On that day, she watched Elmore and Marshall exchange bitter words while Virginia watched from her car. And Jodie heard every hateful word that Marshall said.

"Mother didn't even like her! She wrote me!" Marshall shrieked.

"At first, son," Elmore replied. "But she got to where she loved Jodie like one of her own, and Jodie loved her. I could tell."

"The POOR thing," Marshall said, his voice at soprano heights. "And you couldn't wait to marry her. A PHELPS! White trash! Her mother's the biggest whore in the county. You've DISGRACED Mother! You've disgraced us!" He waved his finger in his father's face. "What's next, a little brother or sister…six months from now. How disgusting!"

"Shut your mouth, boy! It's not like that! There's not going to be children. I…there won't be any."

"Ha. So you say. You don't know what she's been doing!"

Elmore's jaw tightened.

"Her mother was a whore. She must have learned a few tricks whoring around with her."

Elmore slapped Marshall across the face and knocked him to the asphalt. He looked up at his father, a bewildered look on his face. Elmore stepped toward him. He cringed and rolled back.

Elmore reached down to help him up. "Sorry, son. I guess I lost my temper." He pulled Marshall to his feet and brushed him off.

"I've heard stories about Lizzy Phelps. She was a rough woman, but Jodie isn't like that."

Marshall fingered the gold locket he wore around his neck.

When Elmore saw, he exploded. "But I don't reckon YOU'D be able to tell the difference anyway! Wearing your mother's gold locket around your goddamned neck like a—" He stopped, unable to concede, even in fury, his son's aberration.

"Whore!" The word still reverberated in Jodie's thoughts. She was not a whore. Elmore knew that from their wedding night.

Elmore drove them to the coast for a honeymoon after a justice of peace wedding. He'd promised a place at the beach but, claiming tiredness, stopped at the first motel they saw.

Check-in wasn't quick enough, but made it through. Finally. He locked the door behind them and sighed to himself. Ruth's long illness frustrated his sexual gratification for a long time, but that was soon to end, by god! He was alone in a motel room with a young woman, his wife. He throbbed with insistence.

"No flies on me," he mumbled then told Jodie, "Go...get ready." He nodded to the bathroom and began to remove his shirt and trousers. He slipped out of his underwear and crawled between the cool sheets of the bed to wait. The passion that gripped him was so overwhelming he gave no thought to the flesh that sagged on what had once been a powerful chest, nor to the white, brittle hair on it.

Jodie lingered in the bathroom after she slipped a flimsy pink nightgown over her naked body. What Elmore wanted so desperately, she wanted just as desperately to avoid. The thought of having that old man touch her made her want to crawl out the bathroom window. And she might have if there had been one that would open.

"Jodie Mae," he barked from the bedroom.

Might as well get it over with, she thought. Lizzy said it'd only last a few minutes. She remembered Steven and shook her head to rid it of the thought. With a deep breath, she turned the knob and opened the door. Elmore had left the light on.

She eased into bed. Elmore panted with anticipation as he removed the nightgown from her trembling body. He wanted to see full out what she'd brought to his marriage bed. It was a man's right.

"My god," he mumbled without realizing that he had. The sight of her two full, erect breasts, tipped by protruding nipples, brought a second, involuntary, "My god," from his lips.

Jodie steeled herself against his assault. She shut her eyes and fought the urge to push his head away. She began counting to herself, one, two, three…It wouldn't last forever. She counted.

Elmore's hand followed the curve of her torso past her waist to the hair-shrouded nexus between her legs. One hand lingered while the other slid down the length of her leg. He abruptly threw back the cover and stared at her legs. "Don't you shave!" he shouted.

"Shave?" She knew the hair on her legs had gotten longer and darker during the past few years, but thought nothing about it.

"Go shave your goddamned legs."

When she returned, the light was off. She crawled into bed. He rolled over, hoping to recapture some of the urgency that had filled his body. He found her knee and slid his hand slowly upward.

"Ah, shit!" He recoiled at the feel of razor nicks and patches of hair she missed. The botched shaving job brought her a reprieve until the next morning when Elmore awoke ready to go. Jodie satisfied her part of the marriage contract. As Lizzy promised, it took no more than two hundred and twenty-five counts for the rutting Elmore and never longer since that night.

CHAPTER 13

Marshall's sharp rap on the door wrenched her back from the distasteful recollection.

"Merry Christmas!" she greeted them and opened the door wide.

They echoed her greeting as if no hard feelings had passed between them, though Marshall's greeting was subdued. Virginia touched her left cheek to Jodie's. When Jodie offered her hand to Marshall, he brushed past. She helped Virginia out of her coat and hung it on the coat tree next to the door. Marshall slid their presents under the tree then strolled about the apartment to see what was changed. His thin smile, more of a smirk, never left. He switched the radio on.

Jodie wore a bright green dress for the occasion because it was so totally unlike anything their mother had. Jodie did wear some of Ruth's old things, but not that day. To wear one of their mother's dresses might remind them that she'd taken her place. Her hair was tied simply behind her head.

"It smells so good in here," Virginia said.

"Cinnamon apple pie and oatmeal cookies," Jodie responded.

"And the tree," Virginia went on. "Mother used to trim the tree so beautiful."

His living room inspection completed, Marshall pushed past them. "Father here?" He followed his nose into the dining room.

Jodie said that Elmore was in the store. "He'll be thrilled to see you."

Marshall grabbed a handful of cookies and flitted out.

Virginia milled about the living room and scrutinized everything.

"The coffee is fresh. Would you like a cup and an oatmeal cookie?" Jodie asked.

Virginia plopped down on the sofa. "Maybe just one. I shouldn't eat cookies."

Jodie agreed, but not out loud. She turned to leave the room as Virginia wiped a finger over the lamp table. Jodie couldn't restrain a smile.

She'll find no dust there, Jodie thought.

She returned with the tray of cookies and coffee for the center table then filled their cups with the steaming liquid.

"Where are your children?" Jodie asked. She knew that Virginia was married but didn't dare ask about her husband in case they were having a pre-Christmas spat or something.

"Umm…" Virginia answered between bites. "My dear sweet mother-in-law is keeping them." She invited Jodie to admire the stack of photographs she pulled from her purse.

"How beautiful! I can tell they take after you," she said.

Virginia nodded her assent.

"You still going to JC?"

"I graduate next spring. I've been taking mostly business courses." Her professors encouraged her to continue her education, but Jodie didn't mention that. Nor did she expect to continue her education.

"Are you going to work in the store?" It slid out so easily Jodie should have been suspicious.

"I hope so," Jodie said then wished she'd said no. Elmore was reluctant to let her visit the store, much less work there.

"Mother never did!" Virginia said. "Before she got sick, she was happy just to take care of Dad."

"Mrs. Jackson was a wonderful woman." Jodie said.

The sound of shoes wiped on the doormat caught their attention. Marshall burst through the door first. Elmore, with a grip on Marshall's shoulder, was half a pace behind.

"They said I was the fastest meter reader in Mobile's history," Marshall tossed the words over his shoulder.

"The fastest. Well, well. I'm proud of you, son." He patted his son's back. Marshall beamed.

They yanked off their ties and tossed them on the coffee table. Marshall unbuttoned the top two buttons of his shirt. Elmore got out a bottle of bourbon whiskey and a couple of glasses. "The real stuff," he told Marshall, "from New Orleans."

Virginia, trailing cookie crumbs, rushed to embrace her father.

"Dad," she said, "are you happy? You look so tired."

"Hell, I'm fine. I feel great."

They reminisced over whiskey and mended the Jackson family fences. Jodie excused herself to finish dinner preparations.

No one said anything about the Christmas green tablecloth and matching napkins during dinner or the polished silver or the good china Jodie had unpacked. Not even the porcelain candelabra handed down from Mrs. Jackson's mother got a mention. But Jodie noticed that no one left the table hungry.

During dessert, Virginia interjected, "You should get one of those new televisions, Dad."

"Wouldn't do HIM any good!" Marshall boomed, not just a little bit tipsy. He and Elmore had sipped bourbon and water all through dinner. "Jodie would be watching *Howdy Doody* all the time." He doubled over in laughter. His mother's locket fell from inside his shirt and thumped against the table. His head jerked around to see if Elmore saw. Elmore, peeved at the ill-disguised reference to Jodie's age and, by inference his, glared at him. Marshall tucked the locket back into his shirt. He said very little after that.

Virginia persisted, "It would give you something to do when you retire."

Elmore stiffened in his chair so abruptly the chair legs scraped the floor. *The bitch*, Jodie thought. Everyone knew Elmore was sensitive about his age!

"Who said I was retiring?" he demanded. "I'm not old yet." He flexed his muscle.

A bite of apple pie froze on Jodie's fork.

"I just thought, uh, naturally, that Jodie would manage the store after she graduates. She said…" Virginia shrugged.

Elmore faced Jodie with a scowl, a slap harder than his hands ever could. "What did you say?"

"Nothing, Mm…Elmore." She almost called him Mr. Jackson. "I never said anything." She tried to sound calm, but her voice trembled.

Virginia reached across the table and touched Jodie's hand as though they were the best of friends. She said, "I'm sorry, I thought that's what you said."

"By god!" He threw his napkin on the table. "I've run that store, MY damn store, since it opened and I'm not done yet! Retirement be damned!" he said with a snapping jerk of his head.

They finished dessert in silence.

Virginia's vindictiveness shook Jodie. Lying in bed that night, a wave of insecurity passed over her. She had planned to work in the store after graduation. Elmore's arthritis was worse, and notwithstanding his protests, he would have to cut back sooner or later.

Virginia can go to hell, Jodie decided. *I am paying for that damn store in five-minute installments, and by god, I intend to get what I pay for!*

The aroma of bacon and eggs brought them yawning to the breakfast table. Marshall nursed a hangover and poked at his food. Elmore was distant, depressed. Virginia was ebullient. "You've been so nice to us, Jodie, hasn't she, Marshall?"

Jodie wanted to drop a hot frying pan on her frumpy head.

Marshall stared at the cup of black coffee on the table in front of him and nodded. "Yeah. Never had such a good Christmas three days early."

"Marshall's going back to business school," Virginia announced to Elmore.

Elmore looked up in surprise. His face changed from gloom to glow. "Is that true, son?"

Marshall frowned at his sister and shrugged. "Been thinking about it, that's all."

"He's in his first year," Virginia beamed.

"Good news," Jodie said with a smile then pushed the point to get Marshall's reaction. "Won't it be something to have two Jacksons on the floor?"

Marshall's mouth flew open. He looked first at Jodie and then at Virginia.

"Well, that's just great, son! Just great! Best Christmas present I've had in a long time. Damn good news!" He reached across the table and slapped his back. Marshall looked as if he might have to rush to the bathroom, but managed a weak smile. "Thanks, Dad."

After breakfast, presents were opened. Elmore received a new robe and slippers. Marshall got a new pair of work clothes and Virginia a dress, all from the store. Virginia couldn't hug and praise her father enough until he confessed that Jodie had picked it out.

Jodie gave him a belt. He'd been grumping about his old one. She received a housecoat from Elmore and a cookbook—*For Kitchen Beginners*—from Virginia and Marshall.

"I need this," she said with a laugh but cursed them inside. Marshall and Virginia also laughed. Elmore stared at his two children with a stern look on his face.

"It was a good Christmas dinner you cooked, Jodie," he mumbled. "You cook good."

They packed to drive back to Mobile. Marshall would spend his Christmas with Virginia and her family as always even though Elmore asked him to stay.

Virginia promised to bring her children next time. As was their habit during a visit, Marshall and Virginia made a free shopping tour through the store before they left.

Thank God it's over, thought Jodie as she and Elmore watched and waved from the landing. *I have to clean up the messes—the easy one they left in the apartment and the hard one Virginia left in Elmore's head.*

The next few days passed without mention of Virginia's "slip" about Elmore's retirement. Jodie was relieved, but had not given up her plan to work in the store after graduation.

Elmore woke early on Christmas day. When Jodie came into the living room, he sat and stared at Ruth's picture.

"Merry Christmas," he said without enthusiasm and set the picture on the table. Jodie returned his greeting and went into the kitchen.

After breakfast, during which neither spoke, she asked, "Do you mind if I go see Mama today? I haven't seen her new house." It was three miles out of town. Lizzy had sent her a postcard.

"No," he said. "Take that fruitcake." He pointed to the sideboard. "I'd just as soon put Christmas behind me." Marshall and Virginia took most of the leftovers home with them.

When she walked out the door, he picked up the framed picture of his deceased wife and stared at it.

Cold gravel crunched under her shoes as she hurried toward her mother's home. It had not rained in a while so none of the road's red clay stuck to the soles. No cars were on the road to stir the dust. People were at home for Christmas, building memories.

So absorbed was she in her thoughts, it was a surprise to see her mother's house, a square box with unpainted pine siding and a black tar paper roof. It sat near the road on a flat, treeless two-acre parcel. A double-rutted drive, with a scant covering of gravel, led to a side door which opened into the kitchen. There was a front door, but only bill collectors used that.

Lizzy bought the land with the two hundred dollars "loaned" her by Elmore. She exchanged her beer bar for a load of lumber and began to build. To support herself and buy more lumber, she worked two jobs, one as a part-time waitress and another as a piecework presser in a laundry. While waiting tables, she met Jim Watson, a huge man with the temperament of a sheep dog, just her opposite. Eight years younger than Lizzy, he worked for a roofing contractor. It helped that he had a new pickup truck.

He wanted to get married but she put him off. "I can't think of nothing but getting a roof over my head. After I do that, I'm gonna get my younguns back. If you still want to get hitched after that, I'm willing."

Lizzy greeted her with a steaming mug of coffee, black and strong. The mug was stained almost beyond recognition of its original color and chips marked the rim. Jodie would have been surprised at anything else. How long anything stayed in Lizzy's house depended on whether it worked, not on how it looked.

"Come on in! We're having Christmas!" Barefoot as usual, she'd let her hair return to its natural brown color, now graying, and had gained weight. It was the first time Jodie had seen her since she'd married Elmore. Jodie handed her the fruitcake and took the coffee, a hearty chicory brew.

"Well, how do you like my house?" Lizzy asked.

Two-by-four wall studs showed along with the roof rafters. Pictures of children in happier times hung from nails driven into the studs. The plank flooring was bare of cover. A roll of off-white linoleum lay against one wall ready to be installed. The kitchen had a gas stove and the house had electricity.

"It's better than that shack the KKK ran us off from," Jodie said. "No field hands going to move in here."

"That's the truth if I ever heard it!" Lizzy crossed to the front wall and pounded it with the palm of her hand.

"Ain't no wind gonna whistle through that wall. Next spring I'm gonna add two more bedrooms and panel the insides. A man'll sell me seconds at the plant, dirt cheap. Ain't nobody gonna notice if they's mismatching."

Jodie studied her mother. She was happier than Jodie had ever seen her. "It's a good Christmas present."

"Once I get it finished, I'm gonna get my Ted and Emma home. They can't stand their ole stepmama," she said. "I'm through with them ole ways, sugar. Ain't had a drink in over a year." She took out a cigarette and lit it.

"You…doing alright in your marriage?" she asked.

Jodie shrugged. "I'm okay."

Lizzy poured more coffee and Jodie cut the fruitcake. They had a piece.

"Jim went to get my younguns. Chet's ole lady's always glad to get rid of them. They has really growed. They in high school now. Ted wants to quit, Emma too, but I won't let 'em."

"You want them to go to college?"

"Lord no! Ted has his head set on being an electrician. Emma wants to get married. Been sparking a boy at the bakery. She don't know I know." She winked. "What good is a college education, anyway? You still cooking for yours like I cook for mine, and I reckon you're making him happy in bed. Sure don't need no schooling for that."

Jodie didn't answer.

"Taylor wrote," Jodie said. "He's got an apartment in New Orleans. Shares it with some of the people he works with on the barge. Says to tell everybody hello."

Lizzy was glad to hear. All her children had checked in.

A cow lowed outside.

"That's my ole cow. She's gonna find a calf next month. We'll have fresh sweet milk after that. I don't ever want another can of Pet milk in my house." The recollection that she never had sweet milk for her children choked her up. She walked over to the window until it passed.

After a full tour of the house and the two-acre spread, including a short visit with the cow, Jodie said, "I'd better head back. Elmore'll be looking for me."

Lizzy protested but Jodie promised to return soon. At the road, they embraced. The frail woman wiped tears from her eyes. Jodie had not shed a tear since her marriage to Elmore and never expected to shed one again.

CHAPTER 14

In the early summer, Jodie was ready to graduate, and so far, Elmore had said nothing about a job in the store. Then, it became inventory time and Elmore grumped about it all through dinner.

"Have to do it this weekend," he said. "Can't put it off any longer. Gets harder every year. Damned arthritis." He flexed his back. "Gets to where Myrtle dreads it too."

"More coffee?" she asked.

She poured a cup and handed him the pint of whiskey from the floor. He poured a heavy splash into his cup and sipped.

Jodie cleaned the table and returned to rub his back. He always welcomed a back rub when his arthritis bothered him.

"Hmm…" he said and reached for his cup. "You smell good, Jodie. Hmm…"

She had dabbed on something from Ruth's supply, much of which came from Lennox's department store. If Elmore had known, he'd have thrown it into the trash. Mr. Lennox was Elmore's rival. His store was "uptown." The more affluent Jordanians shopped there. Ruth worked for Lennox in the store until she married Elmore.

"Don't talk about it in front of Elmore, Jodie. It upsets him," she told Jodie during one of their walks in the park.

After Ruth married Elmore, Lennox opened an Annex on Front Street as an outlet for the main store's discontinued lines and damaged merchandise, all of which he sold at a discount in competition with Elmore. The men barely spoke after that and only when necessary before that, Ruth had hinted.

"Feels good," he said and reached up to touch her hands. She knew what that meant. It had been awhile.

"I think I'll lay down. Uh, you want to come?"

It wasn't an optional request.

Five or so minutes later, he said, "Think I'll get some sleep. I'm gonna need the rest."

"I wish there was some way I could help with the inventory. I hate for you and Mrs. Ralston to have to do all the work. I wish I knew how to…do whatever it is."

"Take inventory," he said. "Not hard. Myrtle could show you in ten minutes. We have to find out what we've sold so we'll know what to buy…what we have to pay taxes on."

"Buying must be important."

"Most important job in the store! Have to know what your customers want. Takes years to get hold of buying."

"I could help take the inventory…if you want me to. Leave the buying to you and Mrs. Ralston."

"Uh-huh. Well…I don't see why not. Myrtle can show you how." He was asleep in ten minutes. It took a little longer for Jodie. She was excited about her new job in the store, and she didn't have to fight for it.

Myrtle wasn't pleased when Elmore told her. "You might better think about it, Elmore. I just know how bad she'll feel if she messes it up. Uh, if it'd help out, I'll work an extra night by myself."

"I appreciate that, Myrtle, but it's about time she found out what hard work's all about. Besides, I don't want you to come to work Monday all stove up. Me either, come to that."

She later complained to Betty Jarvis, the other female salesperson, "I just know she's going to cause trouble. Just you wait and see."

Betty laughed and said, "You're still mad cause he married that young girl and not you." She pushed her drugstore glasses back into position.

"That's the silliest thing I ever heard. Huh! I never figured he'd marry me anyway. I just hate to see Mr. Jackson hurt, that's all. He's too fine a man."

Betty left to wait on a customer.

I would've made him a good wife, Mrs. Ralston thought. *Why didn't he see that?*

On Saturday, the day Elmore had set aside to take inventory, Jodie showed up after the store closed in a cleaning smock and comfortable loafers. Her hair was tied back with a ribbon to keep it out of the way.

"Elmore told me to help you with the inventory," she told Mrs. Ralston.

"Well, get a tablet and pencil." The woman gestured toward the shelf inside the clerks' stand. "And follow me."

At a rack of dresses, she lifted a tag from the sleeve of a woman's dress and said, "The code number and size have to be listed. Company too, if it's there. You use your common sense as to what else. If this inventory gets messed up, I just hate to think about all the trouble that'll cause."

"How do I know which is the code number? There're lots of numbers—"

"Oh goodness! Code numbers are on the left, I mean the right, except for small items like socks and handkerchiefs and a few others. You can figure it out, I'm sure. Oh, some things have middle-sized tags. The numbers are reversed on them too."

"That's hard." Jodie shook her head.

"Going to JC and all, I wonder that you'd even have to ask questions. I quit high school in the tenth grade, and I never had a lick of trouble catching on."

"You must have a natural instinct for it," Jodie said.

"Humph! Well, that could be," she said then left before Jodie could ask any more questions.

Jodie did not really need to ask questions. She had studied the past year's inventory sheets and reorder forms to see what information was needed. Based on that, she prepared a chart showing codes, item description, size, color, manufacturer, and style.

Jodie loved every minute of the task. She learned the merchandise, what sold and what didn't. Halfway through, she went to the apartment and brought back hot apple cinnamon pie and coffee.

Elmore and Myrtle were partway through the assembly of information for the store's taxes and welcomed the break.

"This inventory taking is hard," Jodie said, taking a deep breath.

"I told you so," Myrtle said.

"I sure do appreciate you taking the time to tell me how to do it. You made it a lot easier. Elmore, Mrs. Ralston knows everything!"

She looked up from her pie and smiled. Elmore nodded and patted his assistant on the shoulder.

"Good pie, Jodie," Elmore said. "And coffee."

Myrtle agreed.

"Uh, how much have you managed to do?" Myrtle asked.

"I only have the underwear to do."

Jodie could tell by the look on her face what she was thinking, *If that girl's finished this soon, it's gonna be a mess.*

Half an hour later, Jodie handed the completed inventory to them. Myrtle grabbed it. "Better let me, Elmore." She sighed.

Jodie left to restock the racks from the storeroom across the hallway from the office.

"Oh, here's, no...ah...now this's, no...Well, it's okay, I guess," Jodie heard the woman say. "Ha! I knew it, here's a...hmm, I guess it'll do." When she finished Jodie's inventory report, nothing had to be rechecked. Nothing was wrong.

"I guess it was good I took the extra time with her." Myrtle handed it to Elmore who quickly scanned the sheets.

"Good idea to add the column about style, Myrtle. That'll save Roy a lot of time." Roy Crawford did Elmore's buying.

"Thank you," Myrtle said.

"I restocked," Jodie announced.

"What?" Myrtle's mouth opened. To take inventory was one thing, but to restock was another.

"I figured I'd better while I had everything in mind. Wasn't that what you had in mind when you told me to check sizes and styles? Did I misunderstand?"

Elmore said, "Damn good idea, Myrtle, restock right after inventory. Give the wrinkles time to straighten out. I guess it's always been so late before."

If Myrtle were a cat, she would have purred. She smiled instead.

They went upstairs early; the first time Elmore could remember. He fixed himself a toddy and went straight to bed.

"Damned arthritis's getting worse," he said.

Jodie climbed into bed and massaged his back.

"Too bad," she said.

Elmore asked, "What's too bad? My arthritis?"

"Nothing. You go on to sleep, Elmore. I was just thinking out loud."

"What's too bad?" he insisted.

"I was thinking about all the time the salespeople lose rummaging around in that stockroom every time they need more stock."

"They do it during slack periods. It's not so bad."

"I guess not. What started me thinking about it was what you told Mrs. Ralston tonight about salesmen being born to it, born to sell. Somehow it doesn't seem right for someone like Mrs. Ralston to get all tired working in the stockroom, when they could be in the store selling or straightening stock."

"I never had a stock clerk. Can't afford one. Old Lennox has two."

"I had a notion to restock for you now that school's about over and all. Especially after what Mrs. Ralston showed me. But I don't see how I could do it. I have to cook and clean, and I don't know the system."

"No different from what you did tonight. Myrtle's taught you all you need to know. Hell, you could restock in the time you've been taking to study. Be a damn sight better than listening to that damned soap opra, Lorenzo Jones and his stupid wife, Bell."

"If you think I could, Elmore, I'm willing to try."

He gave a satisfied snort and began to snore.

Jodie didn't mention her twenty-fourth birthday in April. In fact, she scrupulously avoided all references to age, directly or indirectly. She did remind Elmore about graduation however.

"You want to come?" she asked.

He turned from the radio. "Uh, no, I'd better stay around here. Friday's payday. We're usually busy." He added a muted congratulation.

That was a relief. For sure somebody would come up and ask if he was "proud of his daughter."

In black robes, Jodie took the white parchment from the president of the college and marched from the stage with a determined, proud set to her jaw. There was still a lot of tarnish left to erase, the residue of slurs and jeers, but graduation scraped away the first layer.

The poor southerner's battle cry rang loudly in her mind as she descended the steps, clutching the parchment. "Get yourself an education. Nobody can take it away from you." Well, by god, she had one!

CHAPTER 15

It became Elmore's habit to nap in the apartment after a bowl of chicken noodle soup at noon. One afternoon Betty was at lunch, and Myrtle was at the bank with the store deposits. Fred Stark, the men's salesman, was in the shoe department getting ready for a big shipment. He was a fastidious man, thin and dark-haired with a dark complexion; barely as big as Jodie. In his fifties, he had worked there for five years. Full of energy, he did his tasks with nervous intensity.

Jodie, with several dresses draped over her arm, said hello to him en route to restock the dress racks. So engrossed was she in her task that she did not notice the gray-haired, black woman enter the store.

"Miss," she called, "could you help me?"

Jodie swung around. It was Mrs. Brown from Whitfield! She rushed over to hug the woman.

"Jodie Mae!" Mrs. Brown replied. She reached her arms around Jodie and hugged her like one of her own.

She stepped back and looked Jodie up and down. "My, my, my. How you has filled out. And got so pretty too. Umm huh!"

Jodie thanked her and asked about her children.

"Except for George, they done moved to the Quarter." She referred to Kingston Quarter, the section of Jordan south of the plant where most of the blacks in town lived.

"George got himself a factory job in Detroit. Thomas got on at the plant and Johnny sells used cars. They all married and expecting."

"What about Lillian and Mr. Brown?"

"Mr. Brown's still at the mill. Will be till he's ready for the pine box I reckon. Lillian's working for the Greenwoods on Trace. She's got a boyfriend." Her face beamed with pride.

"What about Willie Bea? Did she go off to college?"

"She did! School by the name of Howard, I think. They say she's gonna make a doctor. Ain't that something?"

"Say hello to everybody for me."

"I will. Goodness sakes, child, I've been talking so, I ain't got to ask about you. You done up and married." She nodded toward Jodie's ring and winked.

It caught Jodie by surprise. She blushed and lowered her eyes. "I…uh, married Mr. Jackson."

Mrs. Brown noticed her embarrassment and said, "Well, well, Mr. Jackson. I knows him. He's a real strong man." She glanced up at the store clock. "I reckon I'd better quit this here gossiping and buy Lillian a dress, like I came in here to do. You help me pick one out. She's your size."

Jodie wanted to help Mrs. Brown but knew Myrtle would raise hell if she did.

"Fred," she called. "Customer."

The dark-haired salesman emerged from the shoe department, held up two dirty hands, and shrugged helplessly.

"You help me, child. He's busy."

So, Jodie recorded her first sale, and Mrs. Brown said she'd tell everyone to come see her. Jodie walked her to the door.

"Jodie Mae, you gonna do fine, just fine," she said.

After Jodie restocked, she returned to the apartment. That evening, Elmore stormed in and slammed the door behind him.

"You made a damn fool out of me today," he shouted with his hands on his hips.

"How?"

"Myrtle couldn't believe you'd up and start selling without so much as asking me. Business is bad enough without you running my customers off."

"Didn't Fred tell you?"

"I told you to restock. That's all. It's like Myrtle says...give some people an inch and they'll take a mile."

Jodie lost her temper. "If you'd shut up for a minute, I'd explain. I didn't—"

Elmore grabbed her by the shoulders and pushed her against the wall. Two of Mrs. Jackson's decorative plates fell from their wall hangers and shattered on the floor.

"You don't tell me to shut up! Not while you're living under my roof, eating my food!" His face reddened and the veins on the side of his face protruded.

Jodie's angry eyes met his. She wanted to reach out and slap him across the face. Instead, she took a deep breath and said, "Well, Mr. Jackson, your wife cooked your food, which is on your table and under your roof. You can eat it by yourself." She turned and left the room.

Elmore, taken aback by her cold defiant stare, stood transfixed and watched her slam the bedroom door behind her. She barely had time to take a deep breath before the door flew open and slammed against the wall.

"You don't run away from me, you sneak." He stepped toward her with clenched fists.

Jodie looked at him in horror. She hung her head and pretended to cry. "I'm sorry, Elmore. It was all my fault. You are right. When Fred couldn't help that woman, I should have let her go to Lennox's, like she said. I didn't know what to do." Her head bobbed in time with her sobs.

The mention of Lennox diverted Elmore's rage. He had disparaged "old man Lennox" in front of her many times. Jodie blinked and rubbed at her eyes with her hands. Placated by the reference to Lennox and unable to resist her tears, he put his arm around her shoulders and urged her toward the dining room table.

"Sometimes I act like a damn fool," he mumbled. "Been a little tired lately. Damned arthritis's been keeping me awake." He pulled the chair out for her.

"Fred went home early. Didn't mean to push you. You all right?" He sat down.

"I won't restock anymore, Elmore. I can tell it's causing trouble between you and Myrtle."

"Hell, Myrtle's set in her ways like me. We both get cantankerous," he said. "Since you started to put out the stock, I haven't heard her complain about her back."

Jodie smiled and heaped a large serving spoon full of mashed potatoes on his plate. He helped himself to the fried chicken.

"No," he said. "You keep on with the restocking. Just leave the selling to Myrtle and them. I won't have the help thinking I can't handle my own wife."

While Jodie did the dishes that evening, Elmore got to his knees and picked the pieces of Ruth's plates off the floor and placed them into a box.

Over the next few weeks, Mrs. Brown's word of mouth about Jodie spread through the black community and every "nigra" that came into the store asked for "Miss Jodie Mae." The first one sent Myrtle into an angry flounce to the cashier's stand where Elmore sat. Betty was busy with sales' slips.

"That uppity ole nigra says she won't buy from anybody but 'Miss Jodie Mae,'" she said, as she mocked the woman.

Elmore craned his neck to see. The thin black woman was wearing a dark hat with a broad brim and an oversized dark brown dress that came to her ankles.

"Who is she?" he asked.

"Never seen her before. Not one of my regulars."

The old woman gazed about the store then took a small can of snuff from her purse and tapped a bit into the lid. She pulled her lower lip out and poured the brown powder from the lid into the space between her lip and gums. Tired of waiting, she shuffled toward the front door. Myrtle bolted away to stop her.

"Go get Jodie!" Elmore barked. Betty hurried from the cashier's stand as Jodie emerged from the stockroom with an arm full of dresses. Without explanation and obviously displeased, Elmore yelled, "Go help Myrtle with that customer."

Jodie lay the dresses on a counter and pursued Myrtle.

"Ma'am!" Myrtle called as she rushed down the aisle. The woman stopped and looked through her glasses. Seeing Myrtle, she shrugged. "I wants Miss Jodie Mae or I'm going on."

"Miss Jodie…" Myrtle scowled. "Here is Jodie Mae!" She waved her arm in Jodie's direction. The woman turned and straightened the wire-rimmed glasses on her nose.

"Miss Jodie Mae?" She smiled, baring her snuff-stained teeth, the dip still very evident within her lower lip.

Jodie reached out, smiled, and took the woman's hand.

"I's Hannah, from South Fourth," she said of her address in the Quarter. "And I wants me a pretty Sunday school dress."

"Mrs. Ralston can help you, Hannah. She's very experienced and knows all the dresses in the store."

That brought a smile to Myrtle's face, but a frown to Hannah's. She again turned toward the front door.

"Rachel says only Miss Jodie. I reckon she knows."

"Oh, for God's sake, help her!" Myrtle said. Elmore moved close enough to listen. Jodie took the woman's arm and helped her to a rack of ladies dresses.

"Let me see," Jodie said as they faced the rack. "I bet you'd like something light and summery." She pushed at the dresses on the rack.

"With flowers," Hannah added.

After going through the rack, Jodie removed the two dresses that brought a sparkle to Hannah's eyes.

"Let's hold them up and see what they look like," she said and showed Hannah to the mirror. One was white with green flowers, the other light yellow with white flowers. Hannah looked at one, then the other.

"Show her a brown one!" Myrtle called. "That's what she wants." She stood along a counter a few feet away.

"No, I don't wants a brown one," Hannah said and gave Myrtle an angry glance over her glasses. "I wants what Miss Jodie's been showing me."

Jodie held them up in front of the elderly woman again.

"Lordy me!" Hannah said. "They's both right pretty."

Myrtle tapped her foot and said under her breath, but loud enough for Elmore to hear. "She's gonna lose that customer."

Elmore said nothing.

Myrtle took the dresses from Jodie's hands. "Suppose I just write both for you." She reached for Hannah's arm to lead her to the cashier's stand.

Hannah pulled away and whispered to Jodie, "She's pushy, ain't she?"

"I thinks this white one. What you think?" she asked Jodie.

"I agree. And I bet you'll be the prettiest young woman in Sunday school."

"Go on with you." Hannah pushed at her.

After writing the sale, Jodie walked her to the door. She dreaded going back to the cashier's stand.

"One of your friends?" Myrtle asked.

"No, I didn't know her."

"You were lucky you didn't lose her. You had the poor woman so confused, she didn't know which way to turn."

"You're right." Jodie shook her head.

"Why'd she ask for you?" Elmore demanded.

"I think Mrs. Brown, the lady in here the other day, must have said something to her."

"Hump, nigras!" Myrtle scoffed.

"Was she a new customer?" Jodie asked.

No one replied.

"Maybe she was one of Lennox's," Jodie said.

Elmore stared at the ladies' wear door. His face broke into a smile. He laughed and said, "That'd be a switch. Wouldn't it, Myrtle?"

"Uh."

"I'm sure sorry I couldn't sell her both," Jodie added.

"I guess you didn't mess up much," Elmore replied. "I bet I got one of ole Lennox's! Be damned!"

Jodie knew she had incurred Myrtle's wrath, so she stayed out of the store as much as possible for the next two weeks. But the referrals increased. Some were men and boys. When Elmore was out of the store, Myrtle took care of a few, but many left. "I'll come back when Miss Jodie's here."

When Elmore was around, he'd send Betty upstairs for Jodie. "Don't want to lose a sale." A sale was a sale, but Myrtle stayed swollen like a toad when Jodie was on the floor.

One night Elmore told Jodie, "I, uh, think you'd better arrange your time to spend more time in the store. Damn fool nigras keep asking for you. If things keep picking up, I might buy a television."

Jodie thought, *If I drank, I'd have a stiff toddy tonight.* She was in the store…at Elmore's request!

CHAPTER 16

A few weeks later, Roy Crawford, a round, short man in his late thirties, with dark hair slicked flat by Vaseline hair oil, pushed into the store like a cowboy swaggering into a saloon after a hard roundup. Roy represented dozens of small clothing stores whose owners lacked the time or inclination to do their own buying. The criterion for most was simple, buy as cheaply as possible. Last year's orders had been mailed in, so he had not been in the store since before Elmore's marriage to Jodie. It was late May, near closing time.

Hearing the swish of the door, Myrtle's body tensed with the expectation of greeting a new customer, but it faded when she saw it was Roy. He wore a pair of green gabardine pants that wanted to ride down on his hips, a matching light green shirt with an open collar, brown sports coat, and white shoes. His receded hairline left him with a broad, moon-shaped face.

"Don't waste a smile, Myrtle! I'm not gonna to buy anything!" He waved. She flounced away. "Now don't you go getting mad, you hear?" He laughed.

As he did periodically, Roy hitched his pants with his elbows and searched the store for Fred. "Fred!" he shouted across the room. "You haven't been doing anything I wouldn't do, have you?"

The salesman forced a smile and waved him away. "I don't know anything you wouldn't do, Roy."

Roy slapped at his pants legs and guffawed. Elmore, at the back, laughed too. Roy's unabashed enthusiasm always fascinated him.

"Betty!" He continued, "When are you gonna to leave that old man of yours and come live with me?"

Betty felt somewhat intimidated by his brashness. She remained cool to his greeting.

"What would I do?" she asked. "Drink coffee with your wife?"

"Hells bells, woman, you'd watch after my body!"

"I wouldn't be able to handle a job that big."

He roared.

Elmore extended his hand. "How are you, Roy? I was just about to mail them in," he said and touched the order sheets on the counter with his hand.

"Glad you didn't, Elmore." He shook Elmore's hand. "Wouldn't have had an excuse to bring this." His free hand held a brown paper sack, which he waved about. No one needed to look inside. In Jordan, a brown paper sack crumpled at the top could only hold one thing, a pint of bourbon whiskey. Elmore glanced around then shoved it under the counter.

"Damn it to hell, Elmore, if you don't get younger every time I see you. How the hell do you do it?" He slapped at Elmore's shoulder.

While Elmore extolled the virtues of hard work, Roy thumbed through the purchase orders. "Hmm…" he mused. "Business is picking up. That's good. Don't you know I love the extra commissions."

He leaned over and talked in hushed tones. Betty retreated out of earshot.

"Let me tell you about this new bathing suit I saw demonstrated last year. French call it a bikini. I was sitting there with a full glass of Seagram's when this little dark-haired beauty comes strutting out wearing one string across her tits and another one across her pussy and ass. It's the God's truth! That room got so hot, my goddamned whiskey pretty near boiled. Um, um, I kept waiting for one of them little titties to pop out. Sheeeit."

Elmore listened to every word. Without thought, he checked the zipper on his fly.

Jodie came in the back door. She had gone to the apartment to cook supper.

"Oo la la!" Roy groaned and leered as she approached. He hitched at his pants. "Wouldn't I just love to see that in one of them bikinis?" He nudged the speechless Elmore with the heel of his hand. "You old fox! Where'd you get her?" He assumed she worked in the store.

Elmore stiffened. Roy's observation of his young wife made him aware of his waning vitality. His lips trembled.

"She's, uh, my wife," he said. "We were married almost two years ago."

A foot-in-mouth faux pas was nothing new to Roy, though few had been quite as egregious. In his trade, he usually spoke first and thought afterward. But, like other survivors, he was just as quick to recover.

"I'm disappointed you didn't send me an invitation," he said and shifted the guilt to Elmore. "Congratulations! She's a fine-looking woman. Perfect match for a stud like you." He punched him softly on the arm. Elmore grinned.

"Hello," Jodie said.

Roy extended his hand and showed all his teeth in his smile. "I'm Roy Crawford," he said grandly, as though it had special meaning.

"He buys for the store," Elmore said.

Jodie took an instant dislike of the man. Loud and crude. She'd seen plenty of them at Lizzy's beer bar.

"Listen, Elmore," Roy faced Elmore and said. "The other reason I came by was to invite you and your bride to New Orleans next month. The rag people're putting on a special show for next year's fashions and things. First time to do it and maybe the last."

Elmore immediately shook his head. His usual response to doing anything new.

"Aw, come." Roy slapped Elmore's arm. "I'll treat you and the misses to dinner at Arnaud's."

"No. Arthritis' been acting up." It had. In fact, it had gotten worse.

"Thank you for asking, Mr. Crawford," Jodie said. "The best thing for arthritis is rest."

Roy sensed an opening, intended or not, and pushed it. "Hell, I understand that. When a man's health goes, he needs a good rocking chair. I get tired myself, and I'm only thirty-five."

"Goddamn it Roy, I didn't say my damn health was failing. Hell, I'm as healthy as ever. When is that damned show? I'll go and see just how much you've been taking me for."

"Uh, oh, I had to open my big mouth." The short man feigned concern then smiled. As he strutted out, he gave Jodie a conspiratorial wink.

Elmore left to shop for a television set.

Jodie and Elmore took the train from Jordan to New Orleans for the special show, a three-hour trip. It was Jodie's first time out of the state.

She had written Taylor as soon as Elmore said they would go, but he hadn't replied. Taylor was her only friend, and she dearly wanted to see him. Sometimes he wrote back in a week, but usually it was longer, depending on when the barge he worked on was next in port.

The show was to be held at the Monteleon Hotel where Roy booked them a room with high ceilings and a private bath tiled with small white octagonal tiles. The room overlooked Royal Street with clip-clopping horse-drawn carriages that ferried tourists about the French Quarter. Watching the street scene from the window was like seeing a movie, and she was in it!

A group of boisterous young men walked by, full of fun and on the prowl for more. She searched their faces for Taylor. It wasn't there. She hadn't expected it to be but looked anyway. She'd brought his address but didn't know if she'd have an opportunity to use it, or whether he would be there if she did.

Elmore took a bottle out of his bag and turned it up. Catching Jodie's look, he said, "I'm on vacation, and I can drink any damned time I please." She brought him a glass.

Delighted the room had a television set, he sipped bourbon from the glass and watched until time to dress for dinner.

Jodie freshened her hair. She wore it almost straight with bangs covering her forehead. The ends brushing her shoulders were curled. She wore her green dress, the newest thing she had.

Roy came by around seven in a white linen suit and tie that matched. He smelled of aftershave from three feet away. "Y'all ready for some of that pampano en papilliote?" he asked. Jodie's puzzled look gave him the opportunity to explain that it was a delicate local fish, richly sauced and cooked in a paper bag.

"I'll have a piece of red meat," Elmore replied. He wore a light brown suit taken from the rack. His strands of white hair were plastered flat by hair lotion.

"Bottle's on the table if you want a drink before we go, Roy."

Roy turned the bottle up and drank several swallows before handing it to Elmore to do the same. "Whooeee!" Roy wiped his mouth. "Hot damn! Burns all the way down! Good shit!"

Excitement built in Jodie on their stroll through the lobby. Heads turned to follow her trim, well-proportioned figure. Elmore saw the stares and pulled at her arm. "Hurry up." Jodie understood and kept her face pointed straight ahead.

Fluttering like an overstuffed butterfly, Roy hurried ahead and handed the black uniformed doorman a bill. Quicker than the eye could follow, the man tucked the bill into a jacket pocket and blew the whistle he carried around his neck. A mule-drawn carriage appeared around the corner. The driver was an old black man dressed in a black coat, top hat, and white gloves.

Even though the first shades of evening covered the street, the heat of the day was ever present and would be until late into the night. Beads of perspiration covered Roy's forehead and began a downward slide, aided by a greasy film of Vaseline hair oil. He dabbed at his face with a big white handkerchief, somehow unable to shove it completely back inside his pants pocket so that its white tail hung out.

Roy urged them into the carriage and managed a quick rub against Jodie's brassiere fastener in the process. Jodie shot him a look and mentally cursed him. He grinned and winked.

"Where y'all be gwain, Gov'ner?" the driver asked Roy.

"Arnaud's." He forked over another bill.

"Much obliged, Gov'ner." The man tipped his hat.

"Sket! Sket! Sket!" The driver drew air between his tongue and teeth to urge the mule forward on the street's uneven bricks. The mule's ears rotated backward, but otherwise did not acknowledge the command. It was repeated to no avail. Finally, the driver laid the frayed rope reins hard across the mule's back. "Get up, Preacher!" At that, the mule moved forward.

"Is that his name, Preacher?" Roy asked.

"No, sir, it ain't. I just calls him that when I commences to get mad. Can't rightly say out loud what I be thinking, but he knows. And when I calls him Preacher, he knows to get going. Get up." The mule pulled the carriage along Royal Street at a steady clip and pushed the still French Quarter air to a welcome breeze against their faces.

"Right cross the street from the hotel where you stays used to be a bank what printed up its own money," the driver began his regular tour dialogue. "Called that money Dixes. Got to where folks here abouts commenced to call New Orleans the land of Dixes. Nowadays, the whole south is called Dixieland. That's how it all come about, from that ole bank. Dixieland!" He tipped his hat at a carriage that passed and rapped Preacher to let him know they were not ready to visit.

The crisp notes of a horn from someplace unseen cut through the early twilight and blended with the delightful smells of baked bread from a kitchen someplace in the Quarter. Along the streets, patrons lingered on spindly-legged chairs drawn up to tables covered in red checked oil cloths. And on second-story balconies, residents stripped off as much apparel as modesty would permit—sometimes more—drank beer from bottles, and took amusement from what moved below.

"On the corner there is Mr. Napoleon's house," the driver said as the carriage approached the three-story building on Chartres. "Course he never live there, but time was when some of them Creole hotbloods got it in their heads to rescue ole Napoleon and bring him here to live. They's somewhat say the pirate Lafitte was gonna help. Anyways, they build this fine ole mansion for him, but he up and died the night they was to sail."

"What's a Creole?" Jodie asked the old black man.

"Some thinks they's mixed colored blood, but they ain't. They's mixed French and Spanish. Now the Cajuns, they's all French, but they lives mostly out of town, and I'm glad." He tipped his hat and smiled to show his teeth. "Get up, Preacher. It ain't quitting time yet."

From Napoleon's house, the old man tugged on the reins and "sket sketed" and continued his running dialogue about the French Quarter until Preacher and the carriage rolled to a stop in front of Arnaud's. Roy handed the driver another bill.

A smallish, dark-haired maître d' in a black coat and white ruffled shirt seated them at a linen-covered table beside a mirrored wall. Soft light bathed the room in a romantic glow.

Glad for Roy's suggestion, Jodie marveled at the white fish in the bag, an Epicurean tour de force not soon to be forgotten. Roy did the same and ordered wine. Jodie, tasting wine for the first time, made one glass last through dinner. Elmore, true to his word, had a rare steak.

"Where're you taking us now, Roy?" Elmore asked, as they left the restaurant. He tried to stand erect, but Jodie could tell his back hurt. The air was still hot and muggy. Roy didn't bother to pocket his soaked handkerchief anymore, just held it out and dabbed.

"Pat O'Briens! You can't come to New Orleans without going to Pat O'Briens."

A few minutes' walk and they were in a large room decorated by colorful mugs that hung from ceiling pegs on rough-hewed beams. The room was filled with tourists in straight-backed chairs at wooden tables singing bawdy old school songs, shouting raucous greetings at people they'd never seen before, and drinking a Pat O'Brien favorite, "Hurricanes," a potent blend of rum and punch. Roy ordered one for Jodie, half of which she left on the table. He and Elmore had two each.

Two women, with more than a few years behind them, sat at back-to-back, copper-decorated pianos on a raised platform, exchanged wisecracks with the patrons, and played everyone's favorite tunes.

No one argued when Roy suggested they go back to the hotel. And while Roy had half-dragged Elmore to Pat O'Briens, on the way to the hotel, it was Elmore, aching back and all, who dragged Roy. Elmore marched along the street with Jodie on his arm and his head held high. His bed was waiting!

At the door to their room, Roy said, "How's about a little nightcap, unless you're too tired."

Elmore sighed. Another drink was the last thing he wanted, but he invited him in.

"I'm going to take a bath," Jodie announced after she thanked Roy for the evening. She luxuriated in a tub of warm, sudsy water and imagined how the evening would have been with Steven then scolded herself for such thoughts. Even so, his face lingered in her thoughts.

She dried herself and was about to roll her hair when the bathroom door opened. It was Roy, with a stupid look on his face.

"Roy!" She clutched the towel tightly about her. "What—"

"Finally drank the ole bastard to bed." He steadied his swimming head against the doorjamb. "What you say, we go to my room? Ole Elmore'll be out for hours."

"What are you talking about?" she asked.

He blinked, trying to get his thoughts into focus and stammered, "Uh, hell, I thought, uh, I mean, shit, didn't you have a good time? I had in mind, you know, well, hell, ole Elmore can't be giving you much peter at his age." He gripped the door facing to keep from falling.

"Let me give you some advice, Roy. Women don't chase 'peter.' Besides, your brain must be pickled if you think I'd let you nasty me up for a fish dinner. You and Parker's dog."

"Whu...dog?"

"Old man Parker had a lazy, egg-sucking, no-good hound dog who thought he could sneak into the henhouse for an egg without getting caught. The dog was about as dumb as you. He shit buckshot for a month." Jodie was surprised at how easily she could draw on the crude, salty language of her youth. It would not be the last time she did.

Roy stood mute. His head bobbed back and forth. He knew he had overstepped his bounds. He turned and staggered toward the door. With one hand on the handle, he hesitated and asked, "You gonna tell Elmore?"

"We'll talk about it," she said.

He accepted that as a temporary reprieve and wobbled out. He bumped and scraped along the corridor wall until he reached his room.

She rolled her hair and crawled into bed. Elmore didn't move. She thanked Roy for a good night's sleep.

CHAPTER 17

It was nine thirty the next morning before Jodie got Elmore to the fashion exhibition held in a banquet-sized room at the hotel. It was three-quarters full, mostly with men who smoked at tables and scribbled on notepads. A catwalk for models extended into the room from a stage. A layer of gray cigarette smoke swirled at the ceiling of the room like a building storm, evidence that the program had been underway for a while.

Roy, red-eyed and nursing a headache, joined them an hour later. A worn, brown order case dangled by his side. As pained as his face appeared, it relaxed noticeably when Elmore acknowledged him with a hesitant wave instead of a curse for his indiscretions last night.

"How are you this morning, Mr. Crawford?" Jodie asked and poured him a cup of black coffee from the table's urn. Roy's mumbled reply was lost in the applause that came at the end of a presentation. He leaned over to Elmore and whispered hoarsely, "North Korea invaded the south. Saw it on the television."

"We going to be in it?" Elmore asked. He was worried about Marshall being drafted. Her thoughts went to Taylor.

Elmore shook his head with concern when Roy said, "Looks like it."

Black letters on a large white placards left and right on the stage announced the Adrian line. Thin aquiline models, with chalky pale faces that showed only a trace of human feelings, strolled onto the walkway in full-skirted evening gowns of floral print. Next, models featured Carnegie's suit-look in women's fashions, trim gray jackets with slanted pockets on the hips, worn over pleated skirts.

"Ole man Lennox carries that line in his main store," Elmore whispered to Jodie. "His boy does his buying, I think."

"Supposed to," Roy added. "I haven't seen either one. Might have mailed the orders in."

More applause as the models completed their tours. Black-coated men worked through the tables, replacing empty coffee urns and water jugs.

Two young women in outfits that showed lots of legs removed the Carnegie placards and replaced them with cards that said "Green."

An announcer in a dark suit followed them out and said, "Next, from New York, Greene Wear Limited will show us the latest in everyday wear." He waved offstage. "Mr. Warren Greene." More applause.

A dark-haired man in his midfifties strode to a lighted podium near center stage where he placed a small sheath of notes. His broad, friendly face wore a relaxed smile. The few extra pounds he carried on his six-foot frame complimented his self-assured, easy manner.

Jodie was impressed by the ease with which he described what they would see modeled and wished she could be like that. He said a few words about the show, the fact that it was out of the ordinary, and might not be repeated.

"A few years ago," he continued, "all we could offer were padded shoulders and short skirts. Ladies had to distinguish themselves by the style and color of the scarves they tied around their heads. Today, thanks to the end of the war and to Dior's new feminine look, we offer everyday dresses with figure-flattering elegance."

With a wave of his hand, models appeared from offstage to travel the length of the catwalk where they twirled once before floating into darkness behind the curtains that framed the stage. The dresses they modeled featured round, unpadded shoulders, shapely busts, and closely defined waists.

"This year's dresses have been padded slightly at the hips for emphasis," Greene said. "Wide, flounced petticoats lined with taffeta give bounce and life to the billowing skirts."

The skirts they wore reached midcalf and were worn with coordinated blouses. Murmurs of approval rolled across the room.

"Are we going to get any of those?" Jodie asked Roy and Elmore.

Roy answered, "Next year I might pick up a discontinued line."

"I doubt it! Ole Lennox gets first crack at Greene's seconds and irregulars for his damned Annex," Elmore said.

"Lennox's main store carries the Greene line," Roy added for Jodie.

Elmore mumbled something under his breath, not complimentary.

"Suzanne is wearing a silk blouse with the skirt worn by Marianne, made possible by this year's coordinated line. One skirt can sell two blouses or one blouse, two skirts."

At the end, he invited buyers to visit their suite.

By eleven o'clock, Jodie had to prod Elmore to keep his nodding head from hitting the table. When the show broke at noon, he told Jodie, "You go with Roy. I want to catch up on the Korean news and take a nap." He didn't wait for an answer.

"When do you place Elmore's orders?" she asked Roy.

"Tomorrow. I buy what nobody else wants, somebody's mistake. I have to buy cheap…for Elmore."

"And get the worst-looking clothes."

"Elmore's Discount ain't exactly Macy's or Lennox when you get right down to it."

She followed him from suite to suite and listened while he negotiated prices and delivery dates. Neither mentioned the night before. She thought that his glad-handing, backslapping personality served him well. His loud, often blunt retorts and objections were welcomed by the sellers who gave as good as they got. Roy's aggressive haggling seemed to relax them.

"Greene's suite," Roy announced as they neared a second floor hotel room. "My last stop. Damn glad." It was a little before four.

"Roy Crawford," a white-shirted man in his thirties said as they entered the room. His dark pants showed a crisp pleat as if pressed only seconds before. Black shoes showed from under their cuffs. "Houston…last year. Right?"

Roy shook his head.

"How have you been?" Roy accepted his offered hand.

"Fine as frog hair, Mark. This is Jodie Mae Jackson, Elmore Jackson's wife. This is Mark Redman."

"Mrs. Jackson," Mark said and took her hand for a quick, gentle squeeze. "So nice to meet you."

"Give me a minute, Jodie," Roy told her.

He followed Mark into the back room of the suite to complete his orders.

The remains of a platter of hors d'oeuvres and a bottle of champagne sat on a table with used glasses and crumpled napkins. On another table were a thin stack of colored brochures and catalogues. Large, colored posters sat against the walls and displayed the Greene mix-and-match clothing line.

Jodie browsed about and admired the displays until they returned.

"You coming?" Roy asked her as he moved toward the door. Mark tidied up the tables.

"No, I want to look at the rest of their dresses." A black satin evening dress displayed on a manikin caught her eye, but she had to work up the courage to actually look at it. Designed to silhouette the body, it featured wide shoulder straps and an open top to expose the neck and shoulders. Shimmering sequins danced in the light that filtered through the windows and brought it to life.

"You remember I'm taking Elmore to that...show tonight."

They'd talked about it last evening, a "lingerie show" for men only, little more than a peep show.

As Roy left, she heard a voice from the hallway say, "The store managers want to see the full line modeled before we make a decision."

"Of course." Jodie recognized the voice as that of Warren Greene from the show that morning.

Greene and a short and balding man with a red nose entered the room. The man thanked Greene and left.

"Mr. Greene," Mark said, "I haven't been able to get a model for tonight. They're all engaged."

"Hmm..." Greene said with a frown. "A problem. Let me think—" He noticed Jodie, stopped whatever he was about to say, smiled, and extended his hand. "Excuse me, I'm Warren Greene. I don't believe we've met."

Jodie said, "No, I just saw your show this morning. I really love your clothes. Lots of people are talking about your mix-and-match line."

"Thanks. I didn't catch your name."

Jodie introduced herself.

"Are you a…buyer?"

Jodie told him that she had accompanied Roy Crawford on his buying rounds. "Roy buys for my husband's store, Elmore's Discounts, in Jordan, Mississippi."

Mark told him, "Crawford buys for small stores, primarily, Mr. Greene. We haven't done much business with Elmore's. Lennox is our main customer in Jordan."

"I see. It's a pleasure to meet you, Mrs. Jackson. Look as much as want. Try the champagne." He turned as if to leave but stopped and said, "Say, Mrs. Jackson. Could you do us a favor? It's worth that evening dress." He waved at the dress on the manikin.

"What?"

"A buyer for a large chain missed our presentation this morning and wants a private showing this evening. Take about an hour or so, maybe two. How about it?" He smiled and held his hands out from his body to emphasize his request.

Modeling! she thought. *What would Elmore say? But Elmore and Roy would be at a "lingerie show."*

"I've never modeled anything," she said, slowly shaking her head.

"Mark will show you the moves. Don't worry. The worst that can happen is that they'll order from somebody else. That's likely to happen anyway if we don't model the line, so what do we have to lose? But you'll do great. I can tell by looking at you." He smiled again and extended his arms, palms out toward her.

"I need to check with my husband first."

"I understand. If he has any questions, have him call me. I'll be here. Can you let me know within the hour in case I need to find somebody else?"

"I will."

"Six thirty. Okay? Oh, if you decide to do it, see Eve in the beauty parlor downstairs. She'll do your hair and makeup. Mark will give her a call."

Elmore was snoring when she entered their room.

"I will do it," she decided. She left Elmore a note that she was going to the beauty parlor. She called Greene on the lobby phone.

Eve, the beautician, was a slim, older woman with a plain face and blond hair that had been almost peroxided to death.

"Mark said you might be by," she said when Jodie introduced herself. "Let me see now." She cocked her head, right then left, as she looked Jodie up and down. "Pretty. He said you were. Can use some work though. I love your blond highlights."

Jodie thanked her.

"Please sit down, but don't speak," Eve said and began a slow move around Jodie. She stared at her as a shopper might stare at something to buy. Now and then, she stopped to touch Jodie's forehead or the crown of her head or her ears.

"Every head is different," she said. "Every face." She bent over and stared for a second then took some strands of Jodie's hair and rubbed it between her fingers.

"Okay. I have it now. Mr. Greene is fussy about his models."

Jodie wanted to say that she wasn't a model but kept her mouth shut.

"I'll part your hair in the center and let it hang in rippling waves down to your shoulders. I'll give the front a lift to show off your forehead. You have an unbelievably exotic face. You want to show as much as possible. That's your strong point. Your eyes are fantastic too, emerald green. They sparkle. Let's get started."

It was five thirty before Jodie returned to the room. Elmore was shaved and showered and dressed, the suit he wore down, less the tie. The television blared about the Korean invasion and what it meant to the United States. Elmore was more interested in the story than he was in Jodie's new hairstyle.

"How do you like it?" she asked.

He turned, stared a second or two, and said, "Why'd you do that? You, uh, can't go to the show tonight."

"I know. But I just had to get my hair done in New Orleans, at least once in my life!"

"Yeah…uh, yeah, women…Humph, spend money like it grows on trees. It looks okay, I guess. It's different."

Jodie wanted to tell him what Greene had asked her to do and felt guilty that she did not but was certain he'd object. She prayed she could get away with it.

CHAPTER 18

Only after Roy and Elmore disappeared into the elevator did Jodie feel safe enough to take the stairs to the second floor. Not only was her stomach was tied in knots thinking about what she was about to do, she couldn't shake the feeling of guilt that she was doing something wrong.

Greene smiled when he saw her. "Beautiful! Quite lovely."

Her anxieties vanished. She smiled, but it was not excessive. Jodie retained the stoic demeanor she'd had since her marriage while Greene stared at her, up and down.

"You look good. Mark will show you what to do," he said and left.

She took a deep breath.

Mark said, "You look gorgeous. You'll do fine. Just relax." He explained the routine she was to follow.

The modeling was anticlimactic. The buyer ordered the entire line.

"I'm glad that's over," Greene said after they were gone.

Jodie was too. *Five changes and I didn't stumble once*, she told herself.

Mark grabbed his coat and headed to the door. Jodie followed him.

Greene paused at the door to turn out the lights. "I almost forgot. Your dress, Mrs. Jackson. Mark boxed it for you."

He retrieved it for her.

As they walked to the elevator, he said, "I don't imagine you've had dinner."

She shook her head.

"I'm having a bite at a small restaurant outside the Quarter. No menu, you just eat what they serve. I like it because I don't have to make decisions. I get tired of making them. Welcome the opportunity to let somebody else do it. Would you be my guest?"

Jodie hesitated. She was married and going to dinner with someone not her husband seemed wrong regardless of the circumstances.

"You're worried about your husband, I imagine. Invite him to come."

She nodded again. "He's at a show."

"I think I know which show it is. Well, he won't be back for a while. We can talk about our clothes. I'd like to hear your comments. I have a daughter nearing your age, well maybe not quite."

She said yes.

Their taxi stopped in front of a weather-beaten cottage with a bricked courtyard. Greene assisted Jodie over the bricks to the multicolored glass-paned front door.

A trim fifty-year-old man with a dark complexion met them with a flourishing gesture. He wore a white shirt and black, open vest.

"Comment allez vous, Anton?" Mr. Greene asked.

"Je vais bien, merci, et vous?" He bowed slightly.

"Bien."

Five tables sat in what was originally the cottage's living room. A sprinkling of guests were already seated and enjoying the restful atmosphere of the quaint cottage with its wood-planked floors, low ceiling, and multipaned windows framed by white café curtains.

"Tonight we are having baked coquille of crabmeat as an appetizer. The entree is noisette of lamb, marinated in lemon and Mama's special spices. For dessert, we serve crepes suzette."

"Sounds great," Greene said.

"We are fortunate to have wine from the village of Puligny-Montrachet, not far from my father's home. Magnifique!"

During the evening, Greene asked Jodie how she got into retail.

She described the years of insecurity that followed the divorce of Lizzy and Chet, the taunts of "white trash," of being chased or burned out, and concluded with the choice of either marrying Elmore or waiting tables until someone from the plant "took a liking to her."

"Quite a story. Not unlike my father's in a general way. He was eighteen when he immigrated to New York. His first job was picking up floor scraps and gofer work. It was one thing to be a Jew, but for a poor Jew, I suppose it must have been equivalent to white trash."

Jodie nodded and sipped her wine.

"Anyway, he figured he had to be rich to be as good as everybody else. 'With money comes self-respect,' he liked to say. Of course, by then we had plenty. But he never stopped…always he had to have more money. He's almost eighty now and has to be worth millions, but he's still not sure he has enough."

"If I had one million, I'd be happy," Jodie said.

"My mother says, 'If you've ever been poor, you can never be rich. So, I don't know if you can ever get enough."

"You're not that way."

"When I was growing up, money wasn't my challenge. My challenge was to do a better job. I don't mean to say ambition is bad. Without ambitious people, regardless of what motivates them, not much would get done. My dad's a huge success, but I don't think he's truly happy."

"At least he can buy what he wants and he's not hungry."

He smiled. "So, what are your future plans? Do you regret your decision to marry Elmore? None of my business of course. Just curious."

"No, I don't think so. I've been able to go to school, and now I'm working in the store." She paused. "I just wish I could get an order of your coordinated line. We've never had anything that looks halfway decent. Your mix and match…wow!"

He shook his head negatively. "I wish I could help, but with your volume, Mark told me what Elmore's does annually, you'd end up paying more than, say Lennox, our regular customer, and your prices would be higher. That wouldn't do you any good. I couldn't cut our prices because in this business loyalty is important, and business is business."

Though she had not expected his response to be any different, hearing it made her sad. "I understand. I didn't mean to…I mean, I wasn't trying to get you to do anything disloyal."

The knowledge that Elmore's was second rate brought to mind the fear that she was also second rate, notwithstanding the fact that an hour or so ago, she'd "been a model."

A fairy tale, she thought.

Beatrice Hansen's condemning words from years ago popped into her mind: "You don't fight with the likes of these." How could she ever escape?

At the hotel, Jodie said, "I really had a good time, Mr. Greene."

"I don't mind being called Warren."

Jodie forced a smile. "Thanks. You don't know how much modeling your clothes meant to me. I felt like somebody for the first time in my life. And the dinner, I'll remember it for the rest of my life."

"I'm sorry I put such a damper on things."

Before she could respond, he continued, "I can't sell you our current line, but we may have some stock left over from preview showings. It won't be quite the same, and I know we don't have much, but with your volume, you won't need much. It won't have our label."

Jodie's face burst into a smile. "Would you do that?"

"Have Mr. Crawford bring Mark an order sheet. I'll let him know."

She rose on her tiptoes and kissed him on the cheek.

"In the years to come, maybe you'll look back and say, 'That was my break,'" he said.

She beamed.

At breakfast the next morning, Jodie told Roy, "Yesterday, after you left, Mr. Greene came in and told the other man they had to dump some mix-and-match clothes left over from a pilot program or something when they were testing the market. He told me to tell you. They have to get rid of them."

"I don't need them. Except for Elmore's, I've filled all my orders."

"Hell, Roy! She said they have to get rid of 'em. I bet you could strike a deal. It's all I've heard since I've been here, coordinated clothes. See if you can get 'em cheap," Elmore barked.

"Not only that," Jodie chimed in. "Since they're leftovers, we should be able to get early delivery, before Lennox."

"Go get them, Roy!" Elmore ordered. "And make sure we get the early delivery!"

He did both.

Jodie and Elmore were on the train back to Jordan that afternoon.

Despite Marshall's assurances that he was not likely to be drafted, Elmore followed the news of the war closely. His preoccupation gave Jodie the opportunity to expand her authority in the store.

She altered some of Ruth's old dresses to mimic Dior. Padding was removed to make the shoulders rounded and more feminine. The bust and waist were tightened and made shapelier. While Dior dresses were padded slightly at the hips, Jodie found her hips didn't need it.

Although Elmore paid little attention to the change in her, others did. Mrs. Ralston, as well as Betty and Fred, began to address her as "Mrs. Jackson."

Elmore's order of the "Greene" line of women's wear was delivered two weeks before Lennox's! The store was filled with such excitement; it was like the air was charged with electricity.

Jodie cornered Elmore after everything was unboxed, priced, and hung. "Mrs. Ralston and I have discussed advertising." Jodie gestured toward Mrs. Ralston. In fact, Mrs. Ralston had listened while Jodie talked. "She makes a good point. We should get an ad in the paper right away."

"Uh, I don't know," Elmore said. "I've never advertised before. Costs money."

"We've never been ahead of Lennox before either."

Mrs. Ralston blurted out, "We'll sell these clothes right away if we get the word out, Elmore." She was, after all, on commission.

Elmore gave his approval. The newspaper ad stressed that Elmore's line of coordinated blouses and skirts, using synthetic cloth, allowed clothes to be washed and worn without dry cleaning. Elmore grumped at the costs but looked at it for a long time at the dinner table and smiled.

And after the ad hit, the store was filled. It was a thrill Elmore had never before experienced. He strutted about like a new father, crowed over the triumph, and forgot for the moment the miseries of his arthritis.

"Goddamn," he chortled. "I've whipped old Lennox's ass this time. Damn, I'd like to see that bastard's face."

Jodie wrote and thanked Mr. Greene for the order and for his suggestion to advertise. He had mentioned it in New Orleans. She also reported the response. "Great," she said and asked, "By the way, do you have any more? We're running out." Just in case, she enclosed another order with her letter. He filled it.

The day the reorder arrived, he called, "Mrs. Jackson, as you can see, you're getting the new line even if it doesn't have our label. Elmore's and Lennox's have both done very well, so I don't feel the slightest bit of disloyalty about filling your reorder."

"I...we can't thank you enough. The store's been filled."

"Good," he said. "Elmore's discount line has whetted people's appetite for the higher-priced stock sold by Lennox's. It's like, 'If Elmore's looks that good at the lower price, Lennox's must look better at the higher price.' You're getting seconds, but most people can't tell the difference and the price is right."

"They look beautiful to us! Thank you, Mr. Greene."

"Warren, okay?"

She hesitated but said, "Warren."

"Are you happy now?" he asked.

"I am."

And she was. She couldn't remember when she was happier. It was like a dream come true.

I have done something! she thought. *I did it!*

CHAPTER 19

"Pick me out a pair of thirty-eights." Jodie heard a man say. It sent a jolt through her body. She could never forget that fuzz-covered voice! It belonged to the deputy who had threatened her on her mother's front porch the day he came to arrest Taylor.

Jodie turned to see the man's bareheaded profile and his crew cut. He and another man sorted through a rack of work pants. When she saw his crew cut, she knew immediately that he was one she'd seen at the creek; that day, the one who had stuck a knife in the giant man's back! She had thought he was the one, but until she saw him without a hat, she couldn't be sure. He now wore the sheriff's insignia and had gained weight, but she knew he was the one who had knifed the giant man in the back and had burned them out afterwards to try and cover it up.

She recalled his arrogance the night they were almost burned to death: "In case a varmint comes out."

"Is that the sheriff?" she asked Betty at the cashier's stand.

"Yes. Sheriff Dagget and Betts, his deputy. He's most likely getting his complimentary purchases."

"What's that?"

"The sheriff is the county tax collector," Betty said in a whisper. "He gets a percentage of what he collects, but he's more lenient on merchants who cooperate. That's why some give complimentary purchases."

That kind of self-interest also permeated the enforcement of liquor laws. Bootleggers who paid off were rarely raided and then only after being warned. Who could count the number of liquor bottles, filled with water, that had been broken on the court house lawn.

"I thought they were supposed to work for us instead of the other way around."

The sheriff plopped his tax-free purchases on the counter for Betty to check. He didn't appear to recognize Jodie at first, but after he studied her face, he said, "Well, well, Miss Jodie Mae. I'll be. Who would've thought it?"

Jodie returned his stare, nodded, and walked away. As they passed her, on the way out, she heard him say, "…Phelps. I ran her old mama out of town years ago."

"Shore looks like her shit don't stink, Sheriff."

"Probably has a pussy as big as your fist, Betts," he said.

The sheriff's face stayed in Jodie's thoughts long after he'd gone. The hate she felt for him never left.

That night after dinner, Elmore watched the television news with a glass of bourbon and fell asleep in his chair. It was something he'd begun to do more and more often. After Jodie got him to bed, she reviewed the sales ledger and opened mail. In the pile was an engraved invitation to attend the Chamber's award banquet.

The main speaker was to be Senator Case, up for reelection to the US Senate. She saw that Steven Jefferson was his local campaign manager. He won the primary but had to go through the motions of a campaign until the November final. The Republicans ran a token candidate.

A small note was penned at the bottom of the invitation. It read, "Mr. Jackson, would you give a few remarks on discount sales at next month's awards banquet?" As far as Jodie knew, it was the first time he'd ever received any recognition beyond their endorsement of his monthly dues check and his title as assistant vice president.

"Must have made them sit up and take notice when he beat Mr. Lennox to the punch with the mix-and-match clothes and the Dior ad." Their preemptive use of "Dior" had forced Lennox to use something less fanciful in his ads. She mentioned the invitation to Elmore the next morning.

He scoffed at the request to speak but would attend and, by god, hold his head high. Elmore's had outsold old man Lennox's Annex! Not even the pain, which streaked across his shoulders, could dull that sweet revenge.

"I'll take care of it," Jodie promised.

She was set to decline the request to speak, but by nighttime, had decided to accept…not on Elmore's behalf, on hers! She was apprehensive. In Jordan, women were to be seen and not heard.

When the day came, Elmore drove his old black Chevrolet into a filling station for a wash and wax. Newer, more expensive cars would be driven to the country club, but none any cleaner.

"Must be going to the chamber banquet," the service station manager said.

"Tonight," Elmore replied.

Jodie lay the black sequined evening dress given to her by Mr. Greene on the bed and stood back to admire it. Her hair was pulled back and tied behind her head. "Haughty for haughty occasions," she quoted Eve's suggestion. "Well, this is a haughty occasion. Now, I just have to be calm and collected like Mr. Greene."

She looked at herself in the hall mirror. Everything was in place. She breathed a sigh of relief and sat down to wait for Elmore.

When he did come into the room, his eyes widened. "Uh, you look nice," he said. "Is that one of Ruth's?"

"Well, you know I altered a lot of her clothes. No need to throw them out."

"I don't remember it. Been awhile I reckon." He shook his head and got up. It was time to go.

Elmore pulled up in front of the white columned country club building and waited as two young attendants rushed to the car and opened the doors. Jodie got out and waited for Elmore to escort her up the steps.

Light from the Club's portico cast her face in a golden glow. Her smile, even and confident, was practiced at length before she deemed it satisfactory. Just enough, but not too much. The soft curve of her exposed shoulders and the gentle swell of her bosom added to the effect she wanted—natural beauty, not flashy glamour. Heads turned as they passed. Ordinarily, Elmore might have been insecure and sulked, but instead, the looks and whispers of the people they strolled past enhanced the pride he felt over his store's success. This was the first time he'd ever beaten Lennox in anything that he cared to talk about.

The cavernous room was filled with tables set for parties of four and eight, with gardenia blossoms that floated in crystal bowls and gave off a sweet scent. Smoke curled upward into currents created by ceiling fans that worked hard to clear the room of stale air.

Dignitaries sat at an elevated head table. Senator Case, the mayor, and some chamber officials stood behind the podium and talked. Steven, in a dark business suit, was with them. It had been a long time since she'd seen him. She marveled at how handsome he looked.

Women wore long gowns. As hot as it was, some displayed furs. Perspiration rolled down their backs and found the crevice near the bottom.

By a strange coincidence, or someone's idea of a joke, Elmore and Jodie were seated at a table with the widowed Mr. Lennox and his son, Tim, whose wife had elected to stay home with their children. Tim was tall and handsome with light brown, wavy hair, and dark brown eyes.

"Humph," Elmore grunted. "How are you, Lennox?" he asked. "Been having a good year?" Elmore pulled out a chair for Jodie then one for himself. They sat down and avoided Lennox's brown paper bag on the floor. Elmore pulled his bag from his back pocket and placed it a few inches away. Brown bags dotted the floor of the room. Though the county was dry, its inhabitants were not.

Lennox leaned over to say, "Mrs. Jackson. My boy Tim." He gestured toward the young man who sat next to him. Jodie nodded with a smile. For an instant, she thought she'd seen Lennox before, but couldn't place where. Maybe not. Her mind was on the speech she was to make.

Tim Lennox suppressed a smile at the sight of his dad and Elmore Jackson as they grudgingly acknowledged each other without an exchange of blows most who knew them might have expected. The mutual dislike of the two men was well known in Jordan.

"Humph, not as good as you evidently," Lennox replied. Though he was on the tall side, like his son, and had been considered handsome when he was young, now he was bald and wide around the waist. "Hear your nigra trade has picked up," he said and reached into his shirt pocket for a cigarette.

"Not just the nigras, Lennox!" Elmore gloated. "Not just the nigras!" Jodie could hear his thoughts: *Goddamn, I have waited a long time for this moment.*

The two men glared at each other for an instant. Lennox angrily snuffed out the cigarette he'd just lit. He'd relight it later.

After a quick look at "the young girl old man Jackson married," Tim asked, "How's Marshall?"

Marshall and Tim played together when they were young. Elmore forbade it, but Ruth allowed it anyway but was careful not to let Elmore know. And they were still friends

"Fine," Elmore answered. "With a utility company in Mobile. Expects another promotion. He'll run the office down there pretty soon."

She almost laughed at that.

Her eyes wandered to Senator Case. The portly, silver-haired, silver-tongued, forever-waving-at-somebody, backslapping, and smiling-without-end senator epitomized southern politicians. "You are all my dearest friends" were the words Jodie would expect him to say, even in his sleep. Never a man to miss a pretty face, he spotted Jodie during her stroll across the room.

"Who's that pretty young thing?" he asked Steven.

Steven stiffened. "That is Jodie Jackson," he said. "She's, uh, the man holding her arm is her husband, Elmore Jackson. He owns a discount-clothing store on Front Street. Has little to do with politics."

"Damned if he didn't rob the cradle. Hell, this *is* Mississippi, I daresay. If I'm any judge, I'd bet a dollar to a donut that she has a brain to go with that body. Get her to help on the campaign."

Steven rubbed his chin. He remembered their last afternoon at the creek. He'd be surprised if the senator didn't have similar thoughts.

Black-coated waiters poured fresh water into glasses, the women's full, the men's half-full by custom, so the other half could be used as "God intended" for good corn whiskey.

Silverstein, the chamber president, a medium-sized balding man with tufts of gray over his ears and a mole on his nose, called the meeting to order. Jodie's stomach tightened. All of a sudden, she felt scared.

What had I been thinking? Speaking to the Chamber! I'll make a complete fool of myself! Why did I do it?

Sheriff Dagget, with an arm full of brown paper bags, hurried to the front. "Look 'a here!" he announced. "This is evidence I picked up behind the colored ball park." He began to hand the bags out. "Just y'all take a look and pass 'em on. I don't suppose anybody's going to complain if some of that evidence spills out on the way." He laughed. And some would…spill into the half-filled water glasses on the tables.

The ballpark was used by one of the biggest bootleggers in the county. The sheriff was coming up for election in two years. He hoped his liquid contribution to the event would yield financial support when he needed it.

"Better let me have a sip of that evidence, Sheriff," Senator Case said and held out his hand. The sheriff handed him a bag.

"Much obliged," the Senator said.

After the invocation and pledge of allegiance, the mayor was introduced. He dispensed self-serving compliments to various people in the room. He also had to stand for reelection.

During a dinner of roast beef with new potatoes, miscellaneous awards were handed out. Grateful recipients rushed up to accept the small plaques. With each announcement, the vise tightened around Jodie's stomach. Soon her name would be called. She took a deep breath.

Stay calm, she told herself. *Stay calm*. She reached for a glass and drank deeply.

Fred Silverstein cleared his throat and began to read from a card on the podium stand. "And now," he paused and drew his head back as if shocked by what he held. "Hmm…Well, now we'll have a few words about discount retailing from…" He looked up, puzzled. "Uh, Mr. Jackson?"

Elmore looked at Jodie, his face white as a sheet. "Didn't you—"

Jodie stood. She touched his shoulder and said, "I took care of it, Elmore." He stared as she strolled toward the head table.

"I mean," Silverstein said when he saw her stand. "Mrs. Jackson."

Whispers followed her to the podium. Most were as stunned as Elmore. No woman had ever made a speech at a Jordan chamber function. It just wasn't done!

Senator Case began the applause, even turned in his chair as she passed. Steven did also. She scarcely noticed. Her hands were like ice. All those people looking at her.

Stay calm, she told herself. *Stay calm…like Mr. Greene.*

Jodie thanked the president with a nod and gripped the podium. Thank God for something to hold on to! Her knees wanted to buckle. Every eye in the room was on her. Elmore sat rigid, his jaw agape, his elbow half-bent, the next sip frozen halfway between the table and his mouth.

Then, a surge of adrenaline flowed through her body and with her first word the butterflies and fears vanished.

"The other day, a woman in a well-to-do part of Jordan mussed up her hair, put on an old pair of shoes and gardening clothes, and picked up her purse and announced that she was going shopping. 'You went shopping yesterday,' her husband said. 'Yesterday,' she told him, 'I looked at some expensive clothes in that other store, but didn't buy anything.'" A ripple of laughter came from the crowd. Most took her words as a reference to Lennox's store.

"'Today I'm really going shopping, and I want to get my money's worth. I'm going to shop at Elmore's. and I don't want to look out of place.'"

Bursts of restrained laughter skipped about the room. Elmore took a long sip of whiskey but was afraid to look up. My god! What the hell is she doing?

"Anybody can walk into any uptown store, including that one, plunk down money…take something home and feel pretty good. No thinking's required, just money. Easy, but…expensive." She paused for a look about the room.

"However, it takes a sophisticated buyer to shop for value, a buyer with a keen eye. Somebody with confidence in their judgment. Somebody who knows that Elmore's sells value every day the sun shines and that Elmore's sells that value at a discount!" The last few words came with an increasing crescendo.

She paused to let that sink in then continued.

"Selling value for less isn't easy. It's part art and part work, lots of work. Meeting the challenge requires the seller to know fashions, to take the time to look at everything offered by the big houses. And when all is said and done, the seller has to negotiate for the smartest-looking, highest-quality clothes…at the lowest possible prices. And that's Elmore's, ladies and gentlemen. Elmore's Discount clothes." Another pause, this time with a smile.

"Well said," Senator Case said loud enough for many to hear.

Polite applause rippled about the room.

"For example, this year's fashions, influenced by Christian Dior's postwar styles, are contoured more to the body. Dior said, 'Women are feminine.' Now isn't that a novel idea? And he designed clothes to celebrate that femininity. All stores sell Dior fashions, but Elmore's sells the Dior look, coordinated mix-and-match blouses and skirts…at affordable prices."

The senator said, "Here, here." It drew a smile and a nod from Jodie.

"The people who buy clothes for Elmore's shop hard so that when Elmore's customers walk out of the store, they know they have bought value for their money." Another look about the room. She added more words about the buying process, about how hard Elmore's buyers worked to find just the right combination of style and price.

She closed with, "And that is the secret of discount retailing. Elmore's buys quality at a discount so that you…can buy that quality at a discount."

Mr. Lennox leaned over and quipped, "More to it than that, I reckon. Your clothes come from Greene's just like mine. Tim tells me your wife arranged it."

Elmore pushed back his chair and made a slight scraping noise as he did. "What? Roy bought leftovers like he always does!"

Lennox winked. "Uh-huh." He reached for another cigarette.

Elmore mumbled, "To hell with you, Lennox. It sticks in your craw that I beat your ass."

Jodie paid special tribute "to Elmore's salespeople who have worked hard over the years and especially to Elmore's loyal customers who come back year after year and, finally, to Elmore Jackson who has brought discount retailing to Jordan and Bucatanna County for all these years and for many more to come."

Senator Case stood to lead the applause. She stayed at the podium only long enough to bob her head and whisper, "Thank you."

She had to restrain herself from smiling on the way back to her seat, but inside she did smile and she was pleased. She felt good.

CHAPTER 20

Senator Case was the event speaker. Steven was given the honor of introducing him. "Nothing wrong with being seen on the same stage with a US senator," his dad told him.

Senator Case who took the podium to drone on about the perils of communism. Jodie, depleted by her effort, sat down. She was aware of Elmore's periodic, sideways glances.

"We'll make those communists register, or they'll wish they had!" the senator said as he concluded. His committee was to begin hearings on the McCarron Internal Security Bill.

Everyone jumped to their feet and enthusiastically applauded. The man was a good American, practically a saint! Damn fine man! Now, can we go home?

And glory be! Silverstein said that they could.

Jodie waited while Elmore detoured to the men's room. Steven brushed against her as he walked past.

With a look of surprise, he said, "Jodie Mae. Enjoyed your speech. I heard that you'd gotten married."

"I imagine you did," she said. "I read about yours."

"Uh-huh. You broke some traditions tonight, by the way."

"I thought I might," she said.

Jefferson Randolph, Steven's father, called, "Steven!" He was tall and austere with gray hair. His face bore a forced smile when he walked over. It faded when he saw Jodie. She began a smile but stopped when she saw the hard look on the man's face. No smile could ever warm that. A frown line creased his forehead at the base of his nose.

Steven glanced at his dad and said, "Have to go. You…look beautiful."

Elmore emerged from the bathroom and took her arm.

"You know who that is?" Steven asked his dad. "That's—"

Randolph took Steven aside and whispered angrily, "Hell yes, I know who she is! She wrote letters…came by the house. Embarrassed the hell out of your mother, crying at the front door like she did. Thank heavens it wasn't more serious, if you understand…no little Stevens. It scared hell out of us."

Steven opened his mouth to speak, but his dad interrupted. "Listen, son, they applauded her tonight…in public, but when some of these old biddies get home, they'll remember who she is. That's what they'll gossip about tomorrow, not what she said tonight or how she looked."

"I don't care—"

"Like hell you don't. We've got clients to think about. Get over to those women and talk about Vicki. They love it when a husband is dutifully concerned." Vicki was due to deliver their baby any day.

In the car, a subdued Elmore said, "You should have told me. Old Silverstein nearly gave me a heart attack when he called my name."

"You had enough on your mind, Elmore, what with all the new customers. The chamber wanted to recognize your contribution. They're proud of you. You deserve a pat on the back for all you've done. I was proud to do it. Proud of you." She touched his arm tenderly.

"Yeah…Well, thanks. Did you see old man Lennox's face when we sat down?"

She mumbled something in agreement though her thoughts were still on her speech.

When they were in the apartment, he said, "I doubt I could have said what you said any better. Uh…by the way…in New Orleans… did you, I mean…ah, to hell with it."

Jodie slept very little that night. It was easily the proudest moment of her life.

And there was something else. For so long, Steven haunted her thoughts like a spell that wouldn't go away. To look him in the eyes and talk to him as an equal after the speech freed her. She was able to let his memory go.

After reading the local newspaper's account of his years of discount service to the community, Elmore began to get his hair cut regularly and took to wearing more youthful, sports clothes. Instead of a scowl when he was in the store, as had become his habit, he began to mingle with the customers and salespeople, even enjoyed an occasional exchange of rejoinders.

Business stayed good.

One afternoon when business was slow, the door into the women's side of the store squeaked. Mrs. Ralston's ears were tuned to the squeak, and when she heard it, she turned and her feet began to move. But when she saw Roy, she turned away.

"You done hurt me, Myrtle. Hurt me bad!" He guffawed.

"Where's Elmore?" he asked as he approached Jodie at the cashier's stand.

His smile gave way to a spiteful look. *An enemy*, Jodie thought, *one she could not afford.*

To disarm him, she said, coyly, "I need your advice, Roy."

His face took on a look of confusion.

"Ah, but first, let me give you this." She handed him a copy of the last reorder. "I added your commission on the bottom."

"Wha—" He scanned the form to tally the commission. "Uh, thanks. I didn't—Well, what advice can I give you?" All smiles again.

"I want to lease the space next door and put in a uniform department. I got the idea from the banquet the other night. All those people who waited tables wore uniforms."

"Yeah," he replied. "There's always a need for uniforms."

"I also want to adopt a layaway plan for the store."

"That's a good idea. Lots of stores do it."

"I'm glad to get your advice. You want to recommend the plan to Elmore with me? You know how to get things done, how to deal with the manufacturers. I think that's important."

Roy bobbed his head. "Heck yeah!"

"He's been grousing about how you almost missed Greene's mix-and-match leftovers. A new way to make money should get him past that." She feigned relief.

"Hell, I didn't even know about the leftovers. You—"

"You know how Elmore is. You're the buyer, not me."

"Well, I guess I'd better go and make my peace," he said.

Roy met Elmore as he walked in the back door. "Damn it to hell, Elmore. You're looking sharp as a pin. I want me some of what you been drinking."

Elmore smiled, extended his hand, and said, "Been getting any lately?" He immediately turned red and wished he hadn't been so bold.

Roy answered, "Hell yes! Don't you just know it! My ole lady was gooood to me last night!"

The men laughed and slapped each other's shoulders and backs. Roy followed Elmore into the small office at the rear of the store.

Elmore tapped his old desk with the edge of the letter he'd brought from upstairs. "Went to the chamber banquet the other night. Old Lennox bitched about us getting an order of Greene's new clothes. Sour grapes because we've been outselling him." He looked straight at Roy and asked, "Anyway, I'm asking you straight out. Were there any shenanigans going on in New Orleans…behind my back…with Jodie?"

Roy's mouth fell open but only for an instant.

"I do remember you saying Greene was a little easier to deal with than you expected."

"Good God, no! Hell, Elmore, your bride's too smart to let anybody get the better of her. Besides, Greene's as straight as they come." Inside, he breathed a huge sigh of relief. He thought for certain that Elmore was asking about his misstep.

Elmore lay the letter to one side.

"You can put that out of your mind. I think he was easier because he thought he'd sold us a bunch of trash. Didn't turn out that way, did it?"

Elmore nodded then picked up the letter on the desk and slid it from the envelope. "Got a letter from Senator Case. He was the main speaker at the banquet."

Roy slapped the desk with his palm. "That old devil would hump an elephant if somebody'd hold the step ladder!"

"What?" Elmore frowned. "Roy, the man's a patriot. He's against the communists. They're killing our boys in Korea right now!"

"Sure, I didn't mean—"

"Anyway, he's asked Jodie to help in his campaign."

"Is that a fact?"

Elmore's head snapped forward.

"I reckon it'd be a damn honor to help a United States senator. You gonna let her?"

Jodie walked in. Elmore handed her the letter.

"Hmm…It's nice that he asked, but I doubt I'll have time." She handed the letter back.

"Says it'll only be for a couple of months. Few hours now and then."

"I don't see how you can rightly refuse…Mrs. Jackson. It's almost like the president himself calling for you," Roy interjected.

"I don't know anything about politics, and besides, I'm busy in the store."

"My back's a lot better, Jodie. I can spend a little more time in the store," Elmore said.

The more she protested, the more Elmore insisted. She agreed, though she never really intended to do much. She was reluctant to leave the store and relinquish her hard-won authority.

"Uh, what the heck, Mrs. Jackson, I'd like to get on with that plan we talked about a while ago," Roy said.

"Yes," she said and looked at Elmore. "We think the store can make more money if we expand into uniforms and adopt a layaway plan."

Elmore listened as she detailed the plan to rent the space next door and to get bank financing for the program so they could sell on credit.

"No," he said bluntly, "I've stayed small since I opened, and I've never missed a meal. I don't believe in credit, and I sure as hell don't want to deal with layaways. Too much aggravation."

"Listen here, Elmore. I know a store in Jackson like yours. It expanded just like we're talking about. Making gooood money."

"I could easily take care of the extra bookkeeping," Jodie said. "The space next door has been vacant for over a year, Mr. Hughes should be happy to lease it to us for next to nothing. Shouldn't take too much of a loan to get us started."

Elmore rubbed his chin, but still shook his head no.

"I'll tell you this," Roy said. "If you aren't interested, I'm gonna talk it around. I betcha one of these old boys 'round Jordan will want to do it. Somebody looking for a way to make an extra buck."

"Damn it, Roy, I'm thinking about it."

Roy and Jodie waited.

"Well," he said, "if you both think it's a good idea."

He fixed his eyes on Jodie and squinted. "But it's your damned responsibility."

"Thank you!" She rushed over and kissed him on the cheek.

"Whoops," he said with surprised amazement and winked at Roy. Roy winked in return.

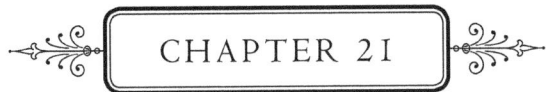

CHAPTER 21

Mr. Hughes wanted more money for the space than it was worth, but Jodie expected that. After negotiations, he agreed on a one-year lease, acceptable to Jodie, with options to renew for a percentage of the profits.

Mrs. Ralston praised the proposed expansion and planned to buy a new washing machine with the extra commissions.

Greene would supply the uniforms.

Armed with sales projections, cash flows, and her own market research, she went to see Mr. Blackledge at the bank. She wore a cheerful blouse and skirt from their new stock. When his secretary told him Mrs. Jackson "was here," he rose from his high-backed executive chair and showed her into his walnut-paneled office. He placed a pudgy arm around her petite shoulder and closed the door behind them.

"Come in. Come in. How is Mr. Jackson, dear?" He complimented her appearance. "Enjoyed your speech at the banquet."

"Thank you," she said and took the chair he offered.

He listened to her presentation. His double chin rested on clasped hands. When she had finished, he said, "I think we can advance Elmore a little on his layaways, but we wouldn't want to finance anything."

"You finance cars."

"We can repossess a car. Security, my dear."

"You'd have security here, the contracts. You'd get paid directly by the buyers."

"What would the bank do about defaults? Even if we could get the uniforms back, they wouldn't be worth anything used…or to us for that matter."

"If a contract goes bad, we take it back and give you another one. We'll handle the defaults. Institutions will be doing most of the buying. You know they'll pay. Can you imagine a hospital that doesn't pay?"

"Let me see, the bank lends you the money to buy the uniforms. You make the sales and give us the contracts. The money we collect on the contracts goes against the loan?"

"That's right. You get the money from all cash sales, less our costs of course. Our profit comes at the end, after the loan's repaid. Your only risk would be if no one ever bought uniforms. How likely is that? Businesses and institutions buy new uniforms every year. I doubt there'd be many defaults."

"Hmm, yes." He looked at the ceiling. "We'd have to discount the value of the contracts to cover our costs, collections, and the like. Our directors are very conservative. That'd cut into Elmore's profit some, but I suppose you've figured that. It'd mean a whole new department here at the bank."

"It's just another way to make a loan, isn't it? That's what a bank does? I can take the deal to National," she said, a reference to Jordan's other bank.

"I didn't say we wouldn't do it, but I think we should discuss this over…lunch. Don't you?" He reached out and covered her hands with his. They were hot and moist. She forced a thin smile and pulled her hands away.

"I believe in business before pleasure, Mr. Blackledge. Lunch would be something to celebrate…after the bank approves the loan." She placed a copy of the plan on his desk, thanked him, and left. Ordinarily he would have stood and accompanied her out, but standing at that moment was out of the question.

Recommended by Blackledge, Jodie's plan was approved, but the bank wanted a mortgage on the store as additional security.

"No! Hell no!" Elmore shouted at Blackledge.

Blackledge said that the bank directors had praised the plan, but that the mortgage was required to satisfy federal regulators.

"We all feel it's a sure thing, Mr. Jackson. You're a preferred customer at the bank. Don't let the mortgage condition bother you," Blackledge assured him.

Elmore signed, but not without a lot of head shaking. The store had never been mortgaged before. He had a sinking feeling in his stomach for days afterward. It was early September 1950.

After the loan was approved, Blackledge pressed Jodie for the lunch "you promised." She managed to put him off with one excuse or another.

Elmore left it to her to get the space ready, although she kept him well informed, should he have a strong opinion about anything or anybody. He signed all contracts.

Steven asked her to help with the senator's campaign. She put him off also. "Too much work in the store. Have to get the new department ready."

One afternoon, while Jodie worked at the cashier's stand, she heard a voice call out. "Jodie Mae!"

Jodie turned to see Willie Bea Hansen headed toward her.

"You haven't changed much," Jodie said. Willie wore a conservatively cut gray suit over a white blouse. Her hair was worn in a bun. "Looks like you had a good Christian raising." Jodie winked.

"Well, you certainly have changed! What have you done to yourself? I hardly recognized you."

Jodie filled in the years and asked, "What about you?"

"I'm interning at the Charity Hospital."

"Dr. Hansen! Well, well. Congratulations!" Jodie shook her hand with heart felt enthusiasm.

"Mama said I was to come by here and see you. 'Course I would have anyway, what with your name in the paper and all. Making speeches now! Next thing, you'll be in politics."

"Ha! You know the woman's place in the home. Barefoot and pregnant," Jodie said. Both laughed.

"I thought you'd forgotten me," Jodie said.

"This black cracker wouldn't forget her white cracker friend." Willie bumped Jodie's shoulder with the palm of her hand. They laughed again.

"Mrs. Brown said Johnny and Thomas and Lillian are doing well. Apparently, George went north."

Willie shook her head. "I don't know about Johnny and Thomas. They're working for Pick Mason. That man's nothing but trouble."

Pick Mason, she said, was a thirty-three-year-old black man, ex-heavyweight boxer, six foot four, 225 pounds of hard muscle. He once fought for the heavyweight title and many thought he'd won. Shortly after the fight, the word was that he knocked out Ezra Charles during a training camp sparring match. As retribution, the promoters quietly pushed him out of boxing. He returned to Jordan to become a small-town thug. He owned a small bar and café called the Blue Goose. He delivered Kingston Quarter's precinct box to the highest bidder. Politicians usually bid from twenty-five cents to a dollar a vote, depending on the stakes.

"I…don't know him."

Willie explained, "Let me tell you. He's into bootlegging, strike-breaking, repossessions. He collects for loan sharks and doesn't care how he goes about it. I'm afraid Johnny and Thomas might get hurt. Pick gets into some awful scrapes."

"Sounds tough."

"More than tough. He's downright mean. Folks in the Quarter cross the street to avoid him." She looked at the store clock then at her watch. "Goodness me, girl. I've got to get back to the hospital. I imagine they've got 'em lined up for me."

They promised to stay in touch. Jodie was glad to see her. It lifted her spirits. She had forgotten what it was like to have a friend, let alone have one drop by to say hello. She felt good and immediately regretted it. Best to be wary, she told herself and thought about what to cook for Elmore's dinner.

She thought about the work on the extension, the fact that nothing had been done. She was anxious to get started, but the builder Elmore wanted for the job, an old customer, was tied up on another job.

One lunch, when Jodie was alone in the store, Steven walked in. They swapped "hellos." He asked how the expansion was "coming along" and praised her efforts. She told him about the hold up in getting the space ready and waited for him to say why he'd come.

He did. "You can't put the senator off forever."

"Frankly, Steven, I don't think the senator needs me. Plenty of people would be glad to help him. He's practically a saint around the state."

"Actually, he did mention it at the banquet, but I'm the one who needs help. I'm a lawyer, not an accountant. I can't keep track of who gave what and how much. All I have now is a bank account and piles of papers with names and numbers, and I'm about to go on another fund-raising trip." His brown eyes looked deeply into hers. She looked away.

"Why collect money?" she asked. "If he dropped dead of a heart attack, he'd still be reelected. He doesn't have to spend a penny."

"Well, people like to give him money. They think they're buying a piece of him. That's politics. I understand that candidates have ways to keep what they don't spend…for their retirement, so the more they raise the better." He flashed a disarming smile.

"Should be illegal."

"Maybe it is, but I still have to do it, and I need your help." He said nothing for a few seconds. "Tell you the truth, I wanted time to…apologize for…you know…Whitfield."

"You don't need to apologize for anything." She turned to move away. "I have work to do."

"I'd sleep better if I knew you didn't hold a grudge." He tilted her face upward with his index finger and looked into her eyes.

In spite of her resolve, the sincerity in his voice and the way he looked into her eyes touched her. And maybe, just maybe, she needed to know that she didn't hold a grudge.

She turned away and said, "If I help, I want Elmore to get a letter from the senator that praises him for his patriotism or something with a copy to the *Tribune*."

"Done," Steven agreed with a smile.

"And I want you to teach me to drive." Each time she asked Elmore, he dismissed it with, "Women don't need to know how to drive. Men do the driving."

"Agreed," Steven said.

So, she would go with Steven on his fund-raising trips. Steven made surrogate speeches and collected checks. At each event, he had Jodie say a few words and, as promised, taught her how to drive a car.

After a few trips, Elmore began to grouse. "I thought you'd be working for the senator," he complained. "Seems to me it's that Jefferson boy you're working for. Ever time I turn around you're going out. You don't have time for the store now. When are we going to start the extension?"

Jodie told him that the builder he wanted wouldn't be ready for another month.

"I don't like it. Going out day and night, mostly night…coming home late. I have to eat by myself half the time."

"I'll quit, Elmore. I'd rather be here with you and the store anyway. About all I do is count money. I've only seen the senator once anyway."

"Hmm, yeah, tell him…No, hell, I guess you can't quit. Damn it! I got another letter from Senator Case. He says you're doing a fine job. I just want it to be over!"

The "campaign" was little more, she thought, than a disguise to collect money anyway. It disgusted her. A down turn in Elmore's health pained her. She didn't like to see him suffer. His arthritis had gotten worse following the brief respite he had after the banquet. In the afternoons, Elmore drank to ease the pain across his shoulders, and in the mornings, he stayed upstairs to nurse his hangovers from the prior nights.

"I don't like you being with that boy all the time. His wife's expecting. He smiles too damn much. I never trust anybody who smiles as much as he does. All his damn teeth showing. Like he's trying to hide something."

"He's a kid, Elmore. Not a man like you."

"Hmpt. I don't like it one damn bit. You tell that boy you have to stop when we get going on the extension! What's holding it up?"

She again reminded him that he'd picked the builder for the job. "If you want me to, I can ask somebody else to look at it."

"No, I gave my word." Elmore eased back in his chair and began to snore. And Jodie continued to help Steven with the senator's campaign.

In October, Whitfield held its annual Founder's Day parade, as much a political event as anything else. Leaves dropped from the trees along the sidewalks and covered the streets with colorful confetti. The morning sun was warm, but late afternoon breezes brought goose bumps to the skin. The parade was scheduled for midday so the dignitaries, including Steven, could ride down Whitfield's Main Street in convertibles. Afterward, on behalf of the senator "who had been called back to Washington for an emergency," Steven mounted a platform in front of city hall and condemned the Chinese for their Korean involvement. After a brief introduction, Jodie collected checks for the campaign.

"What a joke," Jodie said in the car. "Those poor people actually think Senator Case gives a damn about them."

Steven threw his coat and tie in the back seat. "It's kind of like giving to the church, Jodie. It makes them feel good even if all they get out of it is the senator's promise of 'appropriate action.'" He turned the car onto a small gravel road.

"Where are we going?"

"On such a warm day"—he smiled—"I wanted to see our creek one more time. Do you mind?"

"Would it matter?" Her reply was sarcastic and cold.

He shrugged and left the gravel road for a rough-haul road into the woods. After a bumpy quarter of a mile, he stopped and said, "We'll have to walk from here."

Newly fallen leaves crunched under their steps to the creek. Autumn colors surrounded them. Afternoon breezes stirred and cooled the air to add a pink blush to their cheeks.

"It hasn't changed much," Steven said as they gazed out at the rippling waters of the small creek. Shade from the forest trees fell in a mosaic of patches on the earth and the waters. Brown pine needles mingled with yellow and brown leaves and covered the ground with a soft carpet that extended to the water's edge. A sudden breeze whistled softly through the pine needles overhead. Rushing waters of the small stream added percussion.

Jodie said, "No, it hasn't. I used to sit here and let it wash my troubles away."

He picked up a twig and tossed it into the water. "I'm sorry, Jodie."

She looked at him. "I had other troubles."

He shook his head. "Well, for my part then. I'm sorry. Hell, you know how guys are. They take what they can get. Don't give it a second thought."

"No, I don't know, Steven. Girls do give it a second thought."

"The Chamber banquet brought it all back, Jodie. That afternoon in the rain. I keep remembering. It's driving me crazy."

His hands reached behind her back and pulled her close. He looked into her green eyes and kissed her full on the lips. It sent a jolt through his body and hers. She didn't push him away. He kissed her again.

Then, she pushed him away. Her knees did not quiver; her lips didn't tremble. She did not feel weak, and it felt good not to.

"You may want me, Steven, but people don't always get what they want. I ought to know."

"How was I to know how I'd feel?"

"You'll get over it. I did."

She headed back to the car. He followed. Neither spoke. And neither looked at the other. He turned on the car radio on the way back.

CHAPTER 22

Their last campaign event before the election was an evening meeting of the local union hall at the plant. Jodie only agreed to go after Steven assured her there would be no more "side trips."

"Senator Case wants me to speak to the union so the newspapers can report that he supports organized labor," he said.

"Does he?"

Steven laughed. "In politics, what you're for or against isn't important. The important thing is what people think you're for or against."

"Aren't there any real people in politics?"

"As long as people believe in fairy tales, politicians will tell them."

At the union hall, Jodie took chair beside a small table along the wall, near the front. There was no stage, only a small desk in front of fold-up chairs for the rank and file. Steven stood near the desk and talked to the union members while they waited for Charlie Burdette, the union president. He rushed in, stopped at Jodie's desk for an introduction, then took his place behind the desk. On the way, he waved and greeted everybody loudly like it had been ages since they'd seen each other. In fact, he'd been on the line with many that very day. It didn't matter. A loud greeting got everybody's juices going.

"Little late," he said. "Ole lady said I had to eat." He patted his stomach. "Like I need to." They laughed.

He got the job because he was articulate and bright and tough enough to fight when talking didn't work. He was fifty, rawboned with dark hair and a rough, leathery face that shows signs of a hard life. Like other union men in attendance, he wore worn khakis.

After opening the meeting, he introduced Steven who spoke against the Taft-Hartly Act and in support of a minimum wage. He got loud applause for the latter. Afterwards, Charlie pledged the union's support of the senator then waved an arm in Jodie's direction. She stood to face the membership.

"Now, I'm sure glad Mr. Steven Jefferson came down here to tell us what the senator's all about. But I want y'all to take a look at that young lady sitting over to count our money, Mrs. Jodie Mae Jackson. Y'all probably read about her in the papers. Been making speeches, if you can believe it. She's keeping the senator's financial stuff on the up and up." He told all to drop whatever they could afford on the table on their way out.

The members applauded her, perhaps more loudly than they did Steven. She was prettier.

Jodie, in a dark brown wool skirt and tight-fitting light brown cotton blouse, waved at the men whose faces she knew well—the Slims, Smileys, Texs—all rough, unpolished men who worked hard when they couldn't avoid it and who drank hard when they could afford it; men who only beat their wives when they deserved it. Even when they were "stepping out on their ole ladies," they spoke of them fondly and would fight anybody who said an ill word about them.

"Thank you, Charlie," she said. "Although I don't know all your names, I feel like I know you all, like family." More applause.

Charlie eased over and squeezed Jodie under his arm. She smiled.

"You better keep your cotton-picking hands to yourself, Charlie!" someone yelled. Charlie grinned.

"Hardworking people," Jodie said to Steven during their drive back to Jordan after the meeting.

"Yeah. Hardworking and dirt poor and most don't even know it."

"Maybe they're lucky. What they don't know won't hurt them. Once you taste ambition, you want more. You never know if you've climbed as high as you can. There's always another hill."

"You once told me all you wanted out of life was a few acres of land and a house," Steven said. "That seems like a little hill?"

"I'm looking for a little bigger hill now."

"I heard people talk after the banquet," he said, "and at these political rallies. You show something they like, sincerity or confidence, maybe both. I don't know, but I can see it on their faces."

"If that's true, I'm glad. It means a lot to me for you to say so. Whatever I've managed to do, I owe to you. You gave me a reason to be better than I was. I didn't get what I wanted then, but that doesn't matter now."

Little was said after that. She listened to car noises and thought about the union meeting, how she felt when Charlie Burdette asked her to stand to applause. She remembered how she felt at the Country Club and even how she felt when she modeled the Greene line in New Orleans. With each recollection came the realization that she had put a lot of baggage behind her. She no longer felt like a Phelps, even if others still thought she was. What they thought didn't matter anymore. By god, she was herself, Jodie Mae!

He pulled up along the curb in front of the store to let her out. As she got out, he invited her and Elmore to a cocktail party at Chilton Manor, the name of the old home he and Vickie had bought and restored. It was to be a thank-you party for the staff involved in the senator's campaign.

When she opened the door, Elmore stood in the hall. He stared her up and down. "It's late." She could tell he was drunk.

He staggered a step closer. "Hair's messed up. What you been up to?"

She ignored his question and said, "Charlie Burdette said to tell you he was going to bring his whole family in for clothes. He said, 'Elmore's is sure gonna get my business from here out.' He said that in front of everybody at the union hall tonight. Because you've helped Senator Case get reelected."

"Charlie? Charlie said that?" He blinked to clear the cobwebs. "Charlie Burdette. He used to be my customer, before ole Lennox opened his damned Annex. Charlie's coming back." His head bobbed up and down.

"That's what he said."

Jodie took his arm and led him to bed. *He had aged*, she thought, as she looked down at his chalky face, sunken here and there. He didn't have the energy he once had. It made her think of death and hoped she would feel no guilt when he died. There was never any love between them. For her, she was merely a nurse for an old man, even if the old man was her husband.

When Steven arrived home a few minutes later, his father waited in the study. In his hand was half a glass of bourbon. He stared at the fire in the fireplace but looked up when Steven walked through the door.

"Damn it to hell, Steven, I hear you've been waltzing that Phelps girl all over hell's acre!" he said. His expression changed to an angry frown. "What the hell's going on? You lost your damn mind?"

"Listen, Dad, Jodie's bright as hell and does a good job of keeping the finances straight. Senator Case asked me to get her to help. There's been no waltzing!" He didn't say that Jodie had turned him down.

"Bullshit! He didn't give a damn whether you got her to help or not, just his way of wishing he was twenty years younger! Whiskey talk! What do I have to say to get through that thick skull of yours? Or is your skull the problem? Maybe it's lower!"

Steven open his mouth to protest, but his dad held up his hand.

"Let me finish. It doesn't matter that she's bright or that she dresses as well as the next woman. No matter how she well speaks in public, she's a Phelps and will always be a Phelps. Got it!"

"That's not fair, Dad, and you know it!"

"I know that's how it works around here, and you'd better learn it. The women will always be suspicious that she'll corrupt their men. The men will forever see her as another country girl they can take advantage of…just like you did. Don't forget that!"

Steven shrugged off the last and said, "I don't give a damn what some old biddies say. She deserves to be judged by what she is, not by what her mother was. And I can tell you this, I think people do just that. You're out of touch. I'm the one out meeting the folks. She's well liked."

Randolph threw his glass against the back of the fireplace. It shattered and the hundred-proof whiskey inside flamed over the oak logs. He exhaled. "Let me tell you about reality, son, political reality. I can hear it now, 'Young Jefferson's been fooling around with that Phelps girl. There's talk she worked the tonks with her mother before she married old man Jackson for his money.' It doesn't matter if it's true or false. If the voters believe it about her, it'll rub off on you."

"I'm not in politics."

"You will be. Why do you think you got to be his manager down here? Exposure! When people think of Case, they'll think of you. It's how you get ahead in politics. Ride coattails. I've worked hard to get you ready, son. Don't throw it away!" He reached for a cigar.

Steven poured himself a drink from the crystal whiskey container on the bar. Vicki, in her sweat suit, strolled into the room. She had been exercising to lose her pregnancy weight gain. Young Randolf was a little more than a month old.

Vicki was not beautiful; in fact, some thought her face a bit on the plain side, but her figure was the envy of most young women her age, and she was determined to get it back. Her pedigree, though, was the envy of all. Vicki came from the "old monied Jordans" and was considered a prize. The city was named after her grandfather, Andrew Jordan, who founded Jordan Hardboard, the "plant." It was the largest single employer in town.

The Jeffersons were well off but didn't have the pedigree of the Jordans. Randolph's father started the town's first law firm, which had grown with the town and was highly regarded.

"What's this about the Phelps girl?" She shook her head to air out the damp strands of brown hair that brushed her shoulders.

"It's Jackson, Vicki. She's married," Steven said.

"Nothing," Randolph interjected. "Nothing at all."

"I heard you two argue, all the way upstairs. Is something going on? Something I should know about?" Her hands snapped against her hips.

"Hell no!" Steven replied. Angry exchanges had become their pattern since the sixth month of her pregnancy. As far as she was concerned, he had spent too much time away from her. And like many pregnant women, she suspected another woman.

"Were you with her tonight?" she demanded.

"WITH HER? Good God, Vicki! I attended a union meeting at the senator's request, and she collected about fifty dollars in contributions. I hardly call that being WITH HER."

She glared at him.

Randolph crossed to where Vicki stood. He gripped her shoulders gently, looked into her dark brown eyes, and said, "Look, Vicki, I can vouch for Steven. The senator wanted him to use the girl. You know politics, a country girl talking to country people. Steven objected, but I overruled him. I can absolutely assure you there has been nothing untoward between them. I do have my spies."

She looked at Steven for confirmation. He shook his head.

Randolph continued, "Tonight was the last fund-raiser. Steven doesn't think we need her anymore, and I was playing devil's advocate to get the facts out. Old legal habit, I'm afraid. Truth is, I agree with Steven. We should drop her."

"Good!" Vicki said.

Randolph patted Steven's shoulder in a show of camaraderie.

Steven returned his dad's playful pat with a forced smile. "I love only you, Vicki." He took her in his arms and kissed her.

"That's better," she said.

"See," Randolph said, "don't be upset by two old trial horses going at it. It's how we have our fun when court's not in session."

"I was worried that she'd be at our cocktail party next week."

Steven laughed but dreaded the task before him.

CHAPTER 23

Carpenters framed the opening between the men's department of Elmore's and the new uniform department. The winter season was around the corner, and Jodie hoped to have the first order of winter clothes from Mr. Greene soon.

"Hello."

Jodie was startled to hear Steven's voice. She turned.

"I came to apologize," he said and looked down.

Jodie had come to know that look. "Let me guess, the cocktail party has been called off." Since she knew that Elmore would never go to anything on Trace Avenue where most of the town's rich lived, she hadn't mentioned it to him.

"Uh, something like that. Actually, Vicki wants to limit it to— Oh, what the hell! Dad and Vicki are so goddamned worried about my political career, they want to screen my contacts."

Jodie laughed. "I don't blame them. They love you. Worrying about somebody you love is normal. It's a relief to me not to have to go."

He searched her eyes for regret but saw none.

She said, "People like me think differently from people like you. Most of our lives are spent, one way or the other, either headed for trouble, in trouble, or just out of it. Hell, I get nervous when things go right. That party is trouble I can avoid."

She waved her arm about and said, "Now, this is important! Our soon-to-be new uniform department. We finally got started."

Elmore stood at the back of the store and watched. When Steven moved close and looked into Jodie's eyes, he winced. Self-pitying tears filled his eyes, but they were soon chased away by a flash of anger. *By god, she's my wife!*

When Jodie turned away from the young man, Elmore thought, maybe she doesn't like him. Just then, another man entered the store, a dark haired, well-dressed man. It was Mr. Greene. Recognizing him from the New Orleans trip, Elmore straightened up and hurried to meet him.

"How do you do, sir?" Elmore said, as he shoved his bony hand out. "Elmore Jackson. I saw you in New Orleans, at the show."

Mr. Greene gripped it, smiled, and said, "Mr. Jackson. Warren Greene. I was passing through—actually I had business with Mr. Lennox, but I wanted to see your store. We've had trouble keeping your orders filled. And," he said with a wink, "I'm pleased that you'll be buying your uniforms from us."

Elmore beamed as he took him into the space planned for the uniforms where Jodie and Steven talked.

"Mr. Greene!" Jodie exclaimed when she saw him. "I'm…We're glad to see you!"

Steven introduced himself and shook Mr. Greene's hand. He didn't like the way the man smiled when he looked at Jodie or the way she smiled back.

He's old enough to be her father, he thought. *But, hell, she married a man older than her father!*

Steven stood mute as they exchanged small talk about New Orleans. He interrupted to say, "Have to get back to the office."

At the door, he looked back. Jodie seemed to listen intensely to what the man said and fixed her eyes on him with rapt attention. He cursed under his breath.

"I don't have long, Mr. Jackson, but if you don't mind, I'd like to give you some advice about your new department."

"Sure. I'd appreciate it. We would." He nodded toward Jodie.

"Keep your inventory low, just enough for the occasional cash sale. Most of your buyers will order in bulk to get a better price. When you're ready, I'll recommend some numbers. We can fill your orders within two weeks, at the outside. Most of what you need, we have in stock. That way, you keep your overhead low and your profits high. In the future, you can expand into rentals. More management required, but very profitable."

Jodie welcomed his suggestions.

"Take the catalog and a sample uniform or two and call on the institutions and businesses in your area. And keep calling. The more you get to know your customers, the more sales you'll get. Remember, somebody already sells to them. They have to like you or your merchandise better or they won't switch."

"Mrs. Jackson," Mrs. Ralston called, "I have a layaway. Are you free to write it up?"

"Sure."

"No," Elmore interrupted. "You listen to Mr. Greene. I'll take care of it." He shuffled off.

When he was out of sight, Mr. Greene smiled and said, "I'm headed to Houston this afternoon. Your winter clothes will be in New Orleans next week. It's a shipment we diverted from a store in East Texas."

"Great. When will we get them?"

"A couple of weeks. You can save a week if you pick them up in New Orleans. Otherwise, they'll sit in the warehouse until somebody gets around to it. I've heard Mr. Jackson likes to beat Mr. Lennox and vice versa."

"I'll tell Elmore."

"I'd be delighted to have you and Mr. Jackson as my dinner guests if you decide to come. Let me know. The shipment will be at the Terminal Freight Depot, Tuesday."

At noon, she fixed Elmore a bowl of chicken soup laced with black pepper. He dozed in front of the television set to wait.

"Elmore," she said softly.

"Huh, oh." He leaned forward and picked up his spoon.

"Heard a while ago"—he motioned toward the television set and said between slurps—"Mac's gonna run the gooks clear to China if Truman'll let him."

"Mr. Greene said our winter clothes will be in New Orleans next Tuesday if we want to pick them up. He said we could save at least a week if we did."

"Call Roy. Let him do it. He's getting a commission."

She spent the rest of the day tracking down Roy. It was late afternoon before she finally did. "God no!" he told her. "Hell, I have to be in Elba, Alabama, next week. Week after that, I'm free. I'd be glad to do it then."

Jodie told Elmore and suggested that Mrs. Ralston do it.

"No, she's better here. I'll call Marshall. Maybe he'd like a train ride to New Orleans. Might get him interested in the business, especially now that he's taking courses."

To have Marshall interested in the store was the last thing she wanted, but she figured he'd refuse. He didn't.

"But," he told his dad, "I'm not going to be responsible for accepting the shipment. How would I know if it was right or not?"

"Take Jodie with you. She can tell."

So, Marshall caught a bus to Jordan to make the trip. The night he arrived, he and Elmore had a fun time together sipping bourbon and watching television. He seemed strangely excited about the trip.

They caught the train the next morning. The trip down took three hours. Once there, Jodie and Marshall checked into a small motel near the station.

"Dad said not to spend much money," Marshall reminded her.

At least Elmore had agreed to separate rooms, Jodie thought.

Marshall excused himself soon after they'd checked in. She called Warren to let him know they were in town and could pick up the shipment.

"Warren," he said. "It feels younger to be called Warren. Can I call you Jodie?"

She agreed.

"Great then. If you and Mr. Jackson will meet me at the depot in half an hour, I'll help you with it."

"Elmore couldn't make it."

"Hmm. Well, I'll help you."

She met him—Marshall begged off with an excuse about having to meet an old friend—and arranged for the clothes to be shipped to Jordan on the morning train, the one Marshall and Jodie would take.

"I hope you will be my guest for dinner," he said. "Anton's is dark on Monday, but Tujaques is a good Creole restaurant."

Jodie nodded.

He ordered for them—spicy shrimp remoulade followed by superb brisket of beef. The bread, served hot, was a variation of the standard New Orleans French bread and had a unique taste of its own.

After dinner, he looked at her and said, "Every time I see you, Mrs. Jackson…I'd rather call you Jodie, but only if you'll call me Warren."

She hesitated before saying okay.

"Good, Jodie. As I was saying, every time, it's something different. Sometimes it's beauty. Sometimes it's femininity. Sometimes it's a rare mystique. If you were a painting, you'd be a priceless work of art. People would stand and stare at you for hours trying to figure out what you were." He smiled. "And enjoy every minute."

Jodie blushed, the first time in years. No one had ever spoken to her like that.

"I, uh, don't know what to say. Thank you," she said.

"You don't have to say anything, really. I'm not making a move on you. I'm married, happily, at least as much so as most men. But if I weren't and twenty years younger…" He shrugged.

"I hoped you'd come alone." He reached over the table and covered her hands with his and caught her eyes with his.

She forced herself to look away and pulled her hands free. "I'm embarrassed…flattered for sure. I like you, and respect you even more. But any feelings I had like that, for another person, died when I married Elmore. Otherwise, I couldn't have done it. The only thing I care about now is the store."

"Maybe your feelings are only dormant."

"I'd like to think that, but I know that tomorrow morning I have to go back to Jordan…to Elmore, my husband."

He reached over and caressed her hand. "I only wanted you to know how wonderful I think you are. I'll settle to have you as a friend."

Later they strolled to the Café Du Monde for chicory coffee, poured into white, chipped, and stained cups with hot milk, and hot beignets sprinkled with powdered sugar.

As they walked along side Jackson Square afterwards, he said, "New Orleans is old and disreputable and sinful, and I love every laid-back inch of it. I don't see how anybody can come down here and not relax."

Jodie was startled to see Marshall bound through the door of a bar. With him was another young man in an army uniform. They held hands and giggled. Jodie stopped dead. So, that's why he agreed to come. That's why he was so excited.

Marshall also came to an abrupt halt. They stared at each other for a scant moment before Marshall hurried past. When they were a step or two down the sidewalk, the giggling resumed.

Jodie explained why she had stopped so suddenly.

"I didn't know he was like that. I'm sorry he saw me. Elmore has been really jealous lately."

"I can't imagine Marshall will say anything, unless you bring it up. I doubt he'd want Mr. Jackson to know. Mr. Jackson didn't strike me as the kind of man who'd tolerate that kind of thing. On a different subject, you can see the boats on the river from my balcony. Do you trust me enough to come up for a cognac? A perfect way to end the evening!"

"I don't know." Notwithstanding what Warren said, she was still worried about Marshall.

"It may be the last time we'll see each other."

"Okay. One. I've never had cognac."

So, Jodie and Warren Greene sat on the balcony of his hotel room, sipped cognac, and watched the passing boats. She didn't like the cognac but enjoyed the ambience. He covered her shoulders with his coat. Marshall seemed miles away. The smaller boats had lights strung from their decks to the tips of their masts and looked like strange Christmas trees cruising to reach a snug harbor in time for presents to be opened. She wondered if Taylor might be on one of the boats.

He reached over and touched her face with the tips of his fingers. "Hmm, Shalimar…" He breathed deeply and added. "I'll always remember it as you. When I catch its fragrance in airports and train stations, wherever I am, I'll think of you."

Jodie blushed crimson.

He offered a second cognac, but she refused.

She dared admit to herself that she thoroughly enjoyed the evening. It scared her.

On the train back, the prior evening's events were not discussed and no questions were asked. Jodie thought about Warren and compared him with Elmore and Steven while Marshall slept. She wondered what he might say to Elmore, wondered more what she could say in response. An involuntary shiver passed over her body.

She went directly from the train station to the apartment. Marshall lagged back. "Something to do first," he said. Jodie was glad for that.

Elmore was asleep; more to the point, passed out. He took advantage of her absence to drink himself into a stupor. He smelled like a beer hall after a hot Saturday night.

"You don't want Marshall to see you like this," she scolded and dragged him into the bathroom for a bath and shave.

"It's my arthritis," he said. "Can't sleep half the time."

Jodie put out a fresh change of clothes for him. He had become more and more reluctant to change and often smelled like an old goat.

Marshall stayed in town long enough to help unpack the new shipment. Since Elmore didn't explode with rage, Jodie knew Marshall had said nothing. Likewise, Jodie said nothing about Marshall.

CHAPTER 24

Vicki had her cocktail party while Jodie was in New Orleans. It was reported in the newspaper—names, pictures, and all the trimmings. It was also her postpregnancy coming out party. She wanted her friends to see how svelte she looked.

Senator Case was the guest of honor but other local luminaries, including the mayor, were on hand for her comeback. All had the good sense to lavish compliments on her. For many women, a first child was the last time they would ever fit into their old clothes, but not Vicki. She was as slim as ever, and all smiles and charm.

"Well, Steven," Senator Case said with a grand gesture near the end of the evening, "whatever happened to that lovely assistant of yours? Jodie Jackson?"

Smiling, the senator turned to Vicki and said, "Though not in your class by any means, Mrs. Jefferson, that young lady was easy on the eyes. Yes, sir."

"She couldn't make it," Steven said. Randolph shot a glance in Vicki's direction. He wished the senator would get on with it.

"Never mind, I'll thank her election night." To Steven's and Randolph's chagrin, he proceeded to brag about the detailed reports Jodie prepared after each event. "Including who was there, what they said and"—he winked—"how much they gave. Kind of detail I keep up with, if you know what I mean." He laughed. Randolph and Steven joined in.

Vicki smiled before flouncing away. Seconds later, Steven excused himself and followed.

When they were safely out of sight, she said, "It still makes me mad when I think of you running around with that girl. I don't give a darn what you say!"

"Sweetheart, she was just another worker. Like the senator said, country folks vote and they contribute. It hurts me to see you upset over nothing. I love you, only you."

She sighed. "Does she have to be at city hall election night?"

"I don't know, you heard what the senator said."

"The Phelps are below the salt! Trashy! What's that country expression—'They'd steal the nickels off a dead man's eyes.' I can hear my friends now. Your husband invited HER?"

"Your friends?"

"I'm organizing an election party!"

"Hmm…The other problem is Mr. Jackson. If I pull her invitation, he might wonder why she didn't get asked. Could be somewhat awkward."

"Well, she's not coming to my party!"

"All she has to do is tally the election results," he said. "She could work in the small office next to the council chambers. The senator can thank her, and she'd be out of the way."

"That's settled then. Let's get back to the party." She took his arm.

On election day, Jodie broiled Elmore a thick steak, medium rare, hoping the "piece of red meat" would pep him up. They usually finished dinner by six o'clock, in time for the news. He voraciously attacked the steak and two baked potatoes that overflowed with melted butter.

Unfortunately, his renewed appetite for food spawned another appetite. He grabbed her arm and squeezed it. She knew what that meant.

Since the marriage, there had been very little affection between them, which Jodie preferred. They talked about current events and ate dinner together. Only when his urges surged, as they did every three or four months, did he even notice that she was a woman.

He pushed the chair back and, as though embarrassed, nudged her toward the bedroom. He threw his clothes on the floor by the bed and crawled in. Jodie meekly lifted her dress over her head and slipped out of her underwear.

"That too!" He pointed to her bra, which she obediently unhooked and threw it over the chair.

"Goddamn!" he said. He liked to see her naked breasts.

When she hesitated, he said, "Come on! Get in!"

She sighed, lifted the cover, and prepared to do her wifely duty. The raw smell of corn whisky from dinner and the smell of blood from his steak threatened to turn her stomach. A sharp rap on the door stopped everything.

Jodie looked at Elmore for instructions.

"Let 'em knock," he said and grabbed for her.

The rap was heard again, this time more urgently. She looked at him again.

"Aw hell, might as well answer," he said. "Get on a robe and see who it is."

She did, thankful that she'd avoided the inevitable once more.

A young man stood outside the door. "Oh, I was afraid you were out," he said. "Senator Case sent me. Can you come to City Hall? He'd like to thank you before he has to leave. He thought you'd be there for the returns."

"I forgot." In fact, she never intended to go.

"Better get dressed!" Elmore said as he emerged from the bedroom, dressed.

"You coming?" she asked.

He sat down and turned on the television.

"No...my arthritis. Ask him in. We can watch the show while you get dressed." Panelist Arlene Francis and host, John Daly, bantered about a guest's occupation. The volume was loud because Elmore's hearing had slipped.

"Mr. Jackson," the aide said. Elmore reached over and turned the television off. "Senator Case asked me to extend his gratitude. Not many men would have been so unselfish as to let their wives serve in his campaign. He said, quote, 'There should be more Americans like

Elmore Jackson.' Here." He handed him a printed commendation, signed by the senator personally...or somebody. The senator printed them by the hundreds for all campaign workers.

Elmore swelled with pride as he stood to shake the young man's hand.

"Hurry up, Jodie Mae!" Elmore called.

She quickly slipped into the beige wool dress she wore in New Orleans, adopted a false smile, and announced that she was ready. As the door closed behind her, Elmore returned to the television. The next guest's occupation was flea catcher.

By the time they arrived at city hall, the refreshments and champagne were gone along with most of the crowd. The senator was headed toward the door, but Randolph grabbed his arm to say something. Vicki, wrapped in a mink stole, strolled over.

An hour earlier, when the election results were fresh, the room was filled with conversation and frequent cheers. Now only a dense layer of smoke and clusters of tired people who wanted an excuse to leave, remained.

"Senator!" the aide called and urged Jodie to follow him.

"Mrs. Jackson!" Senator Case, smiling his love-everybody smile, reached out with his arms and strode forward. He greeted her with his famous bear hug and several pats on the back. He kissed her cheek, thanked her for her devoted service, and with a wink, whispered, "And if you ever want to come to Washington, just you let me know." He could not resist a suggestive pat on her behind. He put his arm around her shoulder and turned to face Randolph and Vicki. Steven was a few feet away, exchanging small talk with the ones who still hadn't figured out a way to get away.

"Picture Senator?" a *Tribune* photographer asked.

"Why certainly! I never refuse a picture. Heh, heh! Better take it shaking hands," he joked, removing his arm. "Don't want to make my constituents jealous."

A click and a flash, and it was done. Jodie and the senator would make the front page of tomorrow's newspaper.

"You must be Jodie Phelps!" Vicki said.

Jodie turned. "It's Jackson."

"Of course. I wanted to thank you for helping Steven. Picking up after the boys, he said," Vicki said, deliberately not introducing herself. It didn't matter. Jodie knew her face from the newspaper story that announced her marriage to Steven. It wasn't one she could forget.

"Collected money for the senator's campaign," Jodie replied curtly.

"How is Mr. Jackson doing?" Vicki asked.

Jodie had an answer on her tongue, but the senator's aide tapped his wristwatch. It was time to go. The senator turned to Vicki and said, "If I'm to see that young son of yours, I'll have to do it on my way out of town."

Vicki took the senator's arm and led him away, the aide a step behind. Jodie wondered how she would get home.

Randolph gave her a nod and turned to leave, but she said, "I suppose, it'll be Steven's time to run soon." It was deliberate on her part, just to force him to speak to her.

"He needs a little more maturity yet. Excuse me," he said and walked away before she could say more.

She shrugged then turned toward the door to walk home.

"Jodie!" Steven called. "I didn't know you were here. I think there's a little champagne left."

He filled two glasses and handed one to her.

"To the senator?" she raised her glass and asked.

"To his early departure," he said with a laugh. His eyes caught hers. He moved closer.

"I'm glad you came," he whispered.

Jodie looked into his pleading eyes. Feelings stirred within her. She closed her mind to them.

"I have to go." She sat the glass on the table. "It's been a long day for me."

"Don't," he said. He reached out for her, but she moved away.

"Goodbye, Steven."

Steven's look brought back memories of Whitfield Creek and, strangely, memories of Warren Greene; the way he had looked at her that night at Tujaques. She forced both out of her thoughts and hurried to her apartment home, hoping that Elmore would be asleep. He was.

She dressed for bed and slipped under the covers. Elmore coughed, then rolled over, and resumed snoring. Jodie was up early and had breakfast on the table when he struggled out of bed. She gave him a brief account of the evening's events. Mostly, he shook his head and drank coffee.

Blackledge continued to press Jodie. "We all have to pay our debts," he trilled over the phone. "You said we'd have lunch after the loan was approved."

"If you want to have lunch, call Elmore. I have a store to run! The bank gets our note payments, Mr. Blackledge, not you!" She slammed the telephone down and hoped that'd be the end of it.

Marshall and Virginia came for a pre-Christmas celebration. They were to stay for one day, according to Elmore. Jodie dropped everything in the store to bake, cook, and decorate.

Marshall was unusually quiet, almost in a daze. Elmore tried to bring him out, but couldn't. Virginia explained, "Oh, he's had some bad news. A friend he went to junior college with was killed in Korea. May the Lord bless his soul."

Marshall snapped Jodie a look. She wondered if the friend was the young soldier he was with in New Orleans. Had that evening been their last before he shipped out?

"I'd rather not talk about it," he muttered and poured another glass of whiskey. He passed out on the sofa before ten o'clock.

At breakfast, he had a surprise announcement. "I'm not going back to my job." Without his friend, Mobile would not be the same. "Can I stay here and help in the store, Dad?"

Marshall's news hit Jodie like a bolt of lightning. She knew that having Marshall around full time would be nothing but trouble for her. She hoped nobody saw the shock on her face.

"Why, goddamn, son! Of course. Your mother and I always wanted you to, and Jodie's new department will be opening up. When, Jodie?"

"When we get our first uniform shipment," she said.

Elmore reached over and slapped his shoulder. "Best Christmas present I've ever had!"

Marshall's decision revived Elmore. He put on a sports coat and tie, but his awkward movements and grimaces told Jodie it was an effort. He took Marshall on a tour of the store and introduced him to the staff and customers. Mrs. Ralston trailed them like a happy puppy. She praised Marshall's every word, no matter how inane.

The day before Christmas, a special delivery package arrived. The return address showed "Taylor Phelps, New Orleans" but it was postmarked in New York. Excitement fluttered through her stomach. Without waiting for Christmas morning, she tore away the wrapping and opened it. Shalimar! She pressed the cool bowl-shaped vial to her face. That afternoon, the Christmas carols in the store somehow seemed less depressing.

"Can I go see my mother?" she asked Elmore on Christmas morning.

"Long's you're back before dinner." He and Marshall were glued to the television watching a parade in New York City.

She pulled on a coat and hurried down the back stairs. She was pleased to have someplace to go. Not only that, the day was cold and dry, perfect for a brisk walk. The sky was without clouds and the bright sunlight touched the earth. Birds, resting in leaf-barren trees, ruffled their feathers to let the warm air touch their bodies.

Lizzy's house soon came into sight. She couldn't help notice the two-colored roof. "But who'll notice," she said and laughed. One close out of shingles wasn't always enough to do the job and a second wasn't always the same color. The color didn't matter to the rain. Both kept it out. Light brown asphalt siding covered the exterior. Before only black tar paper kept out the cold.

"Bigger too." She noticed. "Extra bedrooms? I wonder if Ted and Emma are back?" Her spirits lifted. Even before she knocked, she heard the musical sounds of a radio, a barking dog, and all the Phelps talking at once.

"Was that the door?" she heard Lizzy's muffled voice ask. A straight-backed chair scraped over a wooden floor. Next Jodie heard the familiar barefoot *thud, thud, thud* of the only person in the world who walked like that, Lizzy.

"Come on in, sugar," Lizzy greeted her with a big hug.

She had gained a little more weight and was as happy as Jodie had ever seen her. At the table were Ted and Emma. They turned in their chairs and waved and shouted, "Merry Christmas!" Jim Watson, also sitting at the table, rose to greet her.

Jodie hugged Emma and Ted. Though now practically grown, Jodie still thought of them as her little sister and brother. Emma was seventeen; Ted a year younger.

Another young boy and girl sat at the table with them, friends of Ted and Emma. Emma, tall and slim, had been going steady with the boy and wanted to get married. Lizzy was insisting that they wait until the boy "found steady work."

Jodie agreed. "Good idea." She knew he wouldn't live under Lizzy's roof otherwise.

"My younguns come back to live with me last summer, just about the time them bedrooms was finished. Each one got a room of their own." Lizzy teared up even then, as she recited the event to Jodie. No one mentioned Taylor.

They had decorated a Christmas tree, the first one Jodie could remember since before the divorce. It was scrawny and the decorations were sparse, but Jodie knew it had been done with love and happiness.

"Lookie here!" Lizzy stuck out her left hand. She wore a small wedding ring. Jim, sitting at the table, smiled broadly and shook his head in affirmation to all at the table.

"Me and him got hitched yesterday." At that, Jim stood and put his huge arm around Lizzy.

"I figured it was time to marry up. The honeymoon was damned near over." He laughed. Lizzy punched.

Jodie smiled and reached for a chair when she heard a thump from a back bedroom. She whirled around.

"Jodie!" Taylor called.

"Taylor," she said. "How long's it been?"

"Too long." They embraced.

She stood back and admired him. "You've grown up." He'd filled out.

He and Ted were short like Chet, their father. None were over five foot, seven but both were stout and as hard as fireplugs. Taylor's face bore the markings of a recent fight. His knuckles were also red and abraded. Catching the question in her eyes, he said, "I won."

"You haven't changed," Jodie said.

He had a job on a drilling rig in the Gulf. It paid more money and was more dangerous. Both appealed to Taylor.

"Got married too, but shit fire, she up and left me," he said with a bravado that hid his disappointment.

"I won't have no nasty talk in my house, Taylor," Lizzy warned. Her frequent reminders to the stump-sized Taylor to curb his cursing were just as frequently forgotten.

"Goddamn, sister, you ain't little no more. You got all growed up and pretty too. Ain't seen as pretty as you in the French Quarter."

"You move back to your apartment?" she asked.

He shook his head and asked, "How's that ol—that husband of yours treatin' you?"

"Okay. He leaves me alone most of the time."

"He ever bothers you, let me know."

Jodie nodded.

"I still have Devil," she said and fished through her purse for the red, switchblade knife. She handed it to him. He switched it open like he had years before and looked like he might want to throw it into the wall, but Lizzy's stare dissuaded him.

"You keep it." He handed it back.

It was midafternoon before they knew it and time for Jodie to return to Jordan and Elmore. Taylor had to leave that night. A friend would pick him up. Wary of the sheriff, he dared not go outside even to wave goodbye.

For once, all the Phelps are happy, Jodie thought during the walk back. *Except me.* She would have been as well but for Marshall. His presence cast a pall over her plans, all she had worked for the past few years. She knew there'd be a fight sooner or later. She didn't want to consider the impact Marshall's return might have on Elmore's promise to give her the store.

A cold December wind pushed at her back and whipped around her exposed legs. She shivered and increased her pace along the yellow-brown gravel road as she had done so many times in the past.

CHAPTER 25

It was early January 1951, and freezing cold. In the hours after midnight, a storm began to drop beautiful white flakes on the ground in and around Jordan. By morning, a thick layer of white covered everything, an event that occurred every ten or so years. Adults admired the blanket of white from their porches before they retreated to the warmth of their fireplaces. Kids, on the other hand, grabbed anything that would slide and stayed outside for the two days' school was in recess. Many stayed home in bed for two additional days to recover the colds they came inside with afterwards.

Merchants came in early to move their old stock out of the storage to meet the demand of folks around Jordan without gloves and coats. Old man Lennox was one of those up early. Even though he'd turned over the business to his son, Tim, he wanted to see if "the boy" was ready for the additional customers he knew would pour into the store that day.

He climbed into his old car and turned the key. A cigarette dangled from his lips. The engine grumbled once then *click, click, click*.

"Dead battery," he mumbled.

Since it was too early for servants, he got out and pushed the car along the driveway. At the street, it would coast downhill and pick enough speed to crank, even with a dead battery.

"Ugh, move, damn it," he said. His shoes wanted to slip on the ice. But with a little rocking back and forth, the car began a slow move toward the street. He pushed harder. It picked up momentum. He pushed even harder.

Halfway to the street, the left side of his body exploded in lethal pain. He clutched his chest and gasped for breath, then fell still on the snow-covered grass beside the opened door of his car. His eyes were wide, but they saw nothing. Smoke curled from his cigarette on the ground beside him.

The news was in the afternoon paper that lay in a heap beside Elmore's chair.

"Should have died sooner," Elmore scoffed. "Would have put a lot of people out of their misery." A sudden panic swept over him. *Naw, I've got years to go*, he thought. *Little arthritis's all that's wrong with me.*

"Well, Tim isn't out of HIS misery. His father's dead," Marshall said from where he sat on the sofa. "You're so callused and unfeeling." His voice grew hoarse. "Disgusting!"

"Maybe he'll close the Annex." Elmore smiled. "Be one less worry for him.

"You can joke! I'm going to the funeral!" Marshall said.

Elmore twisted in his chair to stare at his son. Lennox's death had not released Elmore from the hate he held for the man who had dogged him for as long as he could remember and that hate overflowed to include Tim. Elmore bolted from his chair and went into the bedroom. He slammed the door behind him. He fell across the bed and closed his eyes.

Marshall went to the funeral. Nothing more was said about it by either man.

Uniforms were delivered the last week of January. The bank line was drawn against for the purchase. The crates were opened on the freshly waxed linoleum floor of the new department. Uniform racks were made from unpainted iron pipes, in keeping with the philosophy of discount selling.

White uniforms predominated, but there were also black ones with white trim. Some were striped, two-pieced uniforms for nurses' aides and candy stripers. Warren also included green, blue, and white wraparound smocks, clothes for boy and girl scouts, and uniforms for bus drivers, mechanics, service station attendants, and security guards.

Marshall flitted about like a jealous new mother to feel the material, with a stop here and there to adjust the rack spacing between uniforms. He periodically removed uniforms from racks for a personal inspection. After the packing debris was removed from the floor, he waved his arms about and said, "Everyone out! Out! Out! I have to be alone now. I need time to think."

Elmore, accustomed to such outbursts from when Marshall was a teenager, got out of his way, as did everyone except Jodie. Too much work had been put into the department to allow him to take over without a fight. Jodie strolled along the racks to make her own inspection. She heard Marshall's quick footsteps on the linoleum behind her.

"I said get out!" he ordered.

Jodie faced him, stony serious.

"Tag the uniforms and complete an inventory check against our invoices before the opening next week," Jodie said. "And don't tell me to get out. Ever again. You got that!"

"You bitch," he hissed and pushed his face close to hers. "One of these days I'm going to tell Father about you."

Jodie pressed her index finger hard against his chest and replied, "And one of these days, I'm going to tell him about you! Remember that. I know everything."

Color drained from his face. A curse died in his open mouth. He stepped back and squinted but said nothing.

"Let me know when it's finished. I'll inspect your work," she said.

Marshall stared after Jodie. He couldn't wait until that evening to tell Tim. He reached for the clipboard Jodie left, muttered, "Bitch" and began to tag.

On the morning of the grand opening, Jodie was up early, much too excited to sleep. She baked biscuits large enough to take a generous pat of butter and a spoonful of jam. On the stove beside a platter of crisp bacon and scrambled eggs were the grits. Hot sauce was on the table. The coffee had perked.

The aroma of fresh breakfast never failed to draw Elmore from his bed covers. And Marshall, as well, appeared. She left them at the table to get things ready in the store. The chamber of commerce planned a ribbon cutting.

The air was icy enough to frost her breath as she hurried downstairs. No one was expected until ten o'clock, but she needed everything to be in order.

As her hand slid over the wall for the light switch, Jodie saw the lifeless gloom of the store. Only a clock that hung high on a white column showed any life at all. Its minute hand ticked another notch as the hour hand moved toward eight o'clock.

In the shadows, dresses waited for the luminescence glow of the overhead lights to spring to life. The bright, pretty ones would leap into the light and command attention. Others, dull and unwanted, would stay hidden and unnoticed until someone, perhaps with a special need, searched them out.

Displayed in the store's central, open bins, were handkerchiefs, undergarments, and socks, each only a transaction away from being worn under a dress or tucked in a purse or to cover someone's feet. But whether bright and pretty or dull and anonymous, like the children she did not have, Jodie loved every item.

Her fingers pushed the light switches. The relays thumped, banks of overhead fluorescent lights flickered to flood the store with bright light. The shadows were gone! The store was alive!

Jodie checked and rechecked to see that all was in order before the rest of the staff arrived. A broad red ribbon was tied across the opening to the uniform department.

At nine thirty sharp, the *Tribune* photographer struggled through the door with a black wooden tripod in one arm and a camera case in the other. He installed the camera on the tripod in front of the ribboned opening and checked his light meter. He marked the floor with chalk where he wanted the dignitaries to stand.

Marshall, in a new gray flannel suit from the rack, strolled about the new wing and picked up lint. Elmore stood at the front of the store and greeted new arrivals in a double-breasted blue gabardine suite and matching tie. It had been Ruth's favorite.

Silverstein, the Chamber president, appeared—raspy voice, warty nose, and all. He tried to cut down on his smoking but, like most, was only successful a few minutes at a time.

More people arrived. The warmth of the store brought relief to their chilled faces.

Jodie checked her honey-brown hair in the mirror at the cashier's stand. It was pulled back and tied behind her head with a piece of brown braid. The unbound length brushed against her shoulders. Only the slightest bit of makeup touched her cheeks, a touch of blush. Her lips were pink and full.

Her light brown wool suit with trim conservative lapels was quietly purchased a few days before from Lennox's main store. Worn over a white blouse with lacy ruffles filling the "V" between the lapels, it complimented her hairstyle and complexion. She took a deep breath and walked to the dedication area.

Elmore joked with Silverstein and the photographer. Mrs. Ralston watched from main store as did Fred and Betty and others, all in apparent awe of the occasion.

The mayor walked in with Blackledge from the bank. Blackledge eased through the crowd like a snake and waited beside Silverstein. The outside cold had added a red glow to his naturally ruddy jowls. The chamber president tested the large yellow scissors on Blackledge's tie. Both men laughed.

Steven and Tim Lennox drifted in.

Silverstein positioned the men according to their prominence. Jodie waited to be called. Her stomach tightened in anticipation. The Chamber president cleared his throat, adjusted his wire-rimmed glasses and glanced at the white card on which he'd written his notes.

They are going to begin without me? Jodie tried to ignore the dismay racing through her mind. It was Elmore's store after all, and she'd have to wait her turn. The tightness in her stomach intensified.

"Coming through," a young man's voice interrupted. The crowd parted to let a delivery boy struggle through with a huge arrangement of flowers secured to a stand. He placed the stand beside the dignitaries within camera range.

Jodie knew Warren sent them. Elmore read the congratulatory card that came with it. Warren Greene. The crowd applauded.

The mayor heaped five minutes of praise on Elmore for his entrepreneurial courage and the debt owed him by the community and ended with a resounding, "Thank you, Mr. Jackson!"

Pictures were snapped for those present, if any wanted personal copies to show friends and relatives before they threw them in a box, to be forgotten.

The tension in Jodie's stomach turned too pain, the same pain she felt when she and Taylor ate green plums. It always returned when she was tired or under extreme pressure. Her hands were icy cold.

She felt abandoned, alone, just like years before when Taylor left for New Orleans. Warren Greene came into her thoughts. How she wanted him there. He would understand.

Silverstein cut the ribbon with a flourish. The ends fluttered to the floor and the crowd cheered like the Jordan Bobcats had scored a touchdown. That was the end of the opening of Jodie's uniform department.

"God," she muttered. The pain in her stomach brought cold beads to her forehead.

"You should be proud of yourself," Steven said behind her. She gave him a darting look and quick smile.

"Everyone says you'll make money unless there's a strike at the plant this fall," he said. Someone pulled him away before Jodie could reply.

His words burned in her thoughts. She recalled the last strike. For a moment, the pain in her stomach was forgotten. So was the slight. What would a strike do to the credit sales; more importantly, payments on the loan?

Silverstein asked Elmore who would manage the department. Elmore's eyes found Jodie's as they searched about. But his search continued until his eyes found Marshall.

"Marshall will," Elmore said and pointed to his son.

She cursed. It was as though her child, her only child, had just been snatched from her arms.

Paraphrasing the Bible, she thought, *That is my wife, my only wife for whom I paid two hundred dollars. But, Marshall's my son, my only begotten son, of whom I'm very proud.*

People rushed into the new department to view the uniforms. Marshall answered questions.

Blackledge eased alongside Jodie and said, "Mrs. Jackson, perhaps we'll have time for that lunch now."

She looked at him without an answer and walked away.

"Hope for the best, but expect the worst" were words she recalled from an old book. She let down her guard and expected the best. *I won't do that again*, she vowed.

Steven caught her halfway to the rear of the store.

"You look great!" he said. He saw the beads of perspiration on her forehead and pulled out his handkerchief to dab them away. "It was hot in there. All those people."

"Yes," she replied. "A crowd."

"Pardon me, Mrs. Jackson." Tim Lennox, the epitome of a Hollywood leading man, interrupted. His brown eyes twinkled. "Did you see which way Marshall went? I want to congratulate him before I leave." He smiled and dipped close to her face. His eyes searched hers for interest. She showed none.

"It's Mrs. Jackson you should congratulate, Tim," Steven said. "She put this thing together."

Tim's eyes widened. "Well, not only are you beautiful, but intelligent as well. By the way, I loved your chamber speech." With a debonair bow, he took her hand and kissed it.

Jodie told him where Marshall was likely to be and he hurried off, Steven shook his head with amusement and said, "You know, every girl in Jordan chased after that guy. He ended up marrying a tough divorcee ten years older than he is. She has a teenage son. I still can't figure it out."

"Yeah. Who would? By the way, thanks for what you said just now."

"Hell, I was miffed that you weren't asked to join in the ribbon cutting."

"You've heard the old cliché about blood being thicker than water or a marriage license," she said.

In that moment, his eyes stared into hers. He saw the fire that fueled her determination to succeed. He said goodbye.

Jodie rushed from the store and fell onto the sofa, demoralized. The tears repressed downstairs eased down her face. Within minutes, she was asleep. When she awoke an hour later, the pain in her stomach was gone, but not the painful memories.

She touched up her face and prepared to return to the store. It still had to be run. People needed to be served, and by damn, she still intended for the store to be hers. One way or another.

After a supper of baked ham and green beans, Elmore sat down with the newspaper and a glass of whiskey and water. He lowered the paper and with knitted brows to glare at Marshall.

"Saw that Lennox boy sniffing around the store today. You invite him?"

"Tim's my friend. I'll do as I choose," Marshall retorted.

"I never want a Lennox in my store!" Elmore said.

"God, you needn't burst a gasket!"

"Hmpt, you bring him around here again, and it won't be a gasket I'll burst, it'll be your butt!"

"How revoltingly crude! Well, if it's come to that, I might as well tell you, I've decided to rent a place of my own."

To Jodie, he added, "I'll miss your cooking, sweet new mother."

"Not as much as I'll miss you eating it."

Elmore sighed.

"I'm going to need a salary," he continued.

Marshall had not drawn a salary since his return. Jodie managed from the household money, but Marshall had to depend on Elmore's gratuities.

"As manager, I think I should get as much as Mrs. Ralston."

Money demands always upset Elmore. He roared, "Manager's salary! The hell you say!"

"That's what you said this morning. I was going to be the manager," Marshall reminded him and nodded curtly toward Jodie.

"That was for the newspapers! There's just one manager in my store and that's me. You can sell boy, your mother always said you had a gift for it, but by god, there's a hell of a lot more to managing than selling."

He tilted his head toward Jodie but avoided her eyes. "Ask Jodie. She KNOWS about managing. Bookkeeping, layaways, buying, styles, banking. You have to deal with the likes of Blackledge, the money-grubbing son of a bitch!"

She suppressed a smile.

"Managers have to have judgment. No manager of mine would invite a Lennox into the store. I almost went broke while his old man sold his clothes at cost. He could afford it. He had the big store. But your mother and me couldn't. We had to…" He cleared his throat. "Sell your mother's wedding ring. So don't you—"

"Oh god, Father, don't be so damned melodramatic. All he did was offer his clothes at a discount for a few weeks after he'd opened the store. Mother said you were almost broke before that."

Elmore, his face crimson, leaped to his feet.

"Besides," Marshall continued, "I heard the real reason you hated him was because Mother almost married him."

Enraged, he wagged a finger at Marshall and yelled, "Get out of my house, you disrespectful whelp! The sooner the better! You don't bring your dear, sainted mother into this. You hear?"

He snapped on the television set and sat down to watch. Marshall left to pack. Later, he passed Elmore on his way out. Neither spoke.

Elmore switched off Edward R. Murrow and watched at the door. He shrugged his aching shoulders and watched as his son rounded the corner out of sight. Elmore hoped for a turn, a last wave to show he cared. But his only begotten son never looked back.

CHAPTER 26

In March, new plants pushed through the earth and birds returned to trees in bud. The decorator replaced snowflake posters in the windows with posters of butterflies and flower buds. Mittens and wool coats on mannequins were removed in favor of colorful blouses and slacks and scarves.

"A dollar and a half an hour," Elmore agreed, would be Marshall's salary, and he would work a regular shift like everybody else.

Marshall accepted and worked diligently whether in the store or out. He and Jodie called on prospects together. Jordan's economy was good, and they made a substantial number of sales.

Marshall's presence motivated Elmore to hang around downstairs more. He worked the men's department with Fred Stark. Jodie divided her time between the uniform department, much to Marshall's chagrin, and the cashier's stand. Layaway sales grew.

Warren called now and then to see how things were going. His calls always lifted her spirits.

Steven and Blackledge stopped by to inquire about the new business. If no one was within earshot, Steven asked how she was. Blackledge had only one thing in mind. Jodie loathed the insidious man and his abuse of bank power. He appeared immune to Jodie's rude, insulting responses to his suggestive remarks.

Elmore more and more deferred to Jodie. The first real evidence of it came when Mrs. Ralston bustled over to Elmore and said, "I do wish you'd tell HER"—she pointed a finger at Jodie—"not to meddle in with my department." With one of Elmore's mannerisms, she snapped her head forward.

"Myrtle, I swear, you and Marshall complain too much about Jodie. Chances are most of her sales are to her nigras anyway."

"Well, she practically runs the store," she said, her face twisted with anger.

"She works hard, Myrtle, just like you." He lowered his voice furtively and added, "I'm not getting any younger, you either, for that matter. And if I ever retire..." His voice trailed off.

"Elmore, I pray you won't ever retire, but if you do, you won't have to worry none about the store. I can take care of it, me and Marshall."

"Thank you, Myrtle. Now get back on the floor. You have customers."

Later came another suggestion of his deference. Silverstein dropped by the store.

"Elmore," Silverstein said, "we're having the membership meeting tonight instead of tomorrow. At the opening you said you wanted to become more active. This is your chance."

Elmore shook his head. That was then. Things had changed. He had become more active watching television.

"Maybe I'll let Jodie do it. I've been busy in the store," he said.

So, Jodie became an assistant vice president, by proxy. Her presence created tremendous interest in the membership committee, her assignment. She agreed to call on past members to renew their memberships and on those businesses that had never joined.

One day, a rap on the plate glass caught Jodie's attention. The store hadn't opened. She turned to see Willie Bea Hansen at the door in a white hospital smock bearing the words "Jordan Charity Hospital."

Jodie opened the door. "Come in. We're not—"

"Actually," the young black doctor interrupted. "I'm here to ask you to hire a negro salesgirl, a trainee." Willie Bea had asked all merchants to hire more Negroes.

"Willie Bea, this is not my store."

"People in Kingston say you run it."

"That may be, but right now, Elmore owns it."

"He's a businessman, right?"

Jodie nodded.

"Well, most of your customers are Negroes. And your business has increased. But you still have the same number of salespeople, except for Marshall Jackson and he just sells uniforms. You know the hospital bought a bunch awhile back."

"I know and I appreciate that, but even if I were able to ask Elmore before he chopped my head off, the first thing he'd say after the 'hell no' is, 'besides they aren't qualified.'"

"We know that! That's why we'll take a trainee job at minimum wage, Jodie. Is it fair for merchants to take money from the colored community and refuse to help out when we need it?"

"This is Jordan, Mississippi, not Los Angeles or New York. Things don't have to be fair." Jodie shook her head.

"Right now, Negroes can only be maids and laborers. That's what we want to change. And I'll tell you something else, the South is going to change. Negroes are becoming more aware of their rights. They spend money. Smart merchants can avoid a lot of trouble if they recognize that."

"Are you...is that an or-else offer?"

"No. I didn't mean it like a threat. I don't know a single colored who would cause you any trouble even if you are lily white. They trust you. All I ask is for you to give a little of that trust and respect back."

"The KKK'd be all over Elmore."

"If you take that attitude, nothing'll ever change. A black person's going to stay stuck at the bottom and you know it."

"You didn't."

"Neither did you, but I'm talking about most folks, not us. So, are you going to help or not?"

Jodie studied her friend's earnest face. Warren Greene gave her a break when she needed it the most. Maybe it was time to pass it along.

"I don't know what Elmore will do, but send in the smartest one you know. I'll do the best I can."

"Jodie, we don't want a handout. We can get those from do-gooders. Like welfare, it keeps us weak. We want opportunities. We want a chance."

"I'll try," Jodie said.

During supper and afterwards, Jodie waited and watched for an opportunity to raise the question. She rubbed Elmore's aching shoulders, hoping to improve his disposition, but it put him to sleep. She would wait until Willie Bea sent someone. It's easier to sell goods a buyer can see than something he can't.

She didn't have long to wait.

Jodie unlocked the front door to an attractive young black woman who held a piece of paper and a purse. She smiled.

"Come in!" Jodie tried to sound cheerful.

About Jodie's height and a couple of years younger, she was slim and presented herself in a two-piece beige cotton suit and brown leather heels.

"Dr. Hansen wasn't sure when you'd be opening." She extended her hand. "I'm Ruby Martin."

"Jodie Jackson."

"Well, here's my résumé." She handed the single sheet of paper to Jodie. Her hand trembled with nervous anticipation.

They walked to the cashier's stand where Jodie read the statement of Ruby's history. Ruby's gaze shifted about as she tried not to watch, but her eyes returned to see if Jodie's face showed a reaction. Her hands clinched into tight balls.

Jodie raised her eyebrows. "Hmm…Graduated from Tuskeegee State College in Alabama. Business major. Part-time jobs, mostly clerical."

"I have a one-year-old boy to support. His papa left town."

"Well, Mr. Jackson will be down in a few minutes."

Ruby shrugged her shoulders. Her face dropped. One look at her brown skin, and she'd be out the door.

Fred had perked coffee in a tarnished old pot on a table in the ladies' shoe department. Steam from the spout sent the aroma of fresh coffee to the cashier's stand.

Jodie introduced Ruby to him and explained her situation.

He greeted her with open congeniality. As a salesman, his preferences, if he had any left, were subverted to those of his customers. His prejudices were in favor of buyers and against "lookers."

Mrs. Ralston entered the store from the back door. Betty and Marshall entered behind her.

"Mrs. Ralston," Jodie called.

"One of her colored friends," she paused to whisper to Betty with a condescending smile.

"This is Ruby Martin," Jodie said. "She's applying for a job."

Ruby extended her hand, but Mrs. Ralston, stunned by the announcement, ignored it. Ruby let her hand fall.

"I see," the older woman said and turned away.

"You're looking for a job here?" Marshall asked.

Ruby replied, "Yes, sir, I am. You must be Mr. Jackson's son. People here abouts say you're a good salesman. I'm pleased to make your acquaintance." She extended her hand.

The remark brought a smile to Marshall's face. He took her hand, then dropped it, and brushed his hand against his trouser leg. Ruby smiled. She had seen that before.

The back door squeaked open to admit Elmore. Mrs. Ralston nudged Betty and whispered, loudly enough for all to hear and with unrestrained glee, "As Roy Crawford would say, the shit is about to hit the fan."

Jodie, with Ruby in tow, met Elmore in the hall.

"Elmore, I'd like for you to meet Ruby Martin. This is Mr. Jackson."

Elmore, not completely ready for the day, stood mute as he tried to comprehend why Jodie had introduced a "nigra" to him.

Ruby extended her hand and said what a great pleasure it was to meet him. Elmore, in business a long time, had no qualms about shaking the young woman's hand.

"Ruby is applying for a job, Elmore. She—"

"Ahem, well, Ruby, we already have a part-time cleaning girl."

"Could we discuss this in the office, Elmore?" Jodie asked.

Marshall's giggle brought a puzzled look to Elmore's face. More puzzling was the muffled laughter outside when the office door was closed. Ruby waited in the shoe department.

"Well, we don't need any help," Elmore said. "What's all the damned giggling and carrying on about?"

Jodie took a deep breath and explained that Ruby wanted a job as a trainee, not as a cleaning woman.

"A nigra!" Elmore's face reddened and his hand flew out in front of him. He shook his head in disbelief but the look on Jodie's face told him she was serious. "You want me to hire a nigra?"

Jodie nodded and slid the résumé across the desk. He glanced at it.

"We don't need extra help," he said. He looked her squarely in the eye. She returned his look. "And we sure as hell don't need a nigra around here."

"In the last year, our business has increased thirty-five percent. And we've just opened the uniform department."

"Marshall's handling that!"

"All the time? How about lunch? How about when he makes calls on prospective buyers. How about when he's out sick? That goes for everybody in the store. How about vacations? How about when we have sales?"

"We can hire a white girl if you think we need part-time help."

"Two-thirds of our customers are Negroes. And who do you think wears most of our uniforms we sell?"

"She's a nigra, Jodie! A nigra. We only have one bathroom. I couldn't ask Myrtle or Betty to sit down after a nigra. And what do you think it'd be like in August, the smell."

"What did you and Ruth do? You had colored nurses."

"Oh, well they were clean. We, uh, made them wipe the toilet seat after they went."

"I am sure Ruby is just as clean, and I doubt she'd smell any worse than some of the plant hands who come in here at the end of a shift."

"Now, Jodie, I, uh, know you've done a good job with the store. I meant to tell you. Especially the uniform department. But I can't oblige you on this. No sir! I can't go along with this!" He stood to leave.

Jodie bowed her head and reached for the résumé.

She sighed and said, "I suppose you're right. It's just that, well, the coloreds in Jordan look up to you. They say you've always treated them right. I hate to see them disappointed, particularly after all the business they've given you." That part was true. Elmore treated all his customers well.

"If I've heard one, I've heard a dozen say, Elmore's our friend. The onlyest one in town!"

His hand gripped the doorknob, but he turned to hear her out.

"I figured a colored girl, even a trainee, would be good for business." It was time to make the sale. "Look at it this way. We took a chance on the uniform department, and it paid off. Not only that, it gave Marshall a chance."

Even though he and Marshall were still not on the best of terms, he was gratified to see him in the store every day.

"Now we get new customers in the main store when they come in to look at uniforms. We have more customers than we can handle. They wait for help, and if they don't get it, they walk out. A colored trainee would stop all that. We'd increase sales, Elmore!"

"They say I'm their friend?" He sensed Jodie was selling him, but liked what she said.

Jodie shook her head.

"I do treat 'em right. Like white people," he said half under his breath. "I don't know though…hiring a nigra. Nobody in town has." He shook his head.

"It's the right thing," she said. "What if somebody else hires her and the coloreds move their trade? I'm asking you to take a chance."

He continued to shake his head. He had come to rely on Jodie and hated to buck her, but still, a nigra clerk? It wasn't done!

He yanked the door open and called, "Marshall!"

"Did she tell you?" Marshall asked.

"What do you think about taking on a nigra?"

"Ha! I wouldn't, and I bet neither would any of the uptown businesses."

Elmore said, "Most of them said I'd bust my ass down here when I opened up, and I haven't yet. I still make a living when half of them live off family money and act like big shots."

Jodie saw how he tried to convince himself and felt warmly toward him, a rare moment.

"I'll ask Tim what he thinks," Marshall said.

"The hell you will. Goddamn Tim Lennox! What does he know about my store, my customers?" Marshall cringed and stepped back. The discussion was over! The mention of Lennox as having any say so in *his store* brought about an immediate reaction. The time for reasoning was dead.

"Bring that gal in here!" he ordered.

Ruby came in, all smiles, but her stomach was tied in knots as big as her fists.

For thirty minutes, she answered Elmore's questions.

Elmore principally wanted assurance that she would take orders, not one of them "uppity nigras." He casually mentioned the summer heat.

"It sure does get hot, don't it, Mr. Jackson? I takes me a bath every morning of every day." She deliberately spoke with street slang to avoid sounding "uppity." It was something Willie Bea suggested.

"Hmm…We only have one bathroom."

"Oh, I know that Mr. Jackson, sir. I don't mind taking myself over yonder to the colored filling station." She gestured in the direction of the black service station across the tracks.

"We could fix the old bathroom at the back of the uniform department," Jodie offered. "All it needs is a good cleaning and a new seat."

"Uh-huh. Well, Ruby, we'll try you out. For a month, as a trainee. If sales don't increase, we may have to let you go. You understand? It's just a trial."

"I understand! Thank you, Mr. Jackson. Thank you, sir!" She shook his hand.

She started the next day.

Ruby was a fast learner and, under Jodie's tutelage, handled sales after two days. Of course, she only sold when no one else was free. The rest of the time she put out fresh stock, worked on layaways, and posted payments to suppliers. It wasn't long until Elmore stopped spying on her and the whispering in the store stopped.

At Jodie's suggestion, Willie Bea Hansen dropped by and lavished praise on Elmore.

"The black community wants you to know the esteem they feel for you."

Elmore welcomed compliments. More importantly though, business had increased. And, just as important, no one complained about "Elmore's nigra."

That would change.

CHAPTER 27

In April, Jodie took the inventory alone. Elmore and Myrtle dallied over reorder forms and ate hot pie with coffee. And Jodie had the final say on the orders. It was understood.

"I read where the Lennox boy's getting a divorce," Mrs. Ralston gossiped to Elmore.

"Wife most likely caught him with another woman," Elmore said. "His kind stays in heat."

"Like his old daddy," Mrs. Ralston added. "Heard stories about his philandering."

Elmore's head jerked around. "Don't bring him up!"

Marshall had said that Lennox almost married Ruth. Was there more to the story than the Annex? Jodie wondered.

Jodie's twenty-fifth birthday passed without notice. The differences in their ages usually sent Elmore into a weeklong depression.

A month later, Elmore celebrated his with a cake. Marshall stayed after work for a piece and Virginia called. His grandchildren sang "Happy Birthday" long distance. Elmore got so teary-eyed, he couldn't blow out the candles.

Later, Roy Crawford blew through the front door like a hurricane. He laughed and teased with every step. Customers spread from his swagger like chickens flapping their wings to escape a chicken hawk.

"Sorry I couldn't make it for your birthday," he told Elmore, "but I did bring you a present." He pulled out the familiar brown paper sack, crinkled at the top, and handed it to him. It held a pint of bourbon.

"Reminds me of what a customer told me," Elmore said as he stored the bag under the counter. "Said he never had enough money to buy a fifth of bourbon, but had bought an interest in many a case."

Roy laughed and slapped his back.

"Roy, I thought we heard you come in," Jodie said from the back of the store.

"I don't doubt it." He laughed again then said to Elmore, "Hell, you must be fifty by now."

"Gettin' close," Elmore joked back.

"How the hell is business?"

"Must be pretty good, I hear our commissions bought you a new car," Elmore said.

Roy didn't deny it.

"Y'all going to New Orleans this year?" Roy asked.

It seemed more a courtesy inquiry than an invitation, Jodie noted. The debacle last time brought a smile to her face.

"Not gonna be a show, but the manufacturers are going to display. I hear there ain't gonna be much of a change from last year. They're calling it a Clothes Fair," he added. "Gonna have it in July."

"Don't expect I will," Elmore replied. "Can't shake this arthritis like I used to."

Roy's grin broadened in relief, but Jodie was disappointed. That would mean reordering last year's styles or, worse, Roy's choices. She wanted Elmore to change his mind, but would bring it up later. Also, she wanted to see Warren again, if only to say hello. The realization that she'd grown dependent on him for scraps of joy brought a silent curse into her thoughts.

You don't need anybody, she said to herself.

Roy left with the same suddenness of his entry. The store, like a pile of dry leaves lifted by a gust of wind, settled behind him.

After supper, a week later, Jodie brought up the subject. "Don't you think we ought to see the new styles before we make a decision on our orders? I certainly don't want Roy to do our selecting." Last year's styles would probably be okay, she figured, but she was interested in keeping up with fashion changes.

"What choice do I have?"

"We could go to the Clothes Fair."

"New Orleans?" Before she could answer, he said, "Hmm... You got something going on down there I don't know about?" Of late, he'd eyed her when she waited on male customers, younger ones in particular. And he'd skipped attempts at lovemaking for three months, a relief for her, but she wasn't sure what to make of it. He couldn't wait to get from the supper table to the television set and from there to bed.

"No," she answered. "But I do have pride in the store. I want to keep up. Don't you?"

"Hell, can't you see I'm sick? Haven't been able to sleep for a month. Damn tired all the time. Nobody's going to give a damn if we buy last year's stock."

Jodie massaged his back until he drowsed off. She still held out hope that he'd change his mind.

A few days later, she was surprised to hear someone call her name. She'd heard it before, a raucous, flamboyant voice, with a heavy twang. She twisted around to confirm who it was.

"Charlie Burdette!"

His oily black hair was combed straight back, exposing his forehead. He was fifty but didn't act as if he knew it yet, or cared. His face showed deep, carefree smile lines, like Steven's. It was easy to see why the plant hands elected him their leader.

"Haven't seen you since the campaign," she said.

After a few words about "that ole hypocrite Case" he leaned over and whispered, "If I was ten years younger and didn't already have a wife and house full of younguns, and if you wasn't already took, I'd, by god, be chasing after you."

"With that many ifs, I think I'm safe."

He laughed and slapped the top of the counter. "Ain't you just the smartest little lady I ever saw!"

"Besides, Charlie Burdette, if you were ten years younger, you'd have so many farmers chasing you around with shotguns and pregnant daughters, you couldn't stop long enough to get married."

"Ain't it the truth?" They both laughed.

Elmore was out of the store. Otherwise, their unrestrained laughter would have convinced him they were lovers.

"Let me tell you the real reason I came in here. I'm fed up seeing my ole lady in a dress that says 'Wilson Feed and Seed' across the front." He chuckled. Sometimes the lettering would not boil out of the feed and fertilizer sacks country people sewed into clothes. "It's her birthday," he added.

"We only sell the best."

"Hell, Jodie Mae, I don't want the best. I want something I can afford!" He laughed again. "We may have a strike coming up. Management thinks we're making too much money. I'm saying we're not making nearly as much as we need."

A strike! Damnation! She swallowed her concern and asked, "You know her size?"

"About the same as that lady over yonder." He pointed toward Mrs. Ralston. "Maybe a bit broader in the hips. She makes a gooood pan of biscuits, and we don't have leftovers."

Both chuckled at that. He patted a stomach that pushed at his belt.

Jodie picked two dresses, both with bright floral patterns, and held them up. He picked the brightest one.

"What about a strike?" she asked as she handed him the dress.

"Hell, we've been working without a contract for four months. They say we'll come to some sort of agreement, but I ain't sure. We're running three shifts, turning out lots of boards and stuff, like maybe they're stockpiling. I don't trust them. I've been telling my people to save up too. If there is one, it could last awhile."

That sent a wave of fear through her, but she prayed maybe it wouldn't come to a strike.

The loud tick of the clock told her it was noon and time for Elmore's bowl of soup. At the back stairs, she heard angry voices in the alleyway. She looked through the window.

Elmore and a heavyset, barrel-shaped man wearing a wide leather belt faced each other. Jodie recognized him as the man who had knocked Lizzy to the ground in front of the shack they lived in a few days before white robed men burned a cross in the yard. His hair had thinned and his face had wrinkled some, but Jodie didn't doubt who it was. Two younger men in blue overalls flanked them. Elmore and the heavier man paced and circled, growling like two bears reared up on their hind legs ready for the other to attack.

Jodie caught bits and pieces of what the man was saying. "That colored…KKK…ain't heard the last of it."

When his angry shuffling and circling put him facing the stairs, Jodie heard him say, "Our white women ain't safe as it is, Jackson. If you go to hiring coloreds, next thing you know, them colored bucks'll thank they're entitled to our women!"

"Shit, Anderson, you're making a mountain out of a mole hill," Elmore shot back. He stood erect, no sign of his debilitating arthritis.

"You get rid of her! You better hear me, Jackson!" The stout man stuck a finger in Elmore's face.

Elmore's hand darted out and knocked Anderson's finger to one side. He leaned forward to dare Anderson to do it again. The man backed away a step.

"That nigra is my wife's help. You tell me your wife doesn't have help."

"Damned right, but—"

"But hell! There ain't a damned bit of difference. Anyway, she's only going to be in the store a few months. No need to get your bowels in an uproar."

Anderson's face loosened up. He had warned the others that old Jackson would be a tough bastard and he was, but Jackson had "agreed to fire the colored…in a few months." He'd take that away with him.

Elmore came inside.

That evening, Elmore told Jodie that Ruby had to go.

"Why?" Jodie asked. "She's bringing in business." In fact, Ruby had asked Jodie for permission to solicit uniform sales in adjacent counties. Marshall was reluctant to travel outside the county. She also suggested expanding into rentals, one of Warren's recommendations.

"Marshall will just have to take over. She can work on for a couple of months. I don't want to hear any more about it."

Jodie saw that further talk would only infuriate him. She was well aware of what he faced from the KKK. Even though Elmore would never give in to a bully like Anderson, Jodie knew, his common sense would win out. He wouldn't buck the KKK. Ruby had to go. Jodie would try to string the "couple of months" into three or four and hope something would come along to change his mind.

CHAPTER 28

In the dining room of an old frame house on Second Avenue, a single candle flickered over a small linen-covered table set for two. Soft music blended with the candlelight. Warm rolls rested on small plates on the left.

The dim light from the candle cast a half shadow over Tim Lennox's face. In a sport coat and slacks, and perfectly at ease, he could easily be mistaken for a leading man in a movie, soon to be joined by his leading lady.

In the kitchen behind him, an oven door creaked open. Soft steps approached and white hands placed a baking dish of beef Wellington on the table. A curl of aromatic white steam drifted upward from the delicate brown crust of the dish. It was Marshall standing in the shadowy rim of the table waiting for Tim's approval.

"Hmm!" Tim said. His lips curled upward. Beef Wellington was his favorite.

"You, uh, do you do like it?" Marshall asked. He pressed the potholders to the red apron around his front.

"It looks superb!" Tim assured him. "And, umm, that smell, I can hardly wait." He touched the handle of his fork.

Marshall disappeared into the kitchen to fetch the salads. He served each of their plates with a helping of the delicately crusted beef dish, then passed a covered dish of mashed potatoes and small English peas simmered in butter.

"Oh!" Marshall said. "I forgot the wine!" He fetched a bottle of French Burgundy.

"I'm so thrilled you're getting a divorce," Marshall said.

"No choice. She caught me with the maid." Tim smiled. "Whew! Was she pissed!"

"The maid!" Marshall stopped and stared, openmouthed.

Tim shrugged. "I told her before we were married I liked to fool around. I guess she forgot or didn't like the maid."

Marshall, crestfallen, lowered his eyes. The sip of wine on his tongue turned to vinegar. He said, "I thought it was because, you know, because I came back to Jordan."

Tim reached across the table, placed his hand over Marshall's, and said, "Marshall, you are my best friend, my very best friend."

"But the maid!"

"The female body is beautiful, Marshall. I wouldn't turn down your stepmother."

"Ugh! Please, not at dinner!"

"This is delicious," Tim remarked and hoisted his fork to Marshall in salute. He helped himself to another serving.

The first bottle of wine disappeared. The second was sipped more slowly as the dinner wound down. The candle had burned halfway, and as the last drops of wine were emptied into glasses, Marshall said, "I have an extra bedroom."

Tim dismissed the suggestion. "No, I'm going to stay in Dad's old place on Trace till the estate and divorce are settled."

Marshall's face fell. He said, "Father told me the KKK came by a couple of days ago. I think he was shitting in his britches but wouldn't admit it."

"Dad was a member of the KKK," Tim replied with a grin. "I think I inherited his sheet. Why'd they come? The black girl? It's around town that he hired one."

Marshall shook his head and added, "That cheap bitch Father married forced him to hire her. Pulling Father around by his dick. How disgusting!"

"They came by the store, two nigra women, but I didn't need any extra help," Tim said. "Elmore's been taking some of Dad's business."

"Would you have hired one?"

"I don't know, maybe. Depends on what she looked like."

He was incredulous that Tim could be so cavalier about the KKK.

"I don't want the KKK to hurt the store," Marshall said. "It's going to be mine pretty soon. Father can't have many years left. I think his sugar is high, but he won't go to the doctor. He's afraid they'll find something."

"Dad was stubborn like that." Tim's light brown hair glowed a shade of gold in the flickering candlelight.

"What's for dessert?"

Marshall reached for Tim's hand. "Lemon ice box pie. Later."

CHAPTER 29

Jodie waited until Elmore drank a few toddies to press him on the New Orleans trip. She asked, "Clothes Fair is next week, Elmore. Have you decided what you want to do?"

"I said Roy—"

"Roy? You're ready to go back to leftovers and mistakes that nobody else wants. I'd rather have Marshall buy for the store than Roy."

"Hell, no telling what Marshall would come back with. He can sell, but—" He shook his head. "No. I'm not sending him."

"I could go," she said slowly.

"I'm not letting you go to that sin hole by yourself!"

"Marshall could come—"

"I'll think about it, goddamn it. You always push me, Jodie. Can't you see I'm...hell, I'm not getting enough sleep. I'm tired."

The next day, Elmore discussed the fair with Marshall, asking, "What do you think of Roy Crawford, son?"

"Oh, he's crude clod, Father. Has the taste of a hog wallowing in mud."

"He was our buyer, till last year."

"The Salvation Army had better clothes."

"Well, damn it, what the hell am I supposed to do? The goddamned Clothes Fair is next week, and I'm down in the back. Can you go down there and keep an eye—uh, help Jodie buy?"

Marshall, recalling the remorse that followed his last trip to New Orleans, slowly shook his head no.

"I'm never going to New Orleans again."

"Well, I can't let Jodie go down there by herself."

"Ha, from what I've seen, she doesn't need help."

An angry scowl covered Elmore's face.

"What do you mean, boy? If you've got something to say, spit it out!"

"Father, I'll NEVER say anything about my dear stepmother. You must remember that we've discussed her before. I certainly do." He rubbed his jaw to remind him of their alleyway argument shortly after the marriage. "I'd never let her out of my sight, if I were you."

"Damn it to hell, boy! Are you saying she steps out on me?"

"That's as much as I'm going to say. You figure it out," he called over his shoulder.

Elmore scowled. *The boy all but said she's stepped out on me. She spent a lot of time with that Jefferson boy! A lot of time. Boy has all sorts of women chasing after him, I bet. Most likely laughing up his ass about it, damn rich dog.*

He told Jodie that night, "We'll go to that damned Clothes Fair. For one day and night. You can do the goddamned buying." His eyes narrowed. "I hope to hell you're satisfied."

She saw hate in his eyes. He had changed. That scared her, but she put it behind her. The fair was too important to miss.

Elmore grumped all the way to the train. Actually, he started two days before, but they would go.

Jodie listened to the "clickety-clack" of the train's iron wheels and gazed out the window during the trip. Elmore sometimes dozed, but mostly stared straight ahead in silence. Jodie knew something was on his mind.

Between forsaken, marshy swamplands were hilly bumps of high ground, places for shacks and shanties, gravel roads, and railroad crossings. Where the ground was lower, creeks and rivers flowed. Beside some were camps where men came to fish and hunt and drink beer to revel in their freedom and brag about their past triumphs, real and imagined.

Except for the view, only the twist of the black cap on Elmore's bottle broke the silence. That and the gurgle of his upturned bottle.

His sullen face smoldered with resentment and smoldered more the closer they got to New Orleans.

They took a taxi to their hotel. The driver was a "thief" and received no tip. The registration clerk was incompetent, and their room was filthy. The bellboy also left empty-handed.

When Roy came by to make the rounds, Elmore staggered to the door and said, "Not up to it, Roy! Told Jodie I was sick! Nothing would do her, damn it to hell." Jodie didn't move from where she stood beside the window.

Roy waited at the door, bewildered.

Elmore gave a half-wave. "Make the rounds with her. I don't want her to wander around this hellhole by herself."

Roy's eyebrows lifted. This was none of his business.

It neared five o'clock when they stopped by the Greene suite. A number of buyers milled around to examine clothes and fabric samples. Display posters showed that the styles had changed little from the last year. A slim model, in a lacy day dress, twirled into the room for a balding man with thick glasses. Mark, the young man who prepared Jodie for her modeling assignment at the first Clothes Fair she'd attended, busied himself with buyer's questions.

Warren was not there. Jodie could scarcely conceal her disappointment.

"Hi, Jodie. Good to see you. Look around," Mark called to her. "Roy." The men exchanged nods.

The model talked about the hats they featured, worn to draw attention to the face.

Jodie went through the motions. She viewed the dress and hat samples on display and thumbed through the catalogs and completed Elmore's order sheets as she did.

"You can go on if you want," she told Roy.

He grinned. "Elmore says to stay. I'm staying. You know how he gets."

"Let's go then," she said. She handed the order sheets to Roy so he could haggle with Mark later about price and delivery.

She anticipated that Warren would cheer her up, overcome Elmore's depressing melancholy, but that wasn't to be.

That's what comes if you depend on someone else, she thought as they returned to the room.

"Our room." She pointed. "I think you've done your duty."

He shook his head but watched until her hand touched the doorknob before he turned away.

Inside, she found Elmore in his baggy shorts and undershirt. One hand held a fresh bottle of bourbon by the neck. An empty bottle lay on the floor.

"Where the hell have you been?" he demanded and turned the bottle up for another drink. He staggered, but managed not to fall.

"With Roy." She tried to pass, but he grabbed her arm.

"I tol' 'im t' bring you back."

"He did!"

"Get your clothes off! You need a good fucking! By god, I'm going to give you one!" His eyes were red. He reeked of raw whiskey. Whiskey had escaped his numbed lips and left yellow streaks down the front of his undershirt. Likewise, yellow droplets glistened on the gray and white stubble on his chin.

"No!" She twisted out of his grasp. "You're…you need a bath."

Dropping the bottle to the floor, he jerked her backward, onto the bed. It shuddered violently, but remained upright. Elmore fell on top of her.

He fumbled to remove her clothes but when his enfeebled fingers became frustrated, he ripped at the fabric. It was not a new outfit, but it was now ripped beyond repair. Her struggles only intensified his quest. Next came the bra and panties. He threw them on the floor and kicked off his shorts.

"You think I'm too old, don't you? Can't cut the mustard anymore! Hell, I'm plenty young."

She sobbed helplessly under his crude attack and hoped it would soon be over. For twenty minutes, he pinched and squeezed and probed, without tenderness, without caring and…without success. And the harder he tried, the more inept he became.

"Goddamn you! You aren't trying," he cried out and pushed her naked body off the bed. He staggered to his feet and reached for the bottle he'd thrown to the floor, but the nausea boiling in his stomach reached his throat before his hand touched the bottle.

"Uuuup." He twisted and staggered, weak-legged toward the bathroom, but made it only as far as the door. Vomit sprayed everywhere. He clutched at the door for support and heaved again and again; and even when his stomach was empty, he heaved more. Cold sweat dripped from this throbbing head. The acid brine left his throat raw. Deep moans passed through Elmore's mouth as his stomach continued its spasmodic collapse.

"Help me, Jodie," he cried.

She pulled on a fresh dress.

Between heaves, he stuck his head in the porcelain washbasin and ran cold water over it.

There was a knock on the door. Jodie sat down to wait. The water stopped. The knock continued. Elmore peered through the bathroom door.

"Elmore," Roy called through the room door. "You ready?"

Elmore stared at Jodie, a plea formed on his face. She didn't move. He grabbed his old brown robe and opened the door a crack. His body shivered uncontrollably.

Foul air rushed through the crack.

"Shit!" Roy exclaimed. He knew what it was. All heavy drinkers came to know that smell sooner or later. Seeing Elmore's pained face, he declined further comment. He halfheartedly did a bump and grind to remind Elmore about the lingerie show.

"Can't make it," Elmore croaked. "Arthritis."

Roy knew a husband and wife fight when he saw one. "Never heard of arthritis of the stomach," he mumbled and scurried away.

Elmore closed the door. A mask of hate distorted his pallid features.

"Clean it up!" He pointed at the disgusting, simmering pool of vomit. The stench overpowered the room.

"Clean it up yourself. I'm going to see Taylor."

She moved toward the door. Elmore, trembling with rage, stepped in front of her.

"You're not leaving this room till—"

"You gonna beat me now?" she asked and turned her arms to show the red finger marks he had left from his earlier assault.

He reached out with his rough hands and lightly touched the red welts.

"I didn't mean it, Jodie." Gripping her shoulders in his hands, he stared into her eyes and pleaded for forgiveness.

"I don't know what came over me."

"Forget it. It doesn't matter," she said. Though she hated him for what he had tried to do, she wanted to get it behind her as soon as possible. She reached for the doorknob.

"For God's sake, Jodie, don't go. I'll make it up!" His eyes switched about wildly in search of a way to stop her. "I let you hire that nigra, didn't I? And open the new department."

She looked at him without reply.

"I'm begging you to stay, Jodie. I apologize. Goddamn, Jodie, can't you understand? I'm not as young as I—Hell, I'm afraid I'll…" His voice verged on tears. "It eats at my guts that you want a younger man. Marshall said—" He shrugged.

So, that vindictive, insolent Marshall was behind it! All the rage that had been building up since the opening of the uniform department, the rage she felt at being manhandled by a drunken, clumsy husband, the rage she felt toward Mrs. Ralston and Marshall, the rage that had built up since her marriage spilled out.

"That little queer!"

Her outburst took Elmore aback. He straightened himself and glared at her.

"Don't call my boy a queer! You don't have the right to talk about my flesh and blood!"

Forgotten was his apology, forgotten were his pleas for her to remain.

Jodie, still furious, spewed the words out. "He's a vindictive little queer! He most likely hates your guts and you don't even know it."

"Marshall—"

"I'm sick of your slimy son's snide comments behind my back, and I'm sick of your dumpy back-biting, two-faced daughter who bitches about everything I cook as she stuffs it in her fat face with both hands. I'm sick of you and your whole damned family!"

Elmore's face reddened. His fists clinched and his jaw tightened.

"At least they don't walk the streets like the Phelps. You and your mother. Just alike. Marshall always said it. A whore! Well, go on! Go walk the streets like a bitch in heat. That's what you came for isn't it? Get out!"

"You dumb son of a bitch!" Jodie slapped him hard across the face. The stinging blow was all the excuse his bottled-up frustration needed. His fist smashed against the side of her head, knocking her backward. Half-crazed, he seized her shoulders and slammed her against the wall, again and again. Her head bounced off the wall, each thud bringing darkness to her eyes. Fearing for her life, she drove her fists hard into his stomach and raised a knee to his abdomen.

"Ugh!" he grunted, grabbed her hair, and threw her against the metal ball on the top of the bedpost. Her stomach exploded in searing pain as she slid to the floor.

"Aghhh!"

"Get up, bitch!" he yelled. "You want a beating, you're going to get one."

She staggered to her feet and fell against his arm. He pushed her against the door.

"Can't breathe," she whispered, but he didn't hear. He was busy ripping her clothes from the closet hangers. He opened the door of the room and threw them into the hall. When he'd done that, he pushed her out. Two passersby hurried their pace to avoid the scene.

Elmore slammed the door and reached for his bottle. He turned it up to let what was left drain into his stomach. The room twirled around him. He dropped the bottle and fell to the floor, out cold.

Jodie heard the thump and tried to open the door, but it was locked. She knocked, but there was no answer. More people hurried past and paused to glance at the scene. The pain in her stomach brought tears to her eyes. Her head swam. Cold perspiration formed on her forehead, ran down her face, and mingled with the salty tears already there. She gathered her clothes and stumbled into the elevator. She'd go to Taylor's. In the lobby, her head swirled and her knees wobbled under her. She took two more steps and collapsed.

CHAPTER 30

She awoke in a bed. The room was in twilight. Her hand involuntarily touched her stomach. It was sore, but the pain had subsided.

"Well, you survived." Warren leaned over and kissed her softly on the forehead.

Eve saw her fall and called him. He came for her and carried her to his apartment.

"Doctor says you're all right. He just left. I feel like dragging your husband into the street and, to put it in the southern vernacular, kicking the shit out of him. You talked off and on," he said.

"I'm glad you didn't," she said. "He's come to know that he's old and all that comes with it. He should have thought about it a long time ago, but I can't do anything about that now."

"No husband has the right to beat his wife."

"Down here, a man can beat his dogs, his mule, and his wife. It's their right." She forced a smile.

He kissed her again. This time on the lips and let it linger. A warm glow filled her body.

He ordered dinner. She barely managed half a cup of consommé, but it was good. After dinner, they sat on the balcony and talked.

He asked her to come to New York with him. He promised work, modeling, selling, whatever she wanted. She knew there was more to his promise than work. His eyes told her that. And the kiss. She declined.

"I could never see you without knowing I was stealing your wife's happiness and your children's. That's what my dad did to my mother, and I hated him for it." Tears ran down her face. "I finally got used to being sold for two hundred dollars. I doubt your leftover love would be much of an improvement. I won't take what's not mine."

He didn't argue.

Jodie was up early the next morning. The pain was almost gone. Some soreness, and a purple bruise, remained. A shower and makeup covered the red marks on her cheek.

"Hello!" Warren called. She was in her robe.

He put his arms around her. "Your face never leaves my thoughts. I touch you in my sleep, I hear you talk and kiss your lips. When I see your face, it takes my breath away."

Her fingers touched the sweetness of his lips; her eyes searched the depths of his. "You make everything seem wonderful, Warren," she whispered. Their lips touched and lingered and withdrew only to touch again, as though irresistibly drawn together.

He removed his shirt and threw it across the chair. His arms pulled her close. The warmth of his body blended with hers. Her hands stroked the strength of his arms then strayed to his chest.

He untied her robe and let it fall to the floor. She reached her arms around his neck and pulled his face to hers. He picked her up and gently placed her in bed.

They made love, a soft melody that rose with each stanza until the final crescendo. Afterward, they lay still and let the final moment replay.

She fell asleep with her head cradled on his shoulder. When she awoke, he was gone. A note said, "Have to meet buyers. Be back in an hour. We'll go out."

Despair came with the emptiness in the room. She cursed that she wanted him so, needed him. She dressed and packed her belongings and waited.

When he returned, he said, "I've wrestled with it all damn day. I'm not going to let you go back to that man. Whether you come with me or not, you aren't going back to him. Maybe you're right about…what you said…stealing my wife's happiness, but I've never hit her ever!"

"I appreciate what you're saying, Warren. I do, but nothing has changed. You have your life and I have mine. Or did have. I'll stay with Taylor until I can think straight. I've put my soul into that store. That's hard to walk away from." She touched his face with her fingertips. "I will always remember this morning."

"I love you, Jodie. Let me say that."

She shook her head and looked away.

"Okay. I understand that. But at least tell me you'll think about coming to New York."

"I'm certain I'll think of nothing else, but I won't come."

He accompanied her in a taxi to Taylor's apartment.

Taylor was enraged when he heard. "I'm gonna drag the son of a bitch out in the street and beat the living shit out of him!"

"Please don't, Taylor. Half the time he doesn't even know what he's doing. If you hit him, you'll end up in the pen. And for what? I'm okay now."

He stared at her for a few seconds. She was right, and he knew it. "If you say so, little sister."

Warren called the next morning to see how she was.

"I'm not sore anymore, and my blue marks are fading," she told him.

He asked again about New York. She again refused.

She walked to Canal Street and filled out applications for work. Part of her wanted to return to Jordan and the store, but that seemed impossible. Elmore would see her return as an admission that she'd been wrong. There'd be no living with him after that.

Lizzy called two days later. From the graveness of her voice, Jodie knew something was wrong.

"I kind of figured you was with Taylor. He left his telephone number with Ted or I'd never have found you."

"What's the matter?" Jodie asked.

"Sugar, that ole man come out here the other day, I reckon it was the day after the ruckus he said y'all had in New Orleans. His eyes were all red and watering, like he ain't had no sleep. I think he was drinking…smelled like it. I kind of felt sorry for him.

"He didn't believe you weren't here. Anyhow, he apologized all over hisself. Said he was sorry. Blamed in on the whiskey and all. Said to tell you if you did come home, he'd make it up to you. He swore to God he would."

"That's what Chet used to say after he came home drunk and beat you up."

"You right, I reckon. Anyhow, he went on back toward town so me and Jim figured that was the end of it, but it wasn't. When Jim went out to start his truck yesterday morning, he found that old man asleep in his car by the road. We reckoned he'd been out there all night, thinking you was in here. I told him to come on in and have a cup of coffee. He smelled like a jug of pop skull. I wanted him to see you wasn't here. Jim went on to work.

"He drank two cups of coffee and commenced to ask for a third when he just up and keeled over, flat on the floor. I lugged him to his car and drove him to the hospital."

"Heart attack?"

"Nurse said it looked like a stroke. The left side of his face was awfully drawn. Pitiful looking."

"Is he okay?"

"I don't know. I called that shit ass of a son of his, Marshall—excuse my French—but the boy's such a smart aleck he made me mad. Hospital needed a relative to sign papers. He looked bad, Sugar, real bad. I reckon if I was you, I might come back. I just about know what happened between y'all down there, but you might want to be here, in case."

After a pause, Jodie said, "I'll catch the next train."

"Lizzy?" Taylor asked.

Jodie nodded and related the story.

"You ain't really going back?"

"What if he dies? I don't want him on my conscience. It was partly my fault. I shouldn't have said what I did about Marshall and Virginia."

"Shit fire, you only told the truth! What you should do is get a ticket to New York. To hell with that old man. You ain't had never nothing but grief since you married him. Hell, you ain't never had nothing but grief, ever. If that man in New York loves you, that's where you should go."

"And let Marshall have the store? There wouldn't be anything left in a month."

"I say to hell with that damned store, but I reckon you as bullheaded as me," he said with exasperation. "Do what you have to do."

When the train pulled into Jordan station the following evening, Lizzy and Jim were there in Jim's pickup.

"We went by the hospital before we come here. The nurse says he'll live," Lizzy reported.

Jodie breathed a sigh of relief.

They stopped in front of the General Hospital. It was for the sick with money. Others accepted the gratuity of the Charity Hospital. The two-story concrete building looked as gray and somber as she felt. Lizzy handed Jodie Elmore's car keys and told her where it was. Then, she told Jodie some bad news.

"The men at the plant went out this morning. Charlie Burdette says they gonna stay on the picket line till ole man Jordan agrees to pay a fair wage."

God, Jodie thought. *A strike! And Elmore had just drawn against the bank loan.*

"What does Mr. Jordan say?"

"He says they ain't gonna be no compromise. It's gonna be a long strike, most people say."

Jim said, "I done got calls, canceling jobs. People get real tight during a strike. Looks like me and Lizzy're gonna be eating lots of potatoes."

"Thank the Lord I planted us a garden," she said.

During a strike, people got laid off, cars repossessed, businesses closed, and the worst as far as Elmore's was concerned, people quit buying clothes and uniforms and couldn't make layaway payments. And even worse, Elmore's would have no money for payments to the bank on the loan.

Jodie pushed through the front doors into the waiting room, crowded as always with people. Curious children, oblivious to all concerns but their own, looked for distractions. Tired grandparents held grandchildren and waited for the next to be delivered. Men in suits stared at the walls without seeing. Hard-faced farmers in frayed overalls sat proudly erect in hard-back chairs next to sad-faced wives with frazzled hair and wrinkled dresses. Their frayed sweaters barely stretched around their rounded shoulders. But nothing mattered in a hospital waiting room except news and most of it was bad. Some clutched their Bibles. Some mumbled prayers. A few sobbed. Others stared at nothing with empty eyes or gave comfort to those who needed it. Somewhere in a dimly lit room along one of the hospital's gray corridors was a loved one whose fate was "in God's hands."

Virginia was there. She stared at a cross on the wall. Her mismatched clothes appeared none the worse for the abuse they had suffered during the wait. Jodie went past without speaking. A nurse took her to Elmore's room. Connected by plastic tubes to liquid-filled bottles, he lay on a stark white bed gasping for breath. The left side of his face was contorted in a permanent frown of disapproval. As Jodie entered, his eyes blinked. He groaned feebly and called her name. His hand weakly motioned her closer. She pulled a chair up next to the bed.

"S'ry 'bout...New Or—Please forgi' 'e...Whiske—" His words were slurred and forced and came between brief periods of unconsciousness.

"Just rest, Elmore," Jodie said and patted his arm. "Everything's going to be all right."

"Will he recover?" Jodie asked the doctor during his rounds.

He shook his head and said, "There'll be permanent damage on his left side. It could get worse. Strokes are hard to assess. Keep him away from stress and make sure he gets some exercise every day."

Virginia said her goodbye and left.

The next day, Marshall and two ambulance attendants helped Jodie get Elmore up the apartment stairs and into his television chair.

"Don't leave," he said to Jodie and clutched at her hand.

"I'll be here," she promised.

He smiled a twisted smile and fell asleep.

Jodie had to fight herself to keep out of the store, even at night, but she never knew when Elmore would wake up and need something. Marshall came by daily with reports, glowing reports. He stayed with Elmore when she went out for groceries and medicine.

Warren called, ostensibly to ask about Elmore's health, but really to find out how she was. She assured him that everything was fine though she wasn't exactly sure about the store because of the strike.

"I hope Mr. Jackson gets better soon, maybe then you'll be able to get on with your life."

Two weeks passed before she could go downstairs and inspect the store. Elmore had recovered enough to shuffle around the apartment.

Display posters had fallen down. Layaway accounts needed posting. Light bulbs needed replacing, floors cleaned, and clothes reorganized on the racks.

"Where's Ruby?" Jodie demanded of Mrs. Ralston. Layaways and restocking had been her responsibility.

"Uh," the woman stammered and glanced toward Marshall.

"We let her go. I told Father," he snapped.

"While he was half-dead and couldn't hear?" she asked with a scold that shocked both.

"Betty and Fred have been workin' part-time since the strike," Mrs. Ralston volunteered.

"Both of you listen to me!" She waved a finger under their noses. "You are both employees. I have half a mind to fire you both and rehire Ruby."

"You—" Marshall began.

"Shut up! Get this store cleaned up and the racks organized so it looks like we're still in business." She turned to Mrs. Ralston. "You post the layaways. From now on, consult me before making decisions. Is that clear?"

Mrs. Ralston and Marshall nodded.

When Jodie had gone, Marshall said, "That little bitch. She thinks she's so high and mighty. Just you wait till I get this store."

"But she's his wife. Won't it go to her? Unless…"

He gave her a half-smile and hurried off to clean the floors and replace bulbs.

Elmore cried like a spoiled child when she returned.

"Now you just cut that out!" she said. "Get out of that chair and walk around. You have to get more exercise. You're not trying!" She had to speak up. The stroke had affected his hearing.

He protested but struggled to his feet and did turns around the apartment. With his left side partially paralyzed, he had to drag his left leg along the floor. The scuffling sounds of that effort, his labored breathing, and the regular thumps on the wall with his right arm, for support, brought a lump to Jodie's throat.

"I di' it," he called and slumped back into his chair, exhausted. "I di' it, Ruth."

Jodie brought in his noon bowl of soup. He raised his arm and stammered, "You…Jodie? Where's Ruth?"

"Ruth passed away. Remember?"

He shook his head, but a confused look remained on his face. He did improve enough to allow Jodie to spend more time in the store. Business was no better, but at least the store looked better. Betty found another job, and Jodie suspected Fred was looking. She asked Warren to postpone the new shipment. He pressed her anew to leave since Elmore was ambulatory, but she refused.

CHAPTER 31

The strike followed the usual pattern. Burdette and Jordan exchanged charges in the *Tribune*. Both claimed bad faith negotiations. Jordan threatened to move the plant out of town and Burdette threatened an injunction if he tried. Scabs were hired to cross the picket line. They quit after two or three days, tired of having their tires slashed and their windows shot out.

Pick Mason, with his hired security patrols, inflicted an equal amount of damage to the strikers. Burdette's truck windows were smashed. Sugar was poured into strikers' gas tanks. Fights along the picket lines were common.

Jodie called Willie Bea about Ruby.

"Ruby's fine," Willie Bea said. "She's doing books for Lennox. And loves it. She said you were fair to her. I knew you would be." She'd heard about Elmore and kind of figured something had gone wrong between them since Ruby hadn't seen Jodie in the store before she'd been let go. Jodie admitted to a falling out, but didn't go into details.

Steven stopped by to see how they were doing. Jodie told him, "I've cut everything I can, but we're still not breaking even. We have enough stock left over to last the rest of the year. Ordinarily, I would have had two reorders by now." Threating letters from Blackledge at the bank weighed heavily on her mind, she told him. Defaults on their credit sales increased weekly, and they had no replacement sales.

"It's that way all over the county," Steven said. "People are living on their savings, and they didn't have a hell of a lot to begin with. Dad says it might last a year. He's talked to Mr. Jordan."

A feeling of dread passed over her. Elmore had less than a thousand dollars saved. What would they do after that?

The children of Bucatanna County went back to school that year with patched overalls and mended dresses. Fred quit. Mrs. Ralston and Marshall went on part-time. Jodie told Warren to forget their order.

In November, Mr. Blackledge parked out front and walked through the store. Jodie was busy with a rare customer. He asked to see Elmore. Marshall escorted him upstairs. As soon as she could, she bounded up the stairs as Blackledge drove away.

Marshall stood with his hand on Elmore's shoulder. The smug look on his face told her to expect trouble.

"It wasn't your fault, Father," Marshall said and patted his father's shoulder. Elmore's hand trembled. His mouth was opened, but no words came out. His glassy eyes were fixed on the wall.

Marshall leveled a finger at Jodie and shouted. "It's her fault!"

"What's my fault?" she demanded.

Elmore's head bobbed around to face her. "You…you…my store…all gone…my life…all gone." He raised his right arm feebly.

"Mr. Blackledge says the bank is calling Father's loan, the one you forced on him. Now he's going to lose everything. He'll be thrown into the street."

Tears ran down Elmore's ashen face. His eyes glazed over like a gray blanket of death was slowly pulled over him. "Thrown in…street," he mumbled.

Marshall railed on. Every word assigned blame for the foreclosure to her. Elmore began to sob.

She exploded, "Shut up! Both of you. I'll see Blackledge tomorrow. We can't be in any worse shape than the rest of the businesses in town. The bank can't foreclose on the whole damn town."

She stared hard at Marshall. "You'd better hope I'm successful. Otherwise, what the hell will you do? Maybe you should think about that instead of being tickled out of your gourd."

Marshall's face went white.

That night, she rehearsed what she would say to Blackledge. She dreaded it more than she had ever dreaded anything in her life. She wouldn't have slept anyway, what with Elmore sobbing all night. She felt pity for him but had to admit that Marshall was right. The damn loan was her idea. Damn the strike!

Her walk to the bank might just as well have been a funeral march. The clouds overhead were dark and heavy with rain. A chill was in the air.

"Did you bring a check?" the red-faced banker asked even before she sat down.

"No, I—"

"Tsk, tsk, a pity. We'll begin foreclosure next month. I hope it won't be until after Christmas, but who knows?"

Jodie had the urge to smash his ugly face.

"Poor Mr. Jackson. He's worked all his life. Now, I don't know what he'll do."

"You're premature!"

"I suppose you'll have to get a job and support him. What are you qualified to do? Perhaps you can discuss it with your mother."

Her face turned red. Her hands became fists. She raised out of her chair and shook one at him. "You bastard. The bank has never foreclosed during a strike. I'll go to the *Tribune*."

"Oh yes, do. Mr. Polk, the owner, is on our board. He's also a shareholder. An occasional foreclosure is necessary to let everyone know we're not a charity." His eyes lifted in mock surprise. "There's an idea for you. You might try the Salvation Army."

"So, you're saying nothing matters. The bank wants an old run-down store. What the hell are you going to do with it?"

"I wouldn't say…nothing matters." His eyebrows arched.

"I see," she said. "I see." Only the hate she felt for the man kept her from tears. "That. You low-down son of a bitch."

"Calling me names isn't going to help you at all." He shook his head and asked, "Do you want a one-year extension? Or a foreclosure?"

She stared at the floor. Her shoulders slumped. Her thoughts were on Elmore. Would he live? Would he be bedridden if he did? And what about the store? She had put so much into it. But was anything worth the price he asked? She thought of her mother and the decision she must have faced with children to feed. Was the store worth what she faced? She could go to New York and forget it. But she couldn't do that. It was her fault that Elmore faced foreclosure. Her fault that he'd had a stroke. It was her responsibility to save the store for him. The decision was made.

"I'll see the signed extension first," she said.

He instructed the secretary to type a one-year extension for the "Jackson loan" and instructed Jodie to meet him outside.

"I'm going to inspect some property," he told the secretary. He held the extension in his hand.

Outside, he pointed toward a late model, black Buick, not as expensive as a Cadillac, but a notch or two above the Chevrolets and Fords most often seen on Jordan's streets.

"Fitting for a man of my position," he told his wife when he drove it home the first time. It commands the respect of our depositors but doesn't provoke their envy. "That's so thoughtful, dear. Very Christian," she had told him.

Blackledge waved the paper at her before he shoved it into his coat pocket. A victory gloat covered his red, chubby face. He stepped out, elbows flying out from his pudgy body in cadence with every step. He got into his car and motioned her to follow.

She did. The slam of the door sounded like a steel trap had sprung. The stifling aroma of his Old Spice shaving lotion overpowered the car's interior. She opened the window. She couldn't have felt worse if she was being driven to a guillotine.

"You'll like the cabin," he said, breathing noisily.

"Is it only for entertaining bank customers, or does your family get to use it?" she asked caustically.

She didn't catch his mumbled reply.

The car rolled to a stop beside a small log cabin overlooking a lake and a small boat dock. A picnic table sat at the rear.

His tongue pushed at the side of his mouth without purpose as he checked for visitors. No one was in sight. He hopped out and motioned for her to follow. Hatred boiled within her, hate for Blackledge, the sheriff, the KKK, Marshall, all the people who had abused her. She hated them all. *Lord,* she prayed silently, *get me through this and give me the chance to pay them back.*

He pushed the cabin door open and beckoned her in. The interior was covered in dark shadows and filled with a musty smell that choked her breath. The floor creaked under her steps. With one hand, he pushed at the corner of the bed covered with a multicolored patchwork quilt.

"You first," he said timidly, gesturing at her clothes.

Without a word, she removed her coat and threw it over a chair. Next, she unbuttoned her dress and laid it on top. Blackledge stood sideways but watched from the corner of his eyes, his mouth open, his hands frozen on his vest. She turned her face toward him. He turned away, embarrassed.

Jodie reluctantly crawled into the cold bed and pulled the quilt about her. Blackledge undressed behind the chair then shuffled backward to the bed. He turned, his arms held in front of his body, trying simultaneously to keep the layers of white fat around his stomach from sagging while covering his scant masculinity. A large appendix scar showed in the middle of his stomach, a red birthmark marked his right thigh.

He avoided her eyes and motioned for her to throw back the covers. His eyes widened as she complied. She closed hers and tried to pretend it would be no worse than one of Elmore's drunken abuses.

The bed creaked and lurched to one side as he climbed in. Tears washed across her face. Bile, long present in her stomach, churned to her mouth. She felt his hot breath on her shoulder and readied herself for a crude fondling.

Instead, he slid down her body and pushed at her legs to urge them apart. She opened her eyes and saw him hovering over her.

"You bastard!" She kicked him with both feet and sent him tumbling off the bed with a thump.

When he stood, she kicked him in the stomach. He stumbled backward with a grunt.

"Get the hell away from me, you sick pervert!" she screamed.

He stared at her dumbfounded. "What…"

The turmoil in her stomach could be denied no longer. She rushed into the small bathroom and vomited. When she returned, he had put on his pants. He stood meekly by the bed as if waiting for something to happen.

"You lowbred son of a bitch!" she said as she pulled on her dress.

"I'll take this." She slipped the extension from his coat and put it into her purse.

"I'll revoke it," he vowed.

"The hell you will! But if you even think about revoking it, you asshole, I'll personally tell your wife about your scar and birthmark. You know how trashy us Phelps can be about things like that, don't you? Something I did learn from my mother."

"But I didn't do anything."

"And you aren't going to! Ever!" She headed for the door.

"I'm not going back to town yet."

"Good. I'll walk. I'd get sick to my stomach if I rode with you."

When the gravel road to the lake forked, Jodie took the fork that led past a piece of land she had often visited on her Sundays off when Ruth was still alive. It was a hilly piece, just off the road, covered by a grove of great oaks and pines, standing as if prepared to defend the hill against all invaders. She had dreamed of buying the land when she saved enough money.

Her pace increased, but the nightmare with Blackledge could not be outrun. Salty tears reminded her that there was no corner of her mind dark enough to bury his attempted depravity.

She pushed the rusty strands of barbed wire open and eased through, then ran toward her refuge. The trees waved in the rising wind as if to beckon her. Just then, a merciful rain broke, cold and heavy, a cleansing rain. She rubbed the cold water against her face and body and cried as she did, "Mama, I know what hell you must have gone through. I pray the Lord will forgive me for ever thinking you were bad."

She looked up at the sky through the towering, waving trees. "Please God, strike me with a lightning bolt. Please God. I don't want to be here anymore."

A thunderclap answered, but no lightning bolt came. She fell forward onto a mat of wet pine straw and cried freely while the rain beat at her back like the leather strap wielded by Lizzy years before.

A car passed, stopped, then rolled slowly back. Its door slammed.

"Jodie?" She heard. Then a hand touched her trembling shoulder. She rolled to one side. Her eyes blinked open. It was Steven! He knelt beside her.

She reached out and touched his hand. He put his hands under her shoulders and lifted her from the cold wet ground.

She whispered his name and fell into his open, warm embrace. The rain stopped and a calm filled the air. She did not volunteer nor did he question her reason for being under the trees. Jodie was glad, not only that he stopped, but that he did not ask.

He was returning from a court appearance and stopped to see what appeared to be a body under the trees.

He urged her to his car, and with the car's heater on high, he drove into town. He said, "I was coming to see you tomorrow. The senator wants me to arbitrate the strike and Charlie Burdette wants you at the table."

"I don't know anything about arbitration," she whispered. Her throat hoarse from crying.

"Not much to it," he said, noting the hoarseness in her voice and her seeming lack of caring. Whatever had brought her there, he figured, must have been bad.

"We let each side state their case without fighting. We push suggestions, let them respond, and eventually narrow things down to a single question. If they can't agree, we make recommendations. When it's all over, they blame us for the compromise."

His upbeat banter brought her back from despair.

"Uh, I hate to bring it up, but Elmore may have made a will in favor of his children…before you got married. I'm sure he'd want to change it, if you dare bring it up. I'm speaking as your lawyer now." He smiled.

"He promised me the store before we were married, but it's not that important to me anymore," she said.

Because of it, I've shamed myself, she thought. Suddenly she thought about the extension agreement in her purse. Had it gotten wet? Was it ruined? Seized with panic, she snapped open the purse and stared inside. It was dry! *Thank God,* she thought.

He let her out in front of the store with a promise to help in any way he could. She thanked him for stopping and for the ride home. She wasn't sure what she might have done had he not stopped.

CHAPTER 32

When she walked into the apartment, Marshall was with Elmore. Elmore was slumped over in his chair, looking more dead than alive.

"Mr. Blackledge signed a one-year extension," she said and dropped the paper on the table before going into the bedroom to rid herself of her wet clothes, clothes she'd throw into the trash the next day.

When she returned, Marshall gestured with his head toward the extension and said, "I'm still going to run the store. Isn't that right, Father?" He patted the old man's shoulder.

Elmore slowly looked up without comprehending and said, "Yes."

"If the strike continues much longer, there won't be a store left for you to ruin," she replied.

"What?" Elmore's face whipped around to look at her. "No… store?" His red eyes watered and his good hand trembled. He looked at Marshall for reassurance, but Marshall had none.

Jodie smiled. It pleased her to see Marshall confounded, but it gave her no pleasure to witness Elmore's decline. The old man began to sob. She sighed, more in resignation than pity.

"I might as well tell you. I'm leaving."

It was Marshall who looked at her in shock that time.

"Surprised? Well, you can have the store and all that goes with it." She nodded toward Elmore.

"Ruth," Elmore protested. "Don't leave me, please. I can't make it without you." He waved his right hand about.

"Lennox has everything…money…big store. Never did an honest day's work. I've worked for all I have. I understand…you did it. Don't leave me." He stared hard at Jodie.

"I'm Jodie," she said. "Ruth is dead." Just then she recalled her confusion when introduced to Mr. Lennox and his son, Tim, at the Country Club event. She thought she had seen the old man before. Now she knew why or had a damn good idea. And Elmore had practically confirmed it.

Be damned, she thought.

Elmore shook his head. His chin dropped to his chest, and he fell asleep.

She looked at Marshall and said, "I just realized something, Marshall. You may well be a Lennox. My, my, Elmore always said the Lennoxs were bastards. He must have been right."

"You bitch! You're lying."

"No, there's a resemblance, you and the old man. Remember, Ruth worked for Lennox before she married Elmore. What color hair did Elmore have when he was younger? Dark brown, not sandy like yours. Neither was your mother's. I've seen their old pictures. But Mr. Lennox had sandy brown hair when he was young. Your mother told me that in the park, a long time ago. Just think, Tim might be your half-brother? Isn't that a kick in the balls! Well, if you had any." She enjoyed using the crude expression with Marshall.

Marshall's face contorted in rage. He flew at her with hands raised, ready to claw her face. She reached for a candleholder and brandished it in his face.

"Come on. I'd love an excuse."

"You whore! You filthy whore! I saw you in New Orleans."

"And I saw you. You filthy queer."

"I hate you!"

"You hate everybody, Marshall. You hide from it, but it's always there, isn't it? You're just an inadequate, inferior piece of shit." She smiled then added, "And if you think Ruby is suffering, don't. She got another job within a week after you fired her."

"Ha! Sweeping floors?"

"No, bookkeeping for Tim Lennox. A good job. At least she stayed with the family."

The blood drained from his face. His arms dropped limply to his side. He flew from the apartment. The slam of the front door woke Elmore.

"Huh? Jodie, is Mama all right?"

"She's fine, Mr. Jackson." And, she thought, *I'm fine too. I just kicked Marshall's butt.*

A few days later, Jodie agreed to help with the arbitration. She owed Elmore that much, but once the strike was settled, she would leave.

She wrote Warren to tell him her plans. She no longer felt anything for anybody. It gave her comfort to tell him goodbye. Likewise, she stayed out of the store. If Marshall was going to run it, let him. No thought of the store came without the white flab of Blackledge's stomach. She prayed that the recollection would fade in time.

Economic conditions in Jordan worsened. A barren Christmas was certain unless the strike were settled soon. However, the arbitration, which everyone counted on, proceeded slowly. Steven chaired the meetings. Jodie mostly took notes and acted as a secretary.

Marshall stayed with Elmore when she was away. Like everyone else in Jordan, Marshall knew he had no future unless the strike was settled. Virginia also came up when she had the time and a sitter for her children.

CHAPTER 33

It was Christmas Eve. Negotiations were in their third day without a break. Odors from sandwiches and spilled catsup and mustard blended with cigarette smoke and body odor in the plant's conference room. Recesses were only called when someone fell asleep at the table, and they only lasted for two or three hours.

"I'm gonna get my men another ten cents or we're gonna stay out till summer," Charlie Burdette vowed to the *Tribune*.

It was eight in the evening. Smoke hung like a haze over the mahogany table. A half-filled whiskey bottle sat in the middle of the table within easy reach of the negotiators. A pitcher of water sat on a tray in a puddle of moisture. Steven sat at one end of the table, Jodie beside him. Mr. Jordan and his assistant sat on one side of the oval table, Charlie and his assistant on the other.

"Goddamn it, Charlie," Mr. Jordan chomped his cigar and said. "We can't go that high. Turnover is too great. We train you people, pay the higher wage, and then you head out for Houston or someplace."

He had shed his coat and tie and looked as bedraggled as everyone else at the table. Only by their shirts would a third party have been able to tell who represented whom—management's was white, the union's khaki.

"We ain't working no damn slave wages, Mr. Jordan," Charlie's rawboned assistant said loudly. Charlie touched his shoulder to calm him.

"Well, we ain't!" the man reiterated. "My ole lady ain't had a new dress in two years. If it wasn't for the garden, I couldn't eat regular."

"We'll have to shut the plant, maybe move it," Jordan said with cold forcefulness. It was a frequently repeated threat. "Where will you be then?"

"You do what you have to do. I'm not coming out for a contract unless you cough up another dime and build us a hospital clinic. We have a right to medical care same as anybody else," Charlie said. The clinic had long been a bone of contention with the union. Several times during the past few years, management seemed ready to fund it, but each time they backed off.

"You can't be serious," the accountant bristled and searched without purpose through the stack of papers in front of him as though the answer was hidden in one of its sheets. "You expect management to put its working capital into a clinic and then what, another strike?"

"Next year we have to install new equipment," Jordan added. "New equipment so your people will have better working conditions."

"Automation, you mean! To lay more off!" Charlie's assistant stood and pointed over the table at Jordan. "We ain't no fools."

Steven called for calm. "We're off the issue. Ten cents an hour."

Jordan shook his head no and snuffed out his unlit cigar.

"I reckon we'll be here for a while," Charlie said and sipped whiskey.

The arguments continued. Neither side gave ground. Steven thumped his fingers against the top of the table and looked from Jordan to Charlie. It was the only sound in the room.

"It seems to me y'all are missing the point of this thing," Jodie said. It was the first time she'd spoken since the meetings began.

The men around the table turned to face her.

"What do you mean?" Steven asked.

"None of this bickering back and forth makes sense. Mr. Jordan says something." She gestured to the side where he sat with the accountant. "And your side of the table says no." She bobbed her head toward Charlie Burdette. "And that's the way it's been the whole time. One side says this. The other side says that. Looks to me like neither one of you are really trying to settle the strike."

"Suppose you enlighten us as to how we should be doing it, Mrs. Jackson," Jordan said with a sideways look at his accountant.

"I didn't go to Ole Miss"—she waved at Jordan—"but I did take a few business courses at JC. And the one thing I learned is that to make progress you sometimes have to compromise. Each side gives up something. My professor said that the best agreement is when both sides go away mad."

"We're already pretty mad, Jodie, uh, Mrs. Jackson," Charlie said and let his face break into a smile.

Jordan cleared his throat. "We're waiting on you to tell us how to make some progress, Mrs. Jackson." He held out his palms for her to continue. "We're waiting."

"Well, I've heard y'all talk about turnover and paying more money for wages and keeping the plant going between strikes and all you've been talking about is a one-year contract. Just because you've always had a one-year contract doesn't mean you should stay with it. If you'd agree to a three-year contract, you'd have more time to do something."

The accountant glanced at Jordan. His head bobbed forward, almost imperceptibly, but Jodie saw it. Charlie's eyes widened. He'd love to have a three-year contract, but Jordan had always wanted to stay with a short contract.

"You'd have the assurance that the profits would be there to support the clinic. By keeping the union people healthy, productivity would be higher. Right now, they can't afford to see a doctor when they get sick. A sick person can't do as much as a well person."

"That's the Lord's truth!" Charlie's assistant said.

Jordan said, "Business is such…was anyway, that we might be willing to consider something like that…a three-year contract."

"We still need more money," Charlie said. "More if it's a three-year contract."

"How about eight cents the first year, twelve the second and sixteen the third?" Jodie asked.

"Can't. Cut into profits too much," Jordan said. "That's the problem with long contracts. Can't project sales that far out."

"Yet you're worried about turnover. What does that do to profits? And these strikes can't be cheap."

Charlie said, "Well, we damn sure gotta get a raise!"

She looked at Charlie and asked, "Suppose we come at it from a different direction. Suppose the union got eight cents the first year but agreed to put half of it into the pension fund. It'd be the men's money and something they could use later." The company had a pension fund, but contributions had been voluntary, so the fund's assets were negligible.

She turned to Mr. Jordan. "And suppose you matched half the union's pension contribution plus two cents the first year. That'd give the union the ten cents it wants. The company could borrow funds from the pension fund to pay for part of the clinic."

"With interest," Charlie said. "And regular payments to pay it back."

Jodie continued, "The pension fund would give the men an incentive to stay with the company. Turnover would have to drop."

Mr. Jordan and the accountant left the room to discuss it. Charlie and his assistant did the same thing. It was almost midnight. Thirty minutes passed before they came back.

Charlie spoke first. "I'll recommend it if the clinic's built in two years and if we get annual increases, like Jodie, uh, Mrs. Jackson said."

"That's just not acceptable to us. We can't afford capital improvements and the clinic. We can't even afford the pay raises," Jordan said.

Jodie stood, leaned over the table, and said, "I'm going home then. I can't believe what I just heard." She faced Jordan. "You'd be out of pocket eight cents an hour the first year. And half of that would go into the pension fund you could borrow from."

Jordan shook his head.

"I don't think you want to make a deal. I'm going home," Jodie said.

"We want to make a deal," Jordan said. "But that won't work."

Jodie scratched on the piece of paper in front of her and thought. As she did, an idea came to her. "How about this? The extra contribution to the pension fund, the two cents, could be funded by company stock. Compare that with what it would cost to move the company."

"Use company stock for the pension fund?" Jordan asked.

"The company's publicly traded," Jodie said. "Stock would be the same as money, and it wouldn't cost the company anything. The men would have an interest in the company, its profits."

Jordan and the accountant excused themselves again.

They returned glum-faced after a few minutes.

"We can live with it if Charlie can."

"Build the clinic in two years?" Charlie said.

Jordan started to protest but waved his hand and said, "Okay."

"Well, let's go home!" Charlie said. "We're both mad enough." He winked at Jodie.

"No," Steven said. "Nobody's leaving until we get signatures on this agreement."

"Christ, Steven," Jordan protested. "We're tired. Anyway, I'd like a little time to think about it."

"That's why I want signatures."

"I'll write it up. I have all the notes," Jodie said.

While they grumbled and downed the last of the whiskey, Jodie made an outline of the salient points and Steven called the *Tribune* with the news. At five o'clock Christmas morning, they signed the preliminary agreement. The strike was over; a Christmas present for the whole county.

As they opened the plant doors to leave, they were greeted by popping flashbulbs and a round of applause. Local press and radio reporters clamored for details. The mayor, Silverstein, and other local officials were also present, as was Randolph.

"How did you do it?" they asked Steven.

Microphones were stuck into his face and cameras shoved in to get a close up.

"We all did it," he replied. "Actually, Jodie Jackson got things going. Jodie…"

He twisted about to find her, but she was already on her way to the apartment. The important thing to her was that the strike was over, the store would have customers again. And she could get on with her life.

She heard Virginia's voice at the apartment door. "Walk, Daddy." She helped Elmore make a turn in the apartment's hallway. Marshall lay on the living room sofa with his eyes closed.

Seeing Jodie, Elmore called her name.

"Merry Christmas," she said. "The strike's settled. I'll get dinner started."

The old man stumbled. "It's over! The strike's—" He pushed Virginia aside and reached for Jodie with his good arm. His eyes rolled back into his head, his knees buckled, and he slowly slumped to the floor.

"My god! Oh my god!" Virginia screamed. "Daddy's dead!"

He wasn't dead, just a heart attack, the doctor told them at the hospital. "Maybe overexertion, excitement. Not uncommon for a stroke victim. I've put him on oxygen. We'll watch him closely."

Jodie slept on a cot in the room with him.

Elmore stayed weak, unable to get out of bed. He was only awake about half the time and barely lucid then. Jodie fed him the little nourishment he took. She watched the life drain from his face as each day passed.

"His heart suffered damage," the doctor said. "At his age, I don't know how much time he has left. I don't know if you knew, but his sugar is very high."

Marshall and Virginia visited. Marshall ran the store. Business was brisk as customers no longer feared turning loose their money. Mrs. Ralston returned full-time, as did Betty and Fred. Jodie prayed she'd never have to go back into the store.

Steven came by. Jodie talked to him outside the room. "I wanted to see how you were holding up. You've had a rough few weeks."

She did not argue.

"I've read about you in the papers," she said. "Are you going to run for attorney general like everybody says?"

"If Dad has his way. I'm not convinced that I like politics. When I finish a trial, it's over, but politics never ends, nothing is ever finished. I don't know if I like that."

"Not many people have the courage to face themselves. Most people follow the path of least resistance."

"I thought you'd understand." He leaned forward as if to embrace her, but didn't. "I like talking to you. You make me feel good."

She touched his arm and said, "Thank you, Steven."

A rustle of white uniforms in the hallway startled them. The doctor and two nurses rushed into Elmore's room. Jodie followed them. Elmore's eyes were closed as the doctor and a nurse worked over him. His mouth was open, gasping for breath.

"Another heart attack," the doctor said. A nurse tried to get Elmore to swallow a pill. He tried. His lips quivered, his jaw moved. Words formed in his mouth but never came out. The doctor placed his ear close, listened, then motioned for Jodie to come closer.

"He wants to tell you something."

"Jodie," Elmore spoke in a whisper. "Want you to know I love you. Started when you nursed Mama. So sorry I hit you. So sorry. Jealous old man. I understood about Ruby…working in the store, and all that…you saying…Lennox. I didn't mind. I wanted you to know before…" His mouth twitched once and stopped moving. Elmore was dead. It was January 10, 1952.

He knew, Jodie thought. *He knew what I was doing all along. And I thought I was so smart. I feel like a fool.*

A nurse collected Elmore's personal things. The room had to be readied for another patient whose stay could also end suddenly. She handed the assembled toilet articles and items of clothing to Jodie. Jodie failed to notice that Elmore's wooden handled straight razor was not among them.

The funeral came a few days later. A slashing wind tore at the few gathered at Elmore's graveside, adjacent to Ruth's. A green canvas canopy flapped in the wind. Wreaths of flowers anchored to the ground by metal stakes, swayed and shuddered.

Jodie, Marshall, Virginia, the store employees, and half a dozen of the Jacksons' oldest friends sat on hard metal chairs and listened to the preacher spray reverent pronouncements into the wind. Silverstein stood at the rear and coughed into his handkerchief. He'd die of lung cancer in less than a year. Steven, in a heavy overcoat and leather gloves, stood beside him.

"Soon they will be reunited in heaven," the preacher promised. His eyes blinked now and then from the droplets of rain that pelted his face. Some watching thought he blinked from his tears.

Virginia sobbed loudly.

"There, there," Mrs. Ralston patted her arm.

Marshall, like Jodie, watched the ceremony stoically. Jodie was sorry Elmore had died, but there were no tears in her, only pity.

The preacher asked the Lord to take Elmore's soul and said "amen" to end the service. His prayer was for a man he did not know, but he felt no shame for it. The wind ripped pages from his Bible and drove them into the hedge a few yards away. He stared at them and resolved to retrieve them on a calmer day. He hurried to whatever warmth his old car still held and prayed that the battery had enough strength to turn the engine.

CHAPTER 34

The next day, Jodie took Elmore's will from his underwear drawer. It was dated a few months after their marriage. He'd left everything to Jodie Mae with an explanation that since Marshall and Virginia were well situated, he was not providing for them.

"He kept his promise," she said aloud, somewhat surprised. She called Steven to ask what legal steps had to be taken to get the title transferred.

"Let's talk about it over lunch at the hotel."

She agreed. The sooner she could put Elmore's death behind her, the better.

Steven folded his newspaper and stood when he saw Jodie come into the hotel restaurant. After she was seated, he said, "Tim Lennox was killed."

"What?" Jodie couldn't believe it.

"His throat was cut at the store late last night while he and his bookkeeper, Ruby Martin, took inventory. Police think it was robbery. Leroy Martin, Ruby's ex-husband, has been arrested. I think I'll represent him. She was held for a few hours as a possible accomplice but released. She had facial and hand cuts but wasn't seriously hurt."

"Did Ruby say anything?" Jodie thought it a bit strange that they would take inventory this early in the year and that late at night, but didn't know their routine.

"She says she didn't see the attacker. The police think she's covering up for Leroy. They found a straight razor."

"Straight razor?"

"The murder weapon."

Jodie shuddered at the thought.

"So, the will," he said. "Do you have it with you?"

She handed it to him. He glanced at it. It was only one page.

"Looks okay. Shouldn't be a problem. I'll take care of it if you want me to."

She shook her head.

"Are you pleased? To get the store, I mean. You said one time it was what you wanted."

"I don't know. I'm not certain what I'll do. I may sell it or give it to Marshall. Elmore made the will before Marshall came back. I think he wanted Marshall to follow in his footsteps."

"But you were his wife. It's yours. I wouldn't give it away. You've put so much of yourself into it. Besides, what would you do for a living?"

"Maybe go to New Orleans…get a job and start over. I have experience now."

"Damn, Jodie," he said. He reached out with his hand but stopped short. "I had hoped you'd stay here. Don't make a hasty decision."

"I'm trying not to," she said without looking directly at him. She didn't want to show the shame and guilt she felt about the store.

"I'll open probate. It'll give you time to think things over."

Randolph crossed toward their table. He frowned when he saw Jodie.

"Mrs. Jackson." He nodded and added, "Sorry to hear about Mr. Jackson. He was a fine man."

After Jodie acknowledged his condolence, he turned to Steven and said, "Mary said you were thinking about representing Leroy Martin." Mary was their legal secretary.

"Yes."

"I wish you wouldn't. He killed a white man, a leading citizen. I can't believe that kind of publicity will help someone running for attorney general. Have you filed your papers yet?"

"I told you I haven't made up my mind. Just because you and Vicki think it's a good idea, doesn't mean that I do."

Randolph bristled with anger. "Vicki and I think you have tremendous potential and being attorney general would be a wonderful opportunity to do some good in this state. That's all."

"I'm glad, but it's something I have to decide," Steven said.

"Well, while you're standing around with your finger up your ass, waiting for a decision from on high, I suppose, what I've worked so hard to give you is about to be lost." He paused and said to Jodie, "You'll have to excuse me, Mrs. Jackson. That's how I talk."

He turned to Steven. "What I'm saying, son, is that you owe me. I've done a hell of a lot for you. The least you can do is run for attorney general. If you don't like it, what you do after that is up to you. That's all I'm asking, get your feet wet."

"I didn't know, Dad! Law school, the firm, the clients, the house, Lord knows what else you did for me? Why in hell didn't you tell me it came with a price? I might have turned you down. I thought you did it because I was your son, not to bind me to political servitude."

"Don't quibble. You know what I mean. Somebody does something for you, it's a contract, like it or not. You know it. I know it. If you accept the benefits, you have to pay them back. It's the way society works."

"So, if I run, our books are square?"

"Just about."

"I'll think about it…for all I owe you."

"Put it any way you like, son. You're a leader of men. You have principles. You can do things regular politicians can't and won't do. You can make a difference. You were born for public office."

"That's a lot to live up to. I can't say that I agree, but I thank you. I like being a lawyer, and I like making my own decisions. Whether I run or not, I'm taking Leroy Martin's case."

Randolph frowned. "You're as hardheaded as a mule. Okay. I'll drop by the *Tribune* and make sure they put the proper slant on it. Everybody has a right to a fair trial, even a nigra. You'll lose, but… civic duty and all that. Sounds good."

The KKK, led by Caleb Anderson, held nightly rallies in white robes outside the jail. They shouted obscenities and burned a cross on the jailhouse lawn. They rode through Kingston Quarter and fired shotguns at open windows. Fortunately, no one was hurt. The sheriff and police chief ignored it for a while, but when talk of a "lynching" reached them, they moved in to break up the rallies.

"By themselves, they ain't too dangerous, but you let them old boys get together and start egging each other on, all hell could break loose," Sheriff Dagget told the police chief. "I don't know about you, but this is an election year, and I ain't wanting no killings on people's minds when they vote."

Once the sheriff and police began to intervene, things quieted down.

Steven filed to have the will probated and expected a decision as soon as the court was in session. He also announced his candidacy. He was the clear favorite for the primary, and since the Republicans were not expected to offer much of a challenge in the fall, a victory in the primary was tantamount to winning the election.

Jodie went into the store to tell Marshall the store would be his as soon as she could transfer title to him. He was in the uniform department.

"Marshall," she called.

He turned like a snake coiled to strike. She was shocked by the look of pure hate on his face. Though partially covered with makeup, a pattern of scratches showed on his face. Any other time, she might have inquired about them. Today though, she wanted to get her business over with.

"I want you to know—"

"You get your slutty self out of MY store!" He screamed. Even Mrs. Ralston, who had crept into the doorway to listen, was taken aback.

Jodie tried to remain calm. "It's not your store yet, Marshall. That's what I came to tell you."

"Oh, you bitch!" His voice verged on hysteria. "Did you think you could steal my father's store? He left it all to me."

She slapped him hard.

He winced in pain and stepped back. He shoved his hand into his coat pocket and produced a single sheet of paper bearing the title "Codicil." He shoved it at her. "Read that!"

She quickly read the paper. "I leave the store to my son, Marshall." The signature was unmistakably Elmore's. Tim Lennox and Myrtle Ralston witnessed it in December. Jodie was stunned.

"It's mine now. You can't order me around anymore. I'm doing the ordering now! You switch your little ass out of here!"

He pushed at her shoulder to emphasize the point. She turned sideways and yanked at his arm to pull him off balance. He fell flat on his face. Before he could bound up, she looked at him and said, "This is not your store and never will be."

She called Steven with the news.

"Yeah, I heard. Henry Thompson called a few minutes ago. Marshall was in to see him this morning." Henry Thompson was one of Jordan's prominent attorneys. "He tried to talk Marshall out of contesting the probate, but Marshall was adamant. He thinks, as I do, there's a real competency issue here."

"I know Elmore would never let a Lennox witness anything."

"We'll get affidavits from the nurses and his doctor. They were around when Elmore called you, Ruth. I'll file a motion objecting to the codicil next week. In the meantime, stay where you are. Marshall knows he can't do anything without a court order."

Warren called from Houston. "Roy Crawford told me about Elmore and Tim Lennox. Two tragedies in one town. Hard to believe. I have to ask. Did you mean it? What you said in your letter? There's no future for us?"

"So much has happened, Warren." She told him about the will and codicil. "I was about to give Marshall the store and go to New Orleans, but he's so spiteful I'll fight it. I don't know what I'll do after that. Maybe sell it and start over somewhere."

"I'm thinking about leaving Sheila." Sheila was his wife.

"Don't. Not on my account. I don't know how I feel about anything anymore." She choked up. "I have to wait and see."

"Finish your fight with Marshall. I understand that. You can't walk away. When it's over, please, call me. If you don't, I'll call you."

Steven's motion was heard in early May. Jodie, in a gray cotton suit, sat at one table with Steven. Marshall, with Mr. Thompson, sat at the other.

Judge Harvey, almost senile and hard of hearing, sat at the elevated judge's desk. Staring down at them, he paused particularly long at Jodie to note the resemblance to her mother, Lizzy, the woman who had once cursed him in court and accused him of frequenting Ma's place.

Affidavits from the doctor and nurses corroborated Elmore's lack of ability to comprehend what he was doing and affirmed his lack of capacity to make a testamentary disposition. Fred's affidavit supported Jodie's contention that Elmore would never let a Lennox witness any document. Silverstein gave an affidavit regarding Marshall's lack of business experience and how that inexperience would adversely affect the store. That went to the issue of appointing Marshall as executor.

"I don't consider any of these affidavits relevant, Counsel," the Judge told Steven.

"Your Honor, they speak to the heart of the issue, whether or not the codicil is a valid instrument and certainly to the question of Marshall Jackson's competency to serve as executor."

"I'll make that decision when the will contest is resolved."

"With all due respect, that might be next year. The store might be out of business by then. And my client? How does the court propose that she survive for a year?"

"This court is not in the welfare business!"

Steven was furious. "Your Honor! I'm sure you agree there is substantial doubt about the validity of the codicil. Mr. Jackson's doctor said—"

"You're out of order, Mr. Jefferson. You don't tell me what the law is in my court. If you don't like my decision, you can appeal."

"That'll take months and you know it."

The judge hammered his gavel.

"My decision is to deny your motion. If your client goes on welfare, it's no concern of mine. I rather imagine she knows where the office is. I reckon her people can help her find work in some of the cafés around town."

"Your Honor, I object to your abuse of discretion, and I object to your rudeness," Steven said.

"I don't care!" the old judge snapped. "There's no court reporter here. Sit down and shut up while I make my order or I'll call for the bailiff to throw you in jail. Don't imagine it'd do your campaign any good to be in jail."

Steven refused to sit down.

"Sit down!" the judge repeated and slammed his gavel against its wooden plate.

"I'll stand. You'll get the respect a judge deserves when you act like one." He approached the bench. Thompson followed.

"Bailiff!" he shouted and pointed at Steven. The bailiff watched but did nothing. Attorneys approached the bench all the time.

Steven and Thompson faced the old judge.

"I know what's eating on you, you old bastard, and I don't like it. This is a clear case of prejudice and abuse of authority. I never thought I'd see this kind of thing from you," Steven said. "You've thrown out any number of wills on less evidence than this. If you don't back off, I'm going straight down to the *Tribune* and see Mr. Polk. He'd love to print a story about how you forced a widow out of her home and onto welfare. And I'll win the appeal. You can be damned sure of that!"

"I'm a judge. You can't do anything to me. I don't give a red-ass damn about the newspaper."

"Your friends will. Your family will wonder if you're slipping."

"Your Honor," Thompson said. "I suggest leaving the widow in the apartment with a monthly allowance pending the appeal. Would that satisfy your client?" he asked Steven and winked.

The judge blinked. He had waited a long time to redress the humiliation Lizzy Phelps had caused him to suffer, but could he rule against both counsels?

"Get back to your seats. I have a new ruling."

He scribbled on a sheet of paper then said, "I'm keeping Mr. Jackson as executor pending the appeal and the trial."

Steven jumped up to object.

"But I'm leaving Mrs. Jackson in the home and giving her a widow's allowance."

"No!" Marshall shouted. "I want her out!"

"Shut up!" the judge ordered. "Or I'll throw you in jail."

Steven knew further objections would be futile. Jodie was given just enough to avoid being criticized but not enough to avoid being overruled on appeal.

"The appellate court will throw out the codicil," Steven told Jodie afterward. "Probating the will won't be a problem after that. Unfortunately, the appeal won't be heard until late this year. In the meantime, you'll have a place to live and money."

As they walked down the courthouse steps, they passed Sheriff Dagget and a couple of deputies. They stood beside a stack of quart and gallon jars of confiscated moonshine. The deputies passed a jar around for the assembled crowd to smell.

"No water in them jars!" Dagget announced. He would break a few bottles for the onlookers and load the rest on the back of his pickup truck to be thrown into the creek. At least that's what he said.

"Sheriff Dagget's getting ready to run for reelection," Steven said. "Probably his first campaign contribution will be from the bootlegger who gets the rest of that stack."

"Why don't they just legalize it?"

"What? Put the bootleggers out of business and cut into the sheriff's retirement money?" Steven laughed and opened the car door for her.

"One of these days, the voters will rise up and kick him out," Steven said.

"That'll be the day," Jodie answered.

A wild idea crept into Jodie's thoughts just then, so wild it shocked her. It bounced around until he stopped to let her out at the apartment.

He asked, "What are you going to do while you're waiting for the appeal?"

"I need a job, but there's nothing around here. I could go back to New Orleans, but I hate to tuck tail and run. I guess I'm between the rock and a hard place."

"You could help me in my campaign."

"What would Randolph and Vicki say about that? Besides, from what I read, you don't need any help."

"Let me know if I can help you," he said and began to drive away.

"Wait!" she called and ran after him.

CHAPTER 35

He hit his brakes, leaned out the window, and asked, "What?"

"I've decided what I'm going to do! I'm going to run for sheriff!" She was less than a month past her twenty-sixth birthday.

"I'll be damned. I'll be damned. Only you would think of that. Dagget better watch out. I'd like to see the look on his face when the word gets out." He laughed and was still laughing as he drove away.

Warren's response was one of skepticism. "Aren't you the one who said the women down there eat after the men and dogs? Keep 'em barefoot and pregnant."

"I'm sick and tired of getting pushed around. I'm tired of politicians who think the voters are working for them instead of the other way around. I'm tired of two-faced politicians lying to the public. And I'm tired of that arrogant, swaggering crooked Sheriff Dagget."

"But, Jodie, be realistic. You're what, twenty-six, barely, how can you possibly expect to win?"

"I don't, but I'll enjoy telling everybody what a crook Dagget is."

"Won't that be dangerous?"

"Right now, I don't give a damn."

She went to the park and watched the squirrels race the birds for food scraps dropped by children. Did she really want to run, or had she said it to blow off steam? She remembered Lizzy's warning from years before. "Most likely end up in the crazy house or in the swamps with a bullet in your head."

"It's not right to be afraid of the people we elect to protect us! I'm running."

When Jodie told the elderly clerk at City Hall that she wanted to run for sheriff, the woman's mouth fell open. "What? Did you say you want to stand for the sheriff's office? But you're a—"

"I sure am, a woman. And proud of it! Any law against it? A woman running for sheriff?"

The woman shook her head. "Can't think of any. You have to be a registered voter though. Are you?" When Jodie shook her head, the clerk reached into a drawer and handed her a form.

Jodie completed it and handed it back.

The woman said, "Now then, just because you're registered, don't mean you can run." Jodie would need a number of registered voters to sign her petition.

Jodie drove all over the county in Elmore's old car, which had somehow escaped Marshall's attention, to ask people to sign her petition. Most were skeptical, some were belligerent, and some laughed in her face. Nevertheless, by the last week of July, she had collected signatures from people who didn't give a damn one way or the other and from people who didn't like the sheriff, but she was still short.

She remembered Willie Bea and drove to the hospital.

"I need some signatures," she explained to the young black doctor.

"What in the world, Jodie Mae?" She laughed. "I don't believe this!"

Jodie assured her it was real.

"I doubt if any white person has ever asked a black for help in this town, at least above the table. Let me have it. I'll see what I can do."

Jodie left the petition with her.

Steven won his primary as expected. He would be the next attorney general for the state after the fall elections, a perfunctory exercise since the Republicans were a minority in the state. He had to get ready for the Leroy Martin trial however. Randolph had seen to it that the trial and the potentially damaging publicity would take place after the primary.

Two days before the end of July, Jodie heard a knock on the apartment door. It was Thomas Brown.

"Miss Jodie," he said, handing her back the petition, "Dr. Willie Bea asked me to bring you this."

Jodie looked at the petition. About forty signatures had been added.

"We would have got more, but Pick got mad. He said Sheriff Dagget and them city folks wouldn't like us coloreds messing around in their business." He rubbed a swollen lump on his cheek.

"Thomas, I appreciate this very much. You tell Willie...uh, Doctor Hansen, thanks."

"I sure will," he said. "And good luck. We be pulling for you, Ms. Jodie."

She was still short, but the Chamber of Commerce met that evening and she was a member.

As Silverstein called the meeting to order, she mounted the small platform behind the lectern and said, "I'm running for sheriff, and I need a few more signatures to qualify. I've talked to a few of you already, and you wanted to hide. Now, you can't hide."

"Please...get off there, Mrs. Jackson," Silverstein said. "This is no place for politicking."

"I have something to say, and I'm going to say it."

A few chuckles floated around the room. "...woman with spunk," one said.

"Well, be quick about it," he said.

"I want to kick Dagget out of office. I'm offering you a sheriff who won't take kickbacks, a sheriff who works for you, not the other way around. But I need some signatures on my petition." She waved the petition about and invited them to sign.

Nobody moved.

"I thought y'all were tough and ornery, but I guess I was wrong. Y'all act like a bunch of eunuchs, afraid of a potbellied sheriff. This isn't a Chamber of Commerce, it's a Chamber of Cowards."

Silverstein said, "I'll sign the damned thing if you'll get the hell out of here. But just because I am, doesn't mean I'll vote for you. I'm not afraid of the sheriff or you."

He signed and others lined up to do the same thing. She picked up thirty-seven signatures. Still short, and only one day left.

Lizzy! She drove out that night to tell her what she'd been doing and to ask for her help.

"My god, Jodie Mae! You ain't fixing to stand against Sheriff Dagget? You gonna end up in a creek somewhere."

"I sure as hell am, if I can get enough signatures on this petition. Can you help me?"

Lizzy shook her head. "I don't know. I just don't know. You ain't never asked me for nothing before. I sure don't like it. You running against the sheriff," she said.

She asked Jim what he thought.

"Lizzy, I don't reckon that damned sheriff can do anymore to you than he's done already. I'll take an ax handle to him if he tries."

Lizzy returned the petition to her before noon the next day with enough signatures to qualify unless some were struck off. She rushed the petition to the courthouse.

The elderly clerk took the petition and said, "Don't know why you bothering, everybody says Sheriff Dagget's gonna win."

After the clerk checked the petition against the registered voter rolls, she said, "You are close, Mrs. Jackson, but you're short by, let's see, seven, and you ain't got but three hours left, little lady. I don't reckon you gonna make it this time."

Jodie took the petition and went outside. *Where can I get more signatures?* she asked herself.

"Hey!" Charlie Burdette said from behind her. "I said hey, Jodie Mae!"

"Charlie Burdette! I'm sorry. I was thinking," she explained.

"I heard about you taking out papers to run! Everybody's talking about it. Damnedest thing ever to happen in this county. You should have come to see me first. Hell, let's go to the barbershops. I bet we can find seven people who can write their names."

Two barbershops later, she had the signatures.

The clerk examined Jodie's petition again and struck one name off. That left her one short and less than thirty minutes left. Tears formed in her eyes and ran down her cheeks. She turned to leave.

"Wait," the clerk said. "I'll sign your petition. I like the notion of havin' a sheriff workin' for us 'stead of the other way around. Good luck to you, Mrs. Jackson."

She could and she did. She was running for sheriff!

Dagget had also heard that she was running. Far from being concerned, as Steven had thought, Dagget was amused. "Shit, I may not campaign this time. Hell, the voters ought to campaign for me." The sheriff and the four deputies in the room with him laughed. The list of candidates included a retired police chief, a schoolteacher, and Jodie Jackson.

"Start spreadin' the word, boys. The chief took bribes, the schoolteacher likes little boys, and Jodie Mae, God, just tell the truth. She's a Phelps!"

There was to be Clothes Fair in New Orleans that year. Jodie had no reason to go anyway. As far as she was concerned, the store belonged to Marshall, and she felt relieved. The loss of the store made the shame of what she'd almost done to save it disappear. Elmore was easier to forget, though she still had some guilt about his stroke and his deathbed revelation that he'd gone along with her plans because he loved her.

Warren called. "Meet me in New Orleans anyway," he said.

She refused. "My mind's on the election."

"Sorry you filed?"

"No. I'm glad. I can't explain it, but I'm raring to go. I can't wait."

He sent her a campaign contribution, and Jodie began her campaign.

Jodie met the morning shift at the plant, the swing shift and the midnight shift. Charlie put in good words about her. She was energetic, feisty, and above all, pretty.

When she asked a bear of a man who worked in a warehouse for his vote, he grinned and asked, "You willing to take your kickbacks in trade?" He clutched at his thigh in an obscene gesture.

"I imagine if YOU gave kickbacks, there wouldn't be much of a kick," she retorted. The big man doubled over with laughter. She had his vote.

She visited small country churches, even attended some of the services. The people were accustomed to politicians shaking their hands on Sunday and forgetting who they were on Monday. Even so, a few complained.

"It's the Lord's day," a lady in a flowery, cotton dress snapped, but her husband tipped his hat and smiled.

Labor Day was her first opportunity to speak to a large group, a countywide function, complete with soft drinks, a band, lots of games, and above all, plenty of people and plenty of politicians to tell everybody how fine everything would be if only the God-fearing citizens would elect them. Mostly, it would be fine for the ones elected, but nobody said that.

The ex-police chief, a longtime Jordan resident and grandfatherly figure, strolled about and chatted with old friends. Most people called him "Chief Simms." He entered the race just to have something to do. The schoolteacher, after trouble with the school board because of unsubstantiated charges of homosexuality, dropped out. The sheriff, holding a hot dog and Coke, strutted about and told jokes.

When it came time to make speeches, the police chief took the platform and said, "How y'all doing!" He added a few words about the race before he stepped down to loud cheers. The crowd loved short speeches. The mayor called for Jodie, but a deputy blocked her push through the crowd.

"You ain't gonna go up there, are you?" he sneered. The sheriff bounded up the steps instead.

"Just reckon our female candidate couldn't find the way up here." Dagget laughed and tried to deepen his voice.

"Maybe she's busy washing dishes, Sheriff!" a deputy out of uniform shouted, setting off a round of laughter.

"I didn't want to say a woman's place is in the home, but I sure met lots of nice ladies here today. I betcha they make good homes for you, men folks. And I betcha y'all want to keep it that way." The crowd applauded.

He briefly reviewed his record, including a well-publicized raid on a notorious county bootlegger.

"When he hollered he wouldn't come out, I picked up my ax and busted in the door. I don't know how a female sheriff would be able to do that. I just hate to think of any little lady being in danger like that."

"You tell her, Sheriff," a deputy yelled.

The sheriff droned on awhile longer. "Now, my opponent, Jodie Mae Phelps, is sure a pretty little thing. Why don't one of you young men marry her so she can get to doing what the good Lord intended, and that ain't running for sheriff. Y'all know what I mean!" The crowd cheered and applauded. He raised both arms in a victory salute.

The mayor was about to introduce the next wave of speeches, but Jodie broke away from the deputy and interrupted him.

"Hold it, Mr. Chairman. Don't I get to speak at this rally?"

The embarrassed mayor waved her up.

"I'm Jodie Mae Jackson. Turns out that I'm the other woman in the sheriff's life." A few laughed. "The sheriff says he's stomped out crime. I reckon that's why he sits all day with his feet propped up on his desk. He's plumb tired from all that stomping." More laughed.

"The sheriff says he's run the prostitutes out of town. Well, he must have been blindfolded when he did because I'll bet you a dollar to a donut they're right back where they were before he did all that running he was talking about. Of course, they might not have as much money now." Some were shocked that she would openly suggest the sheriff took kickbacks.

"But that's gonna end when I'm elected. A handful of dollars paid under the table won't make prostitution legal. The sheriff doesn't make the law, he enforces it. At least he's supposed to. Has to read it first though."

She talked about the sheriff's abuse of the other side of his job, tax collector, and how he favored merchants that contributed to his personal needs and his retirement fund. "Wouldn't we all like to have a job that paid double?"

The sheriff stood with clinched fists. His face was crimson as he moved toward the podium in a rage. Two deputies restrained him.

"The sheriff says he swings a mean ax. I'd say all he swings is a fork and spoon. Reminds me of a poem. Must've been written for him. The sheriff's getting rich and fat, the rest are getting poor and thin. While our tax dollars go for beer to wash down the sheriff's dinner."

Laughter. The crowd loved a good show.

With that, the sheriff threw the two men aside and charged up the steps toward Jodie. Luck was on her side. He stumbled on the top step and sprawled onto the platform.

"A real gentleman." Jodie laughed. "You don't have to bow, Sheriff. A handshake will do."

She walked down the opposite steps to loud applause. She had made a good account of herself and for the first time people took her seriously.

The newspapers labeled her, "Mrs. Bilbo Jackson," a reference to the infamous Mississippi Senator Bilbo, who was known for his scathing attacks on opponents.

Steven had to explain to Jodie who Senator Bilbo was. "An old-time politician who ridiculed his opponents. Made a lot of people laugh, but he made a few very mad." He raised his eyebrows, suggesting caution.

Caution wasn't on Jodie's mind. Getting the voters' attention was. Though she had spoken out of anger at the Labor Day rally, she liked the response.

However, the sheriff did not like it and arranged a clandestine meeting with the retired police chief. For a few dollars, the old chief agreed to sling the mud so the sheriff could stay above it all.

"I want you boys to bird dog her around the county and ask her about her old mama and anything else you can think of," Dagget told his deputies. "I want that slut to pay for making a fool out of me. Wear your work clothes."

The next time the old chief made a speech, he said that Jodie Phelps Jackson came from the "worst white trash this county has ever seen." It made the newspaper headlines. The sheriff used the quote in his speeches even though he "didn't necessarily agree." He was a gentleman, after all.

CHAPTER 36

Charlie Burdette invited Jodie to speak at the monthly union meeting, a rowdy crowd of about four hundred, mostly men. More came when they heard Jodie was going to speak. They wanted to hear some of her "hell-raisin'."

Raw, uncontrolled energy, smoke, and raucous laughter filled the union hall and greeted her entry. Beer flowed freely. Charlie introduced her as the "little gal who kicked ole man Jordan's butt, Mrs. Jodie Mae Jackson!"

She had two campaign dresses, both simple and cut with straight, neat lines. One was light brown with pockets and buttons up the front, the other a pale gray, unobtrusive cotton print. That night she wore the light brown.

Her makeup was scant. Her hair groomed just enough to keep it out of her eyes. She wanted the audience to be impressed by what she said, not by how she looked.

She took a deep breath. Reverting to her country twang, she said, "I'm running for sheriff of this damned county, and by god, I mean to WIN!" There was no microphone, but her voice was clear.

Cheers and yells answered.

"Y'all probably read about the sheriff and them calling me white trash. It's true, I ain't got no Trace Avenue pedigree, and I can tell you this. If somebody sent me one, I'd send it back!"

"Don't you know it!" the crowd yelled.

"At first, I was a little hurt, you know, them calling me white trash and all. I didn't know what the hell it was they accused me of, but I figured it must be bad or they wouldn't have said it!"

She paused while they laughed and elbowed each other.

"I reckon they want me to be ashamed about living on gravel roads and eating red gravel dust. Holler if you've ever lived on a gravel road!" They yelled.

"Are you ashamed?"

"Hell no!"

"Me either. Maybe I should be ashamed of all the calluses I got on my hands working the fields from daylight to dark. Holler if you've got calluses!" A roar filled the hall.

"Are you ashamed?" Her voice grew louder.

"No!"

"I'm not either. I reckon they called me white trash 'cause of the old rattletraps we had to drive, you know what I'm talking about, the ones with rusted out floorboards. They let us see the road and smell gas fumes while we're riding. Hell, that was fun! Holler if you ever rode to town in one of 'em!" The roars increased.

"Does that make us trash?"

More shouts.

"I used to hate to go to the mailbox because we seemed to get more duns than regular mail, especially when the plant was on strike. Have you ever been a little short?"

"Yeooow!" They had.

"You know what I think?" She panned their faces. "I think, if living beside a gravel road and working from daylight to dark and driving a rattletrap and barely making ends meet is what they were talking about, I reckon they got me dead to rights. I must be white trash!"

She waited till the applause died down. "But you know what else I think, when you boil it all down, what they're really saying is that I'm COUNTRY! Well, by god, if being country makes me white trash, I'M DAMN PROUD OF IT!"

The applause lasted almost a minute.

"Hell, none of us country folks should ever run for public office. We're so ignorant, we're liable to get confused and turn honest. When I'm elected, I want to tax everybody fair and square. I want to get liquor legalized instead of supporting bootleggers, and I want to get the legislature to take tax collecting away from the sheriff. Let's cut out this business of letting the sheriff get fat off the taxes he collects. Our sheriff is fat enough!"

By law, the sheriff kept a percentage of the tax money he collected. That, plus payoffs from bootleggers made most sheriffs rich after a few years.

She waited until the noise died down and waved for quiet.

"I hope Sheriff Dagget heard that. By the way, you ever stop to think what Dagget rhymes with?"

"Whoooeeee!" They did.

"Ain't this fun?" she asked.

They whooped and hollered as she left the hall.

The *Tribune* carried the story. "Jodie Mae started out running for sheriff, but last night she became the general of country people and promised to lead them into the sheriff's office in November. Better pay attention, Sheriff Dagget?"

Steven dropped by to congratulate her. "I heard about the speech. You hit pretty close to home. I live on Trace Avenue, you know."

She winked. "In politics, you told me, it's not what you say, it's why you say it."

Within the week, a scattering of people around the country made cardboard signs for their windows. They read, "Jodie's Army."

Jordan locals said it was a novelty and wouldn't last, but the sheriff took it seriously and paid Charlie Burdette a visit.

"Everywhere I look these days, Charlie, there's one of them damned signs in somebody's window. I don't like it. Haven't I supported the union all these years?"

"Sheriff, these ole boys got to have some fun, let off a little steam now and then. Hell, we all love Jodie Mae, but shit, she's just a woman. You don't think she could handle your job, do you?" He sounded serious. On the inside though, he smiled.

"You make damned sure your people know that, Charlie. I happen to have a picture of a man firing a rifle at old man Jordan's Cadillac during the strike. It wouldn't take much imagination to claim it was you."

"You threatening me?"

"Damned right! You get the word out to take down them damned signs and stop all this idiotic talk about, shit, Jodie's Army." He stomped out.

"Fuck you, Sheriff!" Charlie yelled.

To Jodie, the signs meant that a lot of people were against the established order. They identified with the underdog and she was, undoubtedly, the underdog.

She continued that theme in the speeches she made after that. In between hell-raising and name-calling, she talked sense on the issues—legalize liquor and take the tax collection away from the sheriff.

"Them people out there are gonna start thinkin' about what she's saying," Dagget complained to his deputies. "Even after I whip her ass, they gonna ask why the sheriff has to get a cut when he collects taxes. They gonna think liquor should be legalized? Either one could cost me a hell of a lot of money."

Jodie did what she had done all her life, work as hard as she could for as long as she could. She began early and worked until there was no one up to listen.

One Wednesday night, a preacher at a country church agreed to let her speak a few minutes after prayer meeting. Twenty-five people were in attendance, a typical gathering.

She said, "Taking kickbacks and bribes is a sin against God, and it's time for the sheriff to repent. But if the devil's got him by the throat and won't let him repent, we'll just have to help him out! Out of office I mean."

"Amen, Sister Jodie!"

"I'm asking every God-loving one of you, to join with me. Let's send that sinner back to hell where he belongs."

They applauded even though for the most part, what the sheriff did or didn't do didn't bother them at all. They applauded the sincerity and audacity of her speech. They were God-fearing people, and if the sheriff violated the law, he was a sinner and had to account for it.

Clyde Bush, the assistant sheriff who was told to dog her tracks, waved from the back of the room. He was tall, balding with jug ears and about Jodie's age.

"Mrs. Jackson!" he shouted. Heads turned toward him. "If you're so all fired righteous, why'd you up and marry that old man Jackson for his money? And, talking about sin, weren't you and your ma whores?"

The charge sent a flash of anger through her. With her hands on her hips, Jodie replied, "That's a lie and you know it! But let me ask you a question. Is it true that you have to squat when you pee?"

The farmers slapped their overall britches and guffawed, a good way to end the meeting. Their wives were more subdued, but did smile.

"You slut!" Clyde charged in exasperation.

"Listen, deputy, if a whore charged a dollar a minute, you wouldn't have to pay more than a penny."

Laughter chased him from the church.

Though Dagget did not sling mud—that was the old chief's job—he regularly called attention to her age and sex when he described her as "that little shop girl." And his deputies continued to heckle her when she spoke.

"It's tiresome," she complained to Steven at a café she'd stopped in to leave a poster. "It's getting to where I can't finish a speech."

"That's politics. They're a little afraid of you, actually afraid of what you're saying. Most people agree with you. Liquor should be made legal. Why force people to break the law to get a bottle. Everybody does it. Frankly, I believe you'll make a good showing. There hasn't been this much interest in a local election since, hell, maybe never."

"But can I win?"

"I wouldn't get my hopes up."

"Because I'm a woman?"

"You have to face it, Jodie. Most people, men and women, think of women as put on earth to cook and clean house and have children while the men folk hunt and drink. You know how it goes. This is my ole lady, I love her. Now, woman, get in the kitchen and fix me some grub or I'll have to beat you again."

Warren called, usually late at night at the end of a campaign day. It was such an oddity, a woman running for county sheriff in Mississippi, that the *New York Times* carried an occasional story about the election. She refused his offer of more support, but he sent checks anyway.

Willie Bea arranged for Jodie to speak at a black church. Whites rarely made appearances in the "Colored Quarters," except to pick up their servants and laborers or for payoffs, but Jodie campaigned as hard there as she did every place else.

"The sheriff thinks it's his just desserts to go into a store and pick out a hunting outfit and walk out with it. He got pretty mad the last time he barged into Elmore's and we didn't have his size." She held out her arms to suggest his girth. "We had to tell him we didn't sell tents!"

Clyde nudged Pick who had laughed. The big black man stopped and stood. Like a mountain, he lumbered down the aisle. Jodie watched in silence with everyone else. What was he going to do?

"You best be getting on," he said in a deep vibrating voice.

"I reckon that's only fair, Pick Mason. If the sheriff's too lazy to come down here and speak, I suppose he would object to me coming." There was a giggle or two, but a glare from Pick stopped that.

He turned back to Jodie. "I ain't telling you no more."

"I'm getting," she mocked him. "Hell, I know you need the sheriff's money."

He took a step forward then let her pass. She breathed a sigh of relief.

CHAPTER 37

The case of *People vs. Leroy Martin* was on the criminal court docket for the last week of September. A couple of days before the trial, Steven stopped by Jodie's apartment. He had his briefcase.

"Wanted to see how you were holding up, but I also wanted to ask you about Ruby Martin."

"She was bright and a hard worker."

"Honest?"

"Completely. Why?"

"Well, I have a little problem with her account of the murder. She says she didn't see who attacked them. I went to the store the other night, same time of the murder, and turned off the lights. There is some light coming through the windows from the street. If she was close enough to get cut on the hand like she was, she had to have seen something. At least what color the attacker was."

He snapped open his briefcase and showed Jodie a picture of Ruby's hand. A deep cut appeared in her palm.

"Looks like a razor cut."

"It is." He showed her a picture of the wooden-handled straight razor found beside Tim Lennox's body.

"That's Elmore's razor!" Jodie said.

"Are you sure?"

"No doubt in my mind. I, uh, had to use it one time. But let me check his things." She left the room to look into the bag of Elmore's personal things given to her by the hospital nurse.

"It's not there," she said. "See, a brad is missing from the handle. It's definitely Elmore's."

"That's a big help. Leroy says he doesn't have a straight razor. The prosecutor says that proves he's lying. 'All black men have straight razors,' he said."

"I can testify if it'll help."

"It will. Now, if I can get Ruby to talk."

"Call Dr. Hansen." Jodie wrote down her telephone number. "She knows Ruby. If anybody has any influence on her, Willie Bea does."

At the trial, Jodie identified the razor as Elmore's. A murmur of shock spread through the courtroom. The district attorney looked perplexed.

Next, Steven called Elmore's nurse who testified, "I shaved him with it."

"Was it with the things you returned to Mrs. Jackson?"

"Now that you mention it, I can't recall that it was."

"Excluding yourself, did anybody else use the razor?"

"No one. Well, Marshall shaved with it one morning. He'd been there all night."

Leroy Martin was never seen at the hospital, so it was unlikely that he took the razor. Steven also established that Leroy Martin did not return to Jordan until the day Tim Lennox was killed, several days after Jodie had picked up Elmore's personal effects.

"Your Honor, in light of this evidence, I move to dismiss all charges against the defendant," the district attorney said.

The judge granted the motion.

Steven was hailed for his efforts. He kept an innocent man from going to prison or worse. Of course that did not answer the question of who did kill Tim Lennox but, the whole town and state, knew it was not Leroy Martin and gave praise to the next attorney general, Steven Jefferson.

"Did you get anything else from Ruby?" she asked.

"Yes. Well, it seems they weren't taking inventory at all. Tim had something else in mind. That's why the lights were off. Ruby was taking her clothes off in one of the dressing rooms when she heard a loud scuffle. When she came out to see, Tim fell into her, knocking her down. That's why she didn't see who it was. Her hand was cut when she reached up to ward off the attacker. Apparently scratched whoever it was. She was positive it wasn't Leroy. The way she put it was, if it had been Leroy, she'd have been dead."

Jodie recalled Marshall's scratched and bruised face but said nothing. She wasn't certain her suspicions weren't based more on her hate of Marshall than any real evidence, but he could easily have taken the razor from the hospital.

The first week of October was Fair week, an event everybody in the county awaited. Farmers could show off their livestock and produce and young people couldn't wait to ride the carnival rides and see the "hoochie coochie" shows. And young women got to be with their "fellers." In fact, the fair was such a prominent event some people marked time by it. If someone was uncertain as to when something happened, they could date it with the question, "Well, was it before the Fair or after the Fair." It worked every time.

Wednesday night was awards night, and lots of people filled the stadium to see who won what. It also meant that lots of politicians showed up to make speeches, including Jodie and Sheriff Dagget.

That night, a bunch of young men with guitars and fiddles got on the platform and played Blue Grass. Men grabbed their women by their backsides and did the two-step in the sawdust in front of the grandstand. Smoke-filled aroma from open grills reminded young and old alike that hot dogs and hamburgers were for sale.

Speeches went before the awards. If they came after the awards, the politicians would likely speak to an empty grandstand.

The sheriff went first. He bragged about the bottles of "stump hole" whiskey he'd busted, the bootleggers he'd put out of business, and the young women he'd delivered from a life of sin. He closed with a biblical swipe at Jodie.

"Now, I know this young woman had been criticized by Chief Simms and others, and I know she's run around the county making fun of me, but I remember the words of Jesus. If someone slaps you on the right cheek, offer up your left. Do unto others as you would have them do unto you. I pray every time I'm in church to keep the Lord's commandments. I have no malice toward her! God bless you all!"

He bowed and left. The people, full of celebration, applauded loudly with scattered shouts of "Amen, brother!"

Jodie waited a bit for the applause and shouting to die down before she took the podium.

When she did, she said, "I don't know why I've been so ignorant. I should've known the sheriff was a religious man. The good book says to tithe, give a share of your wages to help the Lord do his work. Well, the businessmen of this county have been giving a share of their wages to the sheriff for years. I guess he's been doing the Lord's work all this time, and I never knew it!"

The crowd laughed. "She's just getting warmed up," someone shouted.

She challenged the sheriff to name one bootlegger he'd closed down then dared him to tell the voters how much money he made from tax collections.

"I wouldn't embarrass the God-fearing sheriff by asking him how much he got under the table from the bootleggers. It wouldn't be right to make a man with a gut that big squirm."

After a few minutes of telling people how she'd change things, she waved and stepped down. Rebel yells mixed with raucous laugher trailed her into the crowd. People patted her on the back and wished her well.

Later, as she searched the parking area for Elmore's car, she heard someone say, "It's over here."

Taylor was home!

"It's so good to see you! When did you get back?"

"About an hour ago. I heard your speech. Shit, big sister, you ain't half bad. Hell's bells, I came back to help when I read about you. Hell, I reckon you don't need none."

"I do, Taylor. I need help." She told him about the sheriff's deputies and how Pick Mason wouldn't let her campaign in the black part of town. "I'm tired out and my stomach's acting up. I glad you came."

For the next two weeks, she toured gatherings and meetings, large and small, around the county and Taylor went with her. When a deputy heckled, Taylor invited him outside. The heckling stopped.

She continued her attacks on the sheriff's kickbacks and payoffs from bootleggers and the inequities in the liquor laws that forced people to become sneaks. Driving home after a PTA meeting, a sharp pain in her stomach forced her to stop the car.

"Cramps," she told Taylor. "They've been getting worse."

"Female problems?"

"No. I've had stomach pains since that trouble with Elmore in New Orleans."

Taylor drove the rest of the way.

At the apartment, they saw the sheriff's car parked besides the stairs. The sheriff leaned against the hood and stared at the landing. Taylor stopped and turned off the lights.

"I better stay here," he told her.

Jodie willed away the knot in her stomach and walked the rest of the way.

"Hold it right there, Mrs. Jackson," the sheriff called. "I hear that you're harboring a known fugitive."

"What are you talking about?" Jodie asked.

Two deputies got out of the sheriff's car.

"We've come to arrest that half-pint brother of yours," Clyde drawled. "Car theft."

"Are you talking about the charge you made over six years ago?"

"Don't make no difference. He still stole it, and I'm gonna arrest you for harboring a known fugitive," the sheriff said.

"I don't see a harbor around here," she snapped. "Or a fugitive."

"Don't sass me!" He lunged at her. She stepped back. Taylor watched from a shadowed doorway across the street. He started to charge but held up when a deputy grabbed the sheriff's arm.

"Hold it, Boss. Might not look so good right now," Clyde whispered. "They's some who might hold it against you. We can settle with her later. Let's go find that thug brother of hers. Probably at his ole ma's."

Jodie went upstairs and drank a glass of soda water to calm her stomach. It helped a little.

Later, Taylor crept up the stairs.

"I figured they'd have forgot about that by now," he said.

They took turns at the window. Each car rolled through the alley had to be checked. Around midnight, they decided it was safe and went to bed.

It was daybreak when Dagget and his two deputies returned. They shattered the door and burst inside with shotguns.

"Hands up!" the sheriff yelled. Jodie and Taylor sat at the kitchen table with cups of coffee. "You're both under arrest."

Newspaper reporters from the *Tribune* and the state paper were invited to see the sheriff make the arrest. They took pictures of the handcuffed "felons."

Jodie was thrown into a cell with two prostitutes, a drunk, and two women who had been arrested for fighting. The cell smelled of urine and vomit. There was no place for her to sit, so she stood and remembered years before when her mother was in a similar cell.

The reporter from the *Tribune* called Steven for comments on the arrest. Steven told him the sheriff had used the public trust of his office as a political forum. "Politics at its worse," he said. "Clear misuse of his office." Next, he called the sheriff's office and was told the sheriff wasn't in.

"Listen, I know he's in so you'd better put him on."

Clyde covered the phone and said, "It's Jefferson, that lawyer."

"Shit!" The sheriff grabbed the phone and told Steven, "I don't give a rat's ass—"

"Shut up, Sheriff! I'm calling about my client, Jodie Mae Jackson. Have you ever heard about due process?"

"What's that got to do with a damn thing?"

"Tell me what's she's charged with, and I'll explain it."

The sheriff related the charges. "I got 'em dead to rights."

"After six years? Are you senile?" Steven yelled. "No indictment was ever filed! The criminal statute on an unserved warrant is five years! Don't you know the law you say you're enforcing?"

"I'll get a new one."

"You have a witness?"

"Uh…"

The black man whose car was stolen, but returned, had been dead for two years and the sheriff knew it.

"So, this is just a little political horseshit," Steven railed. "You must be afraid that little country girl's going to whip your ass!"

The sheriff slammed down the phone. "Let 'em out," he ordered Clyde.

"But—"

"Just let 'em the fuck out!" he yelled. Veins protruded from his neck. "I got out of it what I wanted anyway."

Steven waited for them outside.

"It'll be in the papers, front page, I'd guess. Even with the rebuttal, it won't do you any good, but at least you're not in jail," Steven told them.

Jodie and Taylor thanked him for getting them out.

"I'm glad to be out of that hellhole," Jodie said.

"You think I should leave town?" Taylor asked him.

"Might as well stick around," Steven said. "I doubt anything more will come of it. He did what he needed to do—put Jodie in a bad light. Dirty politics."

"Is there any other kind?" Jodie asked.

As predicted, a photo of Jodie, handcuffed and in the custody of the sheriff, made the front pages of all the newspapers. The rebuttal appeared on page two.

The talk was all over town by noon. Most folks relied on the adage, "Where there's smoke there's fire."

Jodie was depressed. Though she hadn't really expected to win, the progress she'd made was unfairly snatched away. It didn't help a damn bit to assign it to dirty politics. The next time she made a speech, she was booed and stomped down.

"I wish I could catch Dagget in something bad," she told Taylor who blamed himself for her troubles.

"You want me to ask around?"

"And get your head bashed in?"

"*Tribune* says you should quit." Taylor threw down the newspaper he held.

"I'm not quitting. I'll die first."

"I reckon there's some thinkin' that very thang."

CHAPTER 38

That night, she paced the apartment and searched her mind for ideas. She had to come up with something big and did. That's when she recalled the cold November day when she witnessed Deputy Sheriff Dagget kill a man!

The next day, she went to the *Tribune* to read old issues. Two hours later, after a discussion with Steven, she called a press conference on the courthouse steps at noon, time to make the afternoon editions. The sheriff and several newspaper and radio reporters were present. To her delight, a television reporter from the state capitol was in town. He set up his camera.

"I have proof," she said and waved a handful of papers in the sheriff's direction, "that Sheriff Dagget, who was then a deputy, was responsible for the disappearance of Bud Larson and two deputies."

Dagget's mouth flew open. Her charge caught him completely off guard. He'd forgotten that she had seen him.

Jodie recited the story in the *Tribune* about the disappearance of a prominent county bootlegger and two sheriff's deputies without a trace. After an insurance investigation, the men were ruled legally dead, although no bodies were ever found.

"I have a witness," she proclaimed, waving folded sheets of paper. "You were seen, Sheriff Dagget, stabbing Bud Larson in the back!"

"You're a goddamned liar!" the sheriff, pushing past the reporters, shouted. "If you have evidence, let me see it!" He grabbed at the sheets of paper, but she yanked it away.

"And let it disappear like Bud Larson? No, I'll keep it until after the election. Then you can read all about it from your jail cell."

Pretending to read from her papers, she described the leather bag, Bud Larson's black Cadillac, and specific details about the fight. Larson wielded a bat—he was famous for his baseball bat—and the deputies had knives. The details convinced most that she was on to something. The sheriff's protests were ignored.

Those close to bootlegging knew about Larson's big "Caddie" and his black bag. A few knew that he collected payoffs for the sheriff from all the bootleggers in the county and did a little bootlegging on the side. What no one actually knew, though it had been rumored, was that Larson was skimming. Larson liked to brag about it to his women friends.

Some rumors to that effect bounced around the county after he disappeared, according to Steven. One rumor had Larson absconding with the last collections. Another had the other bootleggers taking punitive action against him. A third rumor whispered involvement by the sheriff's department but nothing was ever proven and the matter was forgotten until Jodie's revelation. The fact that the sheriff at that time resigned suddenly became more significant. Dagget was appointed to take his place. By the end of the day, the third rumor became the popular topic of conversation in and around Jordan.

The headlines read, "General Jodie launches a counterattack. Sheriff Dagget implicated in disappearance of bootlegger bagman and deputies. Steven Jefferson promises a full state-level investigation when he's elected attorney general."

People forgot about Jodie's arrest. That was yesterday's news. Dagget's possible involvement in the murder of a bagman for the sheriff was juicier.

The last opportunity for the sheriff and Jodie to confront each other was during Jordan High's homecoming. Political speeches were usually not allowed during a school event, but there was such interest in the sheriff's race the school board made an exception. At halftime, the sheriff was introduced. He reviewed his record and dismissed Jodie's charges about Larson as political imagination.

"That little girl's been imagining all sort of things," he said, "like she could arrest a full-grown man threatening somebody with a broken beer bottle, like I get my clothes free." He reached in his pocket and produced a receipt. "Wonder what she thinks this is. I pay for all my clothes. She imagines that I get rich off of bootleggers. She should talk to my wife. I've done a good job, folks, an honest job, and I want to keep on. On election day, vote for me. Do the right thing. You know it's so." He smiled, waved to his supporters, and sat down.

A Jordan High football game attracted mostly city people and most of those backed Dagget. However, Charlie Burdette got the word out to the union members that Jodie was going to speak and asked as many as could go to the game. "Can't let 'em gang up on her," he told them.

Jodie hopped onto the wooden platform that had been dragged out for the speeches. She had to concentrate to overcome the throb in her stomach.

"Did I imagine that Sheriff Dagget bought a big house over by the country club a few months after he took office? If he's so poor, where'd he get that money? Did I imagine the talk that Bud Larson took money from bootleggers to pay off the sheriff? It doesn't take much imagination to figure that Larson had a fight with the sheriff's deputies and that one of them walked away with the payoff bag! Who suddenly came into money? Makes you wonder, doesn't it?" She waved in the direction of Sheriff Dagget, who stood less than ten feet away. The crowd was stunned, but they loved it.

Clyde shouted something from the stands. Jodie only caught the last part, "…lover." But she knew what the first word was.

"Shut your mouth, Clyde," half a dozen of Charlie's people shouted. He shut up.

"The sheriff and his bunch called me trash," she said, "but that was before they found out there were a bunch of us around. How many brought their signs?"

Enough "Jodie's Army" signs were waved about to make an impact.

"Wave 'em high! Look at those signs, Sheriff Dagget! We're on the march, and we're not going to stop till your office is cleaned out!"

Charlie's people stomped and yelled and waved their signs.

The pain in her stomach brought tears to her eyes. She wanted to bend over, but it'd have to wait. She had more to say.

"If we legalize liquor, the sheriff might not have so many heads to bash in. Besides," she forced a smile, "if you had a choice, who would you rather have arrest you, Sheriff Dagget or me?"

The sheriff's supporters shouted taunts and Charlie's people responded with calls of "Jo-die! Jo-die!"

The football game was anticlimactic.

Jodie was glad she didn't collapse. The pain was worse. Taylor met her outside. Lizzy was by his side.

Lizzy touched her arm in the twilight of the stadium lights and said, "Jodie Mae! I had to talk to you. They was some men come to see me this morning. They said I was to tell you you'd best quit whilst you was ahead or else they'd see to it you left town in a box."

"Shit!" Taylor spit on the ground and twisted his heel in it. "If any's to leave in boxes, it'll be them."

Warren called that evening. The New York papers carried an account of her arrest and her bombshell revelation about the sheriff. "That must be some kind of campaign. Can I help?"

"No. Things are a little better than I hoped. The city people will vote for the sheriff. They own him so they want to keep him. I have a chance to get the country vote. Nobody owns them. Hell, most don't have anything anybody wants. I don't know what will happen in the Quarter. Pick Mason—he works for the sheriff's bunch—won't let anybody campaign for me down there. He'll watch to make sure the folks down there'll vote the way he wants. It'll all be over next week."

"Are you glad? You sound tired. Are you okay?"

"Stomach bothering me, but I'm okay."

"Shouldn't you see a doctor? It might be appendicitis."

"I'll wait until after the election. The sheriff would love it if I got sick. Too frail to handle the job. I can hear it now. I'll wait."

He asked her to call if she needed anything.

The next day, Steven met with her. "From what Dad tells me, you'll carry the country. The city boxes and the box in the Quarter belong to the sheriff," he said. "If you could arm wrestle Pick Mason, you might have a chance in the Quarter. All things considered though, you've done very well. Scared the hell out of a lot of people."

She grabbed her stomach in pain.

Steven helped her to a bench. "Have you seen a doctor?"

She told him the same thing she told Warren.

"I'll get our doctor. He won't say anything."

"No." She grimaced and stood. "It'll pass. I don't want anybody saying I'm sickly." She forced a smile.

The word around town and in the country boiled down to whether Jodie, a young woman, like it or not, could handle a "man's job." Even with that skepticism, many people were so "fed up" with corrupt politicians that they would vote for Jodie to get a change.

The other thing talked about was legalized liquor. Drinking was a sin, but hell, "We drink anyway. Why do we have to sneak around to do it?"

Many were shocked that the sheriff got a percentage of the taxes he collected, not to mention what he collected on the side. The general consensus was that, "It's okay for a politician to take some, just not a lot." It bothered others that the sheriff had "bought that big house by the Country Club. How'd he get that kind of money?"

"That Larson talk has hurt you, Sheriff," Clyde told Dagget.

"I hear the damn union vote'll go for her. I don't think she'll get shit in town."

"Talk is, legal liquor's better than an illegal sheriff," a chubby deputy said but laughed to take away any sting.

"Fuck 'em. We can win without the union vote, but I'm going to have a talk with Charlie Burdette after it's over." Dagget smashed his fist into his palm.

"People around Whitfield remember her from Senator Case's campaign. They're gonna vote for her," Clyde added.

"I burned them out when they lived down there. Trashy people. Still are. When this election's over, she's going to be sorry she ever messed with me." He faced a map on the wall behind his desk and poked lined areas that represented "boxes" with his finger.

"Best she can do is carry these two country boxes. I've got the city boxes and the colored box. Two months' time and nobody will remember how close it was. And she sure as hell won't be around to remind anybody. Mark my words, Clyde."

"Thank God for Pick Mason," Clyde said.

"A little insurance might not hurt though," Dagget told him. "Let's pay a visit to Jackson's boy."

Dagget and two deputies found Marshall in the uniform department of Elmore's. Dagget stood close and leaned over so that his face was only inches away from Marshall's. The two deputies stood so that they surrounded Marshall.

"Boy," Dagget told Marshall, "I want you to have that bitch evicted. Say she messed up the apartment or something, wrote bad checks, anything you can think of."

Marshall objected. "I'm not going back to court. I'm not!" His eyes shifted right and left to search for a way around the deputies. When he took a step forward, Dagget shoved his arm out over Marshall's chest.

"I ain't finished yet. You just might want to rethink that, boy. You see, I have a pretty good idea about who might have cut that Lennox boy's throat. I bet you a plug nickel you don't have an alibi for that night."

All the color drained from Marshall's face. They drove him to the courthouse.

Judge Harvey issued the eviction order before noon. Dagget, in front of reporters, tacked the order on the door himself.

Dagget's lawyer, per his request, came along to explain the reason for the order. "This woman, Jodie Mae, is a vagrant who has lived here at the expense of my client, Marshall Jackson. She refuses to pay rent and has practically destroyed the apartment out of spite. He had no choice but to evict her."

The story made headlines, but because of intense mudslinging that marked the campaign, people read it as just more of the same and paid little attention to it.

Jodie was in Steven's office when the story hit. She had been campaigning all day and was on the way to the apartment but stopped in Steven's office to sign papers to appeal Judge Harvey's ruling on the codicil.

Steven took the call. He hung up, sighed loudly, and turned to tell her. "The sheriff has struck again. I'm going to—"

What he was about to say was interrupted by Jodie's loud, "Ahhh!" She doubled over in pain.

"I don't care what you say," he said. "I'm taking you to our doctor."

She was in too much pain to object.

CHAPTER 39

"Have you been vomiting?" the old doctor asked as he pressed on her stomach and abdomen.

"Once or twice."

"Does it hurt now?" He pressed a spot on the right side of her stomach.

"Yes, oh…" She groaned.

"We'll need some tests, but I think it's an inflamed appendix."

"You mean I need an operation?"

"As soon as possible! Peritonitis, if it bursts, could kill you."

"Could you just give me something for the pain until after the election?" she asked.

He shook his head. "Do you want to die?"

"I want to finish this election. I have to. Every time I try to have anything, somebody comes along and takes it away. This election is all I have left. If I'm going to die, I'd rather go down fighting."

"I don't like it, but I understand." He reached into his desk and pulled out a small box of pills. "Just take one when the pain comes on. If it gets real bad, election or not, you'd better get in here as fast as you can. That appendix needs to come out. I'm serious, it could kill you."

"Doctor said it'd be okay," she lied to Steven. "Gave me some pills to settle my stomach."

"Good," he said. "I'll see if I can get the Supreme Court to issue a writ to void Judge Harvey's eviction order."

"Don't bother," she said. "The damage is done. The election is in three days. I'll issue a statement. The voters will have to decide."

"You have to have someplace to stay."

"I have a few dollars left. I'll stay in the Pinehaven Hotel. After the election, who knows?"

"By then, I'll have you back in the apartment."

She wondered.

Taylor also took a room in the hotel. He drank raw whiskey from a bottle while Jodie talked with Willie Bea about the vote in Kingston Quarter.

"They'd vote for you if they could, Jodie Mae. They like you, always have, but Pick Mason makes his living by telling black folks what to do."

"Maybe if I talked to him."

"Money's the only thing that man hears. You got any money?"

She didn't.

After hanging up, she took a pain pill. It left a bitter taste in her mouth but killed the pain. It also left her light-headed.

Taylor said, "I'm gonna go down there and talk to the Brown brothers. Hell, we practically growed up together. If we stood together, I bet we could talk some sense into Pick."

"Talk?" Jodie tried to smile.

"Gotta start somewhere."

"You can't go to the Quarter, Taylor! Dagget's bunch would as soon kill you as look at you."

He pulled a pair of brass knuckles from his jacket and pounded them against his open palm. "I'll take my friend," he said.

"Please, Taylor, don't go."

"Jodie, you ain't never asked for nothing but a square deal. By god, if I can do something to help, I will." He reached for the doorknob.

"Taylor," she called and tried to stand up. The pain was less, but her legs were so wobbly she could barely stand. He was gone.

Less than half an hour later, she heard a knock on the door. She thought Taylor had returned. "Taylor?" she said and stumbled over and opened the door.

Randolph Jefferson stood in the door, carrying a briefcase. He tipped his hat and said politely, "Mrs. Jackson."

"Come in, Mr. Jefferson."

He accepted a chair and said, "I suppose you could call this a business meeting. You see, Mrs. Jackson, a lot of people around town agree with you about Sheriff Dagget. We've known about the Larson thing for some time. Not too many people get very excited about a bootlegger bagman getting killed, however. And more people than you know agree that his office should be divided into tax collecting and law enforcement. Most of us even approve of legalized liquor."

"But?"

"The problem is…the old system works. Everybody is comfortable with it. Bootleggers make money, taxes get collected, and the sheriff looks the other way when told to. You want to reform everything. That makes people nervous. Nobody knows how that would work out. Whose ox might get gored?"

"So?"

He cleared his throat and opened the briefcase filled with money. "There's ten thousand dollars in here. It's all yours."

"If?"

"You withdraw and leave town. And take your brother with you."

"You'd like that, I suppose, if only to improve Steven's image."

"I wouldn't object at all."

She stared at the money, even picked up a couple of packets.

"If I take this money, I'd be no better than Sheriff Dagget. Take a payoff and shut up."

"That's a moral issue, Mrs. Jackson. This is business. You're going to lose. Surely you know that. If you leave, however, the town will avoid the strife of a close election and all this reform business you've talked about will fade away.

"Steven will get Judge Harvey's probate order reversed. You'll be able to sell the store. With what you get plus what's in here"—he tapped the case—"you can go someplace and start over…with no baggage."

"Seems so easy."

"Sometimes the easy way is the better way."

She reached over and closed the briefcase lid.

"I don't say the offer isn't tempting. It is. I've never seen that much money. But I represent the only people in this county worth a damn, and I'm not going to let them down, even if I end up with nothing. If I back out, they lose. Country people don't quit. You can kick us, call us names, even starve us, but we'll fight you till our last breath."

He opened his mouth to say something, but she wouldn't let him. She walked toward the door.

"When you're born poor—something people like you can't understand—you expect hard times, but we keep thinking there'll be good times up ahead, so we keep going. We don't quit. In this race, I'm the best candidate." She held the door open. "And, by god, I will not quit."

He tipped his hat and left.

She fell into a chair and worried about Taylor. Where was he? She dozed off and didn't wake until midnight. Taylor had been gone five hours. She paced about the room and stared out the window at the street below. The pain pills had worn off, but her concerns overshadowed the knotted throb in her stomach.

The phone rang in the early morning hours. It was Willie Bea.

"Jodie Mae!" She sounded distraught. Jodie knew it was trouble. "There's been a bad fight. Taylor's in the hospital. Hurt bad, real bad."

The doctor told Jodie, "He's busted up pretty bad, Mrs. Jackson, broken jaw, wrist, shattered kneecap, multiple lacerations, contusions, broken arm, and concussion. Maybe a fractured skull."

"He went down there to help me," she told him. A tear rolled down her cheek.

"A black man brought him in. Johnny somebody," the doctor repeated what he was told. Five people were involved in the fight, three blacks, Taylor, and another white man.

"I don't know who the others are, but an orderly at the community clinic called a while ago and said that Clyde Bush, one of the sheriff's deputies was brought in unconscious. He may not live. The sheriff claims he was beaten during an attempted arrest. They say your brother took on four men! Unbelievable!"

He hurried off. The emergency ward was full of broken bodies.

Jodie choked up. Taylor was in critical condition because he wanted to give her a chance to win. She vowed to avenge him.

Jodie spent the night in the waiting room. The doctor let her see Taylor in the recovery room.

His left eye flicked open when she called his name. The right one was black and swollen shut. He tried to smile, but couldn't. His jaw was wired together because of the break, but he managed to speak in a whisper.

"Was four, I think. Big black guy, Pick, watched and laughed. When I was whipping 'em, son of a bitch hit me over the head with a pipe."

"I saw Willie Bea a while ago. She says everybody in the Quarter is talking about what you did. They are going to vote for me regardless of Pick Mason." She lied, but didn't want him to think he'd taken a beating for nothing.

He tried to say something else, but fell asleep again.

Jodie staggered out. She planned to be at the plant gate for the shift change. It was Saturday morning. The election was Tuesday. She told Charlie and the others what had happened.

"We'll do our best for you, Jodie Mae," Charlie promised. "We'll get the word out." He stared at her for a second then said, "You look like you could use a good night's sleep. Go on home and rest. Ain't a hell of a lot you can do these last two days. Most people have made up their minds by now."

Dagget told the *Tribune* that Clyde Bush was killed arresting a bootlegger. "I was there," he told the reporter. "I can tell you, that wasn't a job I'd send a woman out to do."

Jodie went back to the hotel and called Willie Bea.

"Would it help if I—" She paused to let the wave of nausea pass. "If I came down to the Quarter Monday and talked to the businessmen and the preachers?"

"Jodie Mae, I don't want you to end up like Taylor. The people down here are mad about it, but we can't do anything. You can't ask these people to get killed."

"You're right. It's my fight, not theirs."

She awoke Sunday morning with a desperate idea, which, even if it failed, could avenge the beating Taylor took for her.

She washed down four pills with a glass of water, two more than the doctor said, but they let her walk without pain. She went to see Taylor. He was allowed to take liquid nourishment and sit up. They talked a little.

"Be out next week," he said.

"They'll have it in for you."

"New sheriff'll protect me." He grinned.

Her smile was without conviction.

"Medication time," the cheerful nurse said. Jodie left. Her head felt like it was going to float off her shoulders.

She planned her move for right after dark. She sat in the hospital waiting room and waited. The pain came and went, even with the pills. It was getting worse.

"I can't give up, Lord. I can't." If anyone heard her, they paid no attention. Most had their own prayers.

CHAPTER 40

When it was good dark, she swallowed the last of her pain pills. The bitterness stayed in her mouth like foul bile, no matter how much water she drank.

She trudged along the street headed to the Quarter. Bitter memories pushed into her thoughts. Called white trash, run off from the shotgun shack by the KKK, burned out by Sheriff Dagget, being "sold" to Elmore, shamed by a slimy banker and finally her store stolen from her. Now somebody wanted to steal the election from her. Anger began to shove the bitter memories aside.

She was outside Pick's place at nearly seven thirty. She had called the *Tribune* to say she would meet with Pick Mason at eight o'clock that evening. However, she planned to be there earlier. Jodie also called the city police department, anonymously, to expect some excitement at Pick Mason's place a little around eight. "It involves that Jodie Mae Jackson woman," she said.

A white and red neon light flicked on and off announcing, "Blue Goose - Eats and Drinks." Three black men sat on a sidewalk in front of the nightclub with amber-colored bottles, talking back and forth. They took no notice of Jodie's arrival.

The two windows in front of the club were painted black and covered by iron bars. Its wooden front door opened into a dark, dimly lit cavern.

A gaunt black man in a white shirt sat on a bench near the door. He watched as Jodie moved up the wooden steps. She gripped the door facing and looked inside. Except for a bartender who washed glasses behind a long bar and two men who argued at a table, it was empty.

"Where can I find Mr. Mason?" she asked the bartender. He looked at her as though she had lost her mind. White women never came to the Blue Goose. In fact, neither did white men.

He pointed to a door at the end of the bar marked "Manager."

"I'd knock if I was you," he cautioned.

She did.

"Come on in!" Pick's deep voice answered.

Most of her courage and conviction, her pent-up anger, abandoned her. Nevertheless, she pushed herself on. What choice did she have? This was her last chance. She'd decided it'd be better to die than to give up without a fight.

"Mr. Mason," she said. She tried to sound businesslike, tried to squeeze the tremble from her voice, but the big black man scared her like she'd never been scared before. Pick stood. He was scantily dressed in an undershirt and pants. The room was warm for early November. Or so it seemed to Jodie. The ex-boxer stood well over six feet, his arms and shoulders rippled with muscles.

He grinned when he saw her. "You just come right on in."

She took the cane-bottomed chair he offered and said, "I'm Jodie Mae Jackson. You remember me? I'm running for sheriff."

"I knows who you are rightly enough. Sassed me at the church. What you coming down here for?" His white teeth gleamed in the twilight gloom of his office. His dark eyes sparkled.

"I would be a better sheriff than Sheriff Dagget. Better for the whites and better for the blacks."

"Honey," he replied, "I don't care what you would be. What you got to offer? I knows you ain't got no money, least that's what Ms. Willie Bea says."

"I'm offering a little good sense!" Her anger flared.

"I was thinking you might have something else to offer." He sat on the edge of the battered old desk and looked at her. He looked like a mountain about to fall. She was terrified. He placed one of his large hands on her shoulder. She pushed it away and stood. Her chair fell backward.

"Hey!" He stood. "You switch your white ass down here, you better have something to offer."

"Shut up and sit down. I have something to say!" she commanded him in a strong, stern voice. It was all bluff, but she hoped he wouldn't notice.

He laughed like he didn't care one way or the other and took a step toward her. "Sheriff done tole me all about you…and your mama." He backed her toward the door.

Her first plan had been persuasion. That had failed.

He suddenly stopped and said, "Shit." He waved both hands at her in apparent disgust. "You ain't worth going before no judge. Anyhow, I've had plenty like you. White trash. Ain't worth nothing."

Jodie took a deep breath. "You Uncle Tom–colored trash."

He had turned away but when she said that, he twirled around, his nostrils flaring with rage. "What'd you call me? Uncle Tom! I'm my own man."

"Colored trash," she said. "White man's dog. That's what I called you. You give colored people a bad name."

"Nobody comes in here calling me a dog!" he shouted.

She pointed a finger at his face and shouted, "White man's d—"

He flicked out a left hand faster than she could see and slammed her against the wall. Her head was full of buzzing sounds. Her eyes glazed over. The big black man was crazy with anger.

As hard as she tried not to, Jodie began a slow slide to the floor. Like a fighter with an opponent in trouble, Pick moved in to finish the job. She shook her head, trying to regain control of her senses.

"Stay away from me, Pick Mason!" she screamed. "Help!"

"Ain't nobody gonna help you now. You in Pick's place."

His right hand flashed forward. She braced for the blow, but instead, he grabbed the top of her jacket and the blouse underneath. With one motion, he yanked her to her feet and threw her across the room, sprawling on the floor. Her body ached with pain as she rolled to her knees and tried to stand. Her shoulders burned where the fabric had been torn away.

"Help!" she cried again, feebly.

He grabbed her by her neck and yanked her off the floor and held her so high her shoes barely touched the floor. She gasped for breath and fought the urge to blank out. He stared at her like he was holding a chicken ready to have its neck rung.

He turned loose of her neck and slapped her hard before she could fall. Then he hit her with a quick jab in the stomach. Pain spread like an explosion from her stomach into her chest, then into her arms and legs, liquid flames, searing, scorching, and burning, like no pain she'd ever felt before.

The sneer on the man's face blurred. She fought to stay awake but wanted to pass out and rid herself of the pain. He leaned over and slapped her face. As he did darkness began to flood her mind.

"Can't faint," she muttered. "Can't."

She willed her right hand into her dress pocket. Pick heard the sound of devil's silver blade switch open but the blood roaring in his head made him ignore it. As he grabbed the front of what was left of her dress, her right hand flashed upward. Devil's blade glistened in the light and left a silver trail from her side to the spot on the left side of his chest, where Taylor said his heart would be.

Her strength was almost gone. One thrust was all she could make. The tip penetrated Pick's dark brown skin. Blood flowed. Jodie pushed at the handle of the knife with her weight behind it to drive the blade in as far as it would go. Pick ripped at her dress like he had felt nothing.

Why hasn't he stopped? Her quivering hand gripped the handle of the knife, its four-inch blade completely imbedded in his chest. He reached back to slap her again. The palm of his hand was in motion when his movements ceased, everything at once, his face, his eyes. and his mouth. His lips did twitch, as if to speak but no words came. He brought his right hand up to his chest in slow motion. But by the time his hand reached the knife, his knees began to buckle. He fell slowly to the floor and rolled to one side.

The jukebox, which was on outside, was now quiet. The muffled conversations, which had filtered into the room before, were gone. It was like the Blue Goose had been suspended in time. No one moved and no one spoke. The spell was broken as the door opened. It was Joe, the bartender.

"My god! Good God a'mighty! Somebody get help. It's Pick. He's been stobbed." He ran to the pay telephone on the wall and began to dial.

Jodie writhed in pain. Holding the edge of the desk, she pulled herself up, then vomited. Somehow she managed to get the ragged remains of her clothes over her shoulders. The room blurred. Her knees buckled.

"No," she told herself. "…have to finish…can't…bastards whip me. Can't. Help me, Lord. Please." Cold perspiration ran down her face. Her arms and body were cold, clammy cold. She stepped weakly over Pick's body and braced herself against the wall. The wall clock said "eight o'clock." The sound of police sirens pierced the mountain of mist fogging her mind.

Reporters poured into the bar, flashing bulbs and asking questions.

Speaking in a whisper, and struggling not to pass out, she said, "Mr. Mason said his people…vote for the sheriff unless I paid him more…sheriff was paying. I told him…not…pay him anything… people's right to vote…That's when he hit me."

Mercifully, the police arrived. She felt her body dissolve away and remembered nothing after that.

The next thing she heard was someone calling her voice, from far, far away. Like from in a fog. Her eyes blinked. She smelled ether and heard, "They're ready to operate. Let's move her." She passed out.

In the waiting room, reporters fired questions at Steven.

"What's the deal, Mr. Jefferson. Is she going to live?"

"She looked badly hurt."

"Fellows," Steven raised his arms and half-laughed. "Jodie's being treated for an abrasion on her forehead. Mr. Mason hit her in the struggle. That's about it. She wanted to come out but the doctor has advised her to take tonight and tomorrow off. In fact, she won't do any more campaigning. She says to let the people of Kingston know they are now free to vote their conscience."

"Where did she get the knife?"

"Pick Mason's dead. Will she be charged?"

"One at a time." He smiled like it was a parlor get-together. "The knife apparently fell from Pick's pants during the attack. She obviously picked it up and defended herself. No charges for self-defense.

"I would like to make a point. Tonight, Jodie Mae Jackson, the next sheriff of Bucatanna County, showed she can handle the toughest of people. Do you think Sheriff Dagget would have gone down there and tried to reason with Mason, with or without deputies?"

They rushed out to file their stories. Notwithstanding what Steven told the reporters, Jodie was gravely ill and in the operating room.

When the operation was over, the doctor found Steven and told him, "Her appendix burst. It was ready to go. The poison flooded her insides, but we cleaned most of it out. Otherwise, she'd be dead already."

"Will she'll live?"

He shook his head. "I wish I knew. I'm worried about the infection. We'll do all we can." The doctor walked away.

Steven stood with his back against the corridor wall and agonized over whether to say anything or not. He knew what Jodie would want him to do. Wait. And that's what he did.

The story made the front page of the morning papers. The sheriff knew before then, of course, and was on the radio to minimize its impact. Though he didn't say so directly, he suggested that Jodie went to the Quarter with ulterior motives. Primarily though, he avoided direct criticism, resorting instead to innuendo.

"I want the voters to know one thing. Legalizing liquor is the same as legalizing sin. If we did that, it'd be like telling the devil we prefer him to our Lord. I won't stand for that! I won't see our sons and daughters buying whiskey from roadside stands. I know what it means to have children, to worry about their future. I'm a church-going, family man and I know how important it is to have family values. Others in this race apparently do not."

Whether the sheriff's last-minute appeal would turn the voters from Jodie was anybody's guess. When the election began, the sheriff was considered a shoo-in. Now, most still figured he would win, but it was going to be a lot closer than he or any of his supporters had figured. No one had counted on Jodie's Army! It was a small band, but loud and, by god, proud!

The sheriff campaigned hard the last day. He drove everywhere with sirens and loud speakers blaring. "Vote against legalizing sin. Vote Dagget."

On voting day, a calm passed over the town as everybody waited for the polls to open. The campaign had been one of the bitterest ever witnessed. All wanted it to be over.

People voted in record numbers. The sheriff had his people, in uniforms, at every polling station, officially to ask questions, unofficially to intimidate voters, but none of them were in the voting booths.

The polls closed. An hour passed. Steven called the city hall for the early results.

The registrar told him, "It's a horse race. The sheriff has 13,257 votes and Mrs. Jackson has 11,997."

"Are all the boxes in?"

"Only one left is the box from the Quarter. It's been picked up, but I haven't seen it."

That box held about three thousand votes, enough to put Jodie on top but where was it? A box had been known to get lost or held back for "inspection" depending on what the vote count was. Steven knew where the box likely was and knew it would take more than friendly persuasion to convince Dagget to release it.

Judge Harvey refused Steven's request for an order.

He drove home where his father entertained friends and watched the returns. In addition to the sheriff's race, the mayor and other officials were up for reelection.

Steven pulled his father into the study and explained what had happened. "Judge Harvey won't give me an order."

"Why come to me? The sheriff may be a crook, but he's our crook."

"It's IOU time, Dad. I ran and I won. Now I need a favor."

"Damn it to hell, son. Stay out of this?"

"I want that order!"

Randolph sighed and picked up the phone. "Harvey!" The tone of his voice left no room for argument. "Get my boy that goddamned order he wants or you won't hear another case! You understand?" There was a pause then he hung up.

"We'll let the votes be counted," he told Steven. "Are we still friends?"

"Yes."

"By the way, I tried to buy her off. Had some clients who wanted her to drop out. She may have told you."

Steven shook his head no and asked why.

"She's an honest woman, son. It made some people nervous." He returned to the party.

Armed with the order his father enabled him to obtain, Steven walked into the sheriff's office with a police escort. The sheriff sat with a room full of deputies. All drank whiskey from plastic cups.

"Where is it?" Steven demanded.

"Come in, boy. Have some refreshment. We're just testing it. Damned bootleggers may be selling watered whiskey."

"Where's the damned box?"

Dagget's head involuntarily turned briefly toward the corner of the room.

The box was still locked. On a table in the corner were two stacks of ballots, one stack unmarked, the other marked. The deputies stopped marking when Steven entered.

"I see you haven't completed your inspection." Steven picked up the box.

"What the hell you think you're doing. Put that box down!" the sheriff yelled. "That box is in my custody. Election violations! We've had reports that some of them ignorant colords voted three times apiece."

"That's right," a deputy said and nudged his buddy.

Steven slapped the order on the sheriff's desk.

"File your claim with the court. That damned box is going to the city hall to be officially opened."

"Hell, boy, I voted for you. Your pa contributed to my campaign. Lots of people in this town're going to be upset if that white trash…" The look on Steven's face changed his mind about completing the sentence.

"All Jodie ever asked for was a chance, a damn chance to get something. I mean to see that she gets it, if she lives." His voice almost cracked. He had not meant to say anything, but it slipped out.

"I thought something was up," Dagget said

Steven took the box and left.

"Hell, boss, if she kicks off, you'll probably still be sheriff, even if the coloreds did vote for her."

"Pour me a little more of that evidence!"

Steven dropped the box at city hall and waited for the count before returning to the hospital. Word about Jodie's struggle for life leaked out and the parking lot filled with people—black, white, poor, and not so poor. They came in pickup trucks, old Chevys and Fords, and they brought their "younguns" and their dogs.

CHAPTER 41

Spotlights on the pickups and handheld flashlights periodically illuminated the window of Jodie's third floor hospital room. Cigarette ashes flared in the shadows and faded to bright specks in the mouths of men and women as they stared up. Boys and girls played in the parking lot. A few men and women prayed openly. Most said nothing, just watched and hoped. A young man in overalls sat on the hood of an old car strumming a guitar, making up verses as he went along, verses about Jodie Mae Jackson. "Lord God I pray, please save our Jodie Mae," the young man sang.

As he passed the nurses' station, Steven heard, "Mr. Jefferson." A nurse handed him a telephone. He said a few words, listened, and said, "Okay," before he hung up. Warren had tracked her down.

Steven went into Jodie's room. It smelled of hospital cleanliness, alcohol, and Lysol. Only the lights from her parking lot supporters lit the room. Jodie lay back in the white-sheet-covered bed. She turned her head when Steven came in. A smile came to her face.

"How does it feel to be a lady sheriff?" he asked with a broad smile. Jodie had won by 157 votes.

"I won?" She was elated, even over her weakness. The words echoed through her foggy thoughts and filled her weary body with renewed life. "I've won? I've never won anything in my life."

"Now you have," he said.

The doctor came into the room. "She's better."

"Can I let them know?" Steven gestured toward the window. The doctor nodded.

Steven opened the window and shouted, "Jodie Mae won. She won the election! It's Sheriff Jodie Mae now! And she's going to be fine!"

The crowd let out a whoop so loud; it must have been heard all the way to Trace Avenue.

The doctor wheeled Jodie to the window. She gripped the casing and peered down at the waving arms and cheering faces. Tears welled up inside. She waved and began to speak, weakly at first, but increasing in tempo with each sentence.

"They said we were no good! They were wrong! They said we were trash! They were wrong! They said we couldn't win! And, by god, they were wrong again!" Her head swam and her legs wobbled under her, but she held on to the window ledge and waved.

The doctor put his arms around her shoulders and put her back to bed. Steven put a finger to his lips to ask for quiet. They obliged. As she sat down on the edge of the bed, she looked at the doctor and said, "I'd like a bowl of soup. I feel hungry."

The doctor rang for the nurse. She was going to be all right.

In New Orleans, a handsome man with dark hair checked the train schedule to Jordan.

The End

Milton Keynes UK
Ingram Content Group UK Ltd.
UKHW040044180324
439604UK00006B/992